W9-CIA-271

Gettysburg

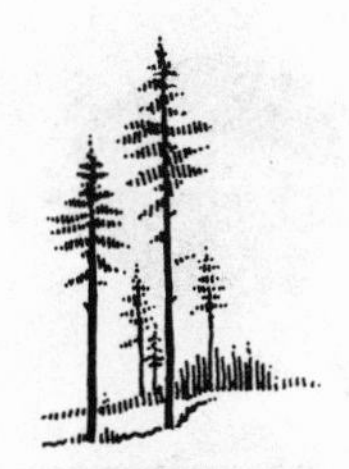

This Large Print Book carries the
Seal of Approval of N.A.V.H.

Gettysburg

A Novel of the Civil War

Newt Gingrich
William R. Forstchen
and
Albert S. Hanser,
contributing editor

Thorndike Press • Waterville, Maine

The photographs on pages 12, 68, 157, 193, 279, 433, 493, 533, 666, 704, 749, and 788 are courtesy Library of Congress; those on pages 352 and 569 are used with permission of R. J. Gibson of Gettysburg.

Published in 2003 by arrangement with St. Martin's Press, LLC.

Thorndike Press® Large Print Basic.

The tree indicium is a trademark of Thorndike Press.

The text of this Large Print edition is unabridged.
Other aspects of the book may vary from the original edition.

Set in 16 pt. Plantin by Myrna S. Raven.

Printed in the United States on permanent paper.

Library of Congress Cataloging-in-Publication Data

Gingrich, Newt.
Gettysburg : a novel of the Civil War / Newt Gingrich, William R. Forstchen and Albert S. Hanser, contributing editor.
p. cm.
ISBN 0-7862-5957-4 (lg. print : hc : alk. paper)
1. Gettysburg, Battle of, Gettysburg, Pa., 1863 — Fiction. 2. Pennsylvania — History — Civil War, 1861–1865 — Fiction. 3. Large type books.
I. Forstchen, William R. II. Hanser, Albert S.
III. Title.
PS3557.I4945G48 2003b
813′.54—dc22 2003060183

For Callista, Sharon, and Krys

National Association for Visually Handicapped
serving the partially seeing

As the Founder/CEO of NAVH, the only national health agency solely devoted to those who, although not totally blind, have an eye disease which could lead to serious visual impairment, I am pleased to recognize Thorndike Press* as one of the leading publishers in the large print field.

Founded in 1954 in San Francisco to prepare large print textbooks for partially seeing children, NAVH became the pioneer and standard setting agency in the preparation of large type.

Today, those publishers who meet our standards carry the prestigious "Seal of Approval" indicating high quality large print. We are delighted that Thorndike Press is one of the publishers whose titles meet these standards. We are also pleased to recognize the significant contribution Thorndike Press is making in this important and growing field.

Lorraine H. Marchi, L.H.D.
Founder/CEO
NAVH

* Thorndike Press encompasses the following imprints: Thorndike, Wheeler, Walker and Large Print Press.

Acknowledgments

All books stand on the shoulders of so many whose names never appear on the cover. First off we'd like to extend our sincere thanks to Jillian Manus, our agent, who believed in this project from the beginning and did a wonderful job of guiding it along and ensuring that it wound up with the right publisher.

The team at Thomas Dunne Books is a true joy to work with. Tom has created a publishing house of the "old school," where editors and staff are directly involved, have a personal desire to see a professional production, and are a real pleasure for any author to work with. Our thanks must go to Tom, our editor Pete Wolverton, his assistant John Parsley, and the rest of the St. Martin's folks in the Flat Iron building.

So many friends had a major impact on how this story shaped out. Early on in the project General Scales and Professor Fohlenkampf of the Army War College at Carlisle, on their own time, took us on one of the famous War College "staff rides," touring the Gettysburg battlefield and the region around it. A wonderful moment for us was when Scales stood on "our ground" at Union Mills, eyes shining, and said, "My God I can see it."

Tom LeGore, a truly gifted historian of Carroll County, Maryland, was invaluable. He perhaps more than any other person knows the history of the Pipe Creek position and guided us over, through, and around it, pointing out so many crucial details, both topographical and personal, that became significant points of our story.

In terms of keeping things organized, Kathy Lubbers, my (Newt's) daughter, was a genius of efficiency, keeping track of appointments, travel arrangements, and just keeping things on schedule with the "business end" of this project. Rick Tyler, who handled a lot of logistical details and the running back and forth with the endless drafts and redrafts of our work, deserves mention as well.

Professor Dennis Showalter of Colorado College, former President of the Society of Military Historians and Distinguished Visiting Lecturer in Military History at West Point, was a wonderful sounding board, especially in the early development of our thesis. He is that rarity in our profession today, a professor of history who also sees the true value of fiction and works such as ours, what we like to call

"Active History," not just as entertainment, but also as a means of analyzing the "whys" of history.

Don Troiani, our cover artist, is a name known to almost anyone interested in the American Civil War. He has an international reputation as one of the leading spirits of the historical realist movement in art. We're honored to have him as our cover artist and thankful for his analysis and advice regarding the historical accuracy of our work.

There are so many others and it is always a fear that if a name is not remembered it means that we have forgotten their help, which is definitely not the case. Friends we met along the way, while walking the ground, doing research, or just talking about the project will always have our thanks.

A final acknowledgment is in order though . . . and that is for those who were there, in the real story of Gettysburg. Both North & South, regardless of their side or the causes they fought for, they represented the highest ideals of our country . . . courage, honor, and chivalry. A hundred and fifty thousand strong they marched the dusty roads of Maryland and Pennsylvania those hot June and July days of a hundred and forty years past, and close to ten thousand would die there.

Most of those who survived would fall on other fields as the war dragged on for almost two more years. Joshua Chamberlain called Gettysburg the "vision place of souls." It is, and from that vision place we should gain renewed inspiration and strength.

No matter how we see this war today, its causes, its results, we should all be united in honoring the memory of those who gave "the last full measure of devotion" and dedicate ourselves anew to the solemn pledge that "government of the people, by the people, and for the people shall not perish from the earth."

Chapter One

June 28, 1863, 8:00 PM

Headquarters, Army of Northern Virginia
Chambersburg, Pennsylvania

The shadows of twilight deepened across the orchards and wheat fields of the Cumberland Valley. The day had been hot, the air heavy with damp heat; now the first stirring of a cooling breeze came down from out of the hills. Fireflies danced through the branches of apple, peach, and cherry trees; crickets sang; and as he rode through the rows of the orchard he breathed the rich evening air of summer, feeling a moment of peace.

He looked up at the moon riding in the eastern sky, nearly full, glowing with an orange warmth, the cold light of the stars beginning to fill the heavens.

As he approached the knoll, the orchard gave way to pasture, the fence dividing the two fields broken down, the split rails so laboriously cut and laid in place gone, except for a few upright posts. He had spoken more than once about this, to not touch the property of these people, but

after a hard day's march such fences were easy to burn, and the pasture ahead was dotted with glowing fires. An entire winter of a farmer's labor to fence this field gone now in a single night.

He reined in, not wanting to venture closer to where the troops were camped. Shadows moved about the flickering lights, the scent of wood smoke drifting on the cool breeze mingled with all the other scents of the army . . . horses, men, food cooking, grease, sweat-soaked wool uniforms, oiled leather, latrines, the heavy mix both repugnant and comforting, the smells that had been his life for over thirty years.

Songs floated on the wind. A boy, Irish from the sound of him, was singing "He's Gone Away." He listened for a moment, feeling a cool shiver, ". . . But he's coming back, if he goes ten thousand miles."

The boy finished. The song had struck a nerve. More than one of the men coughed to hide the tears; there was a forced laugh, then another song; it sounded like "The Girl I Left Behind Me," but the lyrics were not familiar. He suddenly caught one of the stanzas. It was not the traditional song; it was one of the new verses that soldiers always enjoyed making up.

He listened for a moment, and in the shadows he allowed himself to smile. It wasn't as obscene as some and no worse than some of the songs he had sung when a cadet at the Point so many years ago.

He thought of Thomas Jackson. Thomas would have ridden straight into the camp and scattered them, then delivered a stern sermon about such sinful practices, urging the men to pray instead.

Thomas, how I miss you.

The voices around the nearest campfire stilled. Some of the men turned, were looking his way; he heard the whispers.

"Marse Robert. It's him, I tell you. It's General Lee."

He caught a glimpse of an officer stepping away from the fire, coming toward him.

No. Not now.

He lifted his reins; just the slightest nudge and Traveler turned, breaking into a slow canter, and he rode into the shadows. Tracing the edge of the pasture, he followed the broken line of the fence for another fifty yards, the ground rising ahead, climbing to a woodlot. At a corner of the field was a towering oak, gnarled, ancient, a remnant of the great forest that had once covered this land, spared by a farmer long ago, perhaps as a reminder of what the land had once been.

No one was about, and he stopped beneath its vast, spreading branches. Atop the knoll the Cumberland Valley spread out before him, a vast arc of farmsteads, villages, and his army, the Army of Northern Virginia. Ten thousand campfires glowed, spreading up and down the length of the valley, great blazing circles of light. Where the more restless had gathered, there was singing and laughing.

He remembered the night before the Battle of Sharpsburg last fall, the way the Union campfires had glowed on the far side of Antietam Creek and the surrounding hills. As he'd ridden to inspect their lines, he had commented to Jackson on the vastness of the Union host descending upon them.

"Won't be as many of their fires tomorrow night," Thomas had replied coldly.

"Thomas is dead." He whispered the words softly, a simple statement of fact that carried so much weight, perhaps the very outcome of the war.

You have lost your left arm, but I have lost my right. That is what he had sent as a message upon hearing of Jackson's wounding last month at Chancellorsville. And then he had died. How I miss that right arm tonight, he thought sadly. If Jackson were here, I would know without a moment's doubt how to react. But all had changed now.

Where was the Union's Army of the Potomac camped tonight? This morning he had thought they were a hundred miles off, still down in northern Virginia and around Washington. An hour ago he had learned the truth.

The Dutchman, his trusted commander

of First Corps, Gen. James "Pete" Longstreet, had come to him with a spy. He had never liked spies, though they were as much a part of war as any soldier and at times far more important than having an extra division on the field. The spy was an actor Pete had hired on his own.

That in itself said something, that his second in command had spent a fair sum of money to send an actor across the fields, villages, and towns of Maryland and Pennsylvania in search of the Army of the Potomac. That was a job Jeb Stuart and his cavalry were supposed to perform, not someone who strutted upon the stage.

The Army of the Potomac was coming north. It was not in Washington; it was coming north and moving fast. By tomorrow night its campfires would be lit not thirty miles from here.

Stuart had failed him. Reports should have been flooding in, detailing the movement of every division in the Union army. There had not been a single word. For that matter he couldn't even tell for sure where Stuart was at this moment. There was the other side of the coin as well. If Stuart had failed to report in, he had most likely failed as well in his other task of screening the movement of this army.

He had to assume that the Army of the Potomac might indeed know where he was, how his forces were spread out all the way from the Maryland border to Harrisburg . . . and just how vulnerable he was.

I should have known three days back that those people were on the march and following, he thought bitterly. Not tonight, not like this, from a spy slipping through the lines to whisper his report, declaiming his lines as if I were part of a breathless audience hanging on every word.

The anger began to flare. "Damn!"

He knew that if those who followed him had heard that single word it would have sent a shock through the entire army. "The Old Man was so angry he swore," they'd whisper. Staff would have stood stock-still in stunned silence; generals noted for their command of Anglo-Saxon would have been rooted in place.

They make me too much a statue of marble, he thought. I have already become a legend to them. Legends can create victory. Convince your men that they can win, convince the enemy they cannot win, and the battle is half decided before the first shot is fired.

He dismounted, loosely holding Traveler's reins so that his old companion lowered his head to crop the rich clover of the pasture. He sat down under the oak tree, a mild groan escaping him as he settled back, resting his head against the rough bark, and he let the reins go.

They're coming North. That means a fight soon, maybe as early as two days from now, definitely within a week. It is, after all, what I wanted, but not quite yet. And not here, not on the Union army's terms.

A shower of sparks swirled up from the nearest campfire as another rail was tossed onto the flames, another song started, "Lorena."

He listened, humming absently.

"The years creep slowly by, Lorena,

"The snow is on the grass again . . ."

His wife, Mary, loved that one; so had his daughter Annie, the memory of her stabbing his heart.

" 'Tis dust to dust beneath the sod;

"But there, up there, 'tis heart to heart."

Dear Annie, to think of her thus, returning to dust. His youngest daughter dead at twenty-three the winter before. She had gone off to North Carolina to marry, and now she was gone forever.

Only last week a major from a North Carolina regiment had come to his tent, nervous, respectful. He had been home recovering from wounds and just wanted to say that Annie was buried in the churchyard of his village, that the grave was well tended, fresh flowers placed upon it by the local women. The officer had actually choked back tears as he spoke, then saluted as he retired. He thanked the major, closed his tent flap, and silently wept, a rare luxury, to be alone for a few minutes to cry for a lost child before others came, looking for orders, for advice, looking for a commander who could not be seen to weep.

He reached into his breast pocket and pulled out the letter he had been writing to his wife, Mary, until yet again command had interfered, Longstreet arriving with his spy. Though it was dark, he knew the letter by heart already, having labored over it, trying to find just the right tone to still her fears.

My dearest wife,

I take pen in hand praying that this missive finds you well, and that the protection of our blessed Savior rest upon you.

I write to you this evening with news which we must bear calmly. As you know from my last letter our son Rooney was wounded on June 8th in the action at Brandy Station. As I assured you then his injury was not serious; neither bone nor artery was damaged. I stayed with him throughout that night before leaving to embark upon this campaign the following morning. I was just informed this day, however, that Rooney was taken prisoner last week. Captured in the house where he had been resting and has been sent to Fortress Monroe. Thankfully our young Robert, who was tending to him, was able to escape capture and is safely back in our lines.

My dear wife, do not be overly concerned. Though this bitter and terrible struggle has divided our country, it has not severed all bonds of friendship between old comrades nor has it stilled all sentiments of Christian charity. I am certain that friends of old on the other side, upon hearing of our son's plight, will come to his aid and insure his well being and restoration to health.

Though I can ask no special favors, I am certain that our beloved son will soon be listed for exchange and returned safely to our loving embrace.

I know that your prayers are joined with mine for the protection of our son. That we pray, as well, that this campaign shall bring an ending to this bitter conflict.

He folded the letter up, looking back

across the valley. No father should be asked to fight a battle into which his own sons must be sent. When first he had seen them carrying Rooney back from the fight, features pale, thigh slashed open, he had feared the worst and nearly lost his composure. And though he was certain that friends would indeed intervene to ensure Rooney's protection, nevertheless there were some who might do him harm. It was obvious that the cavalry raid to capture Rooney had been launched for no other reason than to seize his son.

So far we've managed to keep the deeper darkness at bay, he thought. In most civil wars Rooney would have been hanged, if for no other reason than to bring me pain. We've fought so far with some degree of chivalry, the memories of old comradeship tempering the fury, but for how much longer can we do that? It has to end soon. It has to end; otherwise the rift will become too deep. It has to end as well, he realized, because if not, we will surely lose.

The song "Lorena" ended; a harmonica struck up a jig; some of the men began dancing, the firelight casting cavorting shadows across the pasture.

He wished he could give them another week, better yet two weeks, of this easy campaigning, living off the rich land, fattening up, getting ready for what lay ahead, but Longstreet and his actor had changed all that.

But while he would have preferred another week, he knew, as well, that he was not up here for a leisurely march; ultimately he was here to fight, and this time to fight a battle that would end the war.

That was the plan he had laid out before President Davis a little more than a month ago. It started when Secretary of War Seddon suggested that part of Longstreet's corps be detached and sent west to relieve the besieged city of Vicksburg on the Mississippi. He had gone down to Richmond to meet with President Davis and the cabinet to present a counterproposal to win the war through a decisive victory in the East.

He tried to remember this Grant who was emerging so rapidly as *the* Union leader in the West and who had been so aggressive in besieging Vicksburg. So many other faces he could recall: comrades of old from Mexico; from the west plains of Texas; from the parade ground at West Point; John Reynolds, who was Commandant of Cadets at the Academy; Winfield Hancock; Fitz John Porter, his old aide-de-camp, all now stood against him — and yet he could fondly remember their voices, their laughter, their friendship.

Many of the younger ones had been cadets at the Point when he was superintendent, a memory that burned hard when he read the casualty lists in the Northern papers and saw more than one name from those days, a boy who had come to a Sunday tea at his home, or one whom he had gently chided for a minor infraction and was now dead, in effect killed by him.

Grant, though, was someone he did not know enough to understand and therefore could not second-guess; and if Grant should win at Vicksburg, he knew they'd bring him east. No, it had to end before then.

He had argued against reacting directly to Grant at Vicksburg. By the time they deployed Longstreet west, the fight might very well be over. Besides, that would leave him with less than fifty thousand men, and surely the Army of the Potomac would come swinging in again, especially if they knew that a third of his forces were gone.

No, take the war into the North. Get into the rich farmlands of Pennsylvania to feed his troops, threaten a state capital, perhaps even take it. That would bring the Army of the Potomac out into the open. We then pick the place, lure them in, and finish it.

Up here in Pennsylvania there would be no falling back; it would be a fight in the open, a chance for an Austerlitz, a Waterloo, the two great battles taught at the Point as classic examples of decisive victory. Do that and end it. Such a victory would leave Washington open for the taking, could perhaps even swing England and France to our side and end the war before winter.

Such a thing, however, required the crucial first step, another slaughtering match with the Army of the Potomac. He knew it would be no easy fight; it would mean yet more losses, ten, maybe twenty thousand men to do it, and as he contemplated that butchering he looked back to the fire, to the singing and dancing and laughing.

They believe in me.

Legend can become a trap if you believe it yourself. Napoleon had six years to contemplate that fact as he rotted on Saint Helena. Santa Anna learned it beneath the walls of Chapultepec. Might I now learn it here?

He stretched, sighing, hands resting lightly on his knees.

The men are ready . . . but am I?

"Sir, we'll storm the gates of hell for

you this day," one of his regimental commanders had cried as they'd charged into the inferno at Chancellorsville.

The impious words haunted him. It had not been a patriotic cry of resolve, a willingness to die for Virginia, or this nation called the Confederacy, or even in defense of home. No, it had become personal with this army; these men would fight and die for *him*.

He could see it in their eyes: the reverent gazes, the way men — even the officers — removed their hats, spoke with lowered voices, fell silent and stared at his approach. He looked back to the men dancing around the fire. They had seen him pass, falling silent, and when they realized he wished to be alone had reverently stood back. Even now, as they danced, more than one stood at the edge of the crowd looking in his direction.

I must be as fit as they are, and of late I have not been. That realization hit with a sharp intensity.

The death of Jackson and the decision to reorganize the army, he sensed, were the core of the problem. He had not felt comfortable with entrusting half the army to a new corps commander and instead had taken Jackson's command and split it into two new corps.

Dick Ewell, one of Jackson's veterans,

out of action since losing a leg at Second Manassas, now had Second Corps. He thought, at first, that the choice was a good one. Yet of late he wondered. Sometimes when a man lost an arm, a leg, something of the old fighting spirit disappeared along with the limb. But two weeks ago Dick's first action in command of a corps at Winchester had been well fought, but far too many of the routed Union troops had been allowed to escape from what should have been a certain trap.

Ambrose Hill, a brilliant division commander, famed for his red fighting shirt and powerful presence in battle, had been given the newly created Third Corps. He had hoped for some of Jackson's mad dash with Hill, a driving spirit that could move a corps twenty-five miles in a day, throw it into battle, and win.

It was not turning out that way. Hill hid it well, but some said he could barely stay in the saddle, that his temper was short, and he was given of late to periods of withdrawal and morose depression. He was sick and barely fit for the next action.

Then there was Longstreet, the third of his commanders, "Pete" Longstreet the old warhorse. Solid, reliable, but everyone knew that he could be too methodical, slow, and firm of opinion.

Pete was not for this campaign. It still touched a bit of a sore point that Pete had gone over his head, taking his case directly to the President, agreeing with Seddon's scheme to transfer his corps to Mississippi in order to relieve Vicksburg. He'd allowed the issue to pass, and since the start of the campaign Longstreet had performed adequately but without real enthusiasm. Adequate was not good enough; he would have to be pushed.

Finally there was Stuart, the boy hero, infatuated with glory. Since the start of the war, the Union cavalry had been a minor annoyance. Brandy Station, fought only three weeks ago, indicated that times were changing. Stuart had been caught off guard. Rooney had said as much.

He wondered now if Stuart's failure to win at Brandy Station lingered and was driving Stuart to seek some new feat of daring and in the process forget what his primary mission was for this campaign, to shield the right flank of the Army of Northern Virginia as it advanced into Pennsylvania.

I have four men who are supposed to be my direct instruments of command. One is still trying to find his way after losing a leg, the second is sick, the third is bullheaded and not fully committed to this operation, and the fourth, well the fourth has simply disappeared.

"Who is truly in command here?" he whispered.

If I am in command, if my men trust me, if they place their very lives into my safekeeping, if my country places in my hands its continued existence, then I must lead with strength. This cannot be another Second Manassas or Chancellorsville, he thought bitterly.

In both actions there had been a moment, like a hazy vision, of what could lie ahead with just a few more minutes of time, luck, and determination. Both times they had come so close to a total victory, and both times the chance had slipped away, once because of darkness, the other because of Jackson's fatal wounding. And both times nearly twenty thousand of his finest young men had fallen.

"I will not let that happen again," and as he whispered those words he looked at the men gathered around the campfire. Some of them will die within the next week, and by God's Grace it must mean something this time.

This army has one more good fight in it, perhaps the best fight it will ever give. After that the numbers, the relentlessly building power of the North, will tell, no matter how valiantly we fight.

Grant struck him as the embodiment of

that new power. He was faceless, remorseless like a machine, it was said, willing to grind down an opponent no matter what the cost. If they take Vicksburg and we do not counter it with a shattering victory in the East, the tide will turn. Grant and his triumphal veterans will be unleashed here or into Tennessee. The noose will tighten, England will stand back, and the Union army will be at the gates of Richmond to stay, with all of his beloved Virginia a scorched battlefield.

He lowered his head.

It is in my hands now, is it not, my Lord? he asked. *The burden is mine, the path ahead is mine, and it rests now with me. That is Your Will. I ask You to give me the strength.*

I will not let this opportunity, this moment, slip away. The rank and file of the army is ready; it is the top, the commanders, who are not. It is I who have been detached, delegating to others. In the next action I must be in control. The old ways of doing things when Jackson was still alive are finished, at least for this next fight. I must lead, or we shall lose this war.

The thought was startling. It was one thing to contemplate such thoughts when studying the history of others, men such as Napoleon or Caesar or even his own stepgrandfather-in-law, George Washington. To think such things in relationship to one's self was to him suspect. And yet, still reeling from the intelligence brought to him by Longstreet, he now knew it to be true as he sat atop the knoll in Pennsylvania. The war rested on his shoulders.

If the killing was to end, he must not waver. That, he knew, was the eternal paradox of command. To command well one had to truly love one's army; yet to command well, one had to order that army into a maelstrom of fire and death.

If they are willing to go there, he realized, I must be willing to lead them, if need be to take direct control and abandon my old practice of delegating. "To take on the aspect of a tiger," was how Shakespeare put it, Lee remembered.

Standing up, he stretched, looking back over at the nearest campfire. With his movement, the men about the fire fell silent. He mounted, taking up the slack reins, and urged Traveler to a swift canter.

As he rode past, the men came to attention and saluted. He removed his hat in acknowledgment, and a cheer echoed across the field.

"Marse Roberts!"

It was picked up, jumping from campfire to campfire, ringing in his ears as he rode back to headquarters, knowing that all things were now possible.

"Marse Roberts!"

Maj. John Williamson of the Fourteenth South Carolina, Perrin's brigade, Pender's division, of the Third Corps of the Army of Northern Virginia, raised his hand in salute as the shadowy figure trotted past the edge of their camp.

He had seen the old man numerous times, had passed within feet of him when going into action at Sharpsburg. His old college roommate, Walter Taylor, was Lee's aide-de-camp, and more than once John had gone to headquarters to visit and seen Lee there. Yet never had John grown used to the presence, to the thrill of it. More than one of his friends said that they were in the presence of a new Washington, a presence they would one day tell their grandchildren about. If they lived to have grandchildren.

"Coffee, sir?"

John turned. It was Sergeant Hazner, holding a tin cup, offering it.

John grinned. Real coffee. Where Hazner had gotten it, he didn't bother to ask. Chances were some shopkeeper down in Chambersburg was tonight clutching a receipt from Hazner promising "payment from the Confederacy for coffee . . . ten pounds, upon the close of hostilities."

There had been strict orders against looting, so now southern Pennsylvania was blanketed with such receipts.

"And try this, sir." In Hazner's other hand was an open tin can.

John took the can, sniffed it.

"What the hell is it?"

"Milk in a can, sir. Never seen the likes of it before. Think of it. Wonder what Yankee thought of it, how many girls he's got squeezing a cow's teat with one hand, holding these little cans underneath with the other."

John laughed, poured half the can into his coffee, and offered it back. He blew on the lip of the cup and took a sip, groaning with delight.

"And real sugar in it, too."

"Hazner, what the hell did you do this time to be bribing me like this?"

"Well, sir, there is that little game tonight, and I was wondering, us not being paid in months . . ."

John shook his head. "George, I'm as broke as you are. Besides, I don't loan out money for gambling. Bad practice; suppose you lose and then get killed in the next fight, where will I be?"

"Without coffee and good grub for starters, sir."

George stepped back to the fire, picked up his own cup, upended the rest of the canned milk into it, and then came back to join his major.

John smiled, glorying in the warmth, the sensation of real coffee, the interesting taste of canned milk.

After a year of campaigning in Virginia, this was close to paradise. Yesterday the regimental headquarters had butchered an entire hog, and not just a skinny runt. This one was a fat sow, and John had woken in the morning to the smell of fresh bacon and for dinner had downed a succulent roast lovingly cooked by Cato, the colonel's servant.

He had on new boots and trousers, yet another Hazner find, and would curl up tonight under a blanket "paid for" by the regimental quartermaster from a store in Greencastle.

The land here was rich, orderly, the fields squared off, the orchards properly pruned, the farmhouses as big as mansions, the barns as big as churches. It was a long way from the hills of Carolina and the fought-over ground of Virginia.

"There's a fight coming on," Hazner ventured.

John nodded, looking over at his friend.

The two had grown up together, George several years his senior and thus always looked up to as the older brother, replacing the one lost to yellow fever when John was just a boy. George was the son of the town blacksmith and had inherited his father's strength, with broad shoulders, a trim waist, and dark, powerful eyes. Being the son of a judge and the largest property holder in the valley had, of course, destined John to another path. Both had accepted that, but they had held to their friendship in spite of the differences of class. With the coming of the war, George had readily accepted that John would be an officer and he would be a sergeant. In front of the men they played their proper roles. In private moments they would let it drop, and John would still look to his friend as he once had, as an older "brother" who would make sure he got through the war alive.

"You think so?" John asked, hiding his anxiety. "I figured we'd have at least a couple of more weeks without any worries."

George nodded sagely, motioning to the darkness that now concealed Lee.

"The old man came out here to think. You go ask your friend Walter about it tomorrow, and he'll tell you that something's up. You could see it in the way the old man rode up here, and the way he left. I tell you, this picnic is about to end, and it's time to pay the bill."

John nodded, saying nothing. He could sense the eagerness in George's voice, the desire to get on with it. He sipped his coffee in silence. He was suddenly terrified.

In the times between battles he managed to keep it concealed, but when the realization came that in a day, a week, he would again hear the thunder in the distance, see the coils of dirty yellow smoke drifting on the horizon, the pace of the column quickening, his stomach knotted and blind terror tore into his soul.

He knew that George was aware of that terror, though no word had ever been directly spoken; such things no one ever spoke of, even to a trusted friend. It wasn't just the terror of what was to come, it was the terror as well of failing, of humiliating himself before his men.

Every battle was the same, the sense of dread, the conviction that fate would finally turn the card of death. Even as he contemplated the thought, he realized that his hands were trembling.

He saw George looking at him from the corner of his eye, and John laughed, trying to cover. "Coffee's strong, gives you the jitters." He downed the rest of the cup and lowered his hands.

"It's alright," George whispered. "Everyone feels that way at times."

"You don't."

"Too stupid, I guess. Shows you what your book learning got you, sir. Makes you think too much."

Think too much. He could imagine a lot of things at this moment, what it felt like to have a leg blown off by a solid shot, to get a minie ball in the guts, to have your manhood shredded by a canister.

He'd seen that, seen the myriad of wounds, the thousand different nuances of how a man could die in battle, all of it taking place under an uncaring heaven, all of it a madness that he was part of and from which there was no escape. He wondered if Lee, by deciding one way or the other how to fight the next battle, had set in motion a path that would lead to his own death.

"What the hell!" George sighed. "Better sooner than later, I say. Let's get it over with now so we can go home."

John nodded. Several men came over, one of them asking George if it really was Bobbie Lee who had just ridden by. George laughed, telling them that Lee had just shaken his hand, and John turned away, walking off into the darkness.

He looked out across the valley, the flickering fires, the moonlight illuminating the hills, and wondered how it would look the day after he was dead.

It would still be the same, going on, continuing, uncaring. George would survive. He had sensed that from their very first day. George was as strong as an ox and as steadfast as one. He was right, as well. He didn't think, didn't worry; he just did his job.

Why did I have to be cursed so? John wondered.

There was no graceful way out, no honorable way to escape this. I'll have to stand again on that damned firing line, unflinching before the others, shouting commands, doing what is expected of the son of a judge, but inside my guts will turn to water. How is it that the others can do it without fear and I cannot?

He thought of Elizabeth, sweet Elizabeth, wondering what she would say of him if he ever confessed his terror. Southern women were told to not tolerate such things in their men, not in this time of national crisis. They were to be as the Spartans, to send their sons, their brothers, their fiancés off to battle with a promise of love held eternal, urging their menfolk to return either with their shields or upon them.

Fine for the poets, for those who stay behind. All he wanted was to be back there, to have married as he had wanted, to have her curled up by his side and, dare he dream it, filled with passionate ardor.

Instead he was here, and he feared that within the week he would be dead.

He walked farther into the field, knelt down and vomited, retching miserably, sobbing with fear, wishing he were anywhere but here in Pennsylvania, marching to battle with the Army of Northern Virginia.

Chapter Two

June 29, 1863, 11:00 PM

Headquarters, Army of the Potomac
Near Frederick, Maryland

Brig. Gen. Henry Hunt, Chief of Artillery, Army of the Potomac, wearily dismounted, barely acknowledging the salute of the headquarters orderly who took the reins of his horse.

Average in height at five and a half feet, showing the first signs of middle-age stoutness, with a full brown beard streaked with wisps of gray, Henry looked typical of the officers of the much battered Army of the Potomac. The hard week of forced marches from Virginia up to the border of Pennsylvania through debilitating heat, relieved only by the occasional thunderstorm, had left all of them dirty, exhausted, stinking of sweat-soaked wool, horse, and bad rations. Once dapper uniforms were now a universal dingy, mud-streaked blue. There seemed to be an infinite weariness to Henry, a hard-edged cynicism, like that of a barroom pugilist who has seen better days and now fights without hope of glory.

Henry walked stiffly; the long hours in the saddle, the grueling heat of the thirty-mile ride, even after the sun had set, had been exhausting. The roads he had traveled had been choked with begrimed, weary men, supply wagons, thousands of exhausted stragglers, and long columns of his artillery, cloaked in swirling clouds of powdery dust that clogged the nostrils and left one's eyes feeling as if they had been rubbed with sandpaper. All of them, near on to a hundred thousand men of the Army of the Potomac, tangled into a sweltering, cursing, tidal mass, were flowing northward and looking for a fight.

A subtle, electric-like sense now permeated the army, knowing that somewhere up ahead a battle was brewing, building like a summer storm concealed on the far side of the mountains but already felt and tasted in the air. It created a strange mix of feelings. The long-ago dreams of glory were dead. The men on the roads were the pragmatic survivors of a new type of warfare fed by factories and railroads. They knew there was precious little glory to be found when charging an entrenched foe. And yet, in spite of their knowledge of the horror that awaited them, there was a grim determination, a desire to be at it and to finish the job. Somewhere up ahead, perhaps just around the next bend, there might be an end to it all, the decisive fight that would decide the issue.

And so the long, swaying columns had flowed along roads stretching from Frederick clear down to the suburbs of Washington, the old Army of the Potomac, which he loved with all his soul and in spite of all its defeats, still they marched. No longer were they boys filled with a dream of some desperate glory . . . they were veterans heading to a fight.

Tomorrow perhaps, the day after, there would be another battle, and more than one of them was walking to his death. As Henry rode among them throughout the long, hot, dusty day, he was filled with a morbid curiosity, looking into faces, wondering how many of them, before the week was out, would never laugh again, would never again write home asking a sweetheart to wait, promising to return, asking a mother to send a favorite treat and a new pair of socks, or manfully telling a father not to worry.

He had reined in and dismounted atop a low rise just before sunset, awed by the panorama laid out before him. Far back to the southern horizon a long column, like a slow-moving serpent or giant prehistoric creature, was crawling toward him. It was a creature of fifty thousand legs, tens of thousands of wheels, flashes of evening light reflecting off steel, iron, and bronze gun barrels, crawling toward him, sweeping past, flowing down into the valley ahead, and the sight of it filled him with wonder.

This is the beating heart of the Republic, Henry thought, men rising up from a thousand hamlets, towns, farms, and cities, all coming to this place, moving now like some great horde from out of ancient history. Shadowy in the dust, he had watched them pass, tin cups and empty canteens clanging on hips, an occasional drum or fife playing in a vain effort to keep up the pace, then falling silent.

Conversations, as if rising from the throats of ghosts, drifted around him, someone talking about a new daughter, proudly showing an ambrotype, a snatch of laughter at the punch line to an obscene joke; a stanza of a song floated in the air counterpointed by a sergeant cursing.

A captain stepped out of the column, helping an exhausted boy to the side of the road, where he collapsed in a clatter of equipment and began to cry as his comrades continued on. The captain gave the boy his canteen before turning to rejoin the never-stopping column. The captain caught Henry's eye for a second. Nothing was said between them, just a sort of embarrassed acknowledgment of this small act of mercy for a boy who was played out and no longer of use to an army that needed men who could continue to march toward death. The boy lay back, features deathly pale, and passed out, canteen clutched in his hands.

Where he had stopped, a dead Confederate trooper and a couple of dead horses lay. A pile of dirt marked where several Union troopers, killed in a skirmish, had been hastily buried by their comrades. Few in the passing column even noticed. Long ago this army had gotten used to fresh graves, dead men, and horses lying by the side of roads, acting as signposts for what was to come.

He casually looked over at the Reb. The heat was beginning to take effect so that his threadbare uniform, which the boy had undoubtedly once been so proud of, was now tight-fitting, bulging, a stir of wind bringing to him the sickly sweet smell as the boy began to return to the earth.

Henry backed away even as a couple of men in the column pointed out the corpse and urged a young lieutenant, obviously new to his job, to go over and take a look. The lieutenant grinned weakly and ignored the jibes, a sergeant threatening the two with a burial detail for the Reb if they said another word.

Having relieved himself by the side of the road, making sure to stand a respectful distance away from the corpse and the exhausted boy, Henry remounted and fell in with the river of men.

The long, flowing column dropped down from the crest of the hill, continuing northward, the land ahead cloaked in twilight. All were disappearing into the darkness, fading from view.

There will come a day, Henry thought, when we shall be no more. Whether we die tomorrow, or die abed fifty years hence, this moment will forever haunt us. We'll remember the sounds, the smells, the feel of this summer evening, and turn back to it in our memories as eagerly as we remember a first love. But even then the memory will fade, and finally it will be lost to the world forever. Perhaps 100, 150 years from now, as an army of ghosts, we might return to this place, to this road in Maryland, marching toward Pennsylvania and a dark rendezvous with death.

Henry looked again at the men around him and wondered how many of them saw it as well and thrilled to the wonder of it, and how many of them would still be alive a week from now. Will I even be alive this time tomorrow? he wondered.

Strange, there was no fear. He smiled at the thought and took a secret pride in it. When he had charged the Mexican line at Chapultepec — a mad, insane dash with a single six-pound gun, galloping to within a hundred yards of their line, unlimbering and opening fire — everyone said he had been fearless. Little did they know the terror of that moment or again at First Bull Run when he'd deployed a battery at the bridge, keeping the line of retreat open for the last stragglers. Those had been terrifying moments; it was simply a question of not showing it.

Something whispered to Henry that death was close, very close, a shadow waiting just on the other side of the next hill. And yet, to have this moment was worth everything. He knew he did not have the words to articulate it, to express either to himself or to the rest the feelings of this instant; others could do that far more eloquently. But there was a deep sense of acceptance; and falling in alongside a regiment from Maine, he pushed on.

The regiment's exhausted colonel, slumped in his saddle, nodded a greeting. They rode together in silence into the twilight until the regiment was ordered to break for the night. Henry rode on alone to the outskirts of Frederick and a meeting with his new commander, George Meade.

He caught the eye of a staff officer and asked directions. A tent pitched at the edge of a peach orchard was pointed out. Henry made his way through the mass of hangers-on, orderlies, staff officers, reporters, all the annoyances that always trailed a headquarters, and was surprised when, after showing the written summons from Meade, he was immediately led into the presence of the new commander.

He had never been close to George Meade, who until less than a day ago had commanded Fifth Corps, but then no one was close to Meade. It struck Henry as a hell of a way to run an army. Here they were heading into a fight, and Washington decides to switch commanders yet again. Joe Hooker was out as commander of the Army of the Potomac; George Meade was in.

For a lot of reasons Henry was glad to see Hooker leave, especially because of the fiasco last month at Chancellorsville. But he should have been fired the day after that battle ended, not with the army on the march, a fight brewing just ahead. He could only hope that Meade would seize control quickly and firmly.

Outside of his previous command with Fifth Corps, Meade was not well-known by the rest of the Army of the Potomac. And in an army that was fond of nick-names, the best Meade could rate was "Old Snapping Turtle" or "Goggle Eyes."

Meade looked up from his field desk, and Henry thought that at this moment he did indeed look like a snapping turtle, balding head a bit too big for his long, skinny neck, eyes bulging, scraggly beard not trimmed in weeks, a decidedly un-attractive man who at first glance did not do much to inspire confidence the way George McClellan, first commander of the Army of the Potomac, could. But then again, what had McClellan accom-plished with all his good looks, bravado, and gold lace except one defeat after an-other?

Maybe, just maybe, Meade would be the kind of snapping turtle who would bite onto Lee and hang on. If only we had done that at Chancellorsville when it was realized that Lee had split his army into two separate wings. Rather than stay on the defensive and let Lee control things, it could have ended right there, rather than turn into yet another debacle of confusion and defeat.

Meade shifted the cigar in his mouth, and with a grunt motioned for Henry to sit in a camp chair, while at the same time sliding over a bottle of bourbon and two glasses with his left hand. As Henry poured the drinks, Meade finished scanning the report in his other hand and then wearily tossed it on the table and with the stub of a pencil wrote a comment on the back.

"The good citizens of Frederick filed a complaint that some of our boys got drunk, broke some windows, and stole a case of whiskey from a tavern," and he motioned to the paper. "I'm to initiate an investigation by order of the War Department."

Henry said nothing.

"Damn War Department, all it knows how to do is needle and harass, and in the middle of all of this I'm supposed to take the time to track down a couple of drunk cavalrymen. Then, in the next breath, they're screaming for me to tackle Lee and finish him. Hell, I'm not even sure where he is."

"Newspapers I saw this morning say he's outside of Harrisburg," Henry offered.

"To hell with the damn newspapers. I got a lost cavalry lieutenant who wandered in a couple of hours ago claiming that Early, with a corps of Confederate infantry, is in York; and a drunk preacher came in here saying that Harrisburg was burned to the ground last night, Lee's across the Susquehanna, and he seen it."

Meade waved his glass of bourbon vaguely toward the north. "All I know is the Rebs are in Pennsylvania, and we are scattered out across a front of damn near fifty miles trying to find them. By God, if Lee should close on us tomorrow we'll get a hell of a drubbing the way we're spread out. Hunt, I've been in command of this army less than a day, and it's taking time to grab hold of the reins."

Meade nodded toward the half-open tent flap and the crowd standing back at a respectful distance. "Nearly all of them are Joe Hooker's old staff."

Henry grunted and shook his head.

"I'm keeping them on for now. There'll be time enough later to switch things around."

"Where are you planning to concentrate?" Henry asked, trying to read the map that was spread out on Meade's desk.

Meade pointed to a penciled-in line he had traced just south of the Maryland-Pennsylvania border.

"I'm ordering the army to concentrate just east and north of here, on a line from Westminster to Taneytown.

"John Reynolds is on the left here at

Frederick with his First Corps, supported by Howard and the Eleventh Corps. Tomorrow they'll push up toward Emmitsburg, while I move headquarters to Taneytown," and as he spoke Meade traced out the movement on the map with a dirty forefinger.

"Reynolds is a good man," Henry interjected. "He'll find them if they're there."

Henry didn't feel it was in any way proper to add that everyone knew that when Joe Hooker had been relieved of command of the army just yesterday morning, word was that Lincoln had wanted Reynolds to take command. Reynolds had refused, and Meade was the second choice.

Meade looked at Henry with a cool gaze, but Henry said nothing more.

"Reynolds has John Buford with a division of cavalry in front of him that has orders to cross into Pennsylvania and take a look up toward Gettysburg."

"Gettysburg, lot of roads junction there," Henry interjected. "It might be worth taking and holding."

"I have a report that some Rebs, Jubal Early's division, passed through there two days ago but then continued on toward Harrisburg."

"And where's our cavalry?"

Meade snorted. "Useless as ever. No

solid reports. They're trailing after Stuart, but they've had no hard contact with Lee's main body."

Henry pointed to the mountain range that arced up through southern Pennsylvania, turning in a great curve from north to east, the Cumberland Valley beyond. Meade nodded.

"I suspect Lee is indeed on the other side of the South Mountain Range, over here at Chambersburg, moving up toward Harrisburg. Buford moving into Gettysburg just might trigger something, cause Lee to feel his rear is threatened and turn back around toward us.

"Lee must have heard by now that we are coming up. He can't leave his rear open," Meade continued. "We'll brush up against his flank. Perhaps I can lure him back down this way to where I want him."

Meade continued to trace out movements on the map, Henry craning his neck to look as Meade pointed out his proposed position along the south bank of Pipe Creek.

"I think it might be good ground," Meade announced. "The south bank of the stream is high, open fields of fire, perfect for artillery."

"It looks like damn good ground," Henry offered. "The question is will Lee bite once he's got a look at it? Usually we wind up fighting on in places he picks."

"Can you suggest anything better?" Meade asked testily.

"No, sir."

Henry nodded. The position Meade had chosen was good. It covered Washington, which would keep the politicians happy, while at the same time forcing Lee to turn away from Harrisburg. But the question lingered: Would Lee accept battle on land chosen by Meade? In every action fought against the Army of Northern Virginia it had always been the Rebs who ultimately selected when or where a battle would be joined.

"We don't know each other very well, Hunt," Meade finally announced after a long, awkward silence, "but I know your work. Last year, at Malvern Hill, you were masterful in the way you placed your guns."

Henry nodded his thanks.

Malvern Hill. The mere mention of those two words triggered the memory of that July 1st, a year ago this week, he realized.

Six days of bitter fighting, retreating from the gates of Richmond, crawling and stumbling through the tangle of woods and marshes, McClellan fumbling the battle every step of the way. But at last

McClellan had turned and given Henry the ground of an artilleryman's dreams . . . open fields, a broad crest of a hill, clear fields of interlocking fire. And he had seized the moment, arraying over a hundred guns, bronze twelve-pound smoothbores, three-inch rifles, even a couple of batteries of heavy twenty-pound rifles for counterbattery work.

Lee had walked straight into it.

That battle had revealed what Henry knew was perhaps the one weakness of Lee, an aggressiveness that bordered on pure recklessness if his blood was up and he smelled victory.

For a commander who normally planned his actions, Lee had allowed the battle to unfold haphazardly, throwing troops in piecemeal rather than slamming them forward all at once. But even if he had sent a full corps up that hill, rather than a brigade at a time, the result would have been the same, and just as ghastly.

Throughout that long afternoon Henry had worked his guns with finesse, sweeping the open fields, solid shot tearing through the columns as they deployed, canisters tumbling over lines of men who fell like broken toys.

The screams still haunted him; five thousand Confederate infantry, damn fine troops, had gone down in mangled, bloodied heaps. He had been awed by the Rebs' audacity, their relentless will, and the sheer madness of their charge. Though he was a professional, the sight of what his guns could do to packed lines of infantry had stunned him. It was, Henry knew, the finest and most terrifying example of the power of artillery yet seen in this war.

"It's how I want to see artillery used in the next fight," Meade continued, interrupting Henry's memories.

Henry leaned forward slightly. He was called Chief of Artillery for the Army of the Potomac, but that was a title he had held in name only for the last six months. Hooker had always suspected that Henry was a "McClellan man"; and in an army torn by political factionalism, such a suspicion, justified or not, had been a kiss of death when Hooker took over. Though he'd managed to hang onto his title, Hooker had relegated him to a desk — and paperwork.

Damned madness. At Chancellorsville, if he had been given a hundred guns to array around the Fairview clearing, he'd have cut the guts out of Stonewall Jackson's charge. But Hooker hadn't listened. He'd panicked and lost the battle.

It's this damn political infighting that is as much the enemy as the Rebs, Henry thought. If only we could get as united as the Army of Northern Virginia was, united with a belief in a single, capable leader, with a single purpose, we could win this war in a month.

"You and Joe Hooker," Meade said, gaze still fixed on his empty glass, "I know what happened between the two of you when Hooker took command of this army back in January."

He stared up at Henry for emphasis. There was no need, Henry thought, for Meade to play this point too hard. There was a lot of grumbling from some about Meade's ascension, especially at this moment. But for Henry the removal of Hooker could only mean the chance to get back his real job as artillery commander in the field, and it was obvious Meade was offering just that.

"I'm putting you back in charge of the Artillery Reserve, active field command."

Good enough. Henry nodded his thanks. But if there was any chance for what he truly wanted it was now, and he had to go for it.

"Sir, am I to be retained as commander of all artillery," he asked cautiously, "or just the reserve artillery attached directly to army headquarters?"

Meade said nothing for a moment.

"What are you pushing for, Hunt?"

Meade finally asked.

"Sir, half of our artillery is assigned to the direct command of headquarters as the Artillery Reserve, which means me. But what about the other half, nearly a hundred and fifty guns divided up into small units and assigned to various corps commanders? Do I have control of those batteries as well."

"Don't push it, Hunt. I was a corps commander until yesterday morning. I didn't take kindly to units being taken from me. Corps commanders like to have a couple of batteries under their direct control."

"In a crisis you need a unified command for artillery," Henry replied. "Allow me to put two hundred, three hundred guns into a unified command, and I'll sweep the field clean. It's concentrated artillery that will decide the next fight, sir. The land up here is open, better fields of fire than in central Virginia."

Henry looked into Meade's eyes, saw the coldness, and fell silent. He knew his enthusiasm, his near fanatical belief, had again run into the politics of command.

Meade replied, his voice cold and threatening, "Yesterday you were nothing but a glorified inspector. Hooker wouldn't have given you a pinch of owl shit to command. I've given you back half the artillery of this army. Be satisfied with that."

"Then why the hell have an artillery commander if half his strength is frittered away?" Henry replied, and he instantly regretted his brashness. But it was exactly what was wrong with this damned army; everything was always a compromise, done in half measures, and the men they commanded suffered as a result.

Meade bristled and leaned forward menacingly. "Do you want the job or not, General? You want it, you take it on *my* terms. If not, I've got fifty men outside this tent who will jump at the chance."

Henry nodded, saying nothing.

"Do we understand each other, General? Corps artillery stays where it is. You may advise in regard to those units, but corps commanders still control their own guns. Take it or leave it."

"Yes, sir. I understand."

"That's settled then. There's something else, though, that I want to ask you."

Frustrated that his hopes had been dashed, Henry lowered his gaze for a moment while pouring another drink for himself. He tried to reason that he was a damn sight better off than he had been twenty-four hours ago; but if ever there had been a chance to create a true unified command it was now, and the chance had slipped away.

"It's the real reason I asked you to come here."

"Sir?" Henry looked back at Meade, wondering what else he wanted.

"You served under Lee before the war in Mexico, didn't you?"

Surprised, Henry nodded. "Yes, we were stationed together at Fort Hamilton in New York City."

"I never knew him that well. I understand the two of you were close."

Henry hesitated for a second. "Professionally, yes."

"Tell me about him."

"Sir?"

"Just that, Hunt. Tell me about him."

Henry looked down at his glass. Lee, in his fatherly way, had chided him on his drinking more than once.

What can I tell him? Henry wondered. If ever an army held an opposing general in awe, it was the Army of the Potomac and Robert E. Lee. He was an endless source of speculation, comment, damning, and grudging praise.

Lee was a hard man to get close to. He had many acquaintances but few true friends. Was I that, Henry wondered, just another acquaintance?

No, it was different, a sense in a way of being a younger brother to an elder, or a favored student to a mentor. They shared a love of the precision of engineering, the bringing of order out of chaos, and a love for gunnery, its history and practice.

Curious, for both of them saw it as an abstraction, an intellectual exercise of trajectories, rates of fire, and the beautiful ritual of drill. Neither of them wanted to think about the end result when it was done for real, the shredded human flesh blasted and burned, the way both of them would see it done a few years later at Chapultepec.

They had spent many an afternoon together on the parade ground, training new recruits. And afterward, when drill was done, the two of them leaning on a gun, admiring the beauty of the harbor and bustling traffic of hundreds of ships, talking about the army, engineering, history, but never quite about themselves. That was something Lee always kept reserved.

"I'm waiting, General," Meade interjected, breaking into Henry's thoughts.

"I doubt if there is anything more I can add to what has already been said," Henry finally replied, a bit self-consciously.

"A lot of men in this army served with him," Meade replied coolly, "but all of them say the same thing, 'He never talked about himself.' "

"Well, they're right."

"Damn it, man, within the week, maybe as early as tomorrow, I'll have to face him on the battlefield. I want something, anything. He sure as hell knows how to read us. I want the same."

Henry was startled. He could see it in Meade's eyes, hear it in his voice, a terrible loneliness, a certain desperation that made Henry uncomfortable. In a way he couldn't blame him. Everyone talked about how a general who brought victory against Lee would save the Republic. Few added the observation that losing a battle might mean the end of the Union. He would not want to be in Meade's shoes right now.

Henry nodded and took another sip of his bourbon.

"He has a gentle soul," Henry finally offered.

"What?" and there was an incredulous look on Meade's face.

Henry leaned back in his chair, looking out the half-opened tent flap, feeling the cool breeze that stirred, causing the canvas to softly crack and flutter. The hint of cool air after the heat of the day was refreshing.

Strange, it reminded him of the night before Chapultepec, the staff meeting with old Winfield Scott, the cool breeze that finally stirred to kill the heat of day.

Maj. Robert Lee sitting in the corner throughout the meeting, taking notes. At the end of the meeting, it had been Lee who'd suggested that they all pray. Lee had led them and not once had he called for victory; in fact, he had asked for God's mercy to be shown on their foe and that the Will of the Lord be fulfilled.

"A gentle soul," Henry continued. "He is devout; we all know that. Yet beyond that there is a profound gentleness. I saw him chew out a teamster for lashing a mule, telling him that cursing would motivate neither man nor beast. From anyone else there would have been derision once he'd walked away; but that teamster lowered his head, ashamed, and once Lee left the teamster patted the mule and led him by the bridle.

"I know that when he was superintendent of West Point," Henry added, "he chided many an upperclassman for hazing a plebe. In fact, personally he hated the tradition of hazing and tried to stop it."

"I heard about that," Meade replied. "Hell, we all survived it. Hazing at the Point toughens a boy into becoming a man."

"He didn't see it that way," Henry replied, and even as he spoke he felt a touch of shame, remembering his own tears at the end of his first day at the

Point, and how only a year later he, too, had harassed new cadets without mercy.

"I'll never forget him coming out to the practice field one day and pulling a young soldier from my gun crew, taking him aside. A letter had just come in with news for the boy that his mother was dead. Lee decided to tell him personally. The boy broke down and Lee held him the way a father would hold a child. I saw the two of them kneeling side by side, Lee's arm around the boy's shoulders."

Even as he described it, Henry fought to control the tightness in his throat.

"He knew every soldier in our command by name. The boys loved it. I can't say that they were close to him the way some commanders allow those under them to be close. Rather, it was a reverent awe. A few saw him as an old granny, especially when he took to praying, but even those would not deny his courage and honesty.

"I think," Henry continued, "that must be paining him now. That boy who lost his mother was killed at Fredericksburg leading his regiment. Lee would remember and pray for him. He remembers all those who've served under him."

"Damn well he should," Meade growled. "He put enough of them in their graves."

"I know he prays for me," Henry added

slowly. "In fact, sir, he'll even pray for you."

Meade looked at him with his cold stare. "If he's so holy, then why the hell didn't he become a preacher?"

"There's the other side," Henry replied, trying not to let a touch of hostility slip into his voice. "He's a fighter. Something comes over him in battle, a sense that it is God's Will, and he must be the instrument of that Will. That is why he is dangerous."

"Why?"

"Because he believes he is right. There are no self-doubts once action is joined. He gives himself over and then unflinchingly flings everything he has into the fight. Only when it is done does he come out of the fog of battle, cover his face, and mourn those whom he has slain.

"When he comes at you in this next fight, he will not hesitate. He wants this war to end, and the only way he sees how is to break our will to resist. Sir, remember, he will seek the battle of decision the same way Napoleon would. Napoleon was someone he admired."

"Lee admires the Corsican?"

"Not for his politics, but yes, for his method of battle. Napoleon was a master at breaking the will to resist, the climax of the grand charge that sends the enemy fleeing the way he did at Marengo and Austerlitz. Lee cannot afford another half victory like the last several fights. It goes against his nature, and it tears at his soul."

"What do you mean, 'tears at his soul'?"

"He wants to believe there is purpose in this world, a logic and reason, God's higher plan, if you will. War, in contrast, represents chaos to him. If he justifies his own actions, it is that he seeks to end the chaos on God's terms, which means a swift victory, brutal in the Old Testament sense if necessary, but a finish."

Meade snorted derisively and poured another drink.

"Fight and the devil take the hindmost," Meade growled. "If you want a purpose, there it is. I never had any use for worrying beyond that. When you are dead, that's it."

"You asked for my opinion on the old man," Henry replied coolly. "Every battle where men are killed — both his and ours — with no conclusive result gnaws at him. It represents chaos to him. He'll want to close it off. The irony is that in so doing he'll create a bloodbath. I expect that when we finally collide, he'll come at us like a wolf at the scent of his prey."

"If we can choose our ground and dig in, then let him come at us."

"Make sure that it's him coming at us and not the other way around," Henry offered.

Meade looked up at him coldly, the glance a signal that Henry was offering advice where it wasn't wanted, but he pushed ahead anyhow.

"He'll come straight at us, but if he can see a chance to flank, he'll do it. He lost Jackson, who was the master of that game. There's a hole now in his command, which I doubt either Dick Ewell or Ambrose Hill can fill. This change in his high command might put him off balance. As a result there's a chance Lee might take the reins himself rather than let his subordinates run things once battle is joined. I heard from a prisoner that he fought the ending of Chancellorsville that way, right down to taking charge of individual brigades. He might do that again next time, and if so, be careful, sir. He'll come in hard then. If blunted, look for a flank. Keep a sharp eye on the flank, sir."

"I appreciate the advice," Meade said coldly, "but it's Lee I want to know about, not your analysis of how I should fight."

"That's about it," Henry replied quietly.

"You liked him, didn't you?"

Henry nodded reluctantly. "I trusted

him. At times he seemed a little too perfect. In peacetime that could put some men off; but in war, a man like that, who can inspire perfect trust . . ." and his voice trailed off.

He realized he had just insulted Meade and, fumbling, he poured another drink for himself, nearly finishing the bottle.

"We probe farther north tomorrow. I want the Artillery Reserve up in support position by Wednesday the first." Meade leaned back over the table and pointed at the map. "As soon as you arrange that, then I want you to go survey the land along the creek up by Westminster. I want you to accompany General Warren. He's my chief topographical engineer, but I want an artilleryman's eyes looking at it as well. See if this could be your next Malvern Hill. We want good ground."

His tone indicated dismissal and, standing, Henry saluted and left the tent.

The camp was quiet. It was past midnight; a mist was rising, cool, pleasant after the heat of the long day. Campfires had burned down to smoldering embers, more than one staff officer curled up on the ground, a few sitting in camp chairs, talking softly. A couple looked up, curious, then returned to their private conversations, ignoring him.

Henry walked back to where he had dismounted, spotted his horse tied to a peach tree, saddle taken off. The orderly had even rubbed him down. Caesar was cropping the rich grass. He looked up at Henry's approach, snorted, and accepted the scratch behind the ears.

Henry had named all his mounts after generals of classical history. Hannibal, the last, had broken a leg at Fredericksburg. Before him there had been Hasdrubal, Pompey, and Vespasian. He sadly wondered how long Caesar would survive.

Never get attached to them, he thought, and never get attached to the men either.

That must be eating Lee alive. He was attached more than any of them to those he commanded. He wanted the killing to end, but he knew as well that in order for it to end he had to be absolutely ruthless. The strain might very well destroy him, but even that he would see as the Will of God.

Henry suddenly felt a terrible wave of sadness, of remorse and pain for the old man.

Damn, he's a traitor, he tried to reason, but at least for this moment he allowed himself a moment of pity.

Leaning against Caesar, Henry watched the moon hanging low in the western sky, wondering where Lee was, what he was

thinking, and wondering as well if he could kill Lee if given the chance.

The chilling thought was there as well that Lee, the gentle, the soft-spoken and kind, would kill him without a moment's hesitation if that was necessary for victory, and Henry knew he had to brace himself to do the same.

Chapter Three

July 1, 1863, 8:45 AM

Union Mills, Maryland

US Henry Hunt reined in, Warren at his side. Warren uncorked a canteen of water and handed it over to Henry, who nodded his thanks. The day was already warm, though a light shower had brushed across the landscape shortly after dawn.

"This is a damn good position," Warren offered, and Henry nodded in agreement.

The ground before them sloped down to a broad, open marshy plain, bisected by a narrow creek. A mill with a pond backed up beyond was to his right. He carefully studied the area, while Warren, with one leg drawn up over the pommel of his saddle, took a small sketchbook out and carefully traced in the topographical details, noting down distances, buildings, roads, elevations.

"Clear fields of fire," Henry announced. "This must have been lumbered off years ago for the mill down there.

God, I could line a hundred guns up along these heights and hold it till doomsday."

"If they come down this far."

Henry, still holding Warren's canteen, leaned over, watching as the engineer drew his map. Personally he found Warren to be difficult at times, a bit too officious; but he respected the man for his eye, his sense of ground, how it affected battle and movement.

"We've got the potential for a remarkable defensive position here," Warren announced, inverting the pencil in his hand, tracing out the line they had ridden along so far with the blunt end. "This creek bottom just east of Taneytown over to here; open fields of fire along the entire length. This is good killing ground, exceptional."

Henry nodded in agreement.

Henry dismounted, one of his staff taking the reins. The men riding with them were nervous. Everyone was on edge, not knowing where the rebel cavalry might be lurking. He walked a few yards along the road they had come out on while riding the ridgeline bordering the creek. The road, he realized, must be the main pike running from Westminster up toward Littlestown and Gettysburg beyond. It was well paved with crushed limestone, but torn up now by the passage of thousands of troops and cavalry. If the fight should come down this way, it would be a main line of advance.

He scanned the ground, a bit rocky but still a good position to dig in guns. Yes, if it should be fought here, along this line, this would be the place to hold.

Stretching, he walked back to his mount and got back in the saddle. Warren was finished sketching, folding up his notebook. Henry passed the canteen back over.

"Pipe Creek," Warren said, "if it's going to be anywhere, I hope it's here. Whoever holds this land will win."

As the two turned to ride on, Henry paused, looking off to the north. He wasn't sure, but there seemed to be a tremor in the air . . . artillery fire. He waited, head raised; again a distant, flat thump, more felt than heard. He looked over at Warren, who nodded in agreement. They waited for a moment, but all that greeted them was silence, and finally they rode off to the east.

July 1, 1863, 9:00 AM

Near Chambersburg, Pennsylvania

C.S.A. "Battalions, forward march!"

The colonel shouting the order sat ramrod straight astride his mount, sword drawn, the tip of the blade resting against his shoulder, obviously nervous that the commander of the Army of Northern Virginia was watching. The young officer's voice echoed across the orchard, picked up by company captains, rippling down the line. He raised his sword and saluted as the column moved onto the Chambersburg Pike and headed east toward the South Mountain gap.

Lee returned the salute, reining in Traveler, and moved to the side of the road, clearing the way for the brigade of Georgia troops that were filing out of the orchard. A lone fifer at the front of the column valiantly tried to play "Dixie." The boy looked over at Lee, turned bright red, and completely fumbled the tune, a ripple of laughter echoing through the column at his discomfort.

Lee smiled and touched the brim of his hat in salute to the boy who, crestfallen, looked as if he was about to burst into tears.

"Don't you worry, General, we can

fight a heap better than Jimmie can play," a wag shouted from the middle of the column.

A piercing cheer erupted, the men raising their caps in salute as they passed Lee.

"They're in good spirits this morning."

Lee nodded, looking over at Pete Longstreet, who was riding beside him. "They're ready for what has to be done," Lee said quietly, watching as the column passed before him. "In spite of the hard marching of the last three weeks, the men look healthier; they're living well off of the land up here.

"You saw the report I sent over to you last night from Harry Heth?" Lee asked, looking back at Longstreet.

"The contact his division made with Yankee cavalry last night near Gettysburg? Yes."

"And?"

"If Stuart was where he was supposed to be, we'd know more about what's down this road," and as he spoke Pete gestured to the east.

"That's what we'll find out today," Lee said. "It might be nothing more than a forward screen, backed up with some militia."

"Or it could be the entire Army of the Potomac concentrating there. We're still spread out, sir."

"We won't be by the end of today," Lee replied sharply. "We are at Cashtown, as planned. If the Army of the Potomac is indeed coming up, as your spy reported, Cashtown is very defendable ground. And don't worry about our young prodigy. General Stuart will be reined in; I've sent couriers out to look for him."

Longstreet said nothing, but Lee could read the doubt in his eyes, the caution that hung over "the Dutchman." In the past it has always been a good balance, the impetuous Jackson, ready to leap off into the unknown, Longstreet the opposite, forever preaching about defense. But Jackson was gone. Longstreet was the senior of the corps commanders now and had to be pushed to show more audacity.

The column continued to pour out of the orchard and onto the road, and Lee felt a thrill at the sight of them. They were typical of the hard-fighting Army of Northern Virginia. Many wore gray four-button jackets, some were dressed in whatever could be found or sent from home. Butternut brown was fairly common, the wool spun, woven, cut, stitched, and dyed by loving hands. Some wore butternut pants as well, but a fair number had on sky blue trousers, taken from Yankee prisoners.

Most of the men had shoes, yet again captured, though more than one boy was barefoot this morning. On the soft dirt roads of central Virginia on a summer day this hadn't been a problem, but this road was a main pike, and as it cut through the South Mountain Range there were sections that had been macadamized with crushed limestone gravel so the going would be tough on bare soles.

In this, the third year of the war, the men passing before him were tough, lean, hard survivors who knew their business. They were stripped down for summer campaigning: a blanket roll over the left shoulder maybe containing an extra pair of socks and shirt, perhaps a Bible stuffed in a breast pocket, a haversack that for once was bulging with rations, a cartridge box with forty rounds, and a good Enfield .577-cal. rifle on their shoulders, in total not more than twenty-five to thirty pounds of equipment.

Headgear in this army truly was a mark of individualism. A few wore kepis, mainly the officers and NCOs; most had on slouch caps, broad brimmed, dirty, sweat stained, more than one on the point of falling apart. A man in the middle of the column was wearing a tall stovepipe, which he courteously removed as he passed, and directly behind him was a redheaded, bucktoothed lad wearing a woman's bonnet, the men around him grinning as he took it off and tried to hide his joke before Lee noticed.

They looked up at him eagerly, eyes bright, some doffing their hats in respect, others saluting, the bolder ones calling out his name, a few asking if the Yankees were up ahead.

It had rained during the night. The air was heavy, damp, coiling wisps of fog trailing up from the mountain range just to the east. The air was rich with morning smells, crushed hay, peaches, and cherries ripening in the orchards. Mingled in, of course, was the smell of the men passing, a rank mixture of scents that every army throughout history cloaked itself in.

Lee edged Traveler onto the road and broke into a smooth canter. Traveler, well rested and well fed for a change, took the pace eagerly. They passed the head of the Georgia column, and this time the fifer boy held his tune.

Next on the road was a battery of three-inch rifles, four guns, battery horses looking like they had just been "requisitioned" from a farm, leaning hard into the ton and a half of gun and caisson. The battery was from Virginia, and he looked at the faces of the boys, wondering if any were the sons of old friends or neighbors from long ago.

The road ahead pushed up through the gap in the South Mountain Range, orchards and split-rail fences flanking the pike, giving way to woods filled with stately old elms and chestnuts that canopied the road. The day promised to be warm, but here in the pass the slanting rays of the morning sun, poking out from a scattered bank of rain clouds, had yet to take off the chill. It was pleasant, like stepping into a dark springhouse on a hot day. Moisture from a shower still clung to the leaves and branches that arced overhead.

The pike was filled with his army — too many men, in fact, for this single road — and at times they were at a standstill, leaning against rifles, waiting for the traffic to clear up ahead. Their spirits were good, though. The day was still young, and they were an army used to triumphs, now moving deep within enemy territory. The world around them was new, fresh, untouched yet by the ravages of war, and thus a world to fill them with curiosity and interest.

But after passing more than a mile of troops frozen in place, Lee felt an increasing frustration. He wanted this army moving, concentrating, not locked in place, and finally he waved for his aide,

Walter Taylor, to come to his side.

"Get a courier forward. I want to know what the delay is up ahead, and tell whoever is responsible to clear the road and keep this column moving!"

Salutes were exchanged, and an eager young boy, delighted with his task, set off at a gallop, knowing that thousands of eyes would be upon him, that he bore an order from General Lee, and perhaps the fate of the Confederacy rested on the safe delivery of the message.

Edging around the stalled columns, Lee and his entourage crested the top of the pass and started downslope, the column ahead still mired in place.

And then he sensed it.

He didn't hear it; rather it was a feeling in the air, a certain tension, a distant pressure. Looking to the side of the road, he saw where several men had broken away from the column, climbed up into trees, and were shading their eyes against the morning sun. They were looking to the east. One of the men was pointing, exclaiming that there was "mischief."

There was a fight up ahead.

The pass came down out of the mountain and into a sloping orchard. Lee turned from the road, weaving through a broken-down section of fence, and cantered through the rows of peach trees, the nearly ripened fruit hanging thick on the branches.

It was ground he had examined on a map, but only now was he seeing it for the first time. Yet already he knew it, the steep, dropping slope that offered a perfect defensive position to either side of the road, the orchards and pastures on the lower slope providing clear fields of fire. It was his fallback position, a place where he had hoped to lure the Army of the Potomac into battle, but what he was feeling in the air whispered to him that such plans were in the past.

Longstreet rode beside him, quiet, his staff trailing behind.

Lee reined in by a small clapboard-sided church and dismounted. There, to the east, was a darker cloud, dirty yellow and gray, eight, maybe ten miles off. A slight tremor in the air, a distant thump of a summer storm far away, of a battle not so far away. Longstreet was still beside him, glasses raised.

"More than a skirmish," Longstreet announced. "Spread out across a half mile or more of front."

"I knew nothing of this," Lee said, looking around at his staff.

They shifted uncomfortably; all were silent.

"Courier coming," Longstreet announced, as the rider approached on a lathered mount, reined in, saluted, and handed the dispatch to Taylor.

"From General Heth, sir," Taylor announced. "He is engaged before Gettysburg. He reports contact with at least one brigade of Union cavalry."

"When was that sent?" Longstreet asked.

"Eight-thirty this morning, sir."

Longstreet pulled out his pocket watch and sighed. "Two hours ago. If it was just cavalry, Harry would have pushed them back by now. I think there's infantry up there, sir."

Lee, still dismounted, said nothing, uncasing his field glasses and slowly scanning the horizon to the east. A shower of rain passing close by half obscured the view. He caught a flash of what appeared to be artillery, clouds of smoke hanging low in the heavy morning air, again blocking off the view.

The courier sent forward earlier to ascertain the reason for the delay on the road came back in and reported. Johnson's division coming down from the north was filing onto the same road up ahead, their supply wagons, thousands of men, creating a snarl of confusion.

Lee looked at Taylor coldly. "That was not the order of march I detailed last night."

"There must have been some confusion, sir."

"Obviously," Lee replied sharply.

He turned away with head lowered, field glasses dangling from his neck, hands clasped behind his back, a gesture that indicated to those around him that he was on edge.

The tie-up on the road was unacceptable. It could be expected with green troops, but this was an army that needed to move fast, especially if a battle was developing just ahead. Someone had "misunderstood" orders yet again. It had happened two months ago at Salem Church, and a certain victory had been thrown away. He would not let it happen again. Not today, especially not today, with so much at stake.

"Colonel Taylor, would you please get out the maps."

There was a scurry of activity. The church was found to be unlocked; a table and chairs were carried out. Lee, like Jackson, refused to use a place of worship for military activities and hesitated even to intrude on a private residence. The furniture was set up under a wide-spread elm behind the church. The headquarters map was unrolled on the table and Lee came over, Longstreet and the staff gathering around.

The courier from Heth was still with them, and Lee looked up. "Lieutenant, is General Heth in the town?" He hesitated, looking again at the map, "Gettysburg?"

The courier, somewhat nervous, came up to the table and shook his head. "Ahh, no sir. There's a big school building up on the crest of the hill just to the west of the town. The Yankees are dug in there. We got right up to it yesterday before retiring back when the Yankee cavalry rode in. I heard the boys say it was a Lutheran Seminary."

"That's west of the town?" Longstreet interrupted.

"Yes, sir."

"Any infantry?"

"We didn't see any, sir."

"They're there," Lee said quietly, looking up from the map and back to the east. "Harry would have driven them by now if it was just cavalry. It's obvious he hasn't; the battle is spreading."

"Heth's orders were to probe, not seek a fight," Longstreet interjected.

Lee nodded.

"We don't know what's up there," Longstreet continued, and he traced the network of roads coming into Gettysburg. "They could be moving up right now, and we're spread out."

"I know that," Lee replied. This time

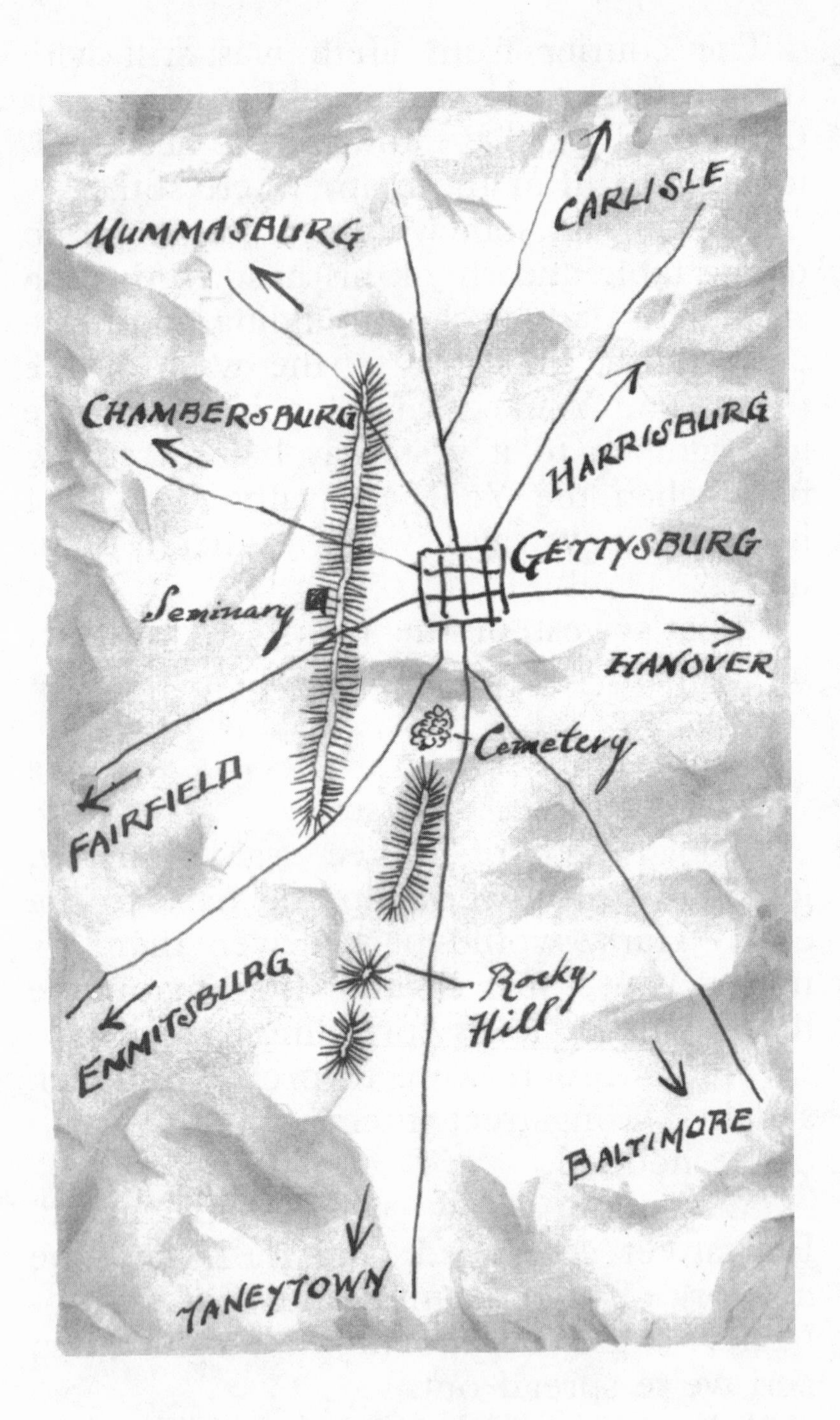
CARLISLE
MUMMASBURG
CHAMBERSBURG
HARRISBURG
GETTYSBURG
Seminary
HANOVER
Cemetery
FAIRFIELD
ENNITSBURG
Rocky
Hill
BALTIMORE
TANEYTOWN

his tone indicated that he wanted silence.

More couriers were coming in as the minutes dragged out while Lee stood silent, gaze locked on the map. Reports now of two Union infantry corps, def-initely the Union's First Corps, possibly the Eleventh as well.

"Sir?"

It was Pete.

"Yes, General?"

"Their entire army might be deploying behind that town."

"You're advising me to break off."

"Sir, Harry Heth stuck his neck into it up there," and Pete pointed off to where the plumes of smoke were boiling up. "There's confusion on the road; we'll be feeding in piecemeal the rest of the day. Pull Heth back. This land right here, sir, it's good ground. They'll come up, just like at Fredericksburg last December. The politicians back in Washington will be screaming at Meade to attack. He's new to his job as commander. He'll feed them in. Atop these heights, we can mow them down."

Lee stepped back from the map, looking to where Pete was pointing. The ground was good, right on the eastern flank of the mountain. Orchards dotted the upper slope, and even as he looked Pete continued to press his case.

"Guns up in the orchards — just drop a few trees for clear fields of fire — infantry farther downslope. Flanks anchored, and a secured line of communications behind us back to Chambersburg. Just like Fredericksburg, even better, sir, with a narrower front. Let them come on, sir."

Lee nodded, then motioned for Longstreet to mount. Lee got into the saddle and rode down the slope, Longstreet coming up by his side. Cutting across an open pasture, reining in at the edge of a cornfield where the stalks were already waist high, they stopped. Lee turned and looked back up the slope. Longstreet was right; the ground was good, very good.

The Dutchman, feeling that he was winning his point, continued to press the argument. "They'll come up these slopes, and it will be a slaughter."

"Malvern Hill in reverse," Lee said quietly. "One year ago today."

Longstreet nodded. Everyone in the army knew Malvern Hill was a sore spot with Lee, a battle he wished he had never fought, a disaster of disorganized brigades charging up an open slope into the muzzles of over a hundred Union guns.

"It will never happen," Lee said quietly,

eyes locked on the slope they had just ridden down.

"Sir?"

"Always consider the position from the view of your opponent. Look at this place," Lee announced, pointing. "Would you attack if they were up there?"

"I don't quite follow you, sir."

"Just that, General," Lee replied sharply. "Neither you nor I would attack if those people were dug in here. We learned that at Malvern Hill. They learned it at Fredericksburg. You have a good eye for ground, General. This position is perfect, and that is why they will never attack us if we dig in here. It's *too* perfect."

"He'll be under pressure from Washington though."

"And we're under a different pressure, General. We can't dig in and wait. Supplies will have to move up through that single road we just traversed. Three, four days and this countryside will be stripped clean of food, and then we'll have to either attack him or pull back.

"No, sir," Lee continued. "Meade will see us dug in here, and he'll wait us out. Then we will have to withdraw, and we will have gained nothing, sir, nothing." He slapped his thigh as he spoke.

"General Longstreet, we cannot continue to fight indecisive battles. Down that road lies defeat. Vicksburg is in trouble; that was part of our reason for coming up north, to try and divert forces away from the fighting in the West. Our own Army of Northern Virginia will never be stronger than it is this week.

"I want this war to end. What will another Fredericksburg give us? Twenty thousand of their men casualties, five to ten thousand of ours, and the slaughter will have given us nothing. Another battle like that just wears us down a little bit more, and they will continue to get stronger in spite of their losses. They can replace their losses in a month; we no longer can.

"We will not end the war fighting defensively in this place, not here. The enemy is up that road, General. General Heth has met them. You saw the map. We know that two of our divisions, Early and Rhodes, are coming down on Gettysburg from the north and northeast. We are coming in from the west. I think, sir, we just might have them. Push in hard, and if God wills it, we can catch part of their army and annihilate it before the rest comes up.

"Our job is to find the right place and shatter the Union army. We have to win a victory so decisive that the North's will to fight will be shaken, and they will agree to a truce. Any victory less than that will ultimately be a strategic defeat. We have had two years of bloody, indecisive fighting. Now is the time for that decision, and down that road toward Gettysburg is where we are going to force it."

"What about Stuart?"

"He'll be found today."

"I hope so."

A rolling thunder, clearly audible now, washed over them, and both looked back to the east.

"General Longstreet, you are now my right arm. I ask you to understand that. I could always count on you in the defense; you demonstrated that at Sharpsburg and Fredericksburg. I need more from you now, General, much more. I need your voice of caution, but I need you to see the opportunity for attack, for audacity."

"I am not Jackson," Longstreet replied coldly.

Lee could sense that he had injured his lieutenant's pride. Jackson had been the darling of the Richmond newspapers, and dead he had been immortalized into an icon that it was impossible to compete against.

"No, nor am I asking that. We have an opportunity here. I want this action pushed, and I am counting on you to see that it is done."

Pete looked back, almost longingly, at the hills he had hoped to dig in on.

"General," Lee asked softly, "if you were Meade, would you attack us here?"

Pete did something that was a rare sight. He smiled and then shook his head. "No, sir. Not here. The ground is too good."

Lee smiled and, turning Traveler, trotted back up the hill to where the staff waited expectantly. Taylor came forward, grinning, holding up a dispatch.

"It's from Stuart," Taylor announced triumphally. "One of the couriers you ordered sent out yesterday morning just reported back in. Stuart was riding toward Carlisle. He is turning about. He'll be here by this evening, and his lead brigade should be in by midnight."

Lee felt a wave of relief. The decision of several nights back to aggressively seek Stuart, to take more direct control, was bearing fruit. He looked over at Longstreet, who nodded, as if the final point had been won.

"Colonel Taylor, it's obvious that battle has been joined, not where we planned, but Providence has ruled differently. Pass the order to all division and corps commanders. Press the action toward Gettysburg and seize the high ground overlooking the town."

He could sense the ripple of excitement sweep through his staff. He nudged Traveler and then turned to look back. "Be certain to return the table and chairs to their proper place, Walter."

Returning to the road, he turned east, heading toward Gettysburg.

1:30 PM, July 1, 1863

Taneytown, Maryland
Field Headquarters, Army of the Potomac

Breathing hard, Henry Hunt climbed the last steps up onto the widow's walk of the Antrim, a mansion at the edge of Taneytown. Meade, with Hooker's old chief of staff, Gen. Dan Butterfield, was leaning on the railing, attention focused to the north.

Henry didn't need to be told where to look. Smoke was boiling up from Gettysburg, ten miles away. Uncasing his field glasses, he leaned against the railing and focused. The church spires of the town were clearly visible, the smoke just to the west. A dull rumble was echoing down, thumping, building, then drifting off.

The day was becoming hot, the morning scattering of showers giving way to a dull sky, not quite clear, not quite hazy, the type of weather that could clear or brew up into an afternoon of fierce storms. The air was heavy, humid, and oppressive.

Turning his field glasses to the west, he clearly saw the Catholic school and convent over at Emmitsburg. Dust was swirling up from the road in front of the school.

"Whose men are those over there?" he asked, looking to one of Meade's staff, who were all silently clustered to either side of the general.

"Dan Sickles's Third Corps."

"Are they moving up?"

"The Eleventh Corps is on the same road and should be in Gettysburg by now," Butterfield announced, not looking back, attention still focused to the north. "We're holding Dan in place for the moment, waiting to see what develops."

Henry nodded and said nothing. He had fairly well memorized the maps of the region over the last couple of days. It was clear that Lee was coming over the South Mountain Range, but was the main thrust toward Gettysburg or was that a diversion and would he hit toward Emmitsburg instead?

He knew the answer without even having to ask it. Lee would move on Gettysburg. It was a better road connection, allowing him to thrust in nearly any direction.

Holding Sickles in reserve at Emmitsburg might be prudent in order to cover the left flank, but Henry sensed it was a waste. Push toward the sound of the guns.

"You hear about Reynolds?" Butterfield asked, turning back at last to look at Henry.

"John Reynolds, First Corps?" He felt a sudden tightness. The old professional army was small, and with every action the rank of comrades thinned.

"Word just came in. Killed a couple of hours ago."

"Damn."

John had always led from the front; it was only a matter of time. He had been Commandant of Cadets at West Point, and many an officer in the army today had first served under him there and worshipped him. Everyone believed John was destined for greatness and that corps command was simply a stepping-stone. It had been, right into a grave.

Henry looked at Meade, who was still hunched over the railing, field glasses trained on the hills to the north. It was Reynolds who was supposed to be commanding this army now. That's who they had really wanted back in Washington. For once the politicians had been right. Meade was good, but John would have been better, a mind perhaps capable of matching Lee's.

But John was dead. He lowered his head, turned, and moved to the other side of the widow's walk, leaning over the side, looking down. Couriers, staff, cavalry escort waited in the open yard below. Dust stirred from farther south and east; columns of troops coming up, Fifth Corps and Second Corps, strung out along twenty miles of road. The entire army was on the move. By tomorrow they'd be concentrated. He looked back to the north, the rumble of fire growing for a moment.

Fight them there or here?

It was a meeting engagement up there, us and them, racing to bring up reinforcements. We win the race, hold the good ground, we roll them up. It was a chance, a roll of the dice, but against Lee that was how things had to be played.

"Hunt."

He stirred. Meade was looking back at him, and Henry stiffened.

"Your report, Hunt."

"I surveyed the ground along Pipe Creek as you ordered, sir."

"Warren has already given me the map."

Henry nodded. Warren had ridden on ahead while he had turned aside for a few minutes to check his batteries parked just outside the town.

"It's a damn good position, sir. Everything you thought it might be. Solid protection on the flanks, clear fields of fire along the entire front, good roads behind the lines to move men, and a rail line just seven or eight miles back at Westminster, linking us back to Baltimore."

"If we can lure Lee down into it," Meade replied. "I'm sending out a circular to the corps commanders that it still might be our position, but it looks like things are being decided differently up there."

Meade pointed toward the north and the distant clouds of smoke.

"You hear about John Reynolds?" Meade asked.

Henry nodded, not saying anything.

"He was in command up there. Now it's General Howard who's senior on the field," and as he spoke Meade gestured toward the dark smudge of smoke rising up into the heavy air.

Henry didn't let his feelings about General Howard show. It wasn't wise to do so when generals were discussing other generals. Some now considered Oliver to be a jinx. He had done well early in the war, losing an arm in a gallant charge at Fair Oaks; but the disastrous rout at Chancellorsville only eight weeks back, when he allowed his entire corps to be flanked and his men panicked, sat squarely on his shoulders. He could be sanctimonious, too, not inspiring confidence when things got tense.

"I've decided to stay here for now," Meade continued. "I've got people spread out from here halfway back to the outskirts of Frederick. John Sedgwick's Sixth Corps is still thirty miles off. The dispatches are coming here, and I'm stuck in this town for now."

Meade leaned back over the railing, gaze fixed on the northern horizon. "I just sent Winfield Hancock forward to take command until the rest of the army comes up."

Henry could not help but let something slip, a nearly audible sigh of relief, and Meade nodded. "Hancock will put backbone into the fight up there. You head up there as well. You might catch Winfield on the road if you move quickly; he left just a short while ago."

"My orders, sir?"

"Organize the artillery. You know your job, Hunt. Put yourself at Hancock's disposal. If it's Gettysburg, and Hancock decides that's the ground to fight it out on, I'll come up later in the day. If not, you help cover the retreat back to here and the line along Pipe Creek. Until we're certain, keep the rest of your Artillery Reserve here in Taneytown, but you are to go forward."

Henry nodded and felt a cool shiver. The long months of exile, of pushing paper, were over. He was being cut loose to fight.

Meade turned away without waiting for a reply, and Henry bounded down the stairs, racing through the broad open corridor of the house and out onto the porch. A young orderly from his staff stood jawing with Henry's headquarters sergeant-major, the two of them relaxed in the shade of the porch. At the sight of Henry's approach, the two stiffened.

Henry pointed at his sergeant. "Williams, get back to my headquarters. Tell them to come up to Gettysburg. You'll find me up there, most likely near where General Hancock is. The Artillery Reserve is to concentrate here, at Taneytown, and await my orders; but get the batteries ready to move at a moment's notice. You got that?"

The sergeant grinned as he swung into the saddle. "Good fight coming, sir?"

"Sure as hell looks that way."

"Don't get yourself killed, sir," and the sergeant was off.

Henry mounted, spurring his horse, orderly falling in behind with guidon. Leaving the grass-covered yard, Henry weaved his way through the town, which was clogged with troops, supply wagons, and, annoyingly, dozens of civilian buggies and wagons filled with curiosity seekers, the vermin who seemed to think that a battle was an event for their amusement.

Several called out, asking what was happening, but he ignored them. One local had had the audacity to set up a stand selling lemonade and cider. Henry made no comment as several men, having drunk their fill, walked off without payment, the proprietor shouting for Henry to arrest them. The man looked healthy enough and should be toting a rifle rather than making a few pennies off men who might be dead by nightfall.

The day was getting hotter, and he reached for his canteen even as he rode, cursing himself for not having filled it at the well back at the house. The lieutenant trailing behind him was new, the boy he replaced having broken a leg in a fall from a horse the day before.

"What's your name, son?" Henry asked.

"Joshua Peeler, sir."

"Where you from?"

"Indiana, sir."

Henry nodded and then let the conversation drop. Never get too close to them. Boys carrying guidons drew bullets, lots of bullets.

Henry gained the road heading out of Taneytown to Gettysburg. Coming up to a low crest just north of town, he could again see the smoke billowing up on the horizon. The field sloping down before him was already beginning to fill with the signs that he was approaching a battle. Skulkers lingered at the edge of the pasture. At the sight of his approach, they ducked back into the woods. The hay in the field was trampled down, fences torn apart, dozens of small, coiling circles of smoke indicating where a couple of regiments had taken a break and built fires to brew up a quick cup of coffee and fry some salt pork before marching on. Half a dozen men were resting under the shade of an elm, and at his approach one of them held up a provost pass, indicating they had been given permission to fall out of the march. They were obviously played out, done in by the heat and the pace of the advance. Several exhausted horses, cut loose from caisson or wagon traces, wandered freely along the road, one of them collapsed in a ditch, gasping for breath.

It was something about the damn war that always affected him. As a boy the sight of an animal in pain had always bothered him. He had once shot a rabbit and not killed it clean. The poor thing started to scream, sounding just like a baby in agony. He couldn't bring himself to kill it, his father having to do it instead. The memory had haunted his childhood nightmares for months. In a world where animals were slaughtered without thought, Henry had been a curiosity, avoiding open mockery only by the strength of his fists.

And yet he had chosen the bloodiest of professions and the bloodiest of arms within that profession. He had seen entire caisson teams, six horses, cut down by a single burst, animals with legs blown off still running, trying to keep up with their harness mates. After Chapultepec, they had burned the carcasses of fifty horses from his battery after carving off the choicer cuts of meat for dinner.

He rode past the collapsed horse, which looked up at him wide-eyed, as if asking forgiveness for being old and weak. He pressed on.

The road dipped down into a hollow, the air pleasant, cool. Fording the calf-deep stream, Henry tossed his canteen to his orderly, who dismounted, went upriver a dozen paces, and filled it.

The shaded glade was peaceful, water swirling around the legs of his horse, who lowered his head to drink. For a moment he could almost forget the war. There was a flash memory of childhood, of playing in the creek on a hot summer day, building dams and little watermills out of sticks and pieces of wood. The lieutenant filling the canteen knelt in the water, splashing some on his face, childlike and innocent, looking as if he were about to challenge Henry to a water fight.

He wanted to forget everything for a minute, to linger here, soaking up the peace, the cool in the midday heat, the quiet without fear of what was to come.

A clattering stirred him from the peaceful moment, and he looked back to the ford. An ambulance was crossing and came to a stop. The driver jumped down, letting the horses drink, and started to fill canteens. At Henry's approach, the driver stood up and saluted.

"From Gettysburg?" Henry asked.

"Yes, sir."

One of the wounded was painfully climbing out of the back of the ambulance, a lieutenant of cavalry.

"Are you with Buford?"

The man, cradling the stump of an arm, nodded. Henry dismounted, took the man's canteen, and knelt down to fill it.

"What's going on up there?"

"Hell of a fight," the lieutenant whispered, "hell of a fight."

"Who were you facing?"

"I got hit early. Kilmer in there," and he nodded to the ambulance, "leg got blown clean off. Mina, he's dead. Died a few minutes ago. Shot in the head; kept calling for his wife."

Henry handed the canteen back to the battle-shocked lieutenant, who was trembling as if the day was icy cold. "What were you facing, son?"

"I heard it was Heth, rest of A. P. Hill's corps behind him. Quinn, I tried to stop the bleeding, but that damn driver wouldn't pull over. Kilmer just needs a drink, and he'll be alright."

Henry spared a glance into the back of the ambulance. It was obvious that the lieutenant's traveling companions were dead, and the boy wasn't far behind. The tourniquet on his arm had slipped.

Henry called the driver over. The driver looked into the back, sighed, and then guided the lieutenant over to the bank of the stream. Sitting him down, he started to reset the tourniquet, the boy feebly struggling to get back up to give a canteen to Kilmer.

"Hospital area's just to the south of town, a few miles back," Henry offered.

Henry's orderly came up and, mounting, Henry started off, looking back at the lieutenant, who was crying like a lost child.

Riding up the slope from the creek bottom, he had to yield the road several times. Ambulances raced past, followed by a lone, panic-stricken rider crying out that the Rebs were into Gettysburg and everyone was dead.

Long experience had taught him that the rear of a battle always looked like a battle lost, and this was no exception. The closer he came to Gettysburg, the more disastrous things appeared. Dozens of exhausted soldiers, collapsing in the July heat, lined the sides of the road, lingering with them the men who had simply collapsed morally and were finding anyway possible to get out of the fight.

A scattering of men were drifting down the pike, obviously having been in a fight. All were dirty, faces looking like they had escaped from a minstrel show, smudged black from tearing open bullet cartridges with their teeth. He caught glimpses of corps badges, the First and the Eleventh. There was no sense in asking them about the fight. These were men who were getting out, and their litany would be the same, that the battle was lost. Things must still be holding up front because there was only one true sign of a general retreat, when the guns fell back.

A dead horse was sprawled in the middle of the road, covered in lathered sweat, next to it an overturned supply wagon filled with rations. A couple of small boys were poking around inside, obviously delighted with all the excitement. Anxious civilians lined the road, all of them asking for reassurance, news. The healthy-looking young men in civilian garb caused his blood to boil, and when several shouted questions he was tempted to pull over, grab them by the collar, put guns in their hands, and push them forward.

Off to his left he caught glimpses of a high, tree-clad hill flanked by a lower rise, and he almost pulled over to climb it but decided to push straight on. An old woman standing by a crossroads held up a small basket with fresh-baked bread at his approach, and he reined in for a moment, grateful for the offering.

"My boy's with the army?" she said, looking at him hopefully. "Jimmy Davidson, Fifty-third Pennsylvania. Do you know him?"

"No, ma'am, I'm sorry I don't."

"He'll be all right, won't he?"

He reached out and touched her arm.

"I lost my youngest at Antietam. You'll see that Jimmy is all right, won't you?"

"I'll see what I can do, ma'am."

She smiled.

"How far to Gettysburg, ma'am?"

"Only two miles or so. The road comes up behind the cemetery where my husband's buried."

"Thank you, ma'am," and he rode on, not looking back as she called out for him to take care of her precious boy.

It was strange but the sound of battle had drifted off, and he half wondered if the engagement had ended and it had, in fact, been simply a diversion. Was Lee up to one of his usual tricks? He felt a vague uneasiness. The entire army was streaming toward Gettysburg, and to turn it about now would be a nightmare.

Along a ridge to the left he caught glimpses of some troopers, mounted, a Union guidon fluttering fitfully in the hot afternoon breeze. Stragglers by the dozens were coming over the ridge, most of them wounded, moving woodenly, slowly, helping each other. A man collapsed and several comrades gathered around to try to bring him back to his feet.

Henry pushed on, caught sight of a rise ahead crested with a graveyard, and felt his pulse quicken. Some guns were up there, the crews digging in, dirt flying. He urged his mount to a swift canter and came up the slope.

There was no need to ask for General Hancock. It was plain to see where he was, marked by his corps guidon and a knot of orderlies and staff. Winfield was in the middle of the road atop the crest, standing out in silhouette like some ancient god of war, wreathed in billowing smoke. He was one of those naturals, Henry realized. You could not help but like him, listen to him, be ready to follow him, even though he was six years younger and not so long ago inferior in rank. War propelled some men forward, and Winfield was one of them.

At his approach Hancock turned, an orderly pointing back down the road, calling attention to Hunt. Winfield smiled and Henry gave a casual salute.

"Good place for your guns here, Henry," Winfield announced, nodding to the cemetery to the left of the road. Henry, saying nothing, appraised the ground. The hill was a clear circular slope, with excellent fields of fire, except for a knoll that extended off to the northeast that would be hard to cover. Ring the upper slope with guns, put a battery or two out on the knoll to secure the flank. Typical of cemeteries, the trees were cut back, well trimmed, the open area beneath the branches offering clear fields of fire for canister. A cemetery makes a damn good killing ground, he thought. He barely considered the irony of the thought.

"Are things simmering down?" Henry asked.

"Hardly. Storm's about to break any second. The Rebs have Early's division coming down on us from the northeast, I'm told. Rhodes's division is to the north, and all of A. P. Hill's corps are hitting us on the far side of that ridge. We had a hell of a fight to the west a couple of hours ago. They drove us back at first; but that's the Iron Brigade up there; and those boys will hold till the bitter end."

As Hancock spoke, he pointed out the lay of the land, the town below them, the open fields beyond to the north. Henry could clearly see dense columns of Confederate troops coming down the road from the northeast, deploying into battle lines, moving through lush, green, patchwork-quilt fields, turning them dark, macabre with their presence, which implied approaching death. Smoke wreathed the hill to the west of the town, but there was little firing at the moment.

"Is this the place for the fight?" Henry asked. "This morning I looked at a place ten miles south of here. It's even better than this. Do you think we could pull Lee down, or is this where we should fight?"

Hancock grinned.

"This is good ground right here, as everyone's been saying, Hunt. Buford saw it, so did Reynolds. We might hold them on the far side of town; if not, we fall back to this crest, dig in, and wait for the rest of the army to come up. For once we have the right position. Put enough guns in the cemetery, and you'll cut the Rebs down like ripened wheat."

Henry nodded. Yes, the guns could do that; the question was, would the infantry support hold?

"Are you in command here, sir?"

Hancock leaned back in the saddle and

laughed softly. "That's what the old snapping turtle back in Taneytown said. You can find Oliver Howard over there," and Hancock pointed to the east side of the road. Less than two hundred yards away was a knot of officers.

"We sort of agreed that he'll handle the situation on the east flank; I'll see to the west. Hell of a way to run a war, but the men will come to me."

"Is that Eleventh Corps deployed north of the town?"

"Yes. Damn Dutchmen, I think they'll break when it hits."

Henry nodded, still surveying the ground. Even as he did so, the pace of fire to the west started to pick up, and then, with a startling roll of thunder, four or five Confederate batteries to the north and east of town opened up.

"Ah, here comes the storm," Hancock announced.

Within minutes it was indeed a storm, a thunderous arch of fire that swept from northeast to due west, across a front of several miles. After gaining the heights west of Gettysburg, the rebels were now advancing to finish the battle off and drive the Union army from the field. Henry was tempted to go farther forward, to look over several batteries he could see north of town; but damn all, they were under the command of Eleventh Corps and he knew Howard would not tolerate any interference.

Half a dozen batteries were atop the crest of the cemetery. That was his place; dig them in, lay out the fields of fire. He had a gut feeling that Reynolds and Hancock had bitten off a bit more than they could chew. Two corps of the Union army were up, but it was evident from the volume of Confederate artillery fire, upward of a hundred guns or more, that perhaps half of Lee's army was beginning to circle in.

If Meade decided that this was a holding operation, it was going to take one hell of a lot of holding, and the cemetery was going to be the key.

Even as he reached that conclusion, Henry could see men breaking out of the battle smoke to the north of town. Tiny, antlike figures, running hard, were zigzagging back and forth, panic-stricken men.

"Goddamn Dutchmen breaking," Hancock snapped. "Just like at Chancellorsville. Can't this army ever hold?"

"I'll see to the guns atop the crest here," Henry said. "I only have one orderly. Can you send a courier back, sir? Tell any batteries on the road to come forward at all possible speed."

Hancock nodded, shouted the order,

and a rider was off.

"Damn all to hell, Henry!" Hancock cried. "Seems like we have one hell of a battle coming down on our necks this day!"

Henry looked at him in amazement. The bastard was actually enjoying it. Thrilling to the challenge, the mastery of it, and even the fear. All he knew was that he was scared half to death at what he was seeing. The Rebs were beginning to break through, on a vast arc, all across the north side of town; and in less than an hour they'd be into his guns atop the hill.

His guns, and he'd better get them ready for it.

Turning away from Hancock, Henry rode through the gate of the cemetery, past the graves, and up to where the guns were digging in.

Chapter Four

4:00 PM, July 1, 1863

McPherson's Ridge
Gettysburg, Pennsylvania

The shell burst knocked him to the ground. Maj. John Williamson, of the Fourteenth South Carolina, felt as if he were floating, not sure if he was alive or already drifting into death. He came back up to his knees. Someone was helping him. He could feel hands on his shoulders, pulling him up.

No pain, just the numbness. The thought triggered a momentary panic. He had seen men eviscerated, entrails looping out onto the ground, stand back up and try to go forward, momentarily unaware that they were dead, until finally the dark hand stilled their heart and they fell.

He started to fumble, feeling his chest, stomach. Where am I hit?

"Sir! Sir!"

Sound was returning. The hazy mist behind his eyes was clearing. It was Sergeant Hazner who was speaking, holding him by the shoulders, turning him around. "Are you all right, sir?"

He tried to speak, but the words wouldn't come.

Someone else came up to his side, Private Jenson, his orderly, eyes wide with fear. "You're alright, sir, just stunned!"

Hazner was shouting, and John looked around. The noise, the noise was returning, a wild roar, the swirling insane thunder of musketry, artillery, men screaming, cursing, crying.

He looked past Hazner. The charge was losing force. The regiment was staggering to a halt, men now crouching in the middle of the open field.

"All right. I'm all right. Keep moving!"

He broke free from Hazner's grasp, and at that instant another shell detonated . . . and Jenson seemed to disappear into pulpy mist, what was left of him spraying over them.

Hazner staggered back, stunned, face covered with Jenson's blood.

John turned away, struggling not to vomit.

"John!"

He looked up; the voice was clear and recognizable, Lt. Colonel Brown, commander of the regiment.

"Goddamn it, John, move these men!" Brown screamed. "We've got to move!"

The sense of what he was supposed to

do, why he was here, returned. He saluted as Brown turned about and disappeared back into the smoke.

John looked down the length of their line. Only minutes before (or was it hours?) they had stepped off, moving past the wreckage of Harry Heth's division, which had fought itself out. Heth's boys had shouted that they were facing that damned Black Hat Brigade of the Yankees' First Corps.

The ridge ahead was wreathed in a dirty yellow-gray cloud of smoke, the only thing visible the pinpoint flashes from muskets and artillery. Above the smoke he caught occasional glimpses of a cupola crowning a large brick building.

"Come on, boys!" It was Brown, stepping in front of the line, waving his sword. "We can't stay out here! Come on!"

The battle line started to surge forward. He heard Brown screaming, urging the men on.

He spared a quick glance for Hazner. The sergeant, face covered with Jenson's blood, pushed back into the line, screaming for the men to keep moving.

"Go, goddamn it, go!" John screamed, adding in his own voice, pushing through the battle line, urging his men forward.

The momentum of the charge began to build again, and he felt swept up in it, driven forward like a leaf, one of thousands of leaves flung into the mouth of a hurricane.

Men were screaming, a wild terrible wolflike cry, the rebel yell.

"Go! Go! Go!"

He kept screaming the single word over and over, urging his men on. Some were ahead of him, running forward, heads down, shoulders hunched, staggering as if into the blast from the open door of a furnace.

He caught a glimpse of the colors. Then the flag bearer spun around, going down in a heap. An instant later he was back up, like a sprinter who had lost his stride but for a second. Disbelieving, John saw that the boy had lost his right arm, blown off at the shoulder. The boy was holding the colors aloft with his left hand, waving them defiantly, screaming for the regiment to press in and kill the bastards.

They were at the bottom of the swale, the ground flattening out, then rising up less than a hundred yards to the crest.

No fire from up forward. Were they running?

The smoke was drifting up, rising in thick, tangled coils.

"Go! Go! Go!"

John caught a glimpse of their line. "Merciful Jesus!" The cry escaped him.

The Yankees weren't running. They had always run when the charge came in. Not this time. They were standing up, preparing to deliver a volley, bright musket barrels rising up, coming down in unison.

A thousand voices all mingled together as one, screams of terror, rage, defiance . . . calls to press on, to charge, to halt, to run. Momentum carried them forward, inexorably forward into the waiting death.

He saw the rippling flash, the explosion of the volley. It swept over them, through them, tearing gaping holes in the line. Men spun around, screaming. The entire line staggered, dozens dropping. Bodies went down in bloody heaps, punched by two, three, even half a dozen rounds.

The line staggered to a halt. Those who were left were raising their rifles, ready to return fire.

"No! Now, charge them now!" The words exploded out of him, and he continued forward, sword raised high.

The mad spine-tingling yell, which had nearly been extinguished by the volley, now redoubled. Men came up around him, shouldering him aside, pressing forward.

The Yankees were so close now John could see their faces, so blackened by powder they looked like badly made-up actors in a minstrel show. Some were frantically working to reload; others were lowering rifles, bayonets poised, others swinging guns around, grabbing the barrels. Yet others were backing up, starting to turn, to run.

The sight of them unleashed a maddened frenzy, his men screaming, coming forward, shouting foul obscenities, roaring like wolves at the scent of blood. They hit the low barricade of fence rails in front of the seminary and went up over it. A musket exploded in his face, burning his check. Clumsily he cut down with his sword, the blade striking thin air, the man before him disappearing.

The melee poured over and around him. They were into the line, breaking it apart. The Yankees were falling back, some running, most giving ground grudgingly, as if they were misers not willing to give a single inch without payment. It was the Black Hats, the Iron Brigade; after their stand at Second Manassas and their valiant charge at Antietam they were the most feared brigade in the Army of the Potomac.

His men surged forward, pressing them across a narrow killing ground, the two lines sometimes touching and exploding into a flurry of kicks, jabs, punches, and clubbed rifles, then parting, firing into each other across a space of less than a dozen yards.

They pushed around the brick building,

crossing over the top of the crest. As the land dropped away, what was left of the Yankee formation broke apart, the last of them turning, running.

John caught a glimpse of men leaping out of the open windows of the seminary, one man dropping from the second floor, his legs snapping as he hit the hard ground. A Yankee officer was by the entryway, wearing a bloody apron, waving a hospital flag.

"Major Williamson! Secure that building! Round up the captives."

He caught a glimpse of Brown in the press, the one-armed flag bearer beside him, still waving the colors.

"Hazner!"

The sergeant was by his side, rounding up a mix of men as John sprinted for the steps. The Yankee officer was still in the doorway; he caught a glimpse of green shoulder straps, a surgeon.

"This is a hospital!" the Yankee shouted.

"Hazner, check the building."

The sergeant shouldered past the Yankee surgeon and cautiously stepped through the door. He hesitated for a second and then plunged into the gloom.

John, the hysteria of the charge still on him, panting for breath, kept his sword pointed at the surgeon.

"I surrender, sir."

"You're damn right you surrender," John gasped.

The surgeon stared, gaze drifting down to the sword that John held poised, aimed at the man's chest.

John suddenly felt embarrassed; the mad frenzy was clearing. The man was a surgeon, a noncombatant. He lowered the sword. "Sorry, sir," he said woodenly.

The surgeon nodded.

"I need help in here," and the surgeon gestured into the building.

The stench was drifting out through the open doors . . . blood, excrement, open wounds, ether; a steady, nerve-tingling hum, groans, cries for water, air, engulfed John as he went inside. He stepped over the body of a Yankee gunner, both legs gone just above the knees, a sticky pool of blood congealing on the floor. The corridor was packed with wounded, men cradling shattered limbs, gasping for air. Frothy bubbles of blood mushroomed from chest wounds. A boy still clutching his fife was crying; a grizzled old sergeant, left foot shot away, sat cradling the lad in his lap.

The sergeant looked up at John, eyes smoldering. John looked away, unable to say anything. He caught a glimpse into a classroom, desks pushed together, a door torn off from its hinges laid across the desks, now serving as a surgeon's table.

They were working on a boy, stripped naked from the waist down, taking his leg off, the meat of the thigh laid open. It reminded John of butchering day, the way the meat of the leg was cut away. He averted his gaze.

"Gave you hell, we did."

He looked down; a lieutenant, pale, sweat beading his face, cradling a shattered arm, holding it tight against his chest, looked up at him defiantly.

"Gave you damn Rebs hell, we did."

John nodded, looking away, trying to find Hazner.

"Reb."

John looked back down.

"A drink. Got anything."

Caught by surprise, John reached around to his canteen and unslung it, handing it down.

The lieutenant tried to reach up, grimacing as he let go of the arm. John could see the white of the bone, arterial blood spurting. The lieutenant groaned, grabbed the arm again.

"Here, let me help," John whispered, as he knelt down, uncorking the canteen, holding it up.

"Whiskey mixed in there; take it slow."

The lieutenant tilted his head back, took a long gulp, choked for a moment, then nodded for more. John held the canteen, let him drink again.

The lieutenant sighed, leaned back. "Ah, that's good, thanks, Reb."

He started to cork the canteen and saw the pleading eyes of a man lying next to the lieutenant, shot through both cheeks, bits of bone and teeth still in the wound. The man couldn't speak, but his desire was clear.

"Major Williamson?"

It was Hazner. The sergeant was standing in the corridor, looking at him.

John handed the canteen to the man shot in the face.

"Take it slow, rinse your mouth out first."

The Yankee nodded, eyes shiny, unable to speak.

"Where you from, Reb?" It was the lieutenant.

"South Carolina." He hesitated, then the question spilled out, "And you?"

"Indiana. Lafayette. Nineteenth Indiana."

"Iron Brigade?"

The lieutenant's eyes brightened. "Yes, by God, and we gave it to you today."

John had a flash memory of the final volley, the way the muskets had caught the sunlight sifting through the smoke, the flashing barrels lowering as if guided by a single hand, the shattering volley at near point-blank range.

"You did well, Lieutenant."

"You won't win this one, Major."

John said nothing.

"We'll keep fighting. Keep fighting, we'll never give up."

"Nor will we," John said quietly.

"Lieutenant, you're next."

Two orderlies stepped to either side of John and reached out with blood-caked hands, helping the lieutenant up. John stood up, motioning for the man next to him to keep the canteen. Inwardly he regretted the decision. It was hot. The day was still long, but he didn't have the heart to take it back as the man raised it up and vainly struggled to rinse his mouth out so he could get a drink, blood, watered whiskey, bits of teeth, and saliva dribbling down his jacket.

John stood, heading toward Hazner. The lieutenant was going through the door into the operating room. The boy on the table before him was dead, two orderlies lifting the body off, clearing the way for the next customer for the knife. John caught the lieutenant's eyes for a second.

"Good luck."

"You too, Reb."

"Major, you gotta see this."

Hazner was by his side, pointing.

John followed as Hazner reached the

staircase and started up.

Damn strange war, John thought. Ten minutes earlier I would have killed him, killed everyone in here; now I leave my canteen with them.

Hazner took the steps two and three at a time, shouldering aside the Yankees who cluttered the way. Surprisingly, some of them were still armed, but he could see the fight was out of them as they leaned against the blood-splattered walls or sat in dejected silence.

Reaching the top floor, Hazner pointed the way to a ladder that ascended into the cupola. One of his men stood with lowered musket, pointing it casually at several officers. One of them made the gesture of offering his sword; John waved him aside.

He followed Hazner up the ladder, and as they emerged through the hatchway, the relative silence inside gave way to a thunderous roar.

John stepped up onto the platform. "My God."

Hazner looked at him, grinning like a child. "Best seats in the house!" the sergeant cried.

John soaked in every detail and knew that if he should live a hundred years, this moment, this place, would forever be etched into his soul.

A great, vast sweeping line, rank upon rank, regiments, brigades, entire divisions were arrayed in a giant arc, closing in on the town of Gettysburg from the northeast, north, northwest, and directly below from the west.

Dozens of battle flags, red Saint Andrew's crosses and state flags marked the advance. Formations moving forward behind the colors looking like inverted *V*s.

They were running, the Yankees were running, and he felt a wave of exultation. All semblance of formation was lost, crowds of men were stampeding, pouring into the streets of the town, surging around the perimeter, jumping fences, stumbling, falling. The roads were tangled knots of artillery limbers and caissons, ambulances, supply wagons. A thunderclap erupted to his left, and John turned, saw the first gun of Pegram's battalion already in place. Other guns were coming up the road, driving hard, swinging into position.

The noise was beyond anything he could imagine, louder even than in the woods of Chancellorsville. It was a wild, steady, thundering roar, punctuated by the shrieking rebel yell as the arc closed in, driving the Yankees.

A hissing scream snapped past the cupola, followed an instant later by another, the shell bursting fifty yards behind them.

He looked past the town. A hill rose up beyond, wreathed in smoke, billowing clouds igniting . . . artillery.

"Here, sir, got this from one of them Yankee officers."

Hazner handed John a pair of field glasses. One of the cylinders was badly dented, the lens cracked. He closed his left eye and focused the one good lens, training it on the hill.

The lower slopes were swarming with men, disorganized clumps, flotsam tossed up on a stormy beach, the tide of defeat sending them up and over the hill. Here and there defiant groups clustered around their flags, turning, firing, then continuing to fall back.

The top of the hill was crowned by a cemetery. Guns ringed the crest. Even as he watched, a battery of three guns laboriously climbed the hill, gunners leaning against the wheels, helping the exhausted horses. Men came running down to help. A mounted officer galloped up to the battery, reining in, gesturing, pointing.

"Digging in up there, sir."

John said nothing, studying the position.

It was good ground for them. He caught a glimpse of a swarm of men, running up the road that crested the hill. An officer cut in front of them, waving a sword. Some of them surged around the officer, continuing in their mad flight, but most slowed, a few collapsing on their hands and knees and then staggering back up, forming around a flag.

John turned and looked back westward. The Cashtown Road, the road they had advanced on only this morning, was clearly visible, all the way back to the South Mountains. It was packed with troops, long, swaying columns. Afternoon sunlight poked through the clouds, flashing on the muskets. He saw a cluster of officers riding alongside the road coming toward him. Men were raising rifles, hats held aloft, a rippling movement that swept down the line as the officers pressed forward at a slow canter.

"Come on!" John cried.

He slid down the ladder, landing hard, and ran down the stairs. Reaching the main floor, he gingerly stepped around the wounded. The surgeon who had surrendered the building tried to say something, but John avoided him, moving fast.

He raced out of the building. All was confusion outside, wounded Yankees, wounded Confederates now intermingled. Those who could walk were coming up from the field where the charge had swept in. Several hundred bluecoats, disarmed, sat around the building, a few sentries guarding them. A column of troops, moving on the double, was coming up over the crest, following their colors, a North Carolina state flag. The men were panting, canteens rattling. A number of men had pairs of shoes tied by the laces and slung over their shoulders or around their necks, booty stripped from the dead, but there was no time yet to try them on. He reached the road just as the knot of officers came up the slope.

Men were stopping, seeing who was coming, cheering.

John took a deep breath and stepped in front of the group. "Walter! Walter!"

One of the officers looked over, saw John, smiled, and reined in.

John, remembering that his old friend was now a superior in rank, came loosely to attention and saluted.

Lt. Col. Walter Taylor, chief of staff to Gen. Robert E. Lee, leaned over and extended his hand. "John, how are you?"

"Tolerable. A hard fight."

"Saw you go in. You were magnificent. The general said it was a proud day for South Carolina."

John caught a glimpse of the general coming up the slope, General Longstreet by his side.

"Walter, can I have a word with the general?"

Walter looked at him appraisingly. He was the gatekeeper, the one who fended off the glory seekers, the hangers-on, the dozens, the hundreds who every day wanted to see Lee.

"Up there, Walter," and he pointed to the cupola. "Go up there. You can see the whole thing. There's a hill beyond the town; that's where they're falling back. I saw everything from up there."

"The cemetery?"

"Yes."

Walter nodded. "Follow me."

Lee approached. John looked up at him. He had seen Lee numerous times. Being an old college roommate of the chief of staff meant that he was often invited to headquarters for a late-night drink or game of cards. Yet every time he had seen him, there was a cold chill, a sense of reverent awe, a belief that if their country was to survive that this man would be the savior. He remembered him from just three nights back, sitting alone in the field, most likely contemplating all that was now happening.

John remembered as well his own panic and terror of that night. It had lingered about him like an unpleasant scent in the air that would not disappear. He had mastered it again for the moment, caught up in the hysteria of the charge, but the fear was still there, whispering to him, warning that something terrible was just ahead.

He forced the thought aside. He was about to speak to the "Old Man," and he had to play his part.

He self-consciously tugged at his uniform and caught a glimpse of Sergeant Hazner by his side, fumbling to button up his jacket.

Walter intercepted Lee; the two exchanged words; Lee looked over, nodded, approached the last dozen yards, and stopped.

John saluted.

Lee, eyes bright, calm, looked down, the touch of a smile on his face. "I trust you are well, Major Williamson."

John, surprised that Lee remembered his name, could barely speak for a moment.

"The blood, sir, are you hurt?"

John looked down at his uniform . . . his orderly, head gone, body collapsing. He shook his head. "No, sir. One of my men . . ." and his voice trailed off.

Lee nodded, a fatherly look of understanding in his eyes. "South Carolina did splendidly today," Lee finally replied. "I saw the charge go in."

"Thank you, sir," and he hesitated, not

sure what to say next.

"You have some information for me?"

John gulped, nodded. "Sir. From up there," and he pointed back to the cupola. "I was just up there. We're driving them, sir, really driving them. But south of the town, they're beginning to reform. Artillery, I'd say at least thirty guns, sir, and what's left of their infantry; most of it is rallying."

General Longstreet reined in beside Lee, catching John's last words. "Fresh troops?" Longstreet asked.

"I didn't see any, sir."

John was surprised at how casually Longstreet had interrupted the conversation, but Lee did not react.

Lee looked over at Longstreet. "We have their First and Eleventh Corps here, and we've defeated them," Lee said. "It might be nightfall before the rest of them begin to come up."

"We are not sure what's beyond that hill," Longstreet replied, pointing east, where the crest of Cemetery Hill was just visible, covered in smoke.

Lee looked back down at John. "Thirty guns?"

"I can't promise that, sir, but I think that's close. I saw a battery coming out of the town and moving into place. There might be more soon."

Lee turned his attention back to Longstreet.

"Sir," Longstreet said slowly, "we've done well today, very well. We don't want to get tangled up in that town. If we try for that next hill now, we might be sticking our necks out."

"General Longstreet, we have them on the run. We will drive these people, drive them, sir!"

He stopped for a second, looking with solemn determination from Longstreet to Taylor, then back to Longstreet again. John stood by, aware that Lee barely noticed that he was there.

"Drive them, sir, drive them. If they are running, I will press them."

As he spoke the last words, he gestured toward the town, to the heart of the battle. John turned to look and sensed that the thunder was abating, the attack dying off even as Lee called for the battle to continue.

"Now is when to press them," Lee said, his voice sharp. "I want those people driven off that far hill within the hour. Colonel Taylor, let us go find General Ewell."

Longstreet began to speak, but a glance from Lee stilled him.

"General Longstreet, return to your corps. Have them come forward with all possible haste. General Hill is not well today. If need be, you are to assume control over his men still on the road and press them forward. I want Johnson and Anderson's divisions to come forward and prepare to go into action."

Without waiting for a reply, Lee reined Traveler around and started toward the town.

John saluted as he passed, but the general did not notice.

"By God, what is going on with him today?" Longstreet asked, looking over at Taylor.

"His blood is up, General. His blood is up."

Walter saluted as Longstreet, features grim, turned his mount and started back in the opposite direction.

Walter looked down at John. "Take care, John. It's a hot day."

John saluted, saying nothing as Walter set off to catch up with Lee.

A hot day. Suddenly he felt very thirsty.

"Sergeant, you got a drink?"

Hazner shook his head. "Gave my canteen to some Yankee."

"Damn it," John sighed.

"Sir, we better get back to the regiment. The Old Man's blood is up, and you know what that means."

John watched as Lee cantered down the

road, heading into the town, hat off, acknowledging the cheers of his men, urging them forward. He could sense the vibrant excitement rushing through the army, the indefinable *something,* the inner spark that Lee could strike and, once struck, exploded into flame. It felt as if they were on the edge of a distant dream, that just beyond the mist, the smoke ahead, were the green, sunlit fields . . . of home.

"Perhaps today is the last day," John whispered. "Perhaps today we will finish it."

5:15 PM

Cemetery Hill

US "That's it Dilger, feed it to 'em, damn them, feed it to 'em!"

Sitting down to see under the smoke, Henry braced his elbows on his knees and trained his field glasses on the column of Confederate infantry cresting over Seminary Ridge.

"Number one . . . fire!"

The first of Dilger's Napoleons recoiled with a thunderclap boom, smoke jetting from the muzzle and touchhole.

"Number two . . . fire!"

Henry waited expectantly.

"Number three . . . fire!"

A yellow blossom of fire ignited fifty yards short of the Reb column.

"Number four . . . fire!"

No detonation from the second . . . "Goddamn fuses," he muttered softly. Number three's shell slammed into the flank of the column and detonated, toylike figures of men tumbling over.

"That's the stuff, number three!" Henry cried, coming back to his feet.

The powder-begrimed crew paused for a second in their labors, looking over at Henry, grinning, but knew better than to revel in their glory, and within seconds were back to work.

"Number one, set your damn sights!"

Captain Dilger, whose Ohio volunteer battery had been in action since midmorning, came up to the colonel. "Sir, ammunition?" Dilger asked, voice barely a whisper.

Henry unslung his canteen and handed it over. The captain took a mouthful, rinsed, spat it out, and then took several long gulps.

"I'm bringing up more," Henry said, "just keep pouring it in."

"Thank you," but his voice still cracked, raw from hours of shouting, breathing the thick, sulfurous fumes, and from sheer exhaustion.

"Pour it on 'em," Henry replied. "You've got infantry columns in flank, by God," and he pointed toward the seminary, where snakelike lines of butternut and gray, following their regimental flags, were pouring over the ridgeline north of town, streaming down into the fields beyond, maneuvering past the town and heading east.

"My God, the arrogance of those people marching like that," Henry exclaimed excitedly. "Just pour it on. I'll make sure you get resupplied." He started to turn away.

"Sir?"

Henry looked back.

"Ah, sir. My men, it's been . . ." His voice trailed off under Henry's icy gaze.

"We hold this hill till the last gun, the last man," Henry replied sharply. "I don't give a damn if you are the last man standing, these guns don't go back another inch."

"Yes, sir."

Number one fired again. He turned his attention back, but the smoke was too thick; it was impossible to see.

"You have the range!" Henry shouted, section commanders and gun sergeants looking back at him. "Smoke or no smoke, keep pouring it on!"

He stalked off, barely flinching as a

shot plowed through the trees overhead, branches ripping off, littering the ground around him.

Looking downslope, he watched as the infantry continued to dig in. Most of them were General Schurz's Germans, the one reserve brigade from Eleventh Corps who had been held back by Howard to fortify the hill. They were the only fresh troops left; and though most of their comrades had broken and run in the debacle north of town, these men still looked fit, eager to prove their name.

A colonel, seeing Henry, came off the line, approached, and gave a friendly salute. "Think the Rebs are going to keep coming?" he asked.

"By God, I hope the bastards do come," Henry growled.

Even as he spoke, there was a flurry of rifle fire, confused shouts. Out of the smoke clinging to the bottom of the hill, shadowy forms emerged, dark blue uniforms, running, most of them unarmed. One of them spun around, going down, his comrades leaving him behind. They reached Schurz's line, refusing to stop, crying that everything was lost and that the Rebs were coming.

Henry watched disdainfully as the men, several of them officers, staggered past. A light breeze eddied across the face of the hill, lifting the smoke, revealing hundreds of panic-stricken Union troops still pouring out of the town.

The infantry colonel, features drawn, looked over at Hunt. "A shameful day for Eleventh Corps," he sighed, shaking his head. "We broke at Chancellorsville and again today. Damn it all, sir, I have good men in my command; its just that we keep getting put out on the flank."

"Redeem it then, Colonel. I'm counting on you to cover my guns. You want to redeem your honor? Then hold, man. You've got to hold."

Dilger's battery fired again, the infantry downslope and in front of the guns crouching low, cursing as the shells screamed over them.

"If it comes to canister rounds, I want clear fields of fire in front!" Henry shouted. "We won't have time to stop for anyone still in front. Make sure of that, Colonel. When the time comes, you pull back in around my guns and clear the field for my canisters."

Henry turned and continued down the line without waiting for a reply. Next to Dilger, to the east and nearly astride the main road to Baltimore, were the three twelve-pound Napoleon smoothbores of Stewart's Battery B, Fourth U.S. Regulars.

Their professionalism showed. At midmorning, on the flank of the railroad cut, the Rebs had surged up to the muzzles of their guns and the battery had held, before being ordered to retreat back to the cemetery.

The intensity of their fight showed. Limber wagons, caissons, and even the field pieces were scored and splintered from rifle fire. The once-polished bronze barrels were blackened, the men grimy, uniforms torn, more than one soldier with a makeshift bandage around an arm or leg. Some infantry had been drafted into the ranks to replace those lost in the final melee, the new recruits serving on the wheels and prolonge to maneuver the pieces back into place after firing. The smoothbores didn't have the range to accurately shell the troops maneuvering to the north of town, so instead they were carefully dropping case shot against any columns of Rebs moving within the town of Gettysburg.

No need to offer advice Henry thought, as the sergeant on the number two piece, not satisfied with the aim, crouched back down, sighting along the barrel, urging the two men working the prolonge to shift the trail piece a couple of inches to the right. Both his hands suddenly went up, signaling that the gun was correctly laid. He barely touched the elevation gear positioned under the breech and detached the rear sight. Reaching into the pouch dangling from his hip, he pulled out a fresh friction primer and inserted it into the breech, then clipped the lanyard to the primer. Stepping back and to the side of the gun, he uncoiled the lanyard until it was taut. The sergeant did his job with an almost detached calm, even though the air was alive with the hum of bullets, the shriek of enemy solid shot, and shells winging in.

"Stand clear!"

The infantrymen pressed into service jumped back from the gun, turning away, covering their ears. The sergeant looked back over his shoulder to Stewart, the battery commander, waiting for the signal. As his gaze swept back, he caught a glimpse of Henry. There was a flash of recognition and a nod. O'Donald . . . sergeant back with Battery A of the Second, long before the war, his first command.

Henry returned the nod and smiled, remembering O'Donald as the quintessential Irish artilleryman, loudmouthed, a first-class brawler who could clear out a saloon, especially if some cavalrymen dared to make a comment about gunners. He was proud of his craft, every inch a professional.

"Number two . . . fire!"

O'Donald jerked the lanyard, turning half away as he did so. The Napoleon let off with a roar. Mingled in with the discharge was the sound that was music to Hunt's ears, the almost bell-like ring from the bronze tube as it belched forth its twelve-pound shot, a sound distinctly different than the sharper crack of the ten-pound rifles.

The crew leapt to work, rolling the gun back into position.

"General Hunt!"

Henry turned. . . . It was Hancock. Winfield Scott Hancock, trim looking, almost dapper in a sparkling white shirt, cuffs and collar still clean. His coat was adorned with two stars on each shoulder and neatly tailored. He was no dandy though. There was a radiant power that generated the instant respect that Henry always felt in his presence. Hancock reined in hard, followed by half a dozen of his staff.

"Glad to see you're still alive, Henry!" Hancock shouted, leaning over from the saddle, extending his hand.

"You too, sir."

Henry grinned. Winfield was his definition of a commander, a man who led from the front and set the example. Another shell whistled past. Winfield didn't notice it, even though those trailing behind him flinched and ducked low in their saddles. "Henry, they'll do it any minute now."

Henry spared a quick glance back to the north. The massive columns, what looked to be an entire division, were still moving, continuing to flank to the east. "They might wait till those reinforcements are in position."

"I think that's Johnson," Hancock replied, "the old Stonewall division, the best they've got. But it'll be an hour or more before they're in position.

"They're pressing hard, damn hard. Bobbie Lee won't wait. He's coming straight in with what he's got."

Bobbie Lee. Damn, how strange this all is. There was a time when I would have led a battery straight into the gates of hell if that old man had asked me.

He can go to hell by himself for abandoning the flag and his oath to it, Henry thought bitterly. Let him come and try to take this hill now.

"Henry, can you hold?"

"Ammunition. Give me enough, and I'll hold this hill until Judgment Day. But if they come on now, I'll need more ammunition for later when Johnson comes in."

"You hold now; I'll worry about later. Give 'em everything you've got!"

As if in fulfillment of Hancock's

prophecy, Henry saw a column of Confederate infantry emerging out of the smoke that drifted along the streets of the town. They were on the Baltimore Pike, charging straight in. Another column poured out of a side street, spreading out, no semblance of order, just a ragged tangle, coming on fast, jumping over fences, moving through back lots, kitchen gardens, and alleyways.

"This is it!" Hancock roared.

Spurring his mount, he tore past Henry, waving his hat, standing in his stirrups, shouting for the men to get ready.

Henry looked over his shoulder. His orderly was still trailing, leading his mount. He ran over, got back into the saddle, and grabbed the reins.

"This road is the Baltimore Pike," and as he spoke he pointed at the road that passed in front of the cemetery gate; "it heads back to Littlestown. There are troops and batteries strung along it for miles. I want you to ride like hell."

The boy nodded, looking past Henry, taking in the sight of the advancing Confederates, eyes wide.

"Look at me, damn you!" The boy shifted his gaze and stiffened under Henry's icy stare.

"Any batteries you pass, tell them I am

ordering them up here on the double. I need ammunition, especially canister. You tell any battery commander you meet, press the ammunition forward. If need be, drive the horses till they drop and then push the damn limber wagons by hand! Now go!"

The boy, impressed with the urgency of his mission, forgot to salute as he reined his horse about and set off at a gallop.

Henry moved along the line, angling downslope to a knoll at the northern tip of Cemetery Hill, where the Reb assault would first hit. Wiedrich's First New York Light Artillery, one of two batteries of Napoleons kept back by Howard and ordered to dig in, held the forward point. The men had been frantically working throughout the afternoon, their efforts undoubtedly spurred on by the sight of the disaster befalling their comrades north and west of the town.

Crescent-shaped lunettes, piles of dirt, fence rails, logs, anything that could stop an incoming round, were thrown up around the four guns. Decimated regiments, what was left of Adelbert Ames's brigade from the battered Eleventh Corps, deployed around the guns, a lone regiment farther downslope. Henry reined in behind the four guns, judging the lay of their fire as the four guns slammed case shot into the advancing enemy.

Red flags — the Saint Andrew's crosses of the Army of Northern Virginia — were streaming out of the town, half a dozen regiments at least, not slowing to shake formation out from line to column; they were coming on at the double.

"Arrogant bastards!"

It was General Ames, face powder blackened, uniform sleeve torn, hat gone, hard pushed but obviously boiling for a fight, standing by Henry's side.

"Land north of town is a worthless piece of shit!" Ames shouted, pointing to the indefensible flat ground. "I told Howard, put us all here, but he sent us over there instead. I lost half my brigade."

Henry said nothing, attention focused on the advancing Rebs, still four hundred yards out. Every gun that could be brought to bear, more than thirty of them, was opening up. Case shot ignited over the enemy lines, dropping dozens. Still they pressed on.

"Good ground here though," Ames continued. "Let the sons of bitches come. You back me up, Henry, just back me up."

Henry remembered Ames as an infantry captain before the war, the star on his shoulders a very recent climb to the exalted rank of brigadier general, supposedly for organizing and training some regiment from Maine to a fighting pitch and leading it into action at Fredericksburg.

"It's the other way around!" Henry shouted back. "Support my guns, and we hold this hill."

Ames, noted for a volatile temper, colored slightly, then broke into a grin. "All right then, damn it, all right."

Ames left him, going on foot down the slope to his forward regiment, the Seventeenth Connecticut, deployed at the bottom of the hill.

Henry rode straight into the middle of Wiedrich's battery, the men working slavishly at reloading, fuses on the case shot cut to two seconds.

Guns recoiled, their thunder joined by the other batteries ringing the hill. He heard the sharp whine of shells from Stevens's guns, deployed on a knoll flanking the east side of Cemetery Hill, the three-inch bolts skimming close to where he stood, dropping down into the rebel lines, detonating with deadly accuracy.

"Canister! Switch to canister!" Henry roared.

Wiedrich's loaders, working at the caissons, deployed twenty yards behind the pieces, picked up the premade rounds, tins holding seventy iron balls and strapped directly to serge powder bags so that the close-in ammunition could be loaded more swiftly. The loaders ran forward, gun sergeants swearing, urging the men on.

Henry watched, always the professional. He carefully eyed the pieces, nodding with approval as gun sergeants actually raised elevation slightly to loft the canister rounds across the three hundred yards to the closing enemy lines. On a flat plain he'd still be ordering case shot, but this high up, canister would plunge down into the Rebs with enough force still remaining to break an arm or smash a skull.

The first gun fired, the other three following suit in a matter of seconds. The deadly dance continued: gunners wheeling pieces back into place, rammers sponging out gun bores to kill any sparks, loaders running up with ammunition, sergeants directing the lay of their piece, depressing elevation slightly, even as the rammers slammed the rounds in. Pieces were primed, crews stepping back, section commanders shouting the order, the one-ton Napoleons lifting up with a terrifying recoil. The hissing scream of canister tins bursting as they cleared the breech echoed around Henry, iron balls shrieking downrange. If close enough, one could hear the sound of that hot iron tearing off arms, legs, killing with a hideous cruelty.

And still they came on. The enemy lines were spreading out, a brigade or more coming straight at Wiedrich and Ames.

The Seventeenth Connecticut, down at the bottom of the slope, opened up with a sharp volley. Schurz's men, on the left flank, opened as well, a good hard volley that cut into the flank of the Reb charge.

Another volley from Connecticut and then the men started to pull back, not running, Ames directing the orderly retreat, his high, clear voice ringing, making it clear he'd shoot the first bastard who tried to run.

The Seventeenth poured up the hill, the sight of their pullback heartening the Rebs, who let loose a triumphal shrieking roar. The defiant note of it, almost a mocking laugh, stiffened the men around Henry.

"Come on and get it, you sons of bitches!" one of the men of the Seventeenth cried as he came up over the lunette of Wiedrich's second gun.

His cry was picked up by others who stood, holding rifles high, bitter men, angry at the beating they had been taking all day, ashamed, and now ready to prove something.

"Come on, come on and get it!" the scream rolled up and down the line.

"All the cowards have run off. What we have left is the steel." It was Hancock, reining in by Henry's side. He stood up tall in the stirrups, right fist punching the air. "Come on, come on and get it, you bastards!"

Henry, looking at him, felt that here was a moment he would forever hold in memory, the late afternoon sun slanting in, illuminating Hancock, behind him and arrayed up the slope of Cemetery Hill, six batteries, thirty guns, firing, smoke billowing, tongues of fire lashing out, and Hancock filling the foreground like a god of war, fist raised high, urging the enemy to just try and take the hill.

The men of the Seventeenth filled in around the guns, hunkering down, rifles poised, flinching as the guns beside them fired yet again. The range was down to less than 200 yards and then to 150.

For a gunner this was a murderous dream, to be up on a good slope, supported by infantry, the enemy in canister range with only a scattering of ineffective counterbattery fire in support . . . it was impossible to miss them.

"They're actually going to try for it!" Hancock exclaimed.

Henry didn't need to be told. Enemy flag bearers were at the fore, colors leaning forward, officers waving swords, the rebel yell echoing.

A hundred yards, they were on the slope, over the low stone wall abandoned by the Seventeenth pouring up the road, breaking into a run.

Madness!

"Wiedrich, load double canister!"

His battery commander didn't need to be told. The charge was coming on fast; Ames's men were pouring it on, volleys by companies and regiments, then the steady staccato roar of independent fire.

Gun sergeants waited, poised, crouching low, holding lanyards taut. The Rebs, seeing what was ahead — a full battery loading with double canister — slowed, until officers and noncoms, screaming for the charge, pushed them forward. In the fore was a lone mounted officer, hat gone, white hair streaming, standing in his stirrups, urging the men on.

"Battery! . . . Fire!"

Wiedrich's four guns recoiled, each piece discharging nearly 150 two-ounce iron balls. Six-hundred man-killing rounds filled the space in front of the battery, screaming downrange, turning the space ahead into an impenetrable killing zone.

The impact was devastating. Entire lines went down. Men were picked up, pitched backward half a dozen yards, decapitated bodies, broken limbs, shattered muskets, torn-up sod, gravel, and dust, the debris swirled up by hundreds of canister rounds flung high into the air.

"That's it!" Hancock screamed. "Again, give it to them again!"

Amazingly, out of the dust and smoke, a rebel battle line emerged. There were gaping holes, but still they pressed on. Rifle fire flickered out of the smoke.

Henry's mount let out an agonizing shriek, rearing up, nearly throwing him. The horse started to roll over on its side. Kicking his feet out of the stirrups, Henry jumped clear, rolling as the horse crashed down, its hooves flaying the air.

Stunned, Henry came back up to his feet and was staggered as the horse, thrashing in its death agony, kicked him just above his left knee, nearly knocking him back over. For a second he thought the leg was broken.

He stepped back and then felt a tug at his left shoulder. He looked down and saw the ragged tear where a rifle ball or a shell fragment had torn off his shoulder strap.

The sound of battle redoubled into a thundering roar. He looked up. Hancock was still mounted, still standing in his stirrups, shouting. A gun sergeant, stepping back, pulling his lanyard taut, ready to fire, suddenly spun around and collapsed, clutching frantically at his throat, bright arterial blood spraying out in a geyser.

The section commander came up, tried to grab the lanyard, and went down as well.

Beyond the gun, Henry could see them pouring in; several of the Rebs, dashing forward with fanatical bravery, were already up on to the lunette, bayonets poised, only to be swept away as the men of the Seventeenth rose up to meet them. Hand-to-hand fighting exploded around the guns.

Henry limped forward into the middle of the melee, ducking low under a musket butt swung by a screaming Reb, who was suddenly tossed backward, shot in the chest. Henry reached down and picked up the lanyard.

He looked forward. Men were coming out of the smoke, a flag bearer in the lead.

He jerked the lanyard taut and then pulled. The Napoleon leapt back with a thunderclap roar. Those in front of the bore simply disappeared, blown into a pulpy spray.

He dropped the lanyard, pulled out his revolver . . . but there was nothing left to shoot at . . . only the smoke engulfing them. He caught shadowy glimpses of Rebs falling back, running, disappearing into the smoke. The charge was broken.

On the ground, in front of the gun he had just fired, was a rebel flag, a red Saint Andrew's cross, torn to shreds, staff gone, a twitching body next to it, the flag bearer, the bottom half of his body nothing but a ghastly tangle of charred flesh that was still smoking from the blast.

One of Wiedrich's gunners scrambled over the lunette and started to pick up the flag. The Reb feebly reached out, trying to hang onto the colors. The gunner stopped, knelt down by his side, and relinquished the flag, gently putting the colors back into the hands of the dying boy. The gunner cupped his hands around the Confederate's, leaned over, whispering something. The eyes of the dying boy shifted, looking up at the gunner. He started to say something, lips moving. Henry heard the words drifting as the two spoke together.

" 'He maketh me to lie down in green pastures . . .' "

The boy shook convulsively and then was still.

The gunner closed the Reb's eyes and then gently pried the bloody fingers loose.

He picked up the flag. There was no triumphal waving of it. The men of the battery stood silent, staring at him. The gunner came back over the lunette, tears streaming down his blackened face.

The smoke was lifting. What was left of the Rebs receded back down the slope. Flanking batteries continued to pound them, bright sparkling airburst of case shot igniting. Stevens's battery had lifted its range, pouring shell into the streets of the town.

"Henry, you all right?"

Still dazed, Henry looked up to see Hancock, blood streaming down his face from a ball that had creased his cheek.

Henry nodded, unable to speak, stunned by all that had happened and what he had just seen.

Hancock motioned for him to step away from the battery. Henry followed and Hancock dismounted, pulled out a clean white handkerchief, and absently dabbed at the nasty furrow plowed across his cheek.

"He came on too soon," Hancock said, voice calm.

Henry looked at him, finding it hard to

believe that only minutes before Hancock had appeared godlike, standing in his stirrups, ignoring the hail of fire, and was now talking quietly, as if they were neighbors sitting on a porch, chatting about the weather.

"A brigade. He thought he could trigger another panic, push us off this hill with just one brigade," Hancock continued, shaking his head. "Damn, is that man arrogant. This isn't Virginia anymore. We're on our own ground now. He came on too soon."

Henry looked past Hancock. The column north of Gettysburg was still moving, flanking around the edge of town, starting to shake out from column into line. A brigade last time, now a division, a full division.

"Look to the seminary; more forming up there."

Henry shifted his gaze. Amid all this madness Hancock was already thinking ahead and had noticed what was going on a mile away.

"Another division over there, I suspect. Maybe fresh, maybe the troops that hit Doubleday earlier. Either way, half hour at most and then they'll come in again, hitting us from both sides of the town."

"Ammunition," Henry said, "I've got to get more ammunition up here, more guns."

"Jones, give your horse to the colonel."

Hancock motioned for one of his orderlies to come over and dismount. The boy offered the reins to Henry.

"Henry, I don't want you down here when they come in again," Winfield said softly.

"Sir?"

"When that division over there charges," and he pointed to the northeast, "they'll roll over this position."

He paused, looking at Wiedrich's men. "God save them, Henry," he whispered, "but they stay here. That charge will have to take this battery first. We'll lose where we are standing, and that battery with it. But we can still hold the crest of this hill, and that is what will count in the end. Get your other batteries ready to enfilade this position as they come up and over it. This fight will be decided farther back, at the cemetery," and he pointed up the hill to the crest.

Hancock remounted, staff gathering around him. "I'll see you at the top of the hill in half an hour, Henry. That's where we stop 'em, teach 'em that they aren't going to take this hill."

Hancock, with a touch of the spurs, turned his mount and galloped off.

Henry looked at the sorry mare that had been passed off to him as a remount.

"Can you get me more ammunition, sir?"

It was Wiedrich, Ames coming up behind him.

"I'll have more canister down to you. Hold your case shot till they start to come in," and he pointed at the rebel division shifting from column to line. Even as he spoke, several shells from Stevens burst over the formation.

"We stay here till we get overrun, is that it?" Ames asked.

Henry couldn't lie. He simply nodded.

"I'll get back the honor of Eleventh Corps right here," Ames said grimly. "We stay with this battery till the end."

Henry dropped the reins of his mare and shook their hands. It was chilling to know that he was shaking hands with men who would most likely be dead within the hour. They knew it as well and didn't flinch from it, and that kind of courage filled him with awe. There was evidence enough of that on this hill, here in Pennsylvania, that they wouldn't back off another inch. Well, if this was a chosen place to die, then so be it, and that thought filled him with a cold and hard-edged resolve to see it through to the end.

"What you do here will mean that this hill holds, that we won't go down to defeat tonight."

Neither of the two spoke. This was not the time for the staged dramatics that some officers favored when the men were watching. This was three comrades, all veterans of the old prewar army, all three knowing what their profession might ultimately demand, and now willing to pay that price.

He started to turn away; then a memory, a grim duty came to him. He walked over to Caesar, lying on his side, breathing raggedly, mouth covered with froth, blood pouring out of the wound that had torn open his breast.

Never get attached to them, he thought, not in this trade. He cocked his revolver and leveled it. Somehow he sensed that Caesar knew what he was doing, why he was doing it, and that it was an act of mercy. The eyes looked up at him. He thought again of the rabbit he had shot as a boy, the creature screaming. His hands started to tremble. He closed his eyes and squeezed the trigger.

Some of the gunners were looking at him, saying nothing. The blood-soaked Confederate flag was draped over the open lid of a caisson, the man who'd taken it standing beside the red flag, eyes wide, vacant, gaze unfocused.

Gen. Henry Hunt, Commander of Artillery, Army of the Potomac, mounted and rode back up the hill to the cemetery.

Chapter Five

6:15 PM, July 1, 1863

The Lutheran Seminary
Gettysburg, Pennsylvania

"Where is Johnson's division?" Gen. Robert E. Lee's gaze locked onto Walter Taylor and the staff arrayed behind the nervous chief of staff.

No one answered.

"Anderson's division is going in." As he spoke, Lee pointed to his right, "But I don't see Johnson!"

Arrayed behind Seminary Ridge, Anderson's division, a battle line stretching for over a quarter mile southward, nearly five thousand men, was moving forward. The first wave of skirmishers crested the ridge, moving at an oblique to the right in order to sweep around the southern flank of the town and hit Cemetery Hill on its eastern flank.

However, there was no sign that Johnson was launching his attack from the east side of town. The signal, Pegram's massed battery firing a twenty-gun salvo, had cut loose more than ten minutes ago, and still no movement . . .

"If they don't strike simultaneously . . . ," and Lee's voice trailed off.

He paced back and forth angrily, hands clasped behind his back. He paused, looking back at his staff. "I thought the first strike by Ewell an hour ago, uncoordinated as it was, could perhaps sweep those people off that hill," he announced.

"It was hard to coordinate from the town," Taylor offered. "Ewell's men fought a running battle for two miles; orders did not get through to everyone."

Lee fixed Taylor with his sharp gaze. "Jackson would have found a way. He never would have slowed for an instant. I directly ordered Ewell to take the hill at once and left him with the understanding that the attacks would push forward."

His frustration, ready to boil over, triggered a response that he had spent a lifetime trying to master, to regain an outward calm. Venting his frustration on his staff would only serve to make them nervous and jittery at a time when he needed them to think rationally and with cool judgment. He knew the impact his slightest gesture or word could have on this army.

He turned away, leading Traveler by his reins. He caught a glimpse of his headquarters detail watching him at a discreet distance, looking anxious. He ignored their concern, his gaze fixed to the southeast.

Anderson's skirmishers swept down onto the open plains south of town. The first wave, moving two hundred yards behind the skirmishers, came over the ridge, the formation breaking up as it scrambled over barricades and around buildings. A cheer erupted from the regiment nearest to him.

The men were looking his way, pointing, an officer pausing, turning, raising his sword in salute.

Lee raised his hand, and the cheering redoubled, picked up, echoing down the line.

Such displays always embarrassed him, and at moments like this left him humbled. In minutes those boys would wade into an inferno of case shot, shrapnel, and canister. More than one was poised at the edge of the eternal.

Why? For Virginia . . . for this thing called the Confederacy? He looked back at Taylor and the others, boys really, just boys dressed up and playing at glory. . . . More than one of them would do it for me. Use such devotion only when you must, when there is no other way, he thought with sharp self-reproach.

The first assault on the hill had placed him in that position yet again. An hour ago he had ridden into town, instinct telling him that Ewell would not press the issue hard enough. He had found his corps commander in the center of the town and issued a direct order to send everything he had in against the hill.

Ewell had argued against it, wishing for Johnson to come up first and secure his own left flank.

"Give me a brigade, sir, and I'll take that hill!"

It was old "Dick" Trimble, attached to Ewell's headquarters, who had interrupted their argument. Essentially a general in waiting, he was ready to be slotted in when a command opened up . . . as they always did on the field of battle.

Lee had looked into Trimble's eyes and seen that gaze, the sense that a man would willingly die at that moment, and all he had to do was nod.

He had made that nod, telling Trimble to round up what troops he could, believing that one more push could trigger another panic in the Union ranks . . . and now Trimble was reportedly dead on that hill, that accursed hill.

He raised his field glasses, scanning to the east side of town. Nothing. It was impossible to see where Johnson was forming, but nevertheless fire from that flank should be increasing; there should be some sign that an attack was underway.

Why wasn't he there?

"Taylor!"

"Sir!"

Within seconds Taylor was at his side.

"Ride. I want Ewell to get his people in there! No more waiting."

"Sir!"

Taylor viciously raked his spurs, mount half-rearing, and he was off at a gallop, leaping the broken fence that lined the Cashtown Road, riding down the hill and into the center of town, where Ewell's headquarters were located in the square.

6:20 PM

Cemetery Hill

US "Here it comes, Howard. My God, what a sight!"

Winfield Scott Hancock reined in, raising his glasses, scanning the Reb battle line cresting Seminary Ridge. One brigade was clearly in view, already passing the seminary, angling to their right. Mounted officers were farther to the right. Now flags were appearing there as well, skirmishers coming forward on the double.

Down in the open fields, Buford's skirmishers, exhausted from having been in action since dawn, were still doing their job of holding his left flank, reluctantly pulling back yard by yard, retreating in relays, a forward line breaking off, mounting, riding back a couple of hundred yards, passing through a dismounted line of their comrades, who then mounted again.

One-armed Oliver Otis Howard, commander of the shattered Eleventh Corps, remained silent watching the display, like Hancock, field glasses raised.

The battle below them spilled out across the pastures and the neatly arrayed fields of summer wheat and cornfields to the west of the road to Emmitsburg.

"Smart of Henry to order his guns to cease fire," Hancock said. "Saves ammunition till they're close and clears the smoke a bit."

Howard nodded.

Winfield looked over at him. Howard was still feeling prickly over the orders from Meade to relinquish field command to an officer who had only been promoted to corps command less than a month ago. He sensed that Howard was still shaken by the rout north of town, but now that the crisis was upon them, nothing showed but a steady calm.

"And still nothing from over there," Howard announced, glasses trained to the east side of town.

One brigade was fully deployed, well over a thousand yards away. Behind it, in the dips and swales, he caught glimpses of columns moving along the road, racing through farmyards, tearing aside fences . . . more troops still maneuvering from marching column to battle line.

Shells flung by Stevens's battery were detonating across the front of the line of the first brigade, where the Rebs crouched in the waist-high corn. To their flank a battery was wheeling into position, a good fourteen hundred yards out.

He grinned. A lot of good those guns would do supporting their attack, firing up toward higher ground at that range. Perfect. There was no real position for the Rebs to establish counterbattery and suppress Henry's guns.

"They're off, Howard. By God, they're off. Damn it, they should either send that brigade in now with whatever they've got in the town or wait the extra half hour until everyone is formed. God, I can't believe Lee is attacking like this."

"In another hour it'll be getting dark. He must push it now while there's still light."

Hancock nodded. It was obvious that the big salvo from the Reb batteries deployed around the seminary was some sort of signal for a general assault. Strange, at times you could hear something like that twenty miles away, and then at other times you could be a mile off and it was barely noticeable.

"Just wait," Hancock muttered, glasses trained on Johnson's men. "Dear God, a half hour is all I ask."

The silence that had hung over the field for the last ten minutes was shattered when a field piece, one of Wiedrich's guns at the tip of the salient on the north slope, fired. A second later the gun to its left kicked back. The salvo raced across the northern and western slope of Cemetery Hill, jumping to Stewart's battery, then Dilger's, and continued.

The first of the shells sparked, igniting in the air near the seminary above a knot of officers. Geysers of dirt shot up; the line seemed to be smothered under a curtain of fire.

"Thirty-eight . . . thirty-nine . . . ," one of his staff was counting, voice pitched high with excitement.

"Forty-three!"

As the explosion from the last gun on the left drifted away, a cheer echoed along the line and within seconds one of Wiedrich's Napoleons finished reloading and cut loose with a second round.

"With the guns on the east flank of this hill, we must have sixty pieces, sir!" one of his staff cried excitedly.

"And enough ammunition for a half

hour at this rate of fire," Howard replied laconically.

Hancock caught a glimpse of Henry galloping past the gatehouse. Several limber wagons were coming up the road, horses covered with sweat, crews lashing teams that were obviously blown, barely able to walk up the final slope. Henry, waving his hat, reined in, pointing for them to cut off the road. Gunners leapt off the wagons; stragglers on the road were pressed into service, helping to tear down the fence flanking it.

From the crest, Henry's guns were tearing into the advancing line with brutal accuracy. In the still evening air, the smoke was quickly banking up around the hill, but the gunners knew enough to keep depressing their barrels and cutting fuses shorter.

Hancock turned to look back down the Emmitsburg Road and then over to the Baltimore Pike. He had sent word down the former to Dan Sickles to bring up his Third Corps, the same order going to Slocum and the two divisions of his Twelfth Corps coming up the Baltimore Pike from Littlestown.

The Emmitsburg Road was rapidly turning into part of the battlefield. Buford's skirmishers lined the post and rail fence, trading shots with Confederate infantry clear down to a distant rise crowned with a peach orchard.

Baltimore Pike was in chaos, jammed with hundreds of stragglers who would dodge into the woods at the sight of a provost patrol, then step back out and press on, mingling with the walking wounded, all of them instinctively heading as far away as possible from the carnage.

And there was no relief in sight.

6:30 PM

Seminary Ridge

CSA "I'm going back down there," Lee snapped to his staff.

Mounting, he spared a final glance toward Anderson's division. A gale of artillery fire swept over them as the forward brigade advanced into canister range, men struggling to get over the heavy fences lining the pike toward Emmitsburg.

He ordered several of his staff to wait at headquarters across the road from the seminary, edged out onto the road into Gettysburg, and set off at a swift canter, guards of his headquarters company swinging ahead and to either flank, carbines and revolvers drawn.

The road into town was a shambles, covered with the litter of war, upended caissons, overturned ambulances, dead horses, dead men, wounded, both Union and Confederate, lying to either side waiting for help, cast-off rifles, cartridge boxes, blanket rolls, uniform jackets, a broken banjo. Hundreds of torn paper cartridges covered the road, and clinging over it all was the heavy sulfur stench of burnt powder and torn flesh.

A column of Union prisoners stood to one side of the road, pushed back at his approach. They looked up at him, some with surprise, others sullen or openly defiant. An officer, bloody bandage around his head, offered a salute, which he returned. "The fight ain't over yet, sir," the Yankee officer announced. "This isn't Virginia. You're in the North now."

Lee pressed on, saying nothing.

Hospital flags, both Union and Confederate, hung from houses marking where surgeons were setting up for business. Blue and butternut wounded mingled together outside the makeshift wards. He tried to ignore the hysterical screams coming from an open window and the glimpse of orderlies trying to wrestle a man up onto a table.

A column of infantry, motionless,

blocked the center of the road ahead, the men standing at ease, a knot of them squatting in a circle in the middle of the road, while one of their comrades carved generous portions from a smoked ham.

At the sight of his approach, they snapped to attention, the corporal dropping his knife and flipping the edge of a blanket over the ham to try and hide the booty.

He rode past, slowing for a moment at the sight of officers at the head of the motionless column. "Whose troops are these?"

A colonel, eyes red rimmed and half concealed behind mud-splattered spectacles, features pale, wearily looked up, staring blankly, then came to attention. "Mine, sir," he announced, voice barely a whisper. "Colonel Bradley, sir, Thirty-fifth Georgia."

"May I ask, sir, what you are doing here?"

"General, kind of a tangle here, sir. I was told to form my men on this road and await orders. No orders have come."

Lee looked down sharply.

The colonel let his gaze drop and then, inexplicably, his shoulders began to quiver, head going down. A sob escaped him.

"Sir? What is wrong?" Lee asked softly.

The colonel looked back up. "My boy, sir, my only son . . ." and he froze, eyes wide and unfocused as he fought to regain control.

Lee looked past him. The men of the colonel's command were watching the encounter. It was obvious their sympathy was with their colonel. Lying by the side of the road was a body on a makeshift stretcher, features calm in death, long blond hair brushed back from the face. One of the boy's comrades sat by the stretcher, crying, head lowered.

He could sense this was a tight-knit regiment, most likely men all from the same town or county, the colonel, older, a schoolmaster look to him, the body on the stretcher a young boy, not more than sixteen, most likely a "pet" of the regiment.

He caught the eye of a major standing behind the colonel. "Take over, Major. I want your men to put pressure on that hill," and Lee pointed to the south.

He leaned over, hand resting on the colonel's shoulder. "Your son is in the care of Our Savior," Lee whispered. "You, sir, shall be in my prayers tonight."

The colonel looked back up. "How can I ever tell my wife?" the colonel replied, voice haunting and distant. He tried to say more but couldn't and turned away, covering his face.

Lee squeezed the man's shoulder and rode on toward the center of town.

What future now for them? he wondered. What comfort can their country ever give them that would repay the loss of an only son.

He thought of his boy wounded at Brandy Station less than four weeks ago, still not recovered. I have four sons, and to lose but one would be all but beyond my heart to bear.

God, I must end this! No more after this. Push it hard today, push it and win so that this madness can finally stop.

The sound of battle echoing from the hill was increasing every second. The crackling of a musket volley ignited like a long string of firecrackers. Passing side streets, he caught glimpses of the smoke-clad heights, ringed with fire, the smoke catching and holding the early evening sunlight, which bathed the landscape in a hellish ruddy glow.

The center square of the town was directly ahead. The press of men, the litter of battle, dead horses, knots of prisoners, all made it difficult to move. His troop of cavalry escorts pressed ahead, clearing the way.

Directly in the middle of the square, sitting in an open buckboard carriage, wooden leg propped up, was Dick Ewell, commander of Second Corps. His coat was open, hat off, thin wisps of what little hair he had left plastered down with sweat. A knot of officers stood around him. Jubal Early, commander of the division that had stormed into the town, was one of them.

At his approach, they stiffened. He had left them in this same spot an hour ago, and it seemed like nothing had changed since.

There was an obvious look of relief on Walter Taylor's face, as if a terrible burden had been lifted. That alone told Lee everything.

"When I left you gentlemen an hour ago," Lee said, deliberately making an effort to stay calm and keep his voice in control, "the understanding was that when Pegram's battalion fired a salvo that would be the signal for you to launch your assault."

"We heard no salvo, sir," Ewell replied.

Lee looked at him, incredulous. It was indeed possible, but somehow he couldn't force himself to believe it.

"Well, can you not hear the guns of those people up there?" and his voice raised slightly as he pointed toward Cemetery Hill. "Is that not signal enough that the attack is pressing in."

"Sir, my men, sir." It was Jubal Early, standing by the side of Ewell's carriage. "They've marched twelve miles, fighting a running battle for the last two. We're still rounding up prisoners. You shouldn't even be in here, sir. This town is not yet secured."

"I need to be where the battle is," Lee replied sharply, "but, sir, it seems as if no battle is being fought on this flank. An hour ago I told you that hill could be taken if pressed quickly enough."

"Dick Trimble died, and a fair part of Gordon's brigade died trying for it, sir," Jubal replied softly. "The first attack was premature."

Lee felt his features flush. He could see the look in Walter's eyes, the boy edging forward, trying to intervene, to head off the confrontation. An icy glance told him to back off. Lee turned his attention straight at Ewell and those gathered around him. "Sir, I want that hill taken!"

He pointed south, arm stiff, his voice ringing so that for an instant it seemed as if everyone tangled up in the confusion-filled square had fallen silent.

"No excuses. I have tolerated such excuses too often in the past when we had the chance to smash them, and always they got away.

"I am not advising you gentlemen; I am

ordering you. I want that hill taken before dark." His voice echoed. All stood silent, stunned by the outburst.

"Where is Johnson? Why is he not going in?"

"He will any minute now," Ewell replied nervously, obviously startled by the outburst. "I sent another courier to urge him to move. One of his brigades somehow took the wrong road and started eastward; he is waiting for them to come about and form. Johnson also reported that Union infantry, coming up from the east and south, are threatening his left flank. He reports it is Twelfth Corps."

"Now! I want the attack now!" Lee shouted, cutting him off. "Anderson is committed. Johnson must press straight in with everything he has and worry about his flank later."

The roar of musketry from the hill was rising in volume.

"Both flanks of the hill attacked at the same time, so they are forced to split their fire. That is what I wanted. We can still do it."

"Sir, we've fought a long fight today," Ewell offered, "trying to coordinate an assault from both wings on the run. It's not easy, sir."

"I know it's not easy!" Lee snapped. "Victory is never easy; only defeat is easy.

We have a chance to smash them, sir. Smash them! I will not let it slip out of our grasp. I am sick of wasting lives in battles that do not bring final victory. No more waste. Not this time."

His voice pitched up as he said the last words, half standing in his stirrups.

Inwardly he was furious with himself for the outburst, the dramatic display, allowing passion to take control. Jackson had been known for such moments. Longstreet was feared for his famed explosions of rage. That was never me though. I've spent a lifetime learning mastery of myself. The realization of it made him even angrier.

"You are to go directly to Johnson and order him to go in with what he has. Do it now!" Lee announced, his voice set at an icy pitch.

He hesitated for a second. "Walter, go with him."

Ewell, obviously startled by Lee's tone, and the none too subtle insult of having Lee's staff officer go along to make sure the order was carried out, simply saluted.

Ewell's driver mounted — wide-eyed in the presence of Lee and the display of temper — grabbed the reins, and swung the carriage around. Lee wanted to shout with exasperation at the sight of Ewell's carriage trying to inch its way through the mad jumble of confusion that filled the square. Wooden leg or not, Ewell should be mounted, not riding around town in a carriage.

Walter, showing initiative, simply left him and disappeared behind a jumble of ambulances abandoned at the east end of the square.

Early was looking up at him, silent, dark eyes penetrating.

"Do you wish to say something, General?" Lee asked.

Early nodded.

"Go ahead then."

"Malvern Hill, sir."

"What?"

"That's Malvern Hill up there, sir. It might look easy from a distance, us having them on the run as we did. But they've got artillery up there, lots of it. A year ago today, sir, we fought at Malvern Hill, and you saw what their artillery did to us there."

"We could have swept them off that hill an hour ago," Lee replied heatedly. "We should have done it."

"We didn't."

Early fell silent as if judging his words carefully.

"Go ahead," Lee said, trying to keep his voice calm.

"Your blood is up, sir. That's all I'll

say, sir. Your blood is up."

Startled, Lee said nothing. Looking away, gaze fixed on that bloody hill, that damn bloody hill.

6:40 PM

Cemetery Hill

His guidon bearer grunted from the impact of the bullet. Hancock reached out, grabbing the boy by the shoulder as he leaned drunkenly from the saddle, half falling, guidon dropping.

The guidon had to stay up. The men had to see it, but he would not let go of the boy.

"I'm sorry, sir, sorry," the boy gasped.

Someone on foot was beside him, reaching up, grabbing the boy, easing him out of the saddle, the youth gasping, clutching his stomach.

Shot in the gut, as good as dead, Hancock thought, trying to stay detached, looking away. A staff officer dismounted, picked up the guidon, and remounted, holding it aloft.

Another volley tore across the western slope of the hill, a rebel yell echoing up. They were charging again, coming up over the fences lining the Emmitsburg

Road. Behind them a battery of four guns was cutting across a field, caissons bouncing, the first gun sluicing around to a stop, preparing to unlimber at murderously close range.

Henry's gunners, following orders, were ignoring it for the moment, concentrating everything they had on the advancing infantry.

A blast of canister, aimed low, tore into a section of fence, which exploded for fifty feet of length into tumbling rails, splinters, and bodies. The charge pressed forward, coming up the slope into the face of forty guns ringing the crest of the hilltop. Gunners, working feverishly, were not even bothering to roll the pieces back into place, simply loading and firing. Some of the crews had even stopped swabbing, running the risk of a hot bore or spark triggering a premature blast in order to save an additional ten seconds.

Shimmers of heat radiated off the guns directly in front of Hancock. Even as he watched, a loader slammed a canister round into the open bore. The rammer pushed him aside, started to drive the round in, and then was flung backward as the powder bag hit a hot spark, seven-foot ramrod staff screaming downrange, rammer writhing on the ground, right hand blown off, shoulder broken, face scorched black.

His comrades pulled him back behind the firing line, the gun sergeant screaming for a replacement ramrod, running back toward a limber wagon.

The Rebs were pushing closer, not coming on in a wild heads-down charge but advancing slowly, pouring in a fierce fire, trying to break up the batteries before pressing the final hundred yards.

Bullets sang around Hancock's ears, his staff ducking and bobbing in their saddles. He rode the length of the line, voice too hoarse to continue shouting. Henry came past, waving his hat, three limber wagons, two chests of ammunition strapped to each, bouncing behind him. He waved them into place, one wagon per battery.

The crest of the hill was crowded with limber wagons and caissons, each with six horses, all of them pressed nearly side to side. Hancock could almost pity the trace riders for the caissons. Regulations stated that when in action the mounted rider of the six-horse team had to remain in the saddle, ready to guide the caisson around if the guns needed to be moved quickly.

It was a ghastly job in the middle of a fight. A man was expected to sit with his back to the enemy, all hell breaking loose, and just wait. It was a type of courage he wondered if he could ever muster . . . to do nothing but wait.

He reached the south end of the battle line, where a low stone wall jutted out to the west for fifty yards, a small grove of trees behind the wall. Buford's skirmishers crouched behind the wall; Calef's hard-fought battery of mounted artillery occupied the angle, pouring shot into the enemy flank. The four Reb guns deployed on the far side of the road opened on Calef, but he ignored them, his men simply ducking as a shell screamed in, then returning to their work of laying down case shot on the road.

He focused his glasses down the Emmitsburg Road, looking south. Something was on it, dark, serpentlike, still distant, but coming. It was Sickles, responding to his urgent plea for immediate support.

"General Hancock, sir!"

He looked back. A courier, one of Howard's men, was riding up hard, waving his hat. "They're coming, sir. The Rebs east of town; they're coming!"

He looked back south. A half hour, maybe more. Damn!

He turned, following Howard's messenger, riding along the crest, looking west, judging the strength and determination of the Reb attack hitting his left flank. A lot of the Rebs were still wearing blanket rolls and backpacks, a sign they had maneuvered straight from the march into battle formation without taking time to form regimental depots, drop-off points for all excess baggage, before going into the fight.

Rather than lose a precious blanket and haversack of food, the men were carrying the extra weight into battle. He wondered if they had been watered before the attack or were coming in with dry canteens.

For whatever reason, their attack was slow. The artillery's concentrated fire had battered Anderson's division down, keeping them pinned along the road. But the guns had to shift if there was any hope of flinging back the new assault on the right. Henry was up at the crest of the hill, frantically waving, directing the redeployment, swinging guns around to face north and east.

The Rebs along the fence, however, had yet to react, to push forward, though they had to have seen by now that the artillery fire was slackening.

He eased his mount through a hole in the cemetery wall and weaved his way past a parked row of caissons. Passing the nearest one, he looked in as a loader pulled a round of case shot out of a storage slot and, with an awl-like punch, set the fuse at two seconds.

"How many left?" Hancock shouted.

The loader looked up, startled by the presence of a corps commander gazing down at him.

"Ahh, three case shot, sir. Half a dozen canister."

"Webster, get that damn shell up here!"

The loader, responding to the cries of his sergeant, tried to salute, gave up, and ran back up to the firing line, Hancock following.

He could hear the cry, the rebel yell. Reaching the battery, he reined in. Through holes in the smoke he saw them coming, definitely a brigade, maybe two, heading straight for the east slope of the hill, advance skirmishers already trading fire on the side of the wooded hill that flanked the cemetery.

"This is where it's going to be decided!"

Henry was by his side, eyes wide with excitement, rivers of sweat streaming down his face. "Got one more battery still coming up!" and he pointed back down the Baltimore Pike.

Struggling up the hill came a battery of six Napoleons, horses covered with foaming sweat, more than one of the mounts all but dead, limp in their traces, oblivious to the whip blows from the drivers.

A thunderclap volley ignited from the north end of the hill. Ames's men, still dug in around Wiedrich's battery, had stood up and fired, the blow staggering the Reb advance, which slowed for a moment then continued on.

"Ammunition?" Hancock shouted, looking over at Hunt.

"Unless Jesus Christ Almighty drops a few limber wagons from the heavens, what we've got here is it. Some of the guns are out of canister; they're shooting solid shot!"

Hancock cast a glance to the western horizon. The sun was blood red, hanging low, soon to slip behind the South Mountains.

A half hour till sunset, a half hour. God, it seemed like an eternity.

The Rebs pressed in, battle lines past the flank of the town, spreading out. A broken line of skirmishers pressing out from the streets formed a loose screen between the two divisions.

Wiedrich's four guns fired in salvo, entire lines going down under the blasts. Stevens's battery was pouring it on, ignoring the increasing fire from long-range skirmishers pressing up the slope of the wooded hill. The six Napoleons coming up behind Henry were swinging into position, forming to face straight down toward the cemetery gate below, knocking over headstones, shattering monuments.

Once the first gun was unhooked from its caisson and positioned, Henry detailed the drivers to head down to Stewart and turn over their caisson of ammunition to the beleaguered battery. The crew assigned didn't look too pleased at leaving their own battery with orders to ride straight into an inferno, but the men lashed their teams and pushed down the slope.

A steady stream of wounded were coming back from the firing line on the west slope. No breakdown there yet. He noticed only a scattering of unwounded trying to get out. Some of the men, as they reached the crest, paused, gazing to the north and east, taking in the sight of Johnson's advance. Several of them, seeing Hancock, slowed and, in spite of their wounds, fell in on the makeshift final line.

The charge was coming on faster, pushing in. Another blast of canister, this one at point-blank range. Stewart's and Dilger's guns, no longer engaged against Anderson, had swung around, and once again were pouring in enfilade fire to support their comrades on the right.

The first line of the charge disappeared, going down, piling atop the dead and wounded from the earlier charge. The second wave, less than fifty yards out, slowed — rifles flashing, lowering, firing a sharp, rippling volley — and then, with bayonets lowered, came in at the charge, high wolf yip shrieks sending a corkscrew down Hancock's spine.

The swarm piled up over Wiedrich's guns, tangling in with the gunners, Ames's infantry, all of them a seething, boiling mass, cloaked in a smoky haze.

A lone caisson came out of the inferno, trying to gain the road, upended, throwing the driver as it rolled over, horses shrieking. Another caisson, down in the middle of the confusion, blew, top lid soaring a hundred feet into the air, flinging men in every direction.

The point of the salient broke, men streaming back, pouring up the road and along the flank of the knoll, followed by the charging swarm. Stewart's guns — now caught fully in flank — turned, continuing to fire, even as the breakthrough spread toward them.

The second line — a hodgepodge of regimental fragments from First and Eleventh Corps — dug in around the gatehouse, stood up, trying to fire over the heads of their fleeing comrades, who, ducking low, scrambled up over the barricades for protection, more than one of them caught between the two fires, going down, struck front and back at the same instant.

Johnson's men, smelling victory, pressed forward, the slope behind them carpeted with casualties as the artillery fired with unrelenting power.

The right section of Stewart's battery was swarmed under, the remaining section retreating slowly up the slope, retiring by prolonge, gunners firing, ropes trailing to the caissons pulling the guns back a dozen yards while the crews reloaded, the last of their infantry support clinging around the pieces, bayonets poised.

The charge kept coming. Hancock caught a glimpse to his left; Anderson's men, at least the regiments closest to Johnson's charge, were up, pressing in as well, heartened by the advance to their flank.

He looked back to the west. The sun seemed motionless.

7:00 PM

Gettysburg

Ignoring the warnings of his headquarters staff, Lee rode

down the middle of the road oblivious to the rain of bullets kicking up geysers of dust in the street, shattering windows, splintering the sides of wooden buildings, and ricocheting off the brick ones.

The head of the charge was up over the forward knoll, pressing up into the smoke that circled the hill, reminding him somehow of an old etching of Mount Sinai, wreathed in eternal storm clouds.

The men, my God, the men, he thought, his stomach knotting. Hundreds of them were down, covering the approaches to the hill. Wounded were coming back up the street, many with uniforms torn and limbs shattered by artillery fire. At the sight of him some held their wounded limbs up, bearing them proudly like holy stigmata.

The gesture was almost frightening to him, a sacrilege. He fixed his gaze on the hill, the bloody hill that seemed to fill the sky ahead.

A glare of light, then a hail of rifle fire exploded in the smoke, followed a couple of seconds later by a storm of bullets sweeping the street. One of his cavalry escorts pitched out of the saddle; another had a horse go down.

"General Lee, you must retire!"

It was Walter Taylor, back from his mission to Johnson, racing out from a side street, moving to place himself between Lee and the rifle fire.

Lee fixed him with an icy gaze. "No. I will not hide at a moment like this."

"Remember Jackson," Walter replied, still moving to take Traveler's reins.

"I do remember Jackson," Lee said fiercely. "If he had been here, this attack would have already taken that hill. Time, Walter, it is always a question of time. We are losing the light."

"Sir, your getting killed will not change any of this now."

"The charge; it looks weak. What is going on?" Lee looked over at Taylor.

"Two brigades only, sir. Johnson claims there's a Union division forming on his left, a couple of miles down the Hanover Road. He's deployed a brigade to contain them. The other brigade is still forming and trying to come up."

Lee motioned him to silence.

The rebel yell!

In the dim light he saw the banners go up over the barricades around what looked to be a gatehouse. Another caisson blew, followed almost instantly by yet another exploding alongside the first.

The yell, the spine-tingling yell. Wounded in the streets paused, looked back, some of them raising their voices, howling. Others stood riveted, watching the charge.

Lee looked around at his staff. All were gazing up at the hill, some shouting. The charge pressed forward, colors dipping, going down, coming back up, going down, then coming back up yet again, still advancing.

My men, though. Oh, God, my men. They were dropping by the scores, the hundreds. "Finish it, for God's sake, finish it." The words escaped him like a desperate prayer.

7:15 PM

Cemetery Hill

"Fire! Fire! Fire!" Henry, screaming like a madman, was on foot, in front of Hancock, in the middle of his guns.

Hancock wanted to scream for him to stop. Some of their own men were still in front, running back from the gatehouse, tangled in with the charging Rebs.

The gunners hesitated; a sergeant looked back at him. Henry shouldered the sergeant aside, drew the lanyard taut, and with a wild cry pulled it.

The Napoleon, loaded with double canister, reared back. As if the gun was a flame that leapt to the other pieces, the batteries fired.

Sickened by the impact, Hancock said nothing, unable to speak as more than a thousand iron balls, a visible blur, slammed into the ranks. A headstone, torn off at its base, flipped high into the air, an ironic sight that frightened him almost as much as the carnage.

"Reload! Reload!" Henry was stalking down the line, clawing at the air, frantically waving his arms.

Hancock wanted to scream for him to stop, for all of them to stop, to end the madness of it. Out of the smoke some of them were rising up, hunched over, pressing forward, a lone color coming back up, then another.

The Rebs were into the guns, but they were too few. The wave broke, collapsing. Some of the Rebs simply stood there in numbed shock and then woodenly dropped their weapons.

Farther down the slope, Hancock saw a column coming up over the knoll where Wiedrich's battery had been. It must be another brigade of Rebs, but they were coming in too late!

"Look, sir, look!"

Hancock turned. A column of Union infantry, coming forward at the double, was spreading out to either side of the Baltimore Pike . . . Twelfth Corps at last!

On his other flank he already knew that the advance regiments of Sickles's Third were coming up. It was hard to see as the shadows lengthened, but he could catch glimpses of a heavy skirmish line pushing up across the fields along the Emmitsburg Road, hooking up with Buford's men.

"Fire, pour it in, pour it in!" Henry, pacing behind his guns, pointed down the slope toward the forward knoll, where the emerging enemy line was trying to shake out into formation. The blasts of canister swept down the hill; the hundreds of men down on the ground in front of the guns and still alive covered themselves, many screaming in terror.

The men of Twelfth Corps, coming on fast, poured down into the narrow valley that dropped down the east flank of Cemetery Hill and then rose up to the knoll where Stevens's overworked battery was still hard at it.

At the sight of their approach, whatever fight was left in the Rebs melted away. Turning, they streamed back down the slopes of Cemetery Hill.

"Reload!"

Hancock edged his mount forward, the horse stepping nervously around a team of six animals, all of them dead, piled up in front of their caisson.

"Henry."

Henry's back was turned, shaking his head as a captain screamed to him that they were out of ammunition.

"Solid shot, you still have solid shot! Give it to them!"

"Henry!"

Henry turned, looking up at him. "Cease fire," Hancock said quietly.

Henry stood there, riveted to the ground, mouth open, shoulders shaking as he gasped for breath.

Gunners around him seemed frozen, looking at the two.

"We held the hill," Winfield said quietly.

Henry simply stood there.

A gunner by Henry's side staggered away, letting his rammer drop, legs shaking so badly he could barely walk. A section commander, leaning against an upturned caisson, slowly doubled over and vomited convulsively, body shaking like a leaf. The men of the battery seemed to melt, dissolve. Some simply sat down, staring vacantly. Others leaned drunkenly against their pieces. A color bearer held the national flag aloft and slowly waved it back and forth, but no cheer sounded; the only thing to be heard was the cries of the wounded.

"Henry, you held the hill."

Henry turned and slowly walked over to one of his pieces, the men around it silent, faces and uniforms blackened.

"No," Henry whispered, nodding toward his men, "*they* held the hill."

Hancock dismounted and went up to his side, putting a hand on Henry's shoulder.

Henry gazed at him, turned away, leaning against the wheel of a gun, his body shuddering as he broke down into silent tears.

No one spoke.

Winfield Scott Hancock looked down across the field of carnage, the cemetery piled high with the harvest of his profession, the results of his greatest victory. Lowering his head, he walked away.

Chapter Six

11:50 PM, July 1, 1863

Westminster, Maryland

Brig. Gen. Hermann Haupt, Commander, U.S. Military Railroads, stepped off the engine cab before the train had skidded to a stop. Exhausted, he stretched, his back popping as he shifted from side to side. At forty-six he was beginning to show the first signs of middle-age portliness. His flowing brown beard was increasingly flecked with gray, and as was so typical of the army, he was wearing a uniform rumpled and stained from too many days of not changing. The uniform was pockmarked with cinder burns, his face streaked with grease and dirt.

The ride up from Baltimore had been a bone-jarring, five-hour ordeal, just to cover thirty miles of track. The track laying of the Western Maryland Railroad was typical of such lines: Slap the rails down as quickly as possible, and the hell with grading and curve radius. Just get the damn thing up and running, then worry later about smoothing things out.

There were no telegraph, no sidings, no fuel or water for the locomotives. He looked around at the small depot of Westminster and the utter chaos that confronted him. Meade had ordered all supply wagons for the Army of the Potomac to concentrate at this point, and it was his job to open up the rail line and organize a depot.

Several miles outside the town, the train had started to pass open fields packed with wagons . . . thousands of them. They were jammed into pastures, wheat fields, cornfields and here in the town the main street was jammed solid. Five thousand wagons, ambulances, reserve artillery limbers, and tens of thousands of mules. Their braying was a maddening cacophony that most likely could be heard clear back to Baltimore.

The sight of it all, the noise, were a shock; and if it wasn't for his innate sense of duty, he would have succumbed to the temptation to simply get back on the train and let someone else try to sort all of this out.

A scattering of infantry was standing about, obviously bored with their duty, though at the sight of a general getting off the train they started to stiffen up a bit in a vain attempt to look soldierly. Civilians milled about, gawking at the jam of wagons, and at the sight of him a delegation swooped down.

He turned and tried to get away, but they were upon him.

"General, are you in charge here?" a portly gentleman wearing a scarlet vest shouted, following after him.

He tried to continue on, walking back along the train, as if inspecting the wheels.

"General!"

Exasperated, he turned. It was always the same: Self-important civilians, who on one hand were damn grateful that the army was there to protect them, but in a heartbeat were ready to switch their song and start complaining.

"I'm in command of the military railroads supporting the army," Hermann replied wearily.

"This, sir, is the property of the Western Maryland Railroad," the loudmouthed civilian replied sharply.

"The army has seized this line," Hermann replied coolly. "It will be returned to civilian control once this campaign is concluded."

"Well, General, there are a few things we need to discuss. No one seems to be in control here. We had a terrible fight here two days ago, several men killed on both sides."

Terrible fight? This pompous ass should

have been at Second Manassas and seen trainloads of the wounded, blood dripping through the floorboards, as they rolled back to Alexandria; his crews vomiting as they scrubbed the cars down afterward; then sending them back to Manassas to pick up another thousand.

"The streets are clogged with your wagons," the civilian continued. "There are soldiers and mule drivers who are drunk wandering about scaring the ladies of the town, and now there's word that the rebels have whipped the Army of the Potomac up at Gettysburg and are coming this way."

Hermann looked around at the self-appointed delegation and sensed that more than one of them might very well be delighted with the last statement.

"And you want me to . . . ?" Herman asked softly.

"Straighten out this mess, General. Straighten it out."

"Precisely my intent. Now if you will excuse me, I have work to do, though I would appreciate some volunteers to help unload the supplies I've brought up with me," Hermann snapped, and without waiting for a reply he stalked off.

Of course they didn't follow, but he could hear their raised voices as they began to argue with each other.

A small knot of officers was under the awning of the depot, nervously looking toward Hermann as he approached.

"Who is in command here?" Hermann asked.

"Ah sir, honestly we're not sure," one of them, a colonel, replied.

That was a bad sign, Herman realized. When things were going well, there would have been an instant argument as to who was, indeed, in command; when they were going wrong, no one wanted that responsibility.

"Well then, I am in command," Hermann offered, and there were no objections.

"What's the situation?" he asked.

"Sir, you've got the supply wagons of seven corps in this town. Meade passed the order this morning for the army to abandon its supply train and have them concentrate here, while the troops moved north toward Gettysburg."

"Troops here in town?"

"Hard to say. Each corps commander detailed off a couple of regiments to accompany their trains. There're a couple of companies of cavalry here, and a heavy artillery regiment out of Washington came in as well. They're hauling those big four-and-a-half-inch guns."

Herman digested the information.

Troops from seven different corps. Regiments assigned were usually units that were either burned out or not of the best quality. No corps commander would detail off his best when there was a fight brewing. Six, maybe eight thousand troops wandering around here, not sure what to do next. No central command at all.

"Your name?"

"Colonel Benson, One Hundred and Third New York, Twelfth Corps."

Herman studied the man for a moment. He seemed alright, no liquor on his breath, unlike a couple of the other men gathered about.

"Fine then, Benson. You're in command of the infantry for this supply depot."

"On whose authority, General?"

"My authority and the hell with what anyone else says. I run the military railroads for the army, and you are now under my command."

"And if my corps commander recalls my unit, General? Damn it all. There's a fight brewing, and we're stuck down here staring at a bunch of goddamn mules."

As if to add weight to his argument, a team of mules, frightened by a blast of steam from the locomotive, took off, braying madly, dragging a wagon up onto the tracks behind the train, the wagon tipping over, mules still tied to their harnesses kicking and screaming.

"You're with me, Colonel. I want the regiments from the various corps rounded up. I'm going to need men here, a couple of thousand at least to off-load trains that will be coming up shortly. I want a defense established around this town. I was up at Hanover earlier today and damn near became a guest of General Stuart."

At the mention of Stuart's name, the other officers started to whisper excitedly.

"That's it exactly. If the Rebs figure out what we have down here, we'll have company soon enough; and as it looks right now an old lady could shoo us out of here with a broom. So get to work. Your men can start by off-loading the hospital supplies I just brought up."

He turned away without waiting for a reply and spied more supplicants, complainers, and the annoyingly curious closing in. Swinging around the back end of the train he had just ridden up from Baltimore, he headed toward a row of parked wagons half-filled with rations and climbed up into the nearest one, drawing the back cover closed.

He was tempted to simply stretch out on the pile of cracker boxes and try to catch some sleep. It had been a mad, impetuous five days. When word had first come in that Lee was across the Potomac, he had gone from headquarters in Washington up to Harrisburg, there to examine the rail lines in case the Army of the Potomac should find itself campaigning along the Susquehanna. As the rebel army approached the capital of Pennsylvania, it was finally decided to drop the bridges spanning that broad river, the one directly in front of the city burning even as Confederate raiders swarmed upon the opposite bank. Leaving Harrisburg, he had routed back through Reading, there stopping to confer with the governor, then to Philadelphia, then back to Baltimore and up to Hanover, nearly running into Stuart's cavalry on the way.

Hanover as a base of supply was out, with nearly twenty bridges destroyed by the raiders. Back to Baltimore once more and now here to Westminster, with rumors swirling that action had been joined at Gettysburg.

His sojourn of hundreds of miles in just five days did not strike him as anything unusual. The locomotive had changed everything. A journey that would have taken Napoleon, or even Scott in the war with Mexico, weeks to complete, could now be done in a day. This war ran on railroads, and it was his job to make sure it ran smoothly, at least up to the point where the railroad ended and the mule-drawn wagons, as ancient as the wars of Caesar, began.

Finding a lantern up at the front of the wagon, he struck a Lucifer on the side of a box of hardtack, lit the wick, and hung the lantern up. Reaching into his oversize haversack, he pulled out a small hand-sketched map of the region and spread it out on a box.

Gettysburg, of course, would be the place they'd collide. He had surmised as much back on June 28th while still in Harrisburg. A beautiful place, rolling hills, rich farmland, a good place for a defensive fight, and with its road network, a natural draw for both armies.

Once the bridges across the Susquehanna went down, Lee would inevitably turn southward, not wanting to get pinned against the west bank of the river. He needed to keep his line of communications open down the Cumberland Valley but at the same time seek out the Army of the Potomac. It would have to be somewhere between Carlisle and Westminster that the two sides would slam into each other, and Gettysburg fit the bill.

Strategy, however, was not his concern. It was railroads, the pulsing arteries of this new kind of war, that he must be concerned about; and that was why he was here at Westminster. Harrisburg as a supply depot was out now that the bridges were down. Hanover was out as well, thanks to the rebels burning most of the bridges along that line. And besides, Hanover was only twelve miles from Gettysburg and not truly secure. Only this morning he had discovered that fact when the train he was on nearly stumbled into a detachment of Confederate cavalry.

That was always the point of vulnerability for a railroad. A regiment of cavalry, in an hour, could wreak havoc that could take days to repair; even a lone bushwhacker with a crowbar could loosen a rail and take a train off the tracks. A depot, and the line behind it, had to be secure. He had to set up that secure base now. At best, the Army of the Potomac could operate for three days, perhaps five at the most, without a supply depot; but beyond that, it would get dicey.

The way this railroad was set up, it would be impossible. Impossible, however, was just the type of challenge he secretly enjoyed facing. Pulling a notepad out of his haversack, he began to jot down what was needed, ideas that had been forming on the gut-churning ride up here.

Given enough time, he'd love to put a thousand men from his Military Railroad command to work grading this line; a couple of weeks' work, however, and by that point the issue would hopefully be decided. No, focus on what can be done now.

There's not enough firewood here. Sending men out to bring in seasoned lumber for the locomotives would be problematic. A lot of good wood had most likely already been emptied out of farmers' woodpiles by the passing armies. Take it from the stockpile in the main marshaling yards for the Military Railroad at Alexandria; a couple of trainloads should see us through for the next several days. Water. There was no tank here, let alone a pump to bring the water up from the stream. We'll need to man haul it up from the creek below the depot. Better get canvas buckets; a thousand should do it. He chuckled at the thought of the fat civilian hauling buckets up out of the creek. No, they'll all disappear once that kind of labor starts.

He began to jot down his list of priorities.

No telegraph to signal trains moving up and back on this single-track line. It'll take at least four to five days to string the necessary wire.

Without the telegraph and with no sidings, each train would tie the track up for hours. We must bring up extra locomotives and cars from the army depot, and then put them on this line in convoys. Five trains, each with ten cars, four hours up, an hour to off-load, then three hours back. As soon as they clear the line, send up the next convoy of five trains. That will give us 150 carloads a day, 1,500 tons of rations, uniforms, ammunition, boots, fodder, grease, coal oil, leather harnesses, horse-shoes, bandages, ether, crutches . . . all of the offerings to war produced by a thousand factories from Chicago to Bangor.

The bridges along this line will have to be surveyed, just in case Confederate raiders do get astride the line and burn them. Once measured, replacement timbers can be cut and loaded back at Alexandria, ready to be rolled up for repairs.

It will take eight hours to turn the trains around, if I can get enough men to unload them once here in Westminster. Too slow though for messages. And though it hurt his pride as a railroad man, he made a note to the War Office to retain the services of the Adam's Express Company. They had the fastest horses in the region, with riders trained to handle them. Ship a dozen horses and riders up here by the next train and use them to run messages and orders back to the nearest telegraph station outside of Baltimore and up to Meade at Gettysburg.

Ironic, he thought. I actually lived there

for a while, teaching college. He wondered if the battle had damaged the college or injured any of his old friends.

Next he drew up a quick report to the War Office, outlining what he had done over the last day, the damage observed to the rail line up to Hanover, and his decision to establish Westminster as the primary depot for the Army of the Potomac.

He double-checked the list of material requested, mentally comparing it to what he knew was stockpiled in the warehouses at Alexandria, already loaded aboard boxcars and flatcars.

What he was doing did not strike Hermann as being all that unique. It was simply how war was now fought, or should be fought, with cool efficiency and the application of a nation's industry to a single goal, something that America, perhaps more than any nation in history, was now ideally suited for.

If the enemy burns a bridge, haul out the prefabricated replacement and drop it in place, and then keep the trains moving. If they burn a depot, set a new one up, as we did after Second Manassas. Just keep the tidal wave of supplies moving until finally they give up . . . or, he thought grimly, we lose our will.

That was impossible. He had come from a Europe that was divided, perpetually at war with itself. No, this place had to be different. And once this was finished, I can go back to other things, other dreams, to run a rail line clear across the continent and then see a hundred new cities spring up in its wake.

A locomotive whistle shrieked, disturbing his thoughts. He pulled back the canvas cover of the wagon and saw that the infantry rounded up by the reluctant colonel had finished unloading the two cars filled with hospital supplies. Folding up his notes, he jumped off the back of the wagon and waded through the tangle of men, climbing up into the cab of the engine. His orderly, a captain according to the military but far more at home at the throttle of a locomotive, was busy studying the water gauge.

"Everything set, Johnson? Enough wood and water to get you back down the line?"

"I think so, sir, but I tell you, this line is a hell of a mess. Not like the B and O, that's for certain."

"Make sure these get handed off," Hermann said, folding up his plans and orders, jotting down addresses on the back of each.

"You staying here, sir?"

"Someone's got to get things organized around here."

Johnson grinned. "Have fun, sir. It looks like a hell of a mess around here."

"Not for long."

"Just don't get in any trouble like you did at Manassas. I like serving with you, sir."

Hermann smiled. That had been a close shave, when the Rebs poured in behind General Pope and cut the rail line back to Washington. He had pushed a train down the line to try and find out what was going wrong and wound up getting chased by Confederate cavalry and nearly killed.

Giving Johnson his orders, Hermann jumped down from the cab. Johnson eased the throttle in, bursts of smoke thumped from the stack, and with a gasping hiss the engine started to back up, pushing the two empty boxcars and wood tender behind it. Someone had finally untangled the overturned wagon and mules behind the train, clearing the track. The shriek of the whistle set thousands of the noisy animals to braying, their cries echoing across the town.

Five thousand wagons, all those damn mules. Have to get that organized and quick, Haupt thought. If a panic ever sets them off, it could turn into the biggest stampede in history.

The train eased around the sharp curve behind the depot and started back toward Baltimore.

Hermann turned, looking around at the pile of boxes littering the side of the track, the hundreds of wagons parked in the fields and along the streets, the milling civilians, the infantry starting to drift back off into the dark.

He caught the eye of the colonel and motioned him over.

"In eight hours, trains are going to pour into this place. I need a thousand men ready to work in relays off-loading the cars. The whole timetable depends on getting the supplies off the cars as quickly as possible.

"I want a loading platform built; I'll sketch it out for you shortly. Next, we need several hundred men to form a bucket brigade down to the creek. All locomotives will be topped off with water before heading back; that will be done at the same time we're unloading. The first two trains up will be loaded with firewood. They're to be unloaded and set up in piles along the side of the track. Teams of thirty men will then be assigned to each pile to load the wood on to each engine as it comes in.

"Next, I'd like to get some kind of

shedding up. It can be open sided, roofed with canvas, but I want the rations and ammunition properly stored. The far side of the shed should have a clear approach for wagons, which will then be loaded up. Traffic has to be sorted out, and wagons cleared from the streets. They'll come in from one direction, load up, then head back out.

"Finally, details to the churches, any large buildings. Hospital supplies can go in there for now. You have that?"

The colonel looked at him, obviously overwhelmed.

"I'll write it all down," Hermann said wearily, pulling his notepad back out.

"And one final order, Colonel."

"Sir?"

"A cup of coffee; in fact, a whole pot if you can get it."

11:55 PM, July 1, 1863

Gettysburg, Pennsylvania

C.S.A.

Riding into the town square, Lee edged Traveler around a line of ambulances clogging the Hanover Road. Torches and lanterns hanging from porches cast a flickering glare on the chaos of vehicles, artillery limbers, dead horses, and a column of troops trying to snake their way through the confusion, heading to the skirmish line on the south side of town.

Dozens of civilians were out in the street, many of them women. He remembered an old saying that when one became a parent, all boys become your children. He paused for a second, looking down at an elderly woman reading a Bible to a tattered barefoot soldier, shirt gone, bloody bandages wrapped around his stomach. The boy was in shock, trembling like a leaf, head resting on her lap. She paused, looking up. There was no hatred or anger, only an infinite sadness in her eyes, and he wondered if her own son was at this moment digging in on that hill south of town. He saluted and rode on.

A smattering of musket fire rippled from the crest of the hill, followed seconds later by the flash of artillery. A shell fluttered over the square, men pausing, looking up. A wounded soldier, eyes bandaged, started to scream hysterically until his comrades quieted him down.

"Walter?"

"Here, sir."

"Flag of truce. Send someone up to that hill. Offer my compliments to General Hancock and please tell him that this town is a hospital area. There are civilians here, and many of their own wounded as well.

Also, we wish to remove our wounded from the front of the hill. Ask for a ceasefire till dawn."

"Sir?"

Lee looked over at him.

"Sir, that is a concession to them, an admission of defeat."

"Just do it. I'll not have these people suffer anymore over a foolish point of military protocol."

Walter saluted, turning back, shouting for an aide.

Was it a defeat? Lee asked himself.

Experience had long ago taught him that in the rear of a battle defeat and victory often looked the same. In the center of the square he paused, looking again to the hill, illuminated by the moon, which shown brightly overhead.

Defeat? Not possible, not with this army. They've checked us for the moment, but in the morning we shall play a different tune.

He opened his jacket and pulled out his watch. It was time for the staff meeting, nearly midnight.

He turned north, riding the short distance to the railroad station that had been designated as headquarters for the army, passing through the line of dismounted cavalry who formed a cordon around the low, single-story brick building. Dozens of horses were tethered or held by orderlies, nearly blocking the entry. The low buzz of conversation stilled at his approach, heads bobbing up, young fresh-faced privates dressed in homespun, staff lieutenants, some of them still sporting finely tailored uniforms of gray, battle-stained brigade commanders, all of them stood silent.

He could sense the mood. They were exhausted. It had, after all, been a very long day, and the night was now half-gone. It had been a day that had exploded with high hopes and triumph and closed with bitterness.

His gaze swept them, each of the men stiffening slightly when they sensed that his eyes were upon them.

I could order them in now, right now, he realized . . . and they would do it. I order men to die and they do not hesitate; they go forth gladly, eager to be the first to fling themselves into the dark mist. If they trust all in me, my God, I must not fail them. I must not.

Slowly he dismounted, someone taking Traveler's bridle. He patted Traveler affectionately. "See that he has water and something to eat," Lee whispered.

"A pleasure, sir."

Lee caught the boy's eyes, smiled. Again the reverent look. He wanted to pause, to ask the boy who he was, where he came from, what regiment he served with. No time for that now. I know what has to be done, and it's time to get to it.

He stepped up onto the siding platform, past the sentries flanking the open doors, and into the waiting room of the station.

A table, a fine dining room table, most likely dragged over from the hotel across the street, filled the center of the room, maps spread out upon it.

The men hunched over the maps looked up as one and came to attention.

They were all here, Longstreet, Ewell, Hill, Jed Hotchkiss, the chief cartographer for Jackson before his death, and finally, standing to one side, the errant Jeb Stuart. His gaze held on Stuart, who stiffened and formally saluted.

"I am glad to see that you are well, General Stuart."

The room was silent. He caught a glimpse of Longstreet standing to one side and could sense the barely concealed anger.

Stuart started to say something, but Lee motioned him to silence.

"General Stuart, there is time enough later for us to discuss what has happened these last few days. The hour is late. I am more concerned with what will happen in the morning."

Though he spoke softly, he fixed Stuart

intently with his gaze, conveying with a single look that the issue would not be forgotten. The man had to be reined in but not broken. A touch of uncertainty at this moment would be good, making him more attentive to the task ahead.

Lee stepped up to the map table, taking off his gauntlets, laying them to one side.

Spread out on the center of the table was a sketch map in Jed Hotchkiss's bold hand of the day's battlefield.

Hotchkiss cleared his throat. "Sir, as you can see, this hill, the locals call it Cemetery Hill, dominates the position south of town. Their First, Eleventh, and we believe a division of Twelfth Corps now occupy that hill, along with sixty pieces of artillery.

"Their left flank, extending on what is called Cemetery Ridge," and as he spoke he traced out the position, "stretches south for a mile, up to this crossroads in the middle of a peach orchard, where the road to Emmitsburg crosses a road that heads west to Fairfield."

"These two hills behind that crossroad?" Lee asked.

"I got a brief look at them just before dark, sir. The higher of the two is wooded. It appears as if they have established a signal station atop it. One of my staff saw flags up there. The lower of the two, with a rocky face, is clear cut on its western slope, facing us, and giving them an excellent field of fire. This left flank, the ridge, the crossroads, the two hills are occupied by Dan Sickles's Third Corps and Buford's division of cavalry."

Lee nodded, finger tracing out the line. "And their right?"

"The locals call this position Culp's Hill."

"Difficult ground," Dick Ewell interrupted. "In our last attack, one of Johnson's brigades swept across the face of it. The crest was occupied by a mix of First Corps and at least a brigade from Twelfth Corps. They're digging in."

"And our own left?"

Hotchkiss looked over at Ewell.

"It's up in the air, sir," Ewell replied hurriedly in his high, piping voice. "That's where the other brigade of Johnson got tangled up. Sir, I assure you, there was a division of Union troops deploying out there beyond Culp's Hill. We even took a couple of prisoners; they're Twelfth Corps."

"Are they still there?"

Ewell was silent.

"Are they?"

"I don't know, sir. The men are exhausted; it's dark. If we had a couple of regiments of cavalry, we'd soon find out," and as he spoke his gaze shifted to Stuart.

"We don't have them yet," Lee replied,

saying each word sharply and clearly.

"My first brigade will be up before dawn," Stuart quickly interjected.

Lee looked up. "I am not looking for excuses, gentlemen. At the moment I am seeking answers."

The room fell silent, the men around him looking pale and drawn as they stood beneath the flickering light of the lanterns suspended from the ceiling.

"I need to know if my flank is secure," he announced after a long silence. "General Ewell, inform General Johnson that I wish an immediate reconnaissance to our left. Inform him as well that General Stuart's men will be coming up the road from Hanover, and that they are to link up and contain any threats developing in that direction."

Ewell nodded and stepped from the room.

Lee returned his attention to the map. Left, center, or to the right?

"What else do we know?"

"Their Second and Fifth Corps are coming up," Jed continued.

"How soon?"

Again silence.

"How soon?" And this time his voice was sharper and more insistent.

"We have to assume they will be up by morning," Longstreet finally interjected.

"To assume otherwise would be dangerous."

"I need to know what exactly is their disposition," Lee replied coldly. "I cannot continue this operation on assumptions. I hear no mention of their Sixth Corps; that's the strongest formation in their army."

"Sir, we brushed around them two days ago down past Manchester," Stuart announced.

"Manchester?"

Jed quickly pointed to the second map on the side of the table, which covered the entire region from Harrisburg in the north down to Washington and west to the valley.

"Here, sir, twenty-five miles to the southeast, nearly halfway back to Baltimore."

"Two days ago. They could be marching behind us even now."

"No, sir," Stuart quickly replied. "My main force is in Hanover. It is, in fact, sir, securing your left flank. No one is moving to flank you."

Lee looked back up at Stuart. He knew the boy was reaching for justifications, to make it appear as if he had been performing a valuable service. Indirectly he had. Sixth Corps, old John Sedgwick's command, could very well be twenty-five miles off. Sedgwick might be popular with his own people, but his performance during the Chancellorsville campaign had been abysmal. By all rights Sedgwick should have been crushed against the river after the battle at Salem Church, Lee thought. Only the incompetence of my own people saved him.

Sedgwick might still be a day away.

The silence dragged out. Left, right, or center?

Too many unknowns with the left. An advance along that axis also drags us farther away from our reserves, communications, and supplies still on the other side of the South Mountains. Any maneuver would be clearly visible from Cemetery Hill as well.

The center? The vision held for a moment, the flags going up the hill, heights crowned with smoke and fire and then the final shattering volley, the men streaming back. So close, so close. And now four thousand of them dead or wounded, the town a charnel house.

My fault. I thought we could push them off. Just one more push. Perhaps if it had been better coordinated, all of Johnson's brigades going in at the same time as Anderson. No matter what the cause, though, four thousand men were dead or wounded for nothing. Tomorrow the Union will have even more forces on those hills, and our casualties would be even greater. I cannot let that happen again.

He kept staring at the map, gauging, judging distances, the ticking of the clock in the stationmaster's office, the steady undercurrent of the ever-present army outside, distant conversations, a horse whinnying in pain, the echo of a pistol shot ending the cries, the creaking of wagons passing, the moaning of the wounded suffering inside the jostling ambulances.

His finger traced across the map of the battlefield one more time.

"Here."

There was a stirring as the men around him leaned over.

"Our left is uncertain. Besides, deployment to that flank will be observed from the cemetery. We tried the center . . ." and he fell silent.

"It is here, on our right. These two hills. Our advance to that position will be covered by this ridge," and as he spoke he pointed out the crest running south from the seminary.

"Deploy by dawn, advance en echelon overlapping the two hills, cutting off this road that goes back to Taneytown. Doing that, we flank Cemetery Hill and cut them off."

No one spoke and slowly he looked up, his gaze meeting Longstreet's.

Longstreet said nothing, unlit cigar clenched firmly in the corner of his mouth. He caught a flicker of a gaze from Ewell, who had come back into the room. Hill, obviously ill, eyes glazed, stared at the map, saying nothing. Jed Hotchkiss, assuming the role of a lowly major in a roomful of generals, stood with gaze unfocused, eyes locked straight ahead.

"General?" Lee asked.

Longstreet took the cigar out of his mouth and finally shook his head. "We were thinking of something different, sir."

" 'We'?"

"Before you arrived here, sir."

Ewell shifted uncomfortably.

Pete fished in his pocket for a match and struck it against the side of the table, puffing his cigar to life.

"You know that I always seek the advice of my commanders," Lee replied evenly. "Go ahead."

"Our opportunity for a decisive victory here is finished, sir."

Lee could feel his features flush. He lowered his eyes, looking back at the map.

"I don't see it that way, General Longstreet," he finally replied.

The tension in the room was palpable,

hanging in the air like the smoke coiling up from Pete's cigar. No one dared speak.

"Do you know why we are here?" Lee finally asked.

"Sir?"

"Here, gentlemen, here," and his voice rose slightly as he stabbed down with a fingertip, pointing at Hotchkiss's map of Pennsylvania and Maryland.

No one spoke.

"Three weeks ago, before we started this campaign, you know that I met with President Davis. Gentlemen, you might be filled with confidence, it is fair to say that our President is confident, but I tell you we are starting to lose this war."

"Sir, that is not true," Stuart interjected heatedly. "Those Yankees run whenever we . . . hit them."

"General Stuart, hear me out!"

Stuart, crestfallen, lowered his head.

"Dispatches from Richmond arrived only three days ago indicating that Vicksburg will most likely fall within the week. You've seen the newspapers we've taken up here; they're already proclaiming the victory.

"In central Tennessee, Bragg is falling back. Before the summer is out, Chattanooga will be threatened; and if that falls, Atlanta will soon be on the front line. A

Union army has landed before Charleston, and even now they are closing the ring on that city.

"General Stuart, I have already heard that you captured a hundred and twenty wagons outside of Washington and that is what slowed your march."

Stuart puffed up slightly, but a glance at his commander warned him to silence.

"How desperate are we for supplies when a hundred wagons and their mules become a major prize?"

No one spoke.

"Don't you see that they can replace those wagons in a day? If tonight we had captured that accursed hill and had taken every gun on it, a day later their foundries would cast a hundred more guns to replace them. Their blockade is strangling us as surely as an executioner's rope."

Lee stepped back from the map table, arms folded, right hand absently rubbing his left shoulder. "We must finish this, and there is only one way to do it. Ours is the only army of the South capable of ending it. We must seek the battle of annihilation. We must bring out the Army of the Potomac and crush it. No more Fredericksburgs, Chancellorsvilles, or Manassases. We must achieve a Saratoga, a Yorktown, a Waterloo."

As he spoke the last words, Lee brought

his clenched fist down on the table, startling Ewell, who looked at him with surprise.

"Defeat the Army of Potomac in detail, force the surrender of their commander, then march on Washington. Even then it will not be over. But it will turn the tide. Such a victory will break the political alliance that Lincoln is barely holding together in Congress. Perhaps, with the Lord's blessing, it would mean, as well, that England and France will at last recognize our government and move to lift the blockade."

He paused, lowering his head, attention again fixed on the map.

"That is why we are here," he whispered. "It's not to seek a half victory; it is to end this war now."

He nodded toward the open window facing the Carlisle Road.

"Those boys out there, they are not immortal. They are mere flesh and blood. They have trusted us with their lives; and we, gentlemen, God save us, are empowered to trade those lives for what we believe in. I will not trade one more life for half a goal, half a victory that simply leads to defeat.

"Realize this. We have but one good fight left in us. We lost fifteen thousand men at Chancellorsville." He hesitated,

"And we lost Jackson . . . then we let them get away. We cannot afford one more battle like that. That is why I want it to end here, today."

"General, today we lost eight thousand men," Longstreet said softly, voice calm, almost like a distant echo.

"God save us, I know."

"And taking those hills south of town, we'll lose eight thousand more."

Lee looked up at him.

"Don't you think I know that as well? Our goal is their army, to defeat it, to finish it, and there will be a bloody price in the doing of it."

"We fought a good fight here today," Longstreet replied, "but the final price, sir, that last charge negated our gains."

"We smashed two of their corps," Lee replied sharply, and then hesitated. "They also lost John Reynolds, one of their best."

"A good man, John." Hill sighed, the first words that had escaped him.

"They checked us though, sir," Pete continued, pushing in. "The last assault . . ."

His words trailed off. Lee knew. Pete was always talking about the defensive, of letting them attack.

"That hill, sir," Longstreet finally continued, "I couldn't have picked better ground. Sir, you spoke against just such an assault only this morning up at Cashtown, and yet we nevertheless charged into such a position just before sundown."

Lee nodded, looking at Longstreet. Yes, that was true. That morning seemed like an age ago. Yes, the land before Cashtown was indeed the same. He nodded for Pete to continue.

"I came to agree with you there, sir, back at the base of the South Mountains. Yes, we do need to seek the final battle, but what happened here this evening ended that chance for this battlefield. Sir, the Union army is concentrated here. We try to flank to that hill south of town here, and in an hour they can shift an entire corps to it, and we are faced with the same problem yet again . . ."

Lee started to speak, to point to the two hills south of town; but as he looked at Pete, he fell silent.

Jackson is gone, he realized yet again. I always listened to Jackson, trusted him; even when he failed before Richmond, I still listened. If this were Jackson before me, offering an objection to a plan, I would listen. I must realize that; otherwise why have commanders who can think? I know now I must take more direct control of this army. His gaze drifted to Hill, then to Ewell, then finally back to

Longstreet. Longstreet is now my right arm more than any other.

"Go ahead, General Longstreet."

"You were focused on that hill, that cemetery. We all were. It was so damn close. We just had to get to the other side, and we thought we could win. Sir, I, too, was caught by it. I saw the tail end of the assault and for a moment I believed we would take it; then their guns, sir, their guns just shredded our lines. And, sir, those guns will still be there tomorrow morning, dug in deeper and resupplied."

Lee nodded slowly. "But I must ask, sir, what is on the other side of that hill?"

Longstreet looked over at Stuart and then to Jed Hotchkiss. "They have two lines of retreat from the far side of that hill," and as he spoke Longstreet traced out the roads back to Westminster and Taneytown. "Sir, it would have been yet another partial victory. Some, perhaps most, of the Yankees would have gotten out along those two roads. And then we would have to fight them again."

He pointed down to the map of Gettysburg and the hills south of town.

"We do this attack tomorrow; and after we take those hills, then what? The road to Baltimore will still be open, and they will retreat. Even if they abandon the army's immediate supply trains, they will get out, dig in someplace else, and then we'll have to attack yet again."

Lee, staring again at the map, did not speak.

"Sir, it's defensive. This ground is defensive. Beyond that there is no barrier we can pin them against to finish it. Jeb and his boys might dream of a glorious saber charge to wipe them out once we get them running, but it won't happen."

"Sir, we could finish it, if you would break them up," Stuart said heatedly.

"No offense, Jeb, but you are not Murat, and this is not Napoleon's army. Those days are finished. These Yankees are not a mob running away, armed with smoothbores, where they can only get one shot off before you are into them. The rifle has changed all that. They might be broken, but you try and charge and they'll shred you at two hundred yards."

"We don't need a discussion of tactics now," Lee interjected.

"General Lee, I beg you to step back and take a look, a long careful look at what you are proposing tomorrow and what will be the result even if we do take those hills."

Lee was silent, gaze locked on the maps.

"Sir?"

He finally looked up.

"Most likely at this very moment General Meade is looking at nearly the same thing. He knows where we are. He knows our line of communication traces back to Chambersburg. Given that we are deep inside their territory, enough civilians have most likely slipped through to tell him that my own corps is still stretched out between Chambersburg and Cashtown, while Hill and Ewell are already up here.

"We know that Hancock was in command of that hill today. He held it. He will wish to continue to hold it. That is most likely what he is advising Meade to do at this very moment. We could ride out of here now, sir, go to the south end of town and listen to them digging in up there. They are digging in on Culp's Hill as well and down along the ridge that stretches to the two hills south of town.

"It's the good position; the roads leading in are good; all he has to do is dig in.

"Let him," Longstreet announced, voice becoming animated. "Then we know exactly where he is. Sir, he will pour into this point like water going down a funnel, and they will pour up the roads from here, here, and here. That sir, is what Meade will see and what Meade will do."

Lee held up his hand, a quiet gesture, not dismissive, simply indicating a wish for silence.

Again he could hear the ticking of the clock, the rattle of an ambulance passing outside the window, the first of a long train of ambulances coming down from the cemetery.

Four thousand men tonight, he thought. And the price tomorrow? If it was worth it, then I would pay it; but if Pete is right, would I have but a half victory here even if we did win . . . and at what cost?

The silence continued. His gaze locked onto the map.

The wrong decision here, and the men being carried past the window would have shed their blood for what? By attacking, does that redeem the mistake of the last charge or just add more to the bill, and without meaning, without results?

Take control back. That is what I resolved to myself back at Chambersburg three days ago. But instead this place, this ground, is now taking control of me. And that realization was fundamental and startling to him.

He noticed that someone, without comment, had placed a tin cup of coffee by his side and, without taking his eyes off the map, he took the cup and sipped.

The pendulum of the clock continued to drift back and forth, measuring out the seconds with a tick-tock steadiness.

He looked up. "General Longstreet, what is your proposal, sir."

Longstreet, normally so rigid in his presence, exhaled. There was no smile, just the slightest of nods, and he stepped to Lee's side.

"Sir, go south of those hills. Here," and he pointed forcefully to the sketch map, the Rocky Hill and the high, wooded hill anchoring the south of the Union line. "A mile, two or three if need be. Swing around their right, sir. Cut the Taneytown Road without a fight. Move toward the Baltimore Road, here, sir, above this place, Littlestown. We do that, sir, and it will dislodge them from here without a fight, and then we pick the ground."

Lee nodded thoughtfully but said nothing, gaze still on the map, the soft murmur of men talking outside and the clock continuing its steady beat.

As Lee studied the map, it seemed as if some lines of movement stood out sharply, like traces of light in his mind, while others faded to a distant blur. Numbers shifted and played in his mind . . . rates of movement, which division where, supply lines, which roads were macadamized and which were but dirt lanes. And of the other side? If they are coming here, then what are their lines of communication? Where is their railhead? They always marry their line to a railhead. Where is that?

The lines on the map led to that point, and in his mind he saw other lines, as if cut with fire, radiating out from it.

"Have any of our supply wagons come through the gap back to the Cumberland Valley yet?" he asked, his voice soft.

"No, sir. General Pickett is still with them," Longstreet replied, "but they have orders to start in the morning to come here."

Lee said nothing. Looking over there on the map, the road from Chambersburg down to here, that line now standing out sharp in his mind as he studied the map, then another line southward, back toward Greencastle, on the Maryland-Pennsylvania border. Another line on the map seemed to shine out now, due west to east, from their railhead, to the South's base of supplies.

"Dear God," and for a moment he was startled, for the words had escaped him, a barely audible whisper, and all in the room were surprised, but none commented.

He took another sip of coffee, put the

cup down, adjusted his spectacles, rubbed his eyes, then looked up at his men.

They were like a frozen tableau.

"We are fighting the wrong battle here," Lee announced, his voice steady.

"Then we flank the hills?" Longstreet asked.

"No, General Longstreet."

"Sir?"

"What you just said, sir, a few minutes ago." Lee looked over at the clock and realized that he had been lost in thought for at least ten, maybe fifteen minutes.

"And that is?" Longstreet asked quizzically.

"About them pouring into Gettysburg like water down a funnel. You are right, General Longstreet. They will all be here by tomorrow morning. Though we do not know for certain the location of their Second Corps, or their Sixth Corps, that is what Meade will do; he will concentrate here and dig in. You are right in that, sir, and they will be ready for us no matter where we strike here.

"Though your plan, sir, is along the right lines, I think we should be more audacious, General Longstreet." And then he traced a line across the map far to the south, Emmitsburg, Taneytown, and then finally Westminster.

"General Longstreet, you spoke with

great clarity just now, sir. We have all become focused on here, on this place, these roads leading to Gettysburg, these surrounding hills, and have forgotten how we have fought in the past, at Chancellorsville and especially Second Manassas.

"If they are here tomorrow, what is behind them? Not just behind the hills, sir, that you suggest we flank, but farther back, ten miles, twenty miles?"

No one spoke.

"Nothing, except their supplies, which are most likely based at Westminster."

He traced his finger on the map, estimating distances, his generals gathering closer.

"Jed, how far would you estimate?" and his cartographer leaned closer to watch.

"Here at Gettysburg, back to Fairfield, then Emmitsburg, then straight to Westminster."

Jed studied the map for a moment. "Thirty-five miles, but that's a rough guess, sir."

"Jackson did over fifty in two days when he marched around them at the start of the Second Manassas campaign," Lee replied, and he chose the analogy deliberately, looking over at Longstreet.

He could see that the comment hit a nerve with Longstreet, who stiffened slightly and then made direct eye contact with Lee and held it.

"Westminster is their supply head; it is the closest railroad," Lee continued, still looking at Longstreet. "Move toward that, gain the march on them, and it will be like Jackson taking Manassas Junction. We will have their supply line and be between them and Washington. Panic will ensue.

"All of the Yankees will be concentrated here at Gettysburg. They'll have to turn around and force march back. It will be a mad tangle. That is the disadvantage this town hides. Getting in is easy; getting back out quickly, that will be a problem. And while they do that, we simply dig in and get ready to receive them."

"How are these roads?" Longstreet asked, at last breaking eye contact with Lee to look at Hotchkiss.

Lee smiled inwardly. Longstreet was rising to the challenge, the bait. It would become for him an issue of pride, to match Jackson and what was now the immortal legend.

"Emmitsburg to Taneytown to Westminster is a good pike, sir," Hotchkiss replied. "Solid bridge over Monocacy Creek."

"I crossed through Westminster, sir," Stuart quickly interjected. "Excellent roads. You could move an entire corps along them without a problem."

Lee held up his hand, indicating for everyone to remain calm. For a moment this afternoon he thought that final victory was, indeed, unfolding before Gettysburg. He realized now that if he had not launched that final, desperate evening assault he would have rejected Longstreet's reasoning, which had triggered this new line of thought, believing that come dawn the fight could be pressed to a successful conclusion on this ground. He knew now that Longstreet, without a doubt, was right. Today, exactly one year later, he had fought Malvern Hill here at Gettysburg on July 1st. He would never make that mistake again.

The battle here at Gettysburg was finished.

"We turn this back into a battle of maneuver, gentlemen, the thing we have always done best, the thing that our opponents have never mastered. But let me say it before all of you quite clearly. I am not seeking a half victory. By abandoning this field, some will see that as an admission of defeat, something we have never yet done, completely abandon a field. In so doing we return to a war of maneuver. We cut their line of supply while at the same time continuing to secure our own line of supply by moving our wagon trains back down to Greencastle. The ultimate goal must be to force the Army of the Potomac to territory that we choose and then fight a battle to finish this once and for all."

He looked carefully at each one in turn. "That is what I will expect from you, what our country expects from all of us, and nothing less is acceptable. We are here to win not just a battle."

He paused for a moment.

"We are here to win a war."

He looked around the room. Ewell's gaze seemed a bit distant; most likely he was still in shock after the debacle before Cemetery Hill, but Longstreet, Stuart, and even Hill had stirred. In their eyes was that light, that terrible fire he had seen before in men anticipating battle and knew could blaze within him as well.

There was a final gaze back at the map of Gettysburg, then over to the other map, his glance catching a creek north of Westminster . . . Pipe Creek.

He took a deep breath and pushed the map of Gettysburg aside.

Perhaps the fate of our nation rests on what I've just done he thought, but that thought held only for a moment until finally, like the map, he pushed it aside as well. Such thoughts, at such moments, could only serve to cripple one's will, and there was a campaign to be planned.

2:00 AM, July 2, 1863

Cemetery Hill

US "It's General Meade."

Henry Hunt, who had fallen asleep sitting against the wheel of a caisson, stirred, looked up blankly. Hancock stood above him, silhouetted by the moonlight.

"Better get up," Winfield said, and leaning over, he offered his hand.

With a groan Henry took the hand, and came up to his feet.

"How long did I sleep?"

"An hour, maybe two."

"Sorry."

"You needed it."

"What about you?"

Hancock chuckled. "No rest for the wicked."

In the bright moonlight Henry could see the cavalcade, a troop of cavalry riding escort, guidon of the Commander of the Army of the Potomac shining silver in the moonlight, staff officers trailing behind as Meade trotted around the side of the gatehouse to the cemetery and came up the hill. One of Hancock's staff rode down to meet them and pointed the way.

Henry stretched, absently tugging at his uniform, trying to smooth it out. His mouth felt gummy, the taste sour. His eyes were scratchy. As he stretched, every muscle and joint ached in protest.

He caught the scent of coffee and nodded his thanks as a sergeant approached bearing a hot cup. He blew on the rim, took a scalding mouthful, and rinsed his mouth out; then he took a deep swallow, the coffee jolting him awake.

Still a bit disoriented, he looked around. In the moonlight it seemed as if the grounds of the cemetery were a seething mass, a strange, almost frightful sight, as if the graves had opened and the dead were rising up.

The men were digging in. Shovels flashed in the moonlight; lunettes were going up around the guns rimming the crown of the hill. Shattered caissons, upended wagons, dead horses, empty limber boxes, anything that could stop a bullet or shell were being piled up, strengthening the defensive line.

Farther down the slope, he could see dozens of lanterns, slowly bobbing and weaving about, stretcher parties working to bring in the wounded.

"Lee asked for a truce a couple of hours ago," Hancock announced. "Their boys and ours are down there helping the wounded. Damn, Hunt, there are places you can barely move the ground is so covered with bodies."

He had a flash memory of the flag bearer torn apart, the ground smeared with blood, entrails, parts of bodies. Lowering the cup of coffee, he caught a scent of the air. It was a mixture of raw, upturned earth (cemetery dirt, he realized coldly), the still-clinging sulfur smell of burnt powder, but layered in was the stench of open flesh, bodies torn open; and though he knew it was his imagination, he felt the air already held the first sickly sweet smell of decay, the flesh preparing to go back into the ground from which it came.

He gagged, then, embarrassed, mumbled that the coffee was strong.

Meade approached, Winfield stepping forward to meet him, offering a salute. Henry put his cup down on a caisson lid and came to stand by Winfield's side.

"Winfield, Hunt, glad to see you're both alive," Meade offered as he dismounted.

"How are things on the road?" Winfield asked.

"Usual. Total chaos. God, is there anything left of Eleventh Corps up here? I swear I saw every last one of them halfway back to Taneytown."

"Some of them held," Winfield offered. "Ames's brigade put up a hell of a fight."

"I heard. Too bad about Ames."

Henry didn't know, and he looked over at Winfield.

"Reb stretcher party brought him in an hour ago," Winfield offered. "He died just after they carried him into our lines."

"Damn," Henry whispered. "A good man."

Meade said nothing, walking up to the line of guns ringing the crest, carefully stepping around the tangle of bodies that still littered the slope. "So they came up this far?"

"Right to the mouth of the guns," Winfield replied. "Henry's people tore them to shreds."

Again the image of the flag bearer, cut in half. Henry pushed the thought away.

"Winfield."

"Sir?"

"Is this position worth holding?"

Henry could see Winfield's features crack into a grin. "It's Fredericksburg in reverse. By God, I hope they come again tomorrow. We have the ammunition now and two more batteries. Let them come."

Meade nodded, looking down the slope toward the town. "So he asked for a truce."

"Right thing to do," Hancock replied. "I was thinking of offering one myself but didn't have the authority. It's ghastly down there. Some of our men were crawling down to offer them water; a couple got shot doing it. I'm glad he offered."

"Not like Lee to make a concession of defeat like that."

"I don't think it was a concession, sir. It was a Christian act."

Meade grunted, saying nothing for a moment. "Think he'll come again?"

Winfield folded his hands behind his back, looked down, and kicked at the ground for a moment.

"Not like Lee to concede ground, especially after he's given blood for it like this. Here, at this point? I don't think so. His stretcher bearers and doctors down there, they'll talk and tell everyone we're digging in even now. If he couldn't take it at dusk with damn near two divisions, he must know he can't take it tomorrow. He must figure we're bringing more men up."

Winfield looked over expectantly at Meade.

"Your corps and my old boys from the Fifth should be coming up by dawn. That only leaves John Sedgwick out of the fight for tomorrow."

"When can we count on him being up though?" and Henry could sense the slight tone of doubt in Hancock's voice. There were some men who swore by old "Uncle John," especially the boys who served under him. There were others though, men like Winfield, who thought he was too cautious and too slow when speed was needed.

"His men should be forming to march even now. I expect them no later than mid-afternoon. But you haven't answered my question."

Winfield hesitated again, attention focused on the town, which was ablaze with light.

"Bobbie Lee's like a pit dog. Once he sinks his teeth in, he worries you to death and won't let go. Sank his teeth into us today, and we broke a couple of them off. That will only serve to get him mad and want to jump in and bite again."

"So you think he'll come at us again tomorrow right here."

"I didn't say that, George."

Meade sighed, features sour, and he rubbed his forehead.

"Sir, I do believe there'll be a fight tomorrow. If we had John up, I'd even say go in after them. Dan Sickles came up here a couple of hours back and we talked. He says the right flank of the Rebs is in the air and wants to push up west and north."

"Dan Sickles always wants to go pushing

when he should be sitting still, damn the man!"

"Just a thought," Hancock replied.

"So you think he'll hit again."

"He has to. He damn near won a major victory today and then threw it away by getting too bold at the last second. He needs to retrieve that tomorrow. He knows just how important morale is with his army. Damn it, he seems to run on little if anything else at times other than sheer brass. He'll come at us."

Meade nodded. "Fine then. It will be here."

Winfield said nothing for a moment. "I didn't say it would necessarily be here, this place."

"Then what the hell are you saying?"

"Watch the flank. With Lee it's always the flank."

"And you said this was a good position."

"That I did."

"Then for once let us have him try our flank while we have the location. Make this hill the center anchor of our line. Artillery up here can dominate everything for a radius of a mile."

Meade looked over at Henry, who nodded in agreement.

"We leave Sickles on the left, but come midmorning we refuse that line, anchor it back. I remember two hills down there, about two miles from here."

"The Round Tops, locals call it," Henry offered. "The smaller is clear cut, excellent artillery ground."

"Fine then. Refuse that flank, pull it back from the crossroads, and anchor it with concealed batteries on those hills. We put Fifth Corps behind the hills as reserve. Winfield, your corps behind this position as reserve covering this hill and that position over there," and as he spoke he waved toward Culp's Hill.

"This is a good site; the roads coming in are good; we'll have our full strength up by late tomorrow; then let Bobbie Lee try and dig us out."

Winfield was silent.

"Don't you approve?"

"It's an excellent position, sir. But I wonder if Lee sees it that way," Winfield said.

"What do you mean?"

"This situation, does he see it as *too* good?"

"Lee's instinct is to attack. He knows we are here," Meade replied sharply. "This whole campaign was to bring us out from Washington in order to engage us in the open. Fine, we want it, too. One thing Lee does not understand is that we are in Pennsylvania now, and the boys will fight like hell to defend it. From everything I heard about this evening's fight, both of you saw that."

"Yes, they fought like hell," Winfield offered.

"He'll come on, and here's where we dig in. Hunt, come dawn, start bringing up the rest of your reserve. I want a firm anchor on the left flank, that hill you mentioned. See what guns you can put on top of the hill to the right of here as well.

"Winfield, I want to meet with all corps commanders in a half hour. There's a house just back down the pike a quarter mile or so; meet me there."

"Yes, sir."

Meade extended his hand. "Winfield, you did well today. Damn well."

"The men did, sir."

Meade grunted and stiffly remounted. Without further comment he trotted off, guidon fluttering behind him.

"I wonder if I should have said more," Winfield said softly.

"Sir?"

"What do you think, Henry?"

"About Lee? Tomorrow?"

"Yes."

"Remember, I served under him at Fort Hamilton."

"I know; that's why I asked."

"A subtle mind, we all know that. Something gets him angry though, and he could be bullheaded. We saw that this evening."

He looked down at the town. A distant cry echoed, a high, pleading shriek that died away.

"Goddamn war," Hancock whispered. "When in Christ's name is it ever going to end?"

"Maybe when the last of us is dead."

Winfield looked over at him.

"You didn't answer my question, Henry."

"Nor did you answer Meade's."

Winfield chuckled softly. "Because I couldn't. When it comes to Lee . . . I just don't know. I'm certain about the flank. That has always been his way. In fact, he surprised me a bit today with the last attack. I'd of shifted, gone for the low ground between here and the Round Tops. I think he got worked up, thought he could push us and we'd crack. Now he knows we won't.

"We whipped him good today. Let's hope it gets him so damn mad that tomorrow he comes straight in across those fields," and he pointed toward the open land west of the hill.

"I think it will be one of two things," Henry finally replied.

"Go on."

"Chancellorsville. Distance is about the same. Swing behind the seminary, head southwest, come out below the Round Tops, then cut in. The flank, just like you said. If so, I'll be on that hill, and by God he'll pay."

"Or?"

"Second Bull Run and he'll march fifty miles to get into our rear."

Hancock stood silent, hands folded behind his back. He finally looked over at Henry and smiled. "Henry Hunt, pray for another Chancellorsville. If Lee tries that on us again, this time we'll bloody him good."

Henry said nothing. Picking up his cup of coffee, he took a sip and grimaced. It had gone cold. He drank it anyhow. Two hours' sleep was enough. It was time to get down to the rocky hill, Little Round Top, and start digging in.

Chapter Seven

4:00 AM, July 2, 1863

Herr's Ridge
Gettysburg, Pennsylvania

"Sir, I think you should see this."

John Williamson drifted in the half-real world of waking and numbed sleep. He tried to ignore Hazner for a minute, to hold on to just one more precious minute of rest, the opiatelike sleep of complete exhaustion, devoid of dreams, of nightmares, of all that he had seen.

"Sir." Sergeant Hazner roughly shook him, and John sat up. Hazner was crouched before him, a dim shadow in the moonlight.

"What is it?"

"Over there by the road, sir. Something is up."

John turned, fumbling for the glasses in his breast pocket. The world around him was hazy, wrapped in early morning mist and smoke drifting from smoldering fires. The air was rich, damp, carrying the scent of crushed hay, and that other smell, the smell of a battlefield. Where the battle had started, dead men and horses scattered about their campsite alongside the pike were beginning to swell.

The camp was quiet, at least nearby, but he could hear low moans, cries from a nearby barn, bright with lights. Even as he put his glasses on, two stretcher bearers staggered toward him, carrying their burden, who was babbling softly, lost in delirium. Even in the dark he could see that the stretcher bearers were Yankees, white strips of cloth tied around their arms to indicate they were prisoners who had given their parole and were now pressed into service.

One of them looked over at John. "Vere the hospital? Ve lost?"

It took him a moment to understand what the Yankee was saying. His accent was thick, German from the sounds of it.

John pointed toward the barn. The Yankee nodded his thanks and pressed on.

John spared a quick glance down at their burden. In the soft glow of moonlight the man they were carrying already looked dead, his features ghostly white, dark, hollow eyes wide with pain. Since he was wrapped in a blanket, it was impossible to tell which side he was on.

Across the gently sloping valley below, lanterns bobbed up and down, like fireflies drifting on a summer night. The rising mists gave it all a dreamlike appearance, of spirits floating in the coiling wisps of fog. A lantern or candle would stop, hover for a moment, and then move on. He watched as one knot of men stopped, lantern laid down on the ground, men gathering around, one going down on his knees and covering his face, while comrades gently picked up a body to carry it off.

Around him all was still, what was left of his regiment lost in druglike sleep. A man cried out softly, tossing, and sat up, breathing hard. Embarrassed, he looked about, caught John's gaze, then looked away, lying back down.

Fires had burned down to glowing embers, thin coils of smoke rising straight up, mingling with the damp night air.

"I think that's your friend, Colonel Taylor, over on the road," Hazner whispered, touching John on the shoulder and drawing him back.

"So?"

"Well, sir, if he's out and about back here behind the lines at this time of the morning, that tells me something is up."

"And you want to know what it is." John sighed. "Is that what you woke me up for?"

"Well, sir, I don't have the social connections you have."

"Goddamn, Hazner. Can't it wait till morning?"

"It will be that in another hour, sir. I was about to get you up anyhow."

Every joint of his body ached in protest, and he was tempted to tell Hazner to go to hell and lie back down. But the sergeant was right. If something was up, it'd be good to know it now.

After the bloody assault of the afternoon, the regiment had gone into reserve. He had watched the final assault go in against that damn hill on the far side of the town, a charge that had gone down into flaming ruin, wiping away the sense of triumph. Perhaps the regiment would be ordered up, and the thought of that knotted his stomach. Not another charge, not like yesterday, God forbid, never another charge like that.

He looked to the road and saw that it was indeed Taylor, half a dozen staff with him. They were dismounted, gathered in a tight circle, one of the men holding a lantern over a map that was pressed against the flank of a horse. John moved toward them, feeling a bit nervous about intruding, but Hazner had set him on a course and he could not turn aside, for now his curiosity was up as well.

As he approached, Walter looked up. "John?"

"How are you, Walter?"

"Good to see you're still alive."

"Same for you."

There was an awkward moment, and John felt he should withdraw.

"A hard night," Walter finally offered.

"How did it go up there?"

"They held the hill. We lost a lot of good men, and now the Yankees are digging in. You can hear them up on that hill moving more men in."

"So that means we attack again come dawn?" John struggled to control the pitch of his voice, offering the words casually, as if discussing a distasteful chore that he simply needed the light of day to accomplish.

Walter sighed. "John, you know I can't discuss that with you."

"I know, Walter. But if my men need to get ready, I'd better see to it."

An approaching horseman, coming from the west, stilled their conversation. John recognized the rider as one of the young couriers on Lee's staff, a cheerful lad still filled with a starry-eyed dream of glory. The boy's mount was exhausted, blowing hard, covered in lathered sweat. The boy reined in before Walter and saluted.

"Sir, I was sent back to tell you that the road is clear all the way down to Fairfield, and that scouts have been posted in that town. A patrol led by Major Hotchkiss is moving toward Emmitsburg but has encountered nothing so far. At least one brigade of

Yankees marched through Fairfield early in the evening, just after dark, coming up from Emmitsburg, but turned east toward Gettysburg, moving on the road that comes out near the rocky hill south of town."

"How do you know that?"

"We captured a few stragglers, sir. Third Corps."

"But the road we want is clear?"

"At least to Fairfield, sir. One of the stragglers said there was nothing behind them."

"Did you hear him say that?"

"Yes, sir. But any man that would talk like that, I wouldn't trust, sir. No honor in a man who would say that to someone on the other side."

One of Taylor's followers snorted disdainfully.

"No honor in any of them bastards."

"Lieutenant Jenson, go tell that to the Yanks still holding the hill," Walter replied softly.

"Did you see General Longstreet on the turnoff to the Fairfield Road?" Taylor asked.

"Yes, sir. I passed the word to one of his staff. They said he was trying to get a few hours' sleep before setting off."

"Jackson would already be moving," Jenson whispered.

Walter turned and looked sharply at his

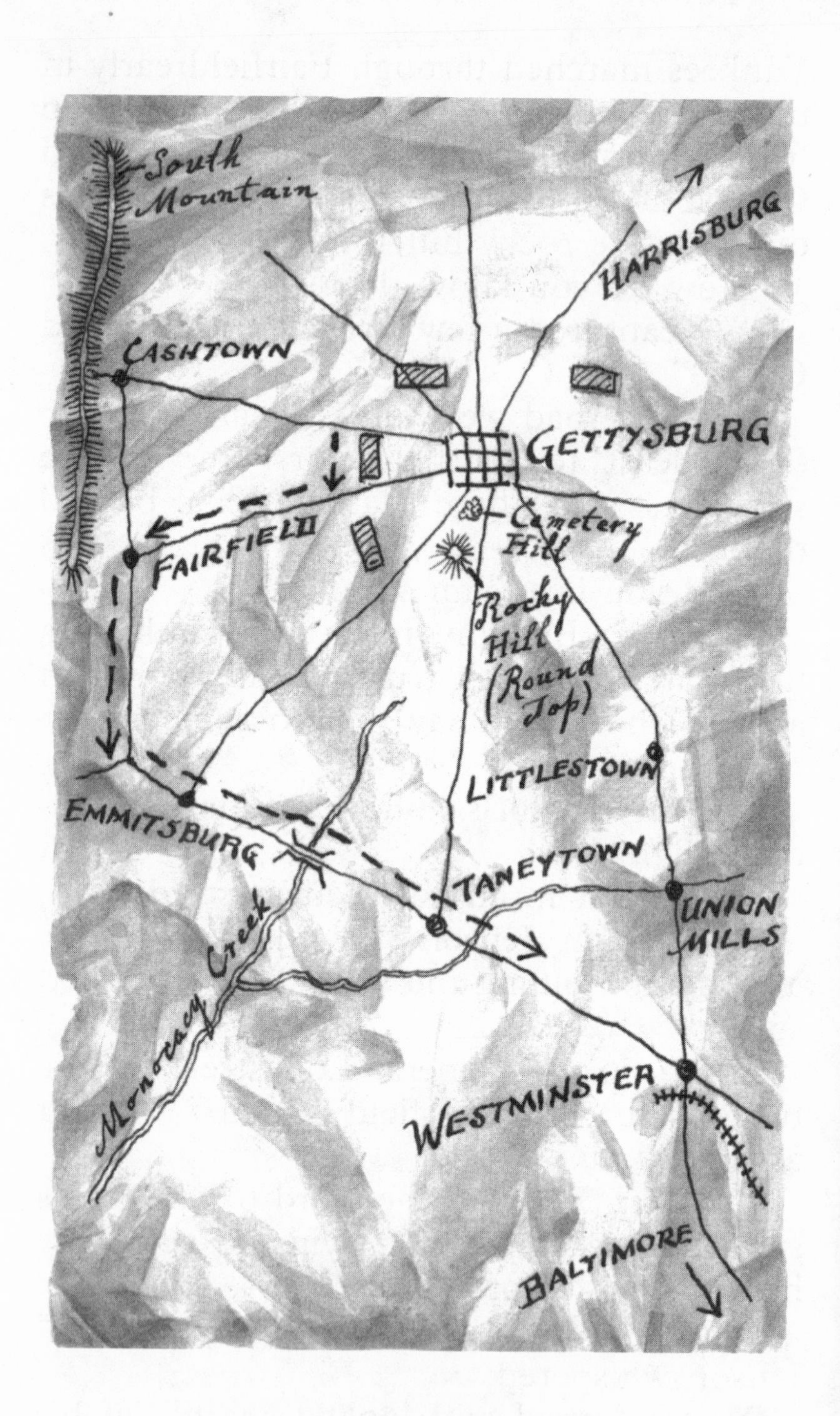
South Mountain
HARRISBURG
CASHTOWN
GETTYSBURG
Cemetery Hill
FAIRFIELD
Rocky Hill (Round Top)
LITTLESTOWN
EMMITSBURG
TANEYTOWN
UNION MILLS
Monocacy Creek
WESTMINSTER
BALTIMORE

companions. “I will not tolerate that,” he replied sharply. “If the general were here, you wouldn’t have dared say that.”

John watched the interchange. Jenson lowered his head and muttered an apology. John could see that Walter was exhausted, leaning against his horse for support. Hazner approached, bearing two cups of coffee, and with his usual good sense he held one out to Walter, who gratefully took the steaming cup while John took the other one. Such a gesture meant that John could linger for a few more minutes and perhaps find out what was brewing.

The first sip was hot, and when it hit his empty stomach, John gagged. He swallowed down the bile, took a deep breath, then another sip, which settled the rebellion. Walter half drained the cup and set it back on an upright fence post. Then he looked up at the courier.

“Good work, Vincent. General Lee is asleep. His headquarters is the house across from the seminary. Report there, but don’t disturb the general. Like Longstreet, he needs some rest, too.”

“Yes, sir.” The boy saluted and tried to urge his mount up to a gallop, but the poor exhausted beast would only give a slow trot as he set off down the road.

Walter looked back at John.

“Emmitsburg, that’s off to the south of

here, isn't it?" John asked.

Walter smiled.

"Just relax, John. It won't affect you for hours. Go back and get some sleep."

Jenson, who was standing behind Walter, turned and, looking back toward the town, stiffened. "Sir, I think that's General Lee approaching."

All turned. John saw Lee, riding alone, coming out of the mist cloaking the road and stopping to take Vincent's report. Again, for John, it had a dreamlike quality. The wisps of fog and smoke drifting, the outline of the seminary up on the next hill, light shining from the windows, and beyond, the glow of distant campfires from what must be the Union lines.

Here and there in the surrounding fields, men were standing up, rising like apparitions from out of this place of battle, watching as Lee approached. The world was still, as if the thunder of the previous day must now be paid for with a vow of silence. The only sound was the soft clip-clop of Traveler's hooves.

Walter stepped away from the group as all stiffened to attention. "Sir, I thought you were asleep," Walter said.

"I wanted to check on things and see General Longstreet off."

"We're working on it now, sir. Sir, you really should get a little more rest."

"Time enough later, Walter. Vincent told me the road is open."

"Yes, sir. Scouts are pushing down toward Emmitsburg."

"The way is clear and can't be observed?"

"We were studying that just now, sir," and Walter nodded toward the map still resting against the flank of a horse. "There's some concern about the rocky hill south of Gettysburg." As he spoke Walter drew a line with his finger across the map.

"This ridge here should block that view. That's at Black Horse Tavern, where Hood's division will pass. McLaws is supposed to come down by a different road farther back. As we move through Black Horse, a regiment of skirmishers will deploy along the ridge in front of the tavern to keep back any Yankee cavalry that might come up. With the rain yesterday, dust should be to a minimum."

"Are the men up yet?"

Walter pulled out his watch and opened it, Jenson bringing a lantern over. "It's just about four-thirty, sir? They should be falling in right now."

"Fine, then let's go and see them off."

"Sir, I can attend to that. Might I suggest you get some rest, sir? I know you haven't had more than two hours' sleep since yesterday morning."

Lee leaned over and put a hand on Walter's shoulder. "Thank you for your concern, Walter, but now is not the time for it. The men must see me; they must understand how important this day is."

Walter said nothing. The staff began to mount, and Walter looked back at John. "Not a word. We don't want wild rumors flying around the camp. You know how men out on a picket line will talk with the other side. Orders will come down soon enough."

"I'll keep it quiet, Walter."

"Take care of yourself, John."

"You too, Walter."

The cavalcade set off, heading west. John watched as they disappeared into the mist. Three times now he had seen Lee in the last five days. And thousands had died across those five days.

"A flanking march, that's it," Hazner whispered, picking up the cup that Walter had left half-empty, draining off what was left.

"Looks that way."

Hazner looked back to the east. "First light," he announced.

It was hard to tell if the glow on the horizon was from the Union campfires or approaching dawn.

"Things have changed." Hazner sighed. "I thought we'd push straight in come dawn."

John said nothing, sipping the last of his coffee, chewing on the grinds.

"I wonder what would have happened if we had. It's not like the old man to break off an action like this," John whispered.

"We'll never know. No sense dwelling on that. It makes a man crazy wondering. Let's just hope it means we stay alive another day and not wind up like those poor bastards in that barn."

"A wonderful thought." John sighed.

"I'm going to get a little sleep, sir," Hazner announced. "You should, too."

"First you wake me up, and now you go to sleep. Thank you."

"Well, my curiosity got satisfied, sir, and now I can rest easy. You heard them talking. Longstreet is off on a flanking march. He'll go slow as he usually does, and that means we can skip getting killed this morning." Without waiting for a reply, Hazner went back to his fire, tossed a few sticks on, and then flopped down on a ground cloth, oblivious to the dead mule that was lying on its back only a few feet away.

If only I could be like him, John thought enviously, to put aside all thought, to sleep next to a dead animal without concern, and awake with a smile, in fact eager for what he calls "the mischief ahead." Whether Longstreet moves slow or not, another fight is still ahead. It's never going to end. It may be mischief for Hazner; for me it's pure terror.

As he rode west Lee's gaze lingered for a moment on an overturned caisson, dead horses collapsed around it. One was still alive, forelegs shattered, its lungs working like a bellows. The earth was torn up from the previous day's battle where Pegram had massed over thirty guns to support the assault . . . . dead horses, plowed furrows of dirt from incoming solid shot tearing in, an abandoned limber wagon with shattered wheels. And more dead horses. Poor beasts. The dying horse cried piteously.

"Lieutenant Jenson," Lee sighed, "please put that creature out of its misery."

Jenson angled away from the group, passing through the shattered fence. Lee did not look back as a pistol shot broke the silence.

The regiments that had fought the previous day's battle were camped in the fields to either side of the road, exhausted men, lost in oblivion. Let them rest; it won't be till later in the day that their time will come. A few, unable to sleep, lined the road, watching as he passed . . . but none spoke. A barn and house to his left were aswarm with activity, hundreds of men lying in the farmyard, around the house, on the porch. Most were silent, a few crying; a knot of men were on their knees, hats off, praying over a comrade. Lee took his hat off, holding it to his breast as he rode past.

He pressed down the road, moving aside to let a train of ambulances pass, followed by several dozen stretcher bearers, Union prisoners who looked up at him curiously. He nodded and continued on. A cluster of tents, pitched next to the road, was ahead; atop the crest of the next hill, the ridge top poked above the fog like an island in a sea of white moon glow. He rode into the mist flanking the hill, the cool dampness soothing, cloaking him for a moment. He entertained a passing fantasy, that he could somehow stay here, let the burden drop away.

I let raw emotion take control. The last assault never should have gone in. And I could see it in the eyes of those around me, the staff meeting at the train station in that accursed town. No one would say it, but I know they were thinking it. I pushed Ewell's men forward, and now thousands are gone from the ranks.

When I stand before God, will those who fell be in judgment? How do I answer for all the blood upon my hands? John Reynolds died near here, supposedly just beyond the hospital barn, a godly man Reynolds.

Out on the frontier, Texas, he remembered how the natives believed that the spirits of the slain lingered at the place where they had fallen.

Does John now linger here? Is his spirit drifting with this fog? The men, Reynolds's valiant men who so manfully held us throughout yesterday morning and afternoon . . . was this mist not a mist at all, but rather their souls?

He shivered. Pagan superstition, don't let it haunt you now.

John, I'm sorry. This war never should have divided us. Duty, you and I lived for duty. We learned that at the Point, taught it to our cadets in turn. We were trained for this, believed it to be our sacred trust. A soldier must not ask why once he has drawn his sword for his nation. He takes his orders and carries them out unflinchingly; thus it was with the Roman Republic, with the Crusaders, with my own father who rode with Washington.

But . . . am I now responsible for all this death? For John, for the bodies that are swelling in the fields around me?

He slowed, suppressing a gag as they edged around a dead horse that had been nearly cut in half by a bursting shell, the broken body of a man twisted up in the offal.

"Lieutenant Jenson, find some men, get that poor man out of that mess, and have them drag the horse off the road. I don't want troops seeing that."

If I start thinking of this now, dwelling on all that this means, it will slow me, make me hesitate. One gets lost in it, the sight of a column of men, buoyant, filled with youthful zeal, marching along the road on a spring morning, their voices rising with the wind, a vast ocean sweeping toward victory, or the lines going forward, the first shock of battle joined, the air splitting with thunder . . . those are the moments we give ourselves over to the dark god.

The duality of man is so apparent then, men like myself who kneel in prayer to the Prince of Peace, who then rise up and go forth, open-eyed, into the red field, filled with mad passion for war and glorying in the moment. It is now, though, that we see the truth in what we do in this darkness before dawn.

No.

And he visibly shook himself, as if trying to cast off a weight upon his shoulders.

Not now. Long after this day is over I can dwell on my sins. I must stay the course with all my strength; to do otherwise is a betrayal of all who have already lost their lives, leading us to this moment.

Traveler's pace slowed as they went up the slope, the mist thinning. He stopped and lowered his head and took his hat off.

"John, old comrade, rest in peace. You did your duty as I must do mine. Forgive me if I have wronged you.

"God, give me strength and Your guidance for this day ahead. Lead me to what is right so that this struggle might come to the end that You decree. Thy will be done.

"Amen."

Startled, he looked to his left, where voices had echoed "amen" in response to his prayer. Several men stood by the side of the road, infantry, staring at him, all with hats off.

"Good morning to you," Lee said self-consciously.

"General, sir. Heard we were marching south. Are we giving up here and headin' home?"

"Just do your duty, men, and all will be well."

The men, ladened down with dozens of canteens dripping with moisture, saluted.

"We was out fetching water for our company," a corporal announced. "Full canteens, haversacks, and eighty rounds per man. Sounds to me, sir, like a fight coming, sir."

"Return to your company, Corporal. You'll be moving shortly."

The men saluted gravely. The crest ahead was a beehive of activity, lanterns casting dim circles of light. But the sky was brightening; and looking back to the east, he could see a band of violet and gold tracing the horizon, the shoulder of Orion, hovering in the morning sky.

"General Longstreet, sir." It was Walter, back at his side, nodding toward the tents.

Longstreet was up, standing over a table, map spread out, men gathered around him. Lee rode up and all came to attention, formally saluting.

"Good morning, gentlemen."

An orderly took Traveler's reins as Lee dismounted, another man bringing up a cup of tea, which he gratefully took, blowing on the rim before taking a sip.

"Another scout just came in," Longstreet reported. "Jed Hotchkiss reconnoitered down to a hill that overlooks Emmitsburg. He reports campfires along the pike road south of town."

"How many?"

"Not many, a couple of regiments, infantry or cavalry, not sure, sir. Lots of signs, though, of heavy troop movements from yesterday."

As Longstreet talked, he nodded to a copy of Jed Hotchkiss's map spread out on the table. John Hood and a couple of his brigade commanders were on the far side of the table.

"Sure would like to have a brigade of cavalry out in front of us on this," Hood offered.

"You have two companies from my headquarters detail," Lee replied.

"And the rest of Stuart's men?" Hood asked, and again there was that slight note of reproof in another man's voice. The universal challenge of the last week: "Where is Stuart?"

"They'll be coming in on our left flank by midmorning. Their arrival will help to keep those people in Gettysburg from looking the other way."

"Still, sir, it would be nice to have a bit more support. We're up north now. I don't have a single boy with us who knows this country the way we did back in Virginia. I'll be running half-blind."

"Jed Hotchkiss will be with you, General Hood, once you reach Emmitsburg, and he has studied this region for months."

Lee drew closer to the table and set his cup of tea down. "Let me make something very clear to everyone," he said slowly, deliberately lowering his voice, forcing those around him to draw closer. "I will not tolerate any more wishes, any more concerns as to what Stuart is doing or not doing, whether we should have taken that hill last night or not." He paused, looking pointedly at Longstreet, "Or any regrets that Jackson is no longer with us. We are in command here. I, and from me to you, down to those boys who trust us with their lives. We must show confidence, gentlemen, as is our duty. Do we understand each other clearly on that, gentlemen?"

"Yes, sir," Hood snapped.

Even as he spoke, Lee could see that the light was shifting. He could see Hood's face by the first touch of dawn.

"This will be like Manassas again. A long, hard march with the army split. Ewell will hold before Gettysburg, drawing back his left flank onto the ridge west of town. Hill's men will wait until late in the day before setting out. General Longstreet, this is the day for your corps to show all that it can do. You must move swiftly and without hesitation. This is not a tactical march, sir, of but a few miles, to swing around the cemetery or even around that rocky hill. You must be audacious and move with the utmost speed. That above all, sir, audacity and speed."

He hesitated, but then decided to add one more thought. It was the type of flourish he did not like, since it smacked of theater, but if it kept their focus then he must.

"Back on the road a few minutes ago three men asked me if by marching south we were going home. That is exactly what we must think on this day, gentlemen. I do not want another half victory or, far worse, what we had yesterday, though some claim it as a victory. Yes, men will die this day, and tomorrow and the day after. I want those deaths to mean something. I want this army to go home after this, the war ended. We can do that. We must do that. After this, I want our army to march south, back home, with victory won."

He lowered his head, his voice barely a whisper. "If we fail in this, gentlemen, then we must answer to all those who have already given their lives to bring us to this moment. Keep that in your hearts this day."

He looked back up. Hood stood before him, silent, and to his surprise several of the men had tears in their eyes.

"Thank you, sir, for this chance," Hood said.

"The South is with you this day, sir."

Hood nodded and looked over to Longstreet. "It's nearly five, John, time to start moving."

Hood saluted, hesitated, then extended his hand to Lee. Lee took it. Though slightly uncomfortable with such displays, he knew that Hood needed this final touch, as if seeking a blessing.

Hood mounted and rode back out to the road. Looking up, Lee could see that the column was just about formed, backed up along the road to Chambersburg. No bugles sounded, no drum rolls or fifers. In the still morning air the sound just might carry far enough to the Union lines.

"McLaws and Pickett?" Lee asked.

"McLaws sets off in another half hour," Longstreet answered. "He'll move down to Fairfield on the next road to the west. Pickett will be sweeping along the flank of the South Mountain on the other side, heading down to Greencastle. There's a good road there, from the head of the pass straight east to Emmitsburg.

"That is one of my concerns. We'll be moving three divisions, plus artillery, through that one town, all of it funneling into one road down to Emmitsburg."

"It was your suggestion, General, that triggered this move."

Longstreet nodded.

"And the road is better than the one Jackson used at Chancellorsville, far better."

Pete stiffened slightly. Good. Let that rivalry play a bit in his mind this day. He knew that Longstreet held a touch of resentment for Thomas, like an older brother who, though he loved his brother, still was bothered by the attention that seemed at times to be favoritism to a younger sibling.

"You have always been the anvil general," Lee said. "Now you must be the hammer."

"Any more word on their movements?"

"We know for certain that four corps are in Gettysburg. Their left wing, which was in Emmitsburg yesterday, the First, Third, and Eleventh Corps, are all in Gettysburg. That move has unmasked their left for what you have proposed. Their Twelfth has moved in on the right flank, the wooded hill above the cemetery."

"So that leaves three corps unaccounted for."

"Your thoughts?" Lee asked.

"They're most likely coming up hard, marching through the night. I don't think Meade will keep anything back."

"I agree. Though not within the realm

of what is proper, still, the truce before that hill resulted in my men mingling with theirs and learning some information. Those people up there were all talking about staying. A doctor helping to move the wounded from before the cemetery gate said that the gunners and infantry were digging entrenchments and gun positions. He also said a couple of Union stretcher bearers claimed that Meade was now on the field.

"I think, General, you will have an open road before you this day. Again, the same as at Manassas."

"Battalion . . . forward march!"

The command was a distant echo, coming from out of the mist, cloaking the road to the west. Lee looked over at Longstreet and nodded as his companion called for an orderly to bring up their mounts. Lee settled into the saddle and with Pete by his side trotted down the sloping ridge to the junction in the road that led toward Fairfield. The head of the column was just at the turnoff, Robertson's brigade of Texans and men from Arkansas in the lead. Brigade colors were uncased, held up, marking the advance.

At the crossroads the command was given for the column to turn to the right, and Lee could sense the ripple of excitement racing down the line. Several men started to cheer, and for a second Lee feared that the cheer would be picked up by thousands of voices. Officers barked commands for silence, and the men settled down.

As the flags passed, Hood and Robertson riding together at the very front of the line, Lee and Longstreet saluted.

"We'll give you that victory, sir!" Hood shouted, and again a suppressed cheer started to erupt.

The First Texas strode past, long-legged men dressed in tattered gray frock coats, many of them barefoot, lean, tough boys born on the frontier, Hood's first command — heroes of the desperate fight in the cornfield of Antietam and the triumphal charge at Chancellorsville. They looked up at him eagerly, some saluting, others doffing their ragged hats.

They were veterans enough to know what was now being done. It would not be an assault forward; this was a flanking march, a march through rich Yankee farmland where the corn was already waist high, the winter wheat was ready for harvest, and orchards filled with peaches were ripening. It was a flanking march and they were in the lead, ready to set a blistering pace.

Columns were formed up in the fields

adjoining the road, preparing to fall into place, couriers riding back and forth, a battery of guns edging up to the road, ready to swing in behind Robertson.

The excitement in the air was electric, for the moment casting aside the dark thoughts of earlier. If only war could be like this, Lee thought. Nothing more than mornings of setting off on the march into new lands, confidence and dreams intact, and no dark, boiling clouds of smoke and fire at the end of the day. For surely that is where these boys were now marching, into those clouds, and yet they were doing so with light hearts this day.

"Your men look ready," Lee offered, and Pete nodded sagely.

"They didn't see yesterday, last night, except for some of the wreckage back here from Heth's attack. They're eager to get into the fight."

Lee looked over at Pete, wondering if there was a note of reproof in what was just said. No, it was just Pete, sanguine in all things, no subtlety or intent other than a calm observation.

"Too bad one of them daguerreotypists isn't around," Walter observed, "this would make quite an image."

Would it? He remembered some of the paintings of Washington, that rather ridiculous one of him crossing the river, or at

Yorktown taking the surrender. Would someone, one day, paint this moment? Lee and Longstreet and the flanking march?

Don't think of such vanities. Too many men in both armies do, and it is sinful to contemplate our actions in such a light at this time.

Behind them Longstreet's headquarters staff was breaking camp, dropping the tents, packing up the map cases and gear, loading only the essentials into an ambulance. Tents and other nonessentials were to be left behind, to follow up after the infantry and artillery had passed. The entire column was stripped down for rapid movement. He could see that his veterans were traveling light, a thin blanket roll over the left shoulder, haversacks stuffed with rations, some men with a chicken or slice of fresh meat tied to their belt, and, of course, cartridge boxes packed with forty rounds and an additional forty rounds stuffed into pockets. With each brigade would go a couple of wagons bearing extra ammunition and a few ambulances. The bulky, slow-moving wagon trains with all those vast impedimenta of war would follow later.

"I think it's time for me to get moving," Longstreet announced.

Lee looked over at his old "war horse."

There was a fire in Pete's eyes, an eagerness to get moving.

"Pete."

Longstreet looked at him, a bit surprised, for Lee rarely used the affectionate nickname by which he was called by nearly everyone else.

"I need to say it one last time. Move with speed. If you must set a mark, then let it be Jackson. Move as he did; slow for nothing. I say that not as a reproach, but simply as an order."

"Yes, sir."

"This is your plan. You were the one last night who caused me to stop, to think, to remember how we did it before. Otherwise I might have gone straight in this morning. If victory comes of it, I shall let it be known to all that you were the one who conceived it."

"No, sir. I was not thinking so much on this scale. But thank you, sir."

"You keep talking of this new kind of war, General. And in some ways you are right. It is all changing, rifled weapons, factories, massed armies of hundreds of thousands. None of that was thought of when I was a cadet at the Point."

"It wasn't for my class either, sir."

"But audacity, aggression still must count. You have a hard march the next two to three days. Fairfield to

Emmitsburg and from there to Taneytown. Once there rest, but not too long; do not slow down. Once you have secured Taneytown, Hill's corps will be on the road behind you. With Taneytown and Emmitsburg secured, I can shift our line of communications, abandon the road to Chambersburg, and march south to Emmitsburg, bringing Ewell up as well.

"I suspect by then that Meade will be onto us and coming down your way. You must push on to Westminster; that is the key. As soon as Hill starts to come up in support of you at Taneytown, then Westminster must be taken. If you can secure that, we will have their supplies and that good base you speak of, the ground south of Pipe Creek. And then you will have the battle you seek, with them coming at you.

"Pete, you might be facing everything they have and doing so alone until the rest of the army comes up. Yet again, it will be like Manassas, when Jackson held alone for nearly two days."

Longstreet shifted uncomfortably. Jackson had been furious over that action, later stating that Longstreet had come up too slowly and taken too long to deploy out while Thomas held alone, his men reduced to throwing rocks at the charging Yankees before Pete's men finally swept in.

"End this war, Pete. And believe me, with you astride their line of communications, cutting them off from Washington, they will come on with a fury. Hill will push in on your flank at the right moment, with Stuart closing from behind. But I need you to move hard and take the foundation to do it on."

"Yes, sir. It will be done."

Lee hesitated. "End this cursed war," he whispered. "I fear we have but one chance left like this. Our final chance."

Startled, Longstreet stared intently at Lee. He drew himself up and saluted. "Yes, sir."

The ambulance ladened with headquarters gear moved to the edge of the road. The last of Robertson's brigade passed, men of the Third Arkansas. The headquarters ambulance rolled into the road behind their two ammunition wagons. General Longstreet, his staff trailing, fell into the road behind Robertson. Morning fog drifted up from the creek flanking the road. Without looking back, General Longstreet disappeared into the mist.

Behind Lee the sun broke the horizon. Dawn of July 2, 1863, had come.

Chapter Eight

8:30 AM, July 2, 1863

Little Round Top
Gettysburg, Pennsylvania

Focusing his field glasses, Henry Hunt scanned the road to Emmitsburg that bisected the open valley below. The road, well built and flanked by post and rail fences, cut straight to the southwest to Emmitsburg, ten miles away. Along a mile of the pike directly in front was Buford's cavalry division, most taking it easy, sitting around smoking fires made of piled-up fence rails. After yesterday's hard fight, they deserved some time to rest.

A thin line of pickets was deployed along the slope rising up from the road to the west, a knot of riders loitering in a peach orchard along the east side of the pike. Focusing on the group, he watched as one of the men gathered handfuls of the nearly ripe fruit, dumping them into a saddlebag. Several troopers were playing catch with the fruit, one of them pitching a shot at the back of an officer riding past. Fortunately for all concerned, the shot missed, and Henry could not help but chuckle.

Raising his gaze, Henry studied the ridge that sloped up to the west. A thin line of dismounted troopers was deployed along the ridge. Occasionally one would pop off a shot, the puff of smoke drifting up. From the next ridge beyond he caught an occasional glimpse of movement, Confederate skirmishers.

It didn't seem threatening, typical of the type of action along the flanks of a battlefield. The skirmishing was halfhearted, just an occasional shot to announce to the other side not to come too close. He lowered his glasses, carefully studying the layers of ridges that marched off westward, climaxing in the South Mountain Range, twelve miles distant. It was hard to discern; the day was humid, a bit hazy, but it seemed as if a low cloud of dust was kicking up between the ridges below the South Mountains.

Not my job to play scout, he thought. I'm here to see to artillery deployment, get the batteries in place up here on this hill, then go back to headquarters behind the cemetery, check on ammunition reserves, and wait to see what comes next.

Behind Henry one battery was now in place, bronze twelve-pound Napoleon smoothbores, perfect for close-in support.

The guns were well positioned, barrels depressed to sweep the lower slope of the hill. A second battery, ten-pound rifled Parrott guns, was coming up now, laboriously making its way through the trees. They had extra limbers to the rear, more than enough ammunition. Things, at least for the moment, were just about taken care of here.

He sighed, rubbing the back of his neck with his free hand.

Perhaps I can finally get a few hours' sleep before things heat up again. They didn't come in at dawn like expected. Maybe we battered them hard enough that Lee will back off. But if he backs off . . . then what?

A coil of cigar smoke drifted around Henry, and he looked over his shoulder.

Damn! It was Maj. Gen. Dan Sickles, commander of the Third Corps, now holding the left flank of the line around the lower end of Cemetery Ridge and the two Round Top hills. Sickles was coming toward him, puffing away like a belching locomotive, holding, of all things, a heavy goblet of cut glass, half filled with brandy. Sickles was short, features florid, mustache drooping around the sides of his mouth. An energetic man with a high-pitched voice. Sickles was the backslapping and hearty manliness type that

Henry found to be distasteful in an officer.

Henry turned away, hoping Sickles would simply wander on. Raising his glasses, he scanned what might be dust drifting along a distant ridge.

"You don't like me, Hunt, I can tell."

Henry lowered his field glasses and looked over at Sickles. He wearily shook his head. "Sir, it's not my place to like or dislike you. You're a general in command of a corps."

"You West Pointers," Sickles announced, as if launching into a speech for the benefit of the men who were digging in to either side of them, only a few feet away, "and I'm not part of your club. You West Pointers, I'm passable as a commander of a brigade of volunteers, but a corps? You just don't feel comfortable with that."

Henry looked pointedly to the infantry, who had stopped their work and were enjoying the confrontation, many of them grinning.

"These are my men, Hunt," Sickles announced with a flourish, the hand holding the glass of brandy sweeping out as if he were about to launch into a speech. "Best damn corps in this damn army. I don't care if they hear what I've got to say."

"I do," Henry replied, his voice pitched low.

"Take Hooker, for example," Sickles continued. "Wouldn't listen to me at Chancellorsville, the stupid son of a bitch. But then again, there was no love lost between the two of you either."

"We saw differently on a few things," Henry replied noncommittally.

Henry slid off the rock he had been perched on and walked down the slope a couple of dozen feet. Sickles followed.

"Sir, such a conversation around the men is not in the best interest of morale," Henry said quietly.

Sickles laughed. "Part of the game at times," Sickles replied, but this time his voice was as low as Henry's. "Troops like it when they feel their commander stands up to the high muckety-mucks. I know these men, Hunt. They're tough soldiers, but they're citizen-soldiers, volunteers, not professionals. They fight for different reasons than you and I. If only someone on top really knew how to lead them, we'd of ended this war months ago.

"You weren't there at the Chancellor House when Hooker got knocked out by that artillery round. All of them, all those damn West Pointers standing around like a herd of sheep, hemming and hawing, no one with the guts to take over. I'd of taken command if I thought the others would have followed, but I didn't have that little date of graduation behind my name. We could have won that damn fight, smashed Lee up good that day rather than the other way around. Then Hooker, his brain all addled, stands back up and everyone starts saluting like god-damn puppets on strings. Puppets, Hunt, we're led by puppets."

Henry said nothing, raising his field glasses back up and focusing on a distant ridge. Actually Sickles was right. If someone had seized the moment before Hooker regained consciousness, had shown a little guts, they might not be sitting atop this hill in Pennsylvania this day, but instead be in Richmond.

"Nice quiet place up there on the Hudson, like some papist monastery," Sickles continued. "But I didn't go hide in some monastery, Hunt. I learned my business on the streets of New York with the likes of old Clinton and Tweed.

"You don't hesitate in that game. You jump in with both feet, grab hold, and thrash your opponent till he begs for mercy and crawls on the floor, and then you kick him in the ass for good measure. That's just as much war as what you learned. Don't let go and always know what the other man is thinking, whether he's your friend or your enemy. That's leadership, Hunt, learning how the other man thinks; then use that to get him with you or get him the hell out of the way."

Henry sighed, trying to keep his field glasses focused, but his eyes hurt, not enough sleep. He lowered the glasses and wiped his face. Already the day was getting warm.

Draining off the rest of the brandy, Sickles set the glass down on a rock. Smiling, he reached into his breast pocket and pulled out a thick cigar, a Havana, and offered it. Henry nodded a thanks, bit off the end, and then fumbled in his pockets for a Lucifer. Dan reached into his breast pocket, produced a match, and Henry puffed the cigar to life.

"I was stationed at Fort Hamilton, New York Harbor, for five years," Henry finally offered. "Even met you a few times at various functions, Fourth of July parades, receptions at City Hall, though I doubt you'd remember."

"Nice place, Fort Hamilton. Right in the harbor, out of the stink of the streets," Sickles replied. "That's when Lee commanded it?"

"Yes."

"I remember him from those times. Elegant, distant, a bit too pious for my blood. Understand you used to pray with him, studied the Bible together."

"Yes, we did." He was surprised that Sickles knew that bit of information.

"A good politician, a good general for that matter, knows such things about his friends and his enemies. You liked him, didn't you, Hunt?"

"Yes, I did."

"And now?"

Henry puffed on his cigar, and Dan chuckled softly.

"It's all right. I'm not one of those damn fire-eating Republicans; you say a good word about that old man on the other side, and next thing you know you've got some damn congressman screaming for your hide before those witch-hunters with the Joint Committee on the Conduct of the War."

"I respect Lee. Anyone who doesn't is a fool, sir."

Sickles laughed. "Would never want to play poker with him. He had that look."

Henry could not help but laugh softly in reply and took another puff on the cigar. It was a good one, the best he had smoked in months. The image of Lee playing poker. No, chess was more his game; poker did not fit with Lee.

"It's always about Lee, isn't it?" Sickles offered. "Always we're wondering what he is thinking, what he is doing, chasing his tail. Politics, Hunt, is like war. The moment you start chasing the other man's tail, you've lost. You've got to keep him off balance, make him dance to your jig. That's why we keep losing. Lee picks the song, and we dance to his tune.

"Chancellorsville, damn it to hell! Hooker knocked out like a cold fish, everyone staring wide-eyed, twittering like a bunch of harem eunuchs."

Henry could not help but smile at the analogy.

"Everyone kept looking at that map, saying we were flanked and Hooker knocked out cold. No one was looking at the map thinking maybe we've got them bastards flanked instead, not just flanked but divided in half, by God. We could of smashed them up good. Meade's entire corps was poised above Jackson's left flank. All that was needed was someone with the guts to go in. Meade lacked the stomach then, orders or no orders, and now he's the one running the show today."

Henry said nothing.

"Meade hates me. I could point to the sun and say it is in the east, and he'll tell me to go to hell, it's in the west."

"I don't think it's that bad," Henry replied.

"I know. Nothing would please him

more than me getting a bullet in the head or my leg blown off."

Henry said nothing, shifting his cigar and raising the field glasses back up. Typical of most politicians, Sickles talked too much. Yet he did have guts, there was no denying that, and even some damn good sense about battle. Though an amateur, he had led his Excelsior Brigade well during the Seven Days and handled a division at Fredericksburg and Third Corps at Chancellorsville. Before Jackson hit the flank, Sickles repeatedly warned Hooker that something was up, first suspecting that the troop movement to his front was a retreat, then just before they got hit, judging it to be an attack about to be unleashed. His troops fought like demons trying to hold back the tide throughout that terrible night of May 2nd, with Sickles on the front line throughout.

It was the other side of him, though, that was unsettling. Though Henry held little truck in how some rambled on about officers having to be gentlemen, nevertheless, Sickles was rather unsavory on many counts. He was a ward heeler out of New York, the kind who used the waves of foreigners pouring into the city as a political army to advance his own power. It was the scandal regarding his wife, however, that had shocked the entire nation.

Discovering that she was having an affair with the nephew of Francis Scott Key, Dan Sickles had confronted the man in Lafayette Park, directly across from the White House, pulled out a pistol, and gunned him down. Then, in a bizarre twist, Edwin Stanton, now the secretary of war, defended him in court, cooking up a strange new plea never heard of before — that he had been "temporarily insane" and thus not responsible. Of course the jury had been delighted with the entertainment provided and let him off. Then Sickles does an about-turn and brings the fallen strumpet back into his bed, showing up in public with her by his side as if nothing had ever happened.

It was all but impossible to understand such a man, such a world. He calls the Point a "papist monastery." Well, better that than the world of a man like Sickles.

Is that what I am fighting for? Henry wondered. I have far more in common with Lee than with this person standing beside me. Yet it is his world I'm fighting for out here, this brawling, strange new behemoth that our Republic is evolving into. Lee fights to preserve a different world, elegant though built on the corruption of slavery, but still elegant, where men are expected to act as gentlemen and ladies, well, to act as true ladies.

Sickles, the boys from the factories of New England, the swarming mobs in the back alleys of New York, the miners coming up out of the pits of Pennsylvania and the smoke-belching iron mills, the Irish and the Germans by the hundreds of thousands swarming off the boats and into our ranks, are something new, different, a strange, vibrant energy that I barely understand.

"You think something is going on over there, don't you, Hunt?"

Henry lowered his glasses.

"Reconnaissance is not my job, sir. I'm up on this hill to place guns."

He nodded back over his shoulder where the Second Battery was laboriously working to bring up their guns, cutting down trees to clear a way, twelve horses, double teamed to a single caisson and piece, struggling up through the woods on the north flank of the hill.

A brigade from Third Corps was digging in along the crest of the slope, piling up rocks, dragging in logs. The front slope of the hill had been lumbered off the year before, thus providing a beautiful field of fire straight down to a jumble of rocks at the base of the hill and out toward an open wheat field beyond. It was wonderful ground. An entire rebel corps would bleed itself out trying to take this hill once they were dug in.

"So why are you sitting here looking west, Hunt, rather than with your guns?"

Henry smiled. "Curious."

"So am I."

"Hard to tell, but it does look like some dust stirring up out beyond that next ridge," Henry noted. "You look close and you can see some Reb skirmishers along that second ridge." Even as he spoke he noticed a bit more dust, a plume rising up from behind the ridge.

Sickles raised his own field glasses and stared intently for a moment.

"Where's General Warren?" Henry asked. "He's the chief topographical engineer. I thought Meade sent him down here to take a look."

"Up on the next hill," Sickles said, pointing toward the large, wooded hill — the Big Round Top, locals called it — that was to their left.

Henry turned his glasses and saw where the Signal Corps had established itself, building a perch halfway up a large tree. There was an occasional fluttering of flags. He had thought about trying to work a battery up that mountain, but a quick survey showed it would have required an entire regiment of men, armed with axes, to clear the way and open out a field of fire. If the battle did spread out there, it would have to be an infantry fight.

"I've got a good regiment up there," Sickles announced, "Second Sharpshooters supporting that signal station. They're tied into a signal station down at Emmitsburg."

"Wonder why Buford down there doesn't push out a bit to the west and see what's up?"

"Go ask Meade," Dan replied. "I just got word from Buford that he's pulling out. Relieved from the field to head back to Westminster to refit after the fight."

"What?"

"One of his staff came up about thirty minutes ago to tell me. They're going down to Taneytown."

"Who's replacing them?"

"I am. I'm sending down Berdan's men, First Sharpshooters."

"No cavalry?"

"Nope."

"Strange, no cavalry on our flank. There's nothing between us and Emmitsburg, is there?" Henry asked.

"My men were the last unit out of there late yesterday. Nothing between us and the Potomac except for the Signal Corps and a regiment or two of cavalry that came in behind us last night."

Henry lowered his glasses and took another puff on his cigar. "I'd better get back to headquarters. My batteries look like they're moving in fine up here."

"My batteries, Hunt. Remember, the corps commander has direct control of his battalion of guns. You just advise."

Henry bristled and looked over at Sickles. The politician turned general smiled.

"Relax, Hunt. You do good work."

"Thanks."

Sickles looked past Henry. "Ah, here comes Warren. Good man, commanded a regiment under me before moving up to headquarters."

Henry looked back over his shoulder. Maj. Gen. Gouvenor Warren, puffing hard, was laboriously walking up the steep slope, trailed by several of his staff.

"A good man even though he's West Point, too?" Henry offered.

"Sometimes it doesn't ruin a man completely. Warren has a good eye for ground."

"West Point training," Henry could not help but say. "You don't learn how to read groundwork wandering around Manhattan."

Sickles chuckled. "Hunt, I might actually like you. You've got guts."

Warren, breathing audibly, approached Sickles, while calling for one of his staff to fetch their mounts. "Feel like a mountain goat going up and down these hills," Warren offered, as he saluted.

"Have a cigar, Gouvernor."

Warren waved the offer off. "I think something is up," Warren announced, bending over slightly to catch his breath. "Signal from Emmitsburg reports dust on the road that goes from Fairfield to Emmitsburg. Also, from up on that hill," and he pointed back to Big Round Top, "you can catch glimpses of some kind of movement, but too much dust to tell."

There was a flutter of signal flags from the perch atop the mountain even as Warren spoke.

Sickles turned and looked back to the west, meditatively chewing on his cigar. Henry uncorked his canteen and offered it to Warren, who nodded a thanks and took a long drink.

"Day's going to get hot real quick," Warren offered. "Maybe we should ask Buford to go over to that next ridge and take a look around."

"Buford is pulling off the line, going back to refit."

Warren sighed, looking back to the west. "Might be nothing. Still think we should take a look."

"I'll send Berdan up, give him a regiment for additional support," Sickles announced.

Henry looked over at the general. "Sir, I remember hearing your orders were to dig in along this line, not to push forward."

Sickles just looked over and grinned. "Hunt, when you get back to headquarters, tell his High Almighty that we might have a problem developing. Also, I think we should put a little more strength down forward, into that peach orchard by the road to Emmitsburg. This hill's a good spot, but my right flank is on low land, no clear fields of fire. If we move out to that orchard and the next ridge, we'll have a better position in case something *is* developing."

"Sir, orders were to deploy along this line," Warren observed. "I was sent here to survey *this* position for defense, not half a mile forward."

Sickles grinned, saying nothing.

Henry nodded. "I'll report it," Henry finally offered.

"I'll ride with you, Hunt," Warren announced.

"Hunt, take an extra one," Sickles said, and he produced another cigar and tossed it over. "One of my old constituents keeps me supplied."

Henry nodded his thanks, and with

Warren by his side they struggled up to the crest. Their mutual staffs were already mounted, and Henry wearily swung into the saddle. For a moment he was disoriented, not sure which way to go. He had come up this way before dawn, and the lack of sleep left him feeling light-headed, dizzy.

"This way, Hunt," Warren said, and they started down the slope.

Henry looked back over his shoulder. Sickles was deep in conversation with an officer wearing the distinctive green uniform of the Sharpshooters.

"I don't trust him," Warren announced.

"Who? Sickles?"

"Exactly. He hates Meade. He most likely vented it on you the same as he did me. It'd be like Sickles to go off half-cocked."

"Do you think something is up?"

"I came up here to survey the land, Hunt, same way you came up here to lay the guns."

"Still, after what happened last night, Lee won't back off. Not now." Even as he said the words, Henry thought of Sickles's comment that we danced to Lee's tune.

"I need some sleep, Warren. Let's just hope nothing happens."

"Where do you think it will happen? Frankly, I hope Lee tries to take those two hills. With Sickles's corps on top, it will be a damn killing ground, just like last night."

Last night. The memory of the rebel flag bearer cut in half, the carnage piled up in front of his guns.

"Where do you think it will hit?" Henry asked.

"South," Warren sighed. "This place is too good. He won't do us the favor of coming straight in. I think he's moving south and coming around our flank."

"Sgt. Major Quinn!"

Sgt. Maj. Michael Quinn, First United States Sharpshooters, knew something was up. Colonel Berdan had come riding into their camp at the base of the rocky hill, shouting for an officers' meeting.

Tossing what was left of his coffee on the ground, Quinn started over to where the officers of the regiment were gathered in a circle around Colonel Berdan. There was no need to be told; the regiment was going out.

Captains were breaking away from the group, shouting orders, as Quinn approached Berdan and saluted.

"Quinn, we're ordered to do a reconnaissance in force. I'll be at the center of the line. I want you down by the right flank. Sickles thinks there's something going on a couple of miles to our front. So push in and don't let any of the boys wander about. I want us to go in there hard and fast."

"Yes, sir."

"Try and gain a high point where you can see something."

Quinn, shifting the plug of tobacco in his cheek, grinned.

"Shoot straight, Quinn."

"Always do, sir."

Berdan swung up onto his gray horse and started out, his famed Sharpshooters deploying into open skirmish order behind him.

The men were skilled, well-seasoned professionals. All the foolishness about keeping alignment, forming into lines, advancing by command was beneath them. They were better than that, and they knew it. Let the others fight the way their granddaddies did, standing in volley line. The Sharpshooters were a new kind of soldier for a new kind of war.

As the three hundred men fanned out, each set his own pace, moving quickly without urging. It was hard to tell the difference between officers and men. The uniforms were the same, dark green trousers, jacket, and green forage caps. Each man was armed with a long Sharps rifle, breechloading, and every one was deadly accurate, expected to hit nine out of ten times at three hundred yards. Besides the forty rounds in their cartridge boxes, each man carried an additional forty to sixty rounds in pockets and haversacks.

Quinn, running back to where his gear rested against a towering oak, swept up his rifle and canteen, then sprinted down to the right of the line, falling in with some of the men from E Company.

"So, Quinn, what're we hunting?" a corporal asked.

"Recon forward. Old Dan thinks the Rebs are moving to our front."

Coming up out of a shallow swale, they passed across the edge of a wheat field, the golden stalks hanging heavy, ready for harvest, then dropped down through a narrow band of forest and rough ground.

The pace was swift. No orders needed to be given, just occasional glances toward Berdan riding in the middle of the line, which was spread out across a couple of hundred yards. Looking back, he could see where a lone regiment was coming out as well, their flag dark blue with a state seal. It looked to be Maine, most likely the Third. One regiment in support then. Most likely not much, just a little skirmishing ahead, something to get the blood moving.

A pheasant kicked up from the edge of

the trees as they emerged into an open pasture, the ground sloping up toward a peach orchard. The man next to Quinn aimed his rifle at the bird.

"Bang!" he cried, and several men laughed, another sighting on a second pheasant and doing the same.

Directly ahead was the cavalry, Buford's men. They were starting to pack up, saddling their mounts. In the past, cavalry had been certain to draw hoots of derision, the usual jibes of "Hey, ever seen a dead cavalryman?" but not today. Word had spread about what Buford's boys had done, and the Sharpshooters approached the camp respectfully, several offering compliments. One of the troopers tossed Quinn a peach, which he grabbed and stuck into his haversack for later.

A cavalry lieutenant rode up to Quinn and nodded, falling in by his side for a moment.

"Take care up ahead, Sergeant. Some of my boys think there's trouble brewing."

"We'll see to it, sir. Aren't you boys joining us?"

"We're ordered down to Westminster, supposed to secure south of here first, some place called Taneytown. Some supplies and such moving through there. So the place is yours now."

The lieutenant fell away as they reached

the edge of the orchard. The post-and-rail fence lining the road was down, consumed as all such fences had been for firewood. Crossing the road, Quinn looked to his left and saw Berdan hold up his hand then point, angling them a bit on the oblique, with Berdan now riding straight up the road that headed due west.

Well, the old man wasn't going to fool around. Follow the road west, and we're bound to run into something. Quinn pushed to the right a hundred yards before turning west again.

They passed a couple of cavalry troopers coming back off the line, one of them cradling an arm that looked to be busted.

"Son of a bitch got me while I was trying to piss," the trooper grumbled, and the men around Quinn could not help but laugh.

"Lucky he didn't shoot off your short arm," a wag replied.

The trooper cursed them all and rode on.

They pushed up over a low crest, and at that moment the old senses began to kick in for Quinn, that strange prickly feeling that he had just stepped across into another world, a place where the game of hunter and hunted was played for real.

Several men around him clicked their weapons to half cock. Quinn did likewise.

"See one," and a man next to Quinn slowed, leaning in against a tree, raising his rifle.

"Not yet," Quinn hissed, "keep moving."

A second later there was a fluttering whine through the branches overhead, a few leaves snapping off a branch, slowly spinning down.

A rifle snapped to the left, a man out on the road, standing near Berdan. The colonel slowed, reining in for a moment, then held up his hand, pointing forward again.

Coming out of the trees, the skirmish line pushed into another pasture. The feeling was not a good one, open field, a marshy creek below, then a low rise ahead. Damn Rebs were most likely up there in the trees, us in the open.

"Alright, boys, let's pick it up!" Quinn shouted, and he started off at the double. Puffs of smoke snapped from the distant tree line. An eruption of torn-up earth kicked up near Quinn's feet. He shifted slightly, zigzagging, running now, heading down the slope, the ground getting thicker with tuffs of high marsh grass, and with a leap he was into the narrow creek, almost completely across. He ducked down, edging up against the muddy bank.

Raising his rifle up, he let it rest on the ground while he scanned the tree line, notching the rear sight to two hundred yards.

A puff of smoke. He took careful aim and squeezed. Another man was beside him, firing at almost the same instant.

Levering the trigger guard down, Quinn reached into his pocket, pulled out a cartridge, and slipped it into the breech, levering it shut, then cocked his piece.

More puffs of smoke rippled along the tree line. Men were hunkered down along the creek bank, firing back. Most of the shots coming in were high, buzzing overhead, but one slammed into the muddy bank, spraying him with mud. Centering on a puff of smoke, he fired again and reloaded.

Leaning up, he looked to his left. Berdan, at the shallow ford across the creek, was shouting for the men to press forward. Behind him the Third Maine was deploying from column into line.

"Come on, boys, let's get this over with."

Quinn stood up, crouching low, and set off. Racing across the meadow, hunkering down for a moment behind a split-rail fence, taking another shot . . . and this time seeing it hit. Dumb fool, looked to be an officer, standing out in the open, an easy shot at 150 yards. The man collapsed, a couple of men running over to him, both going down as well while Sharpshooters to either side of Quinn drew careful aim and fired.

The fire from the crest slackened. Again looking to the left, he saw the Third Maine surging forward, a heavy double line of skirmishers mingling in with the Sharpshooters.

Quinn reloaded, took a deep breath, and stood up, running straight for the slope and tree line. Another round zipped past, this one so close he felt the slap of the round passing his face.

A Reb, not fifty yards off, stepped out from behind a tree, rifle poised, aiming straight at Quinn. The Reb spun around and disappeared.

They were into the trees, the air thick with the sulfurous clouds of yellow-gray smoke. He spared a quick glance around. Ten, maybe fifteen Rebs were down. He pushed up the slope, dodging through the brush, ducking under low-hanging branches, and crossing over the crest. The land ahead sloped away, down to another marshy creek. The Rebs who had occupied the tree line minutes before were out in the middle of the field, running, fifty, maybe seventy-five or more.

It was a slaughter for the next minute.

The Sharpshooters took their favorite stances, some kneeling, others finding branches to rest their barrels on, a few going down on their stomachs. Rifle fire rippled up and down the line. Barely a dozen Rebs made it to the far slope.

"Hey, you're Yankees!"

Startled, Quinn saw a freckled face peeking up from behind an old, rotting tree stump. It was a boy, no more than nine or ten, about the same age as his own son. The boy stood up, gaping.

"Goddamn it, get down!" Quinn shouted, and running up to the lad, he pushed him back down behind the stump.

"Green uniforms. You're the Sharpshooters!" the boy cried happily. "I seen pictures of you in the illustrated papers."

"Sonny, just what the hell are you doing out here?"

"Came out to tell you what was happening, but them dirty Rebs stopped me."

The boy rubbed his backside. "One of them spanked me. Said he was going to take me back to my ma and make sure she whopped me, too."

"He was right, too, you little fool. You should be home."

"Ma tried to keep me in the cellar, but I snuck out."

Quinn sat down by the boy's side. A

couple of men were looking over at the two, grinning.

"Take a hickory stick and give it to him, Quinn." One of them laughed.

The boy looked over at the man and stuck his tongue out.

"Where do you live, sonny?"

"Over the next hill, farm across from the tavern," and as he spoke he pointed off to the west.

"Keep moving!" Berdan was out in front again, back to the enemy, sword held high, urging the men on.

"You stay put right here, boy," Quinn said. "Once we get up to the tavern, I'll send someone back to get you and bring you home. And don't you move an inch till we come back for you. Your ma's most likely worried sick about you."

"Oh, you won't never get to the tavern."

"What?"

The boy puffed his chest out.

"That's why I snuck out; I'm a spy."

"What do you mean we won't reach the tavern?"

"Why, there're thousands of Rebs over there, whole lines of them. They've been marching by for hours. I figured it was my duty to tell you. Will I get a medal for it?"

The men to either side of Quinn were

already up, moving forward.

Quinn watched them heading out, then looked back to the boy. He grabbed him by the shoulders. "Listen, sonny. We're not playing a game now," and as he spoke he squeezed the boy's shoulders. "Tell me the truth. Tell me what's going on over by your house."

"Like I said, sir," and now he could see that the boy was becoming afraid. His eyes were wide, and his voice started to break.

"Rebs, thousands of them on the road, marching toward Fairfield, right past my house, just over the next ridge."

Quinn looked toward the next ridge, where the surviving Rebs had disappeared. Dust appeared to be rising up on the far side.

"Stay here. Don't you move. Don't move."

The boy began to cry.

"I don't want to get whopped. That Reb spanked me awful hard. Don't let Mama whop me too."

"Just stay here, son. I'll make sure your ma doesn't whop you, if you promise to stay here."

The boy nodded solemnly, brushing the tears from his muddy cheeks.

Quinn stood up. The skirmish line was down almost to the creek. He set off hard. Running toward the middle of the line.

Berdan was riding in front, urging the men on. A few shots smacked overhead. The men were eager, pushing forward, already across the marshy ground. The left flank was into a pasture on the far side of the road, the right wading through waist-high corn.

A volley exploded from the woods atop the next crest, several hundred rifles firing at once. In an instant dozens of men were down.

Berdan's horse reared up, shrieking with pain. The colonel hung on as the beast staggered, turned, and then flipped over on its side as another round tore out its throat. Horse and rider rolled over into the stream.

"Jesus Christ Almighty!" Quinn screamed, as he leapt into the muddy water.

Berdan's horse kicked spasmodically, the colonel trapped underneath. Quinn leveled his rifle against the horse's skull and fired.

"Get him out!" Quinn screamed. Half a dozen men struggled with the carcass, pushing and shoving, one of them suddenly pitching over, the back of his head exploding.

Quinn grabbed Berdan by the shoulders

and struggled to keep his head above water. The men dragged the horse a few feet, one of them pulling out a knife to slice a stirrup free and then cut the reins that were tangled in Berdan's limp hands.

"Is he dead?" someone cried.

Quinn felt for the colonel's throat. There was still a pulse.

"You and you! Get a blanket, use it as a stretcher, round up a few more men, and get him out of here!"

Quinn stood up, looking around. Where the hell was Trepp, second in command?

He thought he caught a glimpse of him off to the left, but it was impossible to tell for sure. A captain was suddenly standing over Quinn, looking down in shock as they dragged Berdan up onto the bank of the creek and then rolled him into a blanket. It was Fuller, Company B.

"Sir, there was a boy back up there in the woods we just took!" Quinn shouted. "Says he lives over beyond the next ridge. Says that thousands of Rebs have been marching past his house all morning, moving south toward Fairfield."

"What boy?"

"Sir, a boy hiding up in the woods."

"So?"

Fuller ducked down low as another volley erupted from the next ridge, one of the men attempting to carry Berdan going down with a gut shot.

"Sir, I think we're tangled into something here. Someone should go back now and tell General Sickles that we're facing a large force. A division, maybe even a corps, moving to our left flank."

"What boy? What's his name?"

Exasperated, Quinn stood up. Fuller was obviously rattled, his eyes wide as he looked at the colonel, who was moaning softly, the wounded man next to the colonel curled up into a ball, fumbling to keep his guts in with his hands.

"Sir!"

Fuller looked back at him.

"I didn't ask for his goddamn name. But he's a local boy, sir, and I believe him."

"We get boys telling us tall tales all the time, Quinn. Jesus, am I suppose to tell Sickles we're getting flanked all because of a report from a boy?"

"This isn't Virginia, sir. It's Pennsylvania and I think the boy was telling the truth."

"Get on with your duty, Quinn."

"Sir! I think the general needs to be told."

"I'm getting us the hell out of here, Quinn. The colonel is down. We're going back and sort things out. And I'll be damned if I make a report based on what a boy said."

"Yes, sir. Damn you, sir."

Quinn turned and started back to the right. "Quinn! You might be a pet of the colonel's but goddamn you, you'll face discipline for this!"

Quinn ignored him, sprinting along the creek bed till he reached the right of the line. Turning, he darted into the corn, moving a few dozen feet, falling down, then getting up and sprinting again. Stalks of corn were leaping into the air as minie balls snapped into the field. Puffs of smoke, just ahead, showed where the advance of the skirmish line was.

Quinn, half crawling, pushed through. A lieutenant, obviously frightened, looked over his shoulder as Quinn approached.

"I saw the colonel go down," the lieutenant gasped.

"I know."

"What the hell is going on?" The lieutenant half stood up even as he spoke. "Looks like we're pulling back."

Quinn got up on his knees for a quick glance, then ducked back down. "Lieutenant, sir, we gotta get up on that ridge. Captain Fuller's pulling us back, but I think we should move forward."

"Into *that?*"

"Sir, one good sprint, and we'll be into the woods. We need to get a look over that ridge," and he quickly explained what the boy had told him.

"Hell of thing to get killed for. Some damn loudmouthed brat running around in the middle of a fight."

Quinn said nothing, his gaze locked on the lieutenant.

"All right, Quinn. We get to the top, have your look, and then get the hell out of here."

Quinn nodded.

"Your idea, Quinn. You lead the way."

He wanted to tell the lieutenant to go to hell, but saw that the youngster was trembling like a leaf, though trying to hide it, to make a manful show by courteously offering Quinn the lead.

Quinn knelt up again. "Those of you around me!" he shouted. "I'm making a run for the woods straight ahead. Any of you with some guts, come with me. The rest of you, well, you can go to hell!"

Making the sign of the cross, he took a deep breath, stood up, and started forward at a run. From the corner of his eye, he saw a dozen or more men stand up, going forward with him. Fortunately, the furrows for the cornfield were plowed in the direction he wanted to go. Gasping for air, he continued to run, the wood line less than fifty yards ahead.

Rifle balls zipped past. He heard the

sickening slap of a round striking something hard just behind him. He didn't look back, but somehow he knew it was the lieutenant.

The western flank of the cornfield was bordered by a split-rail fence. He ran straight into it, knocking the fence over, the impact knocking him over as well. Rolling, he half came up and saw a Reb aiming straight at him from not ten feet away. The Reb fired . . . and missed.

The Reb turned and ran. Quinn set off after him, going up into the woods. Another Reb stepped out, bayonet poised. Quinn slowed, leveled his rifle, and fired, knocking the Reb over backward. Fumbling for a cartridge, Quinn levered the breech open, even as he dodged up the slope. The branch of a tree sheered off next to his head, splinters flying from the impact of the round. Quinn dropped, saw the puff of smoke, chambered a round, and took a deep breath, but the man who had shot at him was gone.

He could see the crest just ahead, less than twenty yards off. He looked back and saw half a dozen of his men were into the edge of the woods. From either flank there were shouts, someone screaming that Yankees were in the woods.

Quinn pressed up the hill. Flashes of

fire burst to his left and right. He rushed forward, gained the crest, and dropped behind a rotten log. And saw the boy was right.

There, not three hundred yards away, was the road, packed with infantry, moving like a wave, dust swirling up in low-hanging clouds. A battery was directly below him on the road, bronze Napoleons, sunlight reflecting off their barrels, gunners riding on the caissons. A heavy skirmish line was out in the field directly ahead, deploying out, moving up to add their weight to the fight. He caught glimpses of flags, half a dozen or more marking the line of march, emerging from the dust and disappearing into the dust, all heading south.

Damn. It was big, damn big, and he felt an icy chill with the realization of all that this implied.

"All right, Yank! Don't you move a goddamn inch."

Shit.

"Real slow now, Yank, just let that rifle of yours drop and put your hands out where I can see 'em."

Quinn turned his head ever so slightly. The Reb was standing a bit behind him, twenty feet away, gun nervously trained on his back.

I'm caught.

"That's right, Yank. No fuss now. Just do as I tell ya."

Well, at least I'll live out the day. The thought raced through him . . . most likely paroled after the fighting's over and live awhile longer. Get home alive. Beth, my boy, the farm . . . miserable little patch of land but still, better than what we had in Ireland. . . .

He looked back to the road and before he even quite realized what he was doing he was up and trying to run. Strangely, there was no pain, just a numbed shock that knocked the wind out of his lungs. There was darkness for a moment, and then he was looking up at green leaves, sunlight filtering down.

"I told you not to move, Yank."

The voice was weary, a bit hard to understand the accent was so thick. Deep South from the sound of it.

He felt something tugging at his hands. The man was taking his gun.

"Fine piece you have here, Yank. One of them Sharps rifles, ain't it?"

Quinn tried to speak but couldn't.

"You get him, Will?"

"Yeah. Damn fool tried to run. Y'all get the others?"

"We got 'em."

The man knelt down by his side. Quinn could barely see him; the sunlight behind him was blinding. He looked old, beard gone to gray.

"Sorry I had to kill you, Yank. Like I said, you should'a just been sensible about this."

He tried to breathe and couldn't. He felt as if he were drowning. Then hands grabbed him under the shoulders. The Reb pulled him up. There was a terrible stab of pain now. The Reb eased him back down, sitting up against the side of a tree.

"There, you might breathe easier now."

Quinn could only nod.

"Spit out that chaw, Yank. You'll choke on it."

Quinn opened his mouth, and he was shocked when the Reb, in a fatherly way, actually stuck a finger into Quinn's mouth and helped him clear out the tobacco.

"I think I'll keep this here gun, if you don't mind, Yank."

The Reb casually reached into Quinn's cartridge box and took out the ammunition. Next he went into Quinn's haversack, took out a piece of salt pork and pocketed it, and then hesitated when he drew out the peach, the peach one of Buford's men had given him.

"Mind if I eat this, Yank?"

Quinn shook his head.

"Thank you."

The Reb sat looking at him for a minute. "You got kin?"

Kin? Quinn slowly nodded and feebly touched his breast.

The Reb opened Quinn's jacket, reached into his breast pocket, and pulled out a daguerreotype. The case was smeared with fresh blood, and the Reb wiped it off on his trousers. The Reb opened the case, looked at the image, and sighed. "Pretty wife. Good-looking young boy, too."

Quinn was suddenly ashamed. He was crying. He didn't want this man to think he was crying because he was afraid or because of the pain. No. Not that. He had forgotten. He had become caught up in all of this and forgotten what would be left behind . . . and now would indeed be left behind.

"I know, Yank. I know."

"Come on, Will. We got 'em on the run."

The Reb was squatting beside him and looked up. "I'm comin'."

The Reb put the open daguerreotype into Quinn's hands. "I'm sorry, Yank. I wish the hell you'd just given up. Saw the way you charged in. You was right brave; but damn me, you was a bit too brave today. Just couldn't let you go back and tell what we is doin' over here."

Quinn struggled to keep the tears from coming. All he could do was nod. He tried to look back to the road; it was barely visible. It didn't matter though, not now. His gaze fell on the daguerreotype; the image etched into the mirrorlike surface was lost to view . . . even as the darkness settled and all went still.

Will Peterson, Second Georgia, of Benning's brigade, Hood's division, stood up.

"Nice gun you got off him," someone said.

"Yeah, a real nice gun," Will said softly, as he bit into the peach and walked away.

10:30 AM, July 2, 1863

Gettysburg, Headquarters,
Army of Northern Virginia

Returning the salute, Lee motioned for General Stuart to enter the small room that was now his headquarters. He paused for a moment, looking out the window, across the street to the Lutheran Seminary, which was still serving as a hospital. Even now wagons and ambulances were lined up downslope, out of view of the Union position atop the cemetery. Those men who could be moved were being loaded up, to be taken back to Chambersburg, but according to a report just turned in, at least a thousand men would have to be left behind, their wounds too critical to endure the jostling twenty-mile ride. That was one of the reasons he hated to concede a battlefield; abandoning wounded was disturbing and hurtful to morale as well.

He turned to look back at Stuart, who stood expectant, nervous.

"I trust you have managed to get some rest since last night, General Stuart?" Lee asked.

Stuart hesitated. To answer that might imply that he was not seeing to his work, and yet it was obvious he was exhausted.

"A little, sir."

"You will need all your energy today, sir," Lee replied, deliberately pitching his voice low and soft, a hint of reproach in his tone.

"I'm ready for whatever you have for me, sir."

"Let me make something quite clear, General," Lee said, and he stepped closer.

Stuart gulped and nodded.

"I expect to see your best these next few days."

"As always, sir."

Lee hesitated, but then pushed ahead. "That has not always been the case, especially this last week."

Stuart said nothing, but his features reddened.

"This army cannot accept that, sir. Too much rests upon you. I assume that you are aware by now that I had no word that the Army of the Potomac was moving. None, sir, none until a hired actor, playing amateur spy, came to General Longstreet four days ago bearing the news. That, sir, should have been intelligence brought in by you."

"General Lee, I was shielding to the east . . ." He fell silent as Lee held up his hand.

"It will not happen again," Lee said sharply, fixing Stuart with his gaze.

Stuart gulped and stiffened. "No, sir."

"Then we understand each other and can move forward."

"Yes, sir."

Lee waited a moment, wondering if he should press it further, to make it clear that one more lapse would result in dismissal. He could see the anxious look in Stuart's eyes; gone was any of the defensive bluster of last night.

"Fine. Now come over here."

He drew Stuart over to the table covered with Jed Hotchkiss's map of the region and quickly traced out the line of march that

Longstreet was now taking.

"Risky without cavalry cover," Stuart offered.

Lee looked up at him with some surprise. Was it an admission of his own failure to provide proper support, or a rebuke for going ahead without the cavalry first coming in?

Stuart saw the look and nodded. "I should have had at least a brigade up here ready to march, sir, at the head of this column. I am sorry."

Lee finally offered a trace of a smile. "I thought of ordering Robinson down from the Cumberland Valley," Lee replied, "but decided against it. They are still needed to cover our own supply line. General Longstreet has a small detachment of mounted troops, made up of headquarters guard details. What is the position of the Union mounted forces?" Lee asked.

Stuart quickly traced out the latest intelligence. "Scattered in pursuit of my own forces. It looks as if the largest concentration is near Hanover to the east of here."

"And to the south, down toward Taneytown, Westminster?"

"Perhaps a brigade, sir, under Merritt. That is all I know."

Lee nodded. "When can I expect the rest of your command to be concentrated here?"

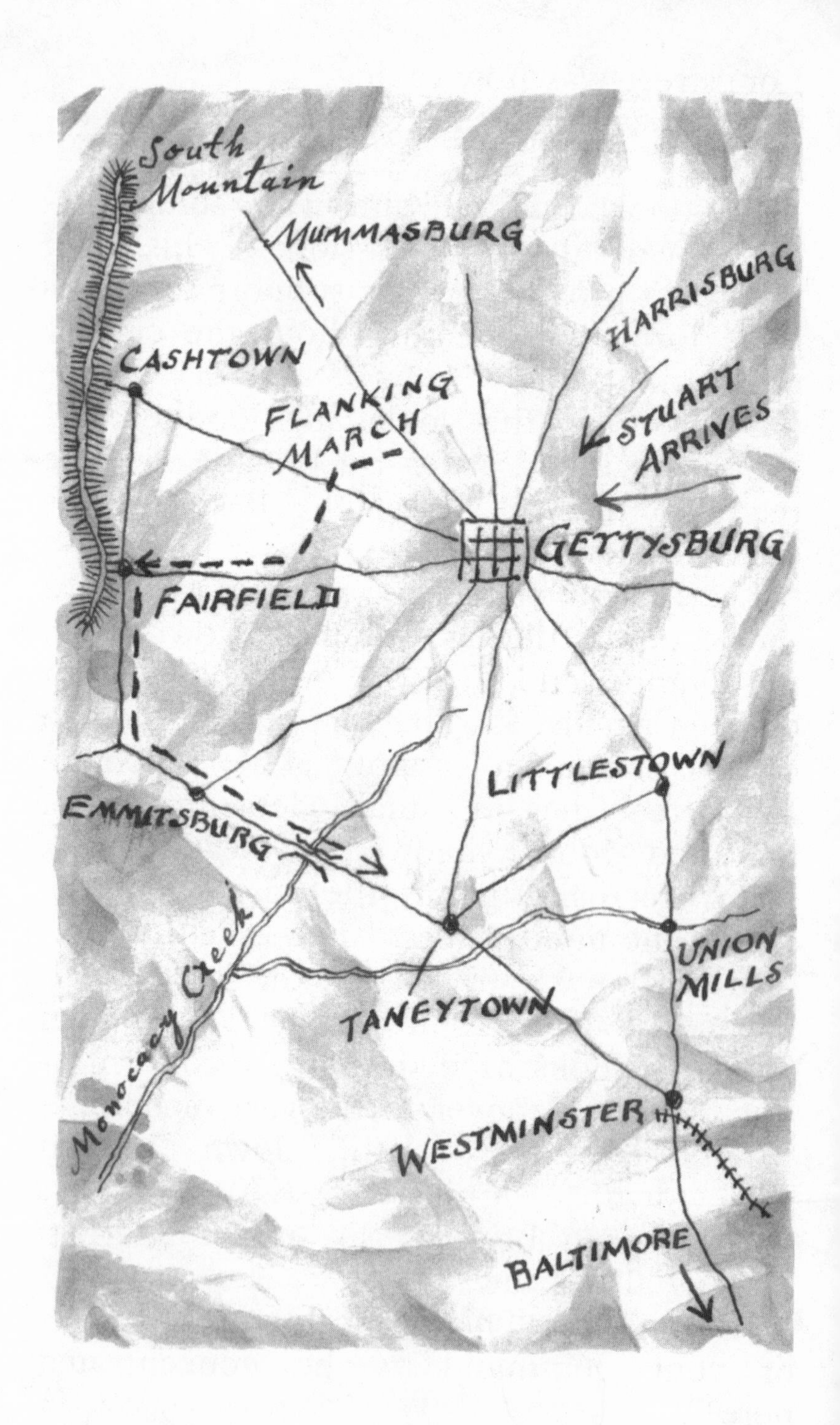
South Mountain
MUMMASBURG
HARRISBURG
CASHTOWN
FLANKING MARCH
STUART ARRIVES
GETTYSBURG
FAIRFIELD
LITTLESTOWN
EMMITSBURG
Monocacy Creek
UNION MILLS
TANEYTOWN
WESTMINSTER
BALTIMORE

"By midafternoon, sir. I have two brigades up ready, deployed, and concealed northeast of town as you ordered, sir."

"Fine then. Once you are concentrated, I expect a sharp demonstration on your part. I want General Meade looking in your direction, not to his own rear. I will concede, General Stuart, that your opponents fear you."

Stuart offered a smile, but a glance from Lee broke that.

"I want them to think that you are the vanguard of some kind of movement to their right. I will temporarily detach one brigade of infantry to you from General Ewell's corps. You will make arrangements with him for that. They will be yours to control until dusk. Use them to create the illusion of a solid infantry deployment in that direction.

"If Meade should move forward, do not get drawn into a direct confrontation, but do not shy away either. Demonstrate, probe; if you see some tactical advantage, hit, but don't become too deeply engaged."

"Yes, sir."

"If all goes well, I will move with the army later today, followed this evening by General Ewell. At that point you, sir, will be in sole command here. Maintain the illusion of a possible attack on Meade's right as long as possible. When General Meade does turn about to meet me, you will then be in his rear. Press and harass him, and keep his cavalry occupied; but General Stuart, you must maintain contact at all times with me. I expect efficient communications at all times. Am I clear on that, sir?"

"Yes, sir, perfectly clear."

Lee hesitated then decided he had to do it. "No mistakes this time, General Stuart."

"No, sir."

Lee gave a curt nod of dismissal.

Stuart saluted and left. Seconds later he and his staff were galloping down the road back into town. Lee watched him go and then let his gaze return to the ambulances swinging out onto the road heading back toward Chambersburg. He watched only for a moment, then returned to his work.

Chapter Nine

11:00 AM, July 2, 1863

Fairfield Road
Emmitsburg

C.S.A.

"General Longstreet?"

The courier was edging along the side of the road, pushing his way around a battery, standing in his stirrups, and looking toward Pete and his staff. The day was getting hot; the courier's horse was lathered, the animal blowing hard, the lieutenant's face covered with dust, traced with rivulets of sweat streaking his forehead.

Longstreet nodded, motioning the boy over. Excited, the courier drew up alongside the general and saluted. "Message from General Robertson, sir," and the boy handed the paper over.

Pete, swinging one leg up over the pommel of his saddle, opened the message and quickly scanned it.

"Robertson has Emmitsburg," Pete announced, looking back to his staff. "They took the signal station up behind a Catholic convent, St. Mary's College," and he paused, looking at the time on the note, "thirty minutes ago."

There were nods of satisfaction.

"Did the signal station get any messages off after we came into view?" Pete asked, looking back at the courier.

"Not sure, sir. They was waving them flags something fierce though as we came through the town. Some mounted boys up front got up there quick and took 'em prisoners."

"Anything else in the town?"

"No, sir, just some stragglers. General Robertson said that it looked like a whole hell of a lot of Yankees were there yesterday though. Stragglers from First and Eleventh Corps, he said."

Pete nodded, pulled a pencil out of his breast pocket, and flipped the message over.

> *Secure road south and north of town; push out pickets. Clear your men from the road. Law's brigade will start toward Taneytown.*

Signing his name, he handed the message back.

"Where is General Hood?"

"Sir, I heard he was reconnoitering east of the town. Moving toward the bridge over Monocacy Creek."

"Get back to Robertson; tell him I'm coming up shortly," and he nodded a dismissal.

As the boy pushed back onto the crowded road, Pete turned to his staff. "One of you stay here in case any more couriers come back looking for me. One of you go back up the road as far as Fairfield, keep them things moving, keep them moving. I'm going up to join General Hood and can be found on the road to Taneytown."

Wearily swinging his leg off the pommel, he slipped his foot into the stirrup and urged his mount to a slow trot. The road was narrow, coming down out of a low ridgeline that cut across the road toward Emmitsburg. The battery that had just rumbled past had come to a stop, and pushing around it, he swore at the sight of an ammunition wagon blocking the way ahead. The driver and half a dozen men were squatting down looking at the rear axle, the left rear wheel splayed out at a drunken angle . . . apparently a lug nut and the wheel had come loose.

"Damn it!" Pete snarled. "Don't just sit there staring; get some men and, if need be, heave that damn thing off this road. You're blocking the entire column!"

"Ah, sir, we can fix this in ten minutes."

"I don't have ten minutes! Heave it off the road now!"

The men saluted and as he rode on he heard one of them whispering that "Old Pete" was in a bad temper.

Damn it, I am in a bad temper! he thought angrily. Two or three breakdowns like that could delay a column for an hour or more. If this was going to work, they had to get into Taneytown before Meade began to shift. He had to assume that the signal station had sent a warning, that even now staff officers were galloping about Meade's headquarters, heading out to the various corps. Fifth and Sixth Corps were still not clearly accounted for. If they were coming up from Westminster or Taneytown, they could be turned around in fairly short order, and the race would be on.

The rear of Law's brigade was ahead of him, swinging down out of the pass, keeping a good pace. An orchard opened up to his right, and he edged his way off the road and into the rows of peach trees. The trees nearest the road had already been stripped by the passing column, but in the middle of the orchard the fruit was still untouched. As he moved up to a slow canter, he reached out and snagged one from an overhanging branch and bit into it, grimacing slightly. The fruit was still hard, not quite ripe. In Georgia they'd be ripe, and he thought for a moment of his boys — a summer evening, picking peaches for a cobbler — and forced that away. They're dead. Don't dwell on that now. My babies are dead and gone from the typhoid.

He rode on, half consuming the peach and then tossing it aside. The orchard gave way to a wheat field. It took a moment to find an opening in the split-rail fence. The wheat brushed against his boots, heavy golden stalks ready for the harvest. In fact, part of the field had already been cut, but no one was working the field today. Not with a war on.

He hated trampling down the hard labor of another. There were more than a few who these last two weeks were taking pleasure from it, making the Yankees feel what a war is like, the men said; but his nature rebelled against such wanton destruction and vandalism. Someday this war was going to be over. If we win, we have to be neighbors once more.

As he reached the bottom of the field he saw the farmer standing by his barn, a portly wife clinging to his arm. Pete tipped his hat, and she offered a wan smile. The farmer just glared at him, saying nothing.

The path from the barnyard led back down to the main road into Emmitsburg, and he followed it. The street was packed with troops, men of Law's brigade. The village was typical of the region, small two-and three-story houses, packed together tightly, their front steps right on the walkways flanking the roadway. Windows were open, curious civilians peering out at the flood of men pouring down their thoroughfare. A tavern had a provost guard outside its door. The troops streaming past peppering him with jests and more than a few barbed comments about good infantry going thirsty while officers lingered inside. He was tempted, just for a second, to actually stop and go in, to see if any officers were indeed malingering within under pretense of securing contraband liquor. The guard nervously saluted as Pete continued on.

The road curved down a gentle slope, past a church that had a Union hospital flag hung from a window. The doors were open and he could see a surgeon at work. Some casualties from the previous day's fight had most likely been moved down here during the night. A dozen soldiers, a mix of Yankees and his own, were on the steps of the church, one rebel boy moaning, holding a crushed foot up in the air, blood dripping from his smashed boot. Several others were obviously sick, one an old man with a waxy pallor and blue lips, wearing a tattered uniform, a soldier from the Texas Brigade.

Several of the Yankees saluted, and Pete returned the gesture as he pressed on. Directly ahead was the intersection with the Gettysburg-Emmitsburg Road. A regiment in open order was deployed in a field north of the intersection, slowly pushing up along either side of the road in a heavy skirmish line. As he reached the junction, he spied Robertson, commander of the lead brigade in the march. Robertson was standing to the side of the road, talking with his staff. Behind him, in the fields to the south of town and below the convent, the Texas Brigade was deployed, guarding the approach to the south.

"How are things here?" Pete asked.

Grinning, Robertson saluted.

"No real trouble so far, sir. Skirmish to take that signal tower," and he pointed up to the high ridge behind the convent. "Gotta figure we just knocked on the back door of the Yankees."

"Why is most of your brigade off that way then?" Pete asked casually. Robertson was a good officer, who knew his business.

"A couple of the stragglers we picked up" — and he gestured to where half a hundred Yankees were sitting glumly in an open field, guarded by several mounted provost guards — "one of them said there was a brigade of Yankee cavalry south of here and coming up this way."

Pete nodded, shading his eyes as he scanned the road to the south. No dust on the road, no sense that anything was coming, but still a brigade of Yankee cavalry slamming into their line of march could play havoc; even a brief delay at the crossroads here would reverberate clear back to Gettysburg, bringing the entire march to a halt. He silently cursed Stuart. Rather than rounding up headquarters details and mounted staff to push the head of the column, it should have been a full division of Stuart's troopers securing the way.

"General Hood?"

"Talked with him about a half hour ago, sir. He's heading east with his staff to scout the bridge at Monocacy. He should be at the front of Law's brigade. The head of their column should be a couple of miles down the road by now."

Pete nodded, gaze still looking south, then turning in the saddle, he studied the road northward. All of the wheat and corn in the fields to either side of the road was trampled down, hundreds of burnt circles marking campfires, clear evidence that a lot of men had been through here in the last couple of days.

"So far though," Robertson offered, "it looks like every one of them Federals hightailed it up to Gettysburg yesterday. Other than that sorry bunch sitting over there, a couple of surgeons and the Signal Corps unit, there was nothing here."

"Could change damn quick though," Pete responded. "Rest your men, then fall in on the rear of Hood's column once the rest of the division has passed. If there's a fight up ahead, I want your brigade of Texans in it. I want to keep my units together as much as possible. But if anything starts to loom up from either direction, you get word up to me quick. I'm going forward, and once into Taneytown I will establish headquarters there. You got that?"

Robertson repeated the orders, and Pete nodded approvingly.

He looked around again. To the west of the north-south road, it was good ground, perfect for a defensive fight; on the other side, however, the land gave way to gently rolling farmland. If this plan worked, the entire Army of Northern Virginia would funnel through here across the next two days. If the Army of the Potomac should react by coming back down the main road to Gettysburg, they could possibly cut his corps off, strung out all the way past Taneytown.

Then it was going to get dicey. We stretch out. If we grab Taneytown and start to move toward Westminster, then we have them. But if they react now, coming south on this road, it will be us who are scrambling.

He looked back to the north.

"If there is cavalry coming up from the south, we can handle it. I'm more worried about a damn corps of infantry coming back down this road from the north. Before you push on, get up this road a bit, scout it out, find a good defensive line to slow them down."

"Yes, sir."

He hesitated for a moment. Perhaps I should stay here, at least till I get a full division forward. He looked back toward the town of Emmitsburg. The torrent of troops continued to pour down the main street, reached the intersection with the Gettysburg Road, and pressed on eastward. The pace was quick. Hood was doing a good job. The men were moving along sharply. Now that they were out of the pass above Emmitsburg and into open country, we should be able to make close to three miles an hour to the Monocacy Bridge. The road was a good one, a pike surfaced with crushed limestone.

Should I stay here to keep an eye on things?

No. That's what I would have done yesterday. Not today. I can't think that way today. Trust Lee's instincts. It was I who first put this scheme forward; I have to keep it moving. The old man was right. Jackson is dead. I have to take his place now. To hell with the myth about Jackson's foot cavalry. Let them see what my corps can do for a change.

He looked over at his staff. The boys were tired. Most had not slept since yesterday morning, and he could see more than one who had that wistful, dogged look in his eyes, hoping he'd declare that here was headquarters and they could grab a few minutes of sleep in the shade.

We do that and it sends a signal to every soldier marching past. Headquarters is here; this is the center; we can begin to slacken the pace.

"Come on," Pete said, "we got some more riding."

None of them said anything. A few were obviously a bit surprised at his determination to go to the front of the march.

Swinging out into the open fields beside the road, Pete urged his mount up to a near gallop, weaving through open pastures, rich land of wheat, corn, apples, and fat milk cows. It was getting decidedly hot, even as he rode, and he took his hat off for a moment, letting the breeze cool his sweat-soaked brow.

Troops marching on the road saw him pass, a few offering a cheer. He wasn't the type that most of the men cheered, no Jackson, but damn it he would show Jackson a thing or two this day. He passed a battery of three-inch rifles, moving at a sharp pace, the road ahead darkened by the swaying column of infantry, the men moving briskly, some of the shorter men pushing along at a slow trot. Something must be up, he realized, an order from forward to come along on the double.

And then directly ahead, he heard it, the patter of musketry, puffs of smoke rippling along the far ridge, a low stretch of ground, the crest, open pasture and fields. Whoever was shooting was down in the wheat and corn. He slowed for a moment, not sure if they had, in fact, run into Union troops contesting their approach, then saw some men in butternut sprinting from the road, deploying out along the base of the ridge and moving up, arms still at the shoulder.

Coming down from the ridge ahead was a knot of mounted men, one of them John Hood, and Pete angled over toward him, coming on fast, his mount laboring hard, exhaling noisily. John was heading for the road but then swerved at Pete's approach and came straight toward him.

"What's happening, John?" Pete shouted, even as he reined in hard.

"Damn Yankee cavalry, that's what gives. The bridge over Monocacy is just on the other side of that ridge. We were just about on it, and then from the other side, out of Taneytown, we saw them coming up, riding hard, a regiment at least and more on the way."

"Can you force it?"

"I'm doing that right now."

Even as he spoke, the volume of fire was increasing. A regiment of troops down on the road was moving forward on the double in columns of four, heading up toward the low rise. As the head of the regiment crested the rise, the racket swelled, and he could see several men tumble out of the ranks. The column slowed and then began to deploy into a battle line.

"We're trying to find a ford so we can flank it, but I think they've beaten us to the bridge."

"Who is it?"

"Buford."

"Damn!" Pete sighed. It would have to be him. A year ago, at Second Manassas, John Buford had put up a hell of a fight and almost delayed Pete's march through the Bull Run Mountains. Reports were he had done it again yesterday before Gettysburg. Why the hell was he here now?

11:45 AM

Gettysburg

US "Sir, maybe you should get up."

Henry Hunt groaned, raising his hat off his face, squinting up at his orderly, who was looking down anxiously.

He wanted to curse the young lieutenant and tell him to go away. The orderly was holding a tin cup of coffee as a peace offering, and Henry gingerly took it by the rim, swearing softly as it burnt his fingers before he could finally take the handle. He blew on the thick brew.

"What's going on?"

"Some real upset, sir."

He stood up, bones creaking from the effort, rubbing his eyes with his free hand and looking around. All was quiet along the brow of the cemetery. There were occasional distant pops from skirmishers off beyond the wooded hill to the northeast. As he faced that way, the thump of distant cannon fire washed over him. The volume picked up even as he stood there.

Are things opening on our right? he wondered. Is Lee trying to flank us there? Around the headquarters, back behind the slope, there was a flurry of activity: staff officers riding back and forth, knots of men talking.

Strange how it worked, so many self-important men around a headquarters, all of them acting as if the fate of the war rested on their ponderings and swapping of rumors. It was like a hive of bees getting riled up whenever something happened.

"What's the upset?"

"Sickles has moved."

"What?"

"You can see for yourself, sir. Apparently he did so without telling General Meade."

The orderly motioned to the west, and Henry followed him, coming out from under the shade of an elm, squinting from the harsh noonday light. Slowly walking up the slope of the cemetery, he sipped the coffee. He hated the feeling when awakening from a midday nap, especially after an exhausting night of work. It was hard to think clearly. You felt sticky, aware of just how long it has been since you had a decent bath, a change of clothes, and a proper meal.

A gun crew was directly ahead, the men standing, pointing off to the south, intent on whatever it was they were watching. As he came up alongside the three-inch gun, he finally saw what they were looking at, a mile away . . . an entire corps of Union troops, flags flying, moving as on parade, sweeping out across the fields toward the Emmitsburg Road. Though long ago cynical about the grandeur of war, he had to inwardly admit that it was a powerful sight.

"General Meade galloped out of here a few minutes back, swearing a blue streak," Henry's orderly said. "Everybody saw it."

"Better get down there," Henry sighed. The orderly, who had been leading Henry's horse, handed over the reins. Henry drained the rest of the coffee, tossed the cup on the ground, and mounted.

"There's more, sir. Right after General Meade rode out, I was talking with a sergeant with the Signal Corps. He said there was some confusion about the signal station down at Emmitsburg."

"Emmitsburg?"

"Yes, sir. It's been hazy all morning, sir. This sergeant said there was some sort of signal, but they couldn't read it clearly. And then nothing. The station atop that big round hill on our left flank has been trying to raise them, but no response. Seems that there's a bit of worry about it."

"Anything else?"

"Well, there're a lot of rebel cavalry coming in around our right. That's the skirmishing you're hearing."

Henry looked toward the northeast. Puffs of smoke rippled in front of the crest locals called Culp's Hill. His orderly was right. It was cavalry, dismounted skirmishers.

"Infantry?"

You can still see what's left of the Rebs who attacked last night; they're on the far side of town.

Worry about that later. Stuart coming in, and on the right flank, might mean a move. Should I check this out? he wondered.

He suppressed a groan as he spurred his mount to a fast canter. Too damn much riding these last couple of days, enough to bounce your guts out. For a brief instant he thought about just turning back to headquarters, finding the shade of the tree that was so comfortable, and waiting it out. But two things drove him. If Sickles was on to something down on his flank as well, he'd better go up and see about the deployment of guns . . . that and he was just damn curious to see what was going to happen.

They followed the crest line down along the position held by Second Corps. The men were up, shading their eyes, looking southwest, watching the spectacle; and it was indeed a spectacle, long battle lines of blue sweeping across the fields. He weaved his way down onto a farm lane that cut through a woodlot and then came out to a narrow road heading west. The pasture to either side of the road was trampled down, clear indication that lines of infantry had just passed through. He turned onto the road and within a couple of minutes came up on the rear of the advancing corps, men moving forward in a vast formation, the sight of which quickened his pulse. The road was jammed with artillery limbers, batteries assigned to Third Corps; and as he passed, several men shouted to him, asking what was happening.

He ignored their calls, weaving in and out through the formation until his orderly pointed toward the knoll crowned by a peach orchard. The confrontation was already on, Meade and Sickles facing each other, still mounted, staff back a couple of dozen feet away, soaking in every word. He edged up to the group and reined in.

"And I tell you," Sickles was shouting, waving an arm toward the west, "there is something big moving out there, at least a division, maybe a corps going for my flank."

"Goddamn it, Sickles!" Meade roared back. "I'll break you for this, bust you out of this army. I don't have time for amateur generals running about whenever the whim seizes them."

"Been going at it like this for the last ten minutes," a guidon bearer whispered, coming up to Henry's side.

He ignored him, trying not to be too obvious a voyeur to the confrontation.

"Listen," Sickles replied, lowering his voice, "it's good ground here; half my corps were looking up at this knoll. Beyond that, I tell you we're getting flanked. The signal station tried to communicate that from Emmitsburg, and now we can't raise them at all."

"How in God's name do you know that?" Meade shouted. "We could barely *see* it yesterday it was so damn hazy. Based on that, a signal station we can't see, and now you're moving without orders?

"Can't you hear the Confederate artillery on the right flank?" Meade shouted, gesturing back to the north. "Lee might very well be moving on our right, and you are overextending the left.

"Goddamn you, Sickles! Damn you! You moved up from Emmitsburg yesterday without waiting for orders. Now you're moving again without orders. Are you in command of this army or am I?"

Sickles said nothing.

"Answer me, damn you!"

"You are," and there was a long hesitation, "sir."

"General Sickles, if you desire to still have your command five minutes from now, you'll listen to me, damn you. Turn your corps around and go back to the position assigned to you."

Dan sighed, looking around at the men watching the confrontation. He wearily shook his head. "At least let me send a brigade forward as reconnaissance, that and send a couple of regiments south toward Emmitsburg to find out what is happening, why we can't raise the signal station down there."

"Your heard me, damn you. Every man back to his original position right now."

Dan looked frantically around, like someone cornered in a barroom brawl, hoping for support. All around him were silent. "Order the men back to their original positions," he finally said to no one in particular, his voice filled with weariness.

Members of his staff sat mesmerized, not moving.

"Do it!" he roared.

Staff officers turned and moved off. Meade, glowering, looked around and with a savage jerk turned his horse about.

"After this is over, by God there will be an inquiry into this, Sickles. I promise you that."

Without another word, the army's commander rode past Henry. Henry watched him go, wondering if he should ask for orders, but figured it was best not to deal with the man at this moment.

The confrontation broke up. Bugle calls echoed across the fields, the vast movement grinding to a halt, like a lurching machine that had suddenly seized up. Thousands of voices rose up, expressing the eternal sentiment of soldiers of the Republic, that the damn officers didn't know what the hell they were doing.

Dan caught Henry's eye, and before Henry could turn away he rode up.

"Can't you talk to him?" Sickles asked, an imploring note in his voice.

"Me? If you couldn't, I know I sure can't."

"You see my point, don't you?"

"It's not my place to say," Henry replied cautiously. Sickles was noted as a damn cagey courtroom fighter. The last thing Henry needed was to be cited as having lent support to Sickles's position. Meade's words were not idle ones; they rarely were. Once the campaign was over, Meade would go after Sickles, political friends be damned.

"You heard about Emmitsburg?"

"Something."

"They couldn't read the signal, but one of my staff was up there, on the Big

Round Hill, and said there was a lot of frantic waving and then nothing. Nothing, I tell you."

"And?"

"Hunt, they're flanking us. You can smell it. The dust in front of my lines; you can see that even now.

"After you left, I sent a probe forward and it got savaged. Berdan is damn near dead, and a hundred men lost. If the Rebs were fighting that hard, just a mile in front of me, that tells me they don't want us looking over that next ridge. It tells me we're being flanked."

"So why advance forward, unmasking your left?" Henry asked, unable to avoid getting sucked in.

"Because if they're flanking us, we should hit them first. It's the same as Chancellorsville all over again. Hit us, fix our attention, then slip around our flank. I said it at Chancellorsville, by God, and no one listened. And now we're doing it again. Twenty more minutes and I'd of been into them, goddamn it!"

"You should have cleared it with him," Henry finally offered.

"I sent half a dozen messengers to him. Half a dozen and always the same reply, that he had things well in hand."

The battle formations to either side of Sickles were at a halt and now facing about, starting the hike back toward the main line half a mile away. Sickles looked around, squinting, features scarlet.

Henry almost felt a moment of pity for this foul-mouthed ward politician turned general. He had been humiliated in front of his entire command. Every soldier, down to the most dim-witted private in the Third Corps, would know about that humiliation within the hour.

"You'd better get back and establish headquarters," Henry finally offered.

"Hunt, would you do me a favor?"

"What, sir."

"Go south. You've got a good mount. Just take that road down to Emmitsburg. You could get there in an hour. Scout it out."

Henry said nothing. Scouting was not his job. It was artillery and Sickles knew that. If Meade found out that the chief of artillery had gone off scouting at the request of Sickles, he'd be out of a job.

Dan lowered his head and turned his mount back. "Hunt, this day will wind up haunting both of us for the rest of our lives." He rode off, leaving Henry alone at the Peach Orchard, except for the orderly, who like all orderlies waited patiently.

Henry nudged his mount forward, the orderly falling in by his side, the young officer knowing better than to say anything. For a brief moment Henry was tempted to detail the lad off, send him down the road as Dan requested. No, one boy wandering off on his own would most likely get lost, or wander into trouble and get himself killed.

All the way back to headquarters, and even as he settled back under the elm tree, Dan's words haunted him. The nap was an unsettling one and brought Henry no rest or peace.

1:00 PM, July 2, 1863

The White House

President Abraham Lincoln settled into the chair by the table covered with maps. Sighing, he adjusted his glasses and wearily looked at them, half listening as Edwin Stanton, Secretary of War, droned on about the situation. To one side of the table were the latest newspapers from Baltimore, Philadelphia, New York, all of them screaming about the rebel invasion.

"The reports indicate that Lee's casualties last night were substantial," Stanton announced. "It's a heartening indicator."

"Strange," Lincoln whispered, "we now

call the deaths of so many young men heartening."

"It's the most successful repulse we've seen yet of an attack by Lee, in fact the first clear defeat since Malvern Hill a year ago. . . ."

"And do you think he will come on again today?"

Stanton nodded.

"Why?"

"It's not like him to back off from an attack."

Lincoln picked up one of the maps brought over from the War Department showing southern Pennsylvania and most of Maryland. Blue and red pencil markings traced out the route of the two armies as they converged on Gettysburg.

"Should we be confident that General Meade will react correctly?" Lincoln finally asked.

"He was chosen by you," Stanton replied cautiously.

"Upon your recommendation."

"He is the only one capable right now. Unfortunately, Reynolds turned it down."

"And now he is dead."

"Yes."

Lincoln nodded, looking back at the papers, one of them dated from Chicago only two days ago. How remarkable, he thought. When I came to Congress from

Springfield only seventeen years ago the journey had taken more than a week. Now papers can be rushed from Chicago in just two days. The Chicago paper's top story was a report from Grant's army proclaiming that Vicksburg would fall within the week.

"There is nothing we can do to affect things now," Lincoln said, again looking back at the map. "Let us trust that General Meade will prove himself worthy of the men who serve him."

Chapter Ten

1:45 PM, July 2, 1863

Battle of Monocacy Creek

Brig. Gen. John Buford fought to regain his saddle, his mount nervously shying back from the shell burst that had detonated a dozen feet away. The trooper who had been reporting to him was down, lying still in the middle of the road, covered in white dust.

"You hurt, General?"

Head ringing from the concussion, John turned. It was Gamble, commander of his First Brigade.

He was stunned from the blast, and it took a moment for his thoughts to clear.

Gamble leaned over, grabbing the reins to John's horse.

"Are you hurt, sir?"

"No, no. I'll be fine in a moment."

"They're spreading the line," Gamble shouted, "extending to our right!"

John nodded, willing the pounding in his chest to settle down, his thoughts to clear.

It was getting decidedly hot, the air thick, sticky. He looked back to the east, toward Taneytown. The rest of Devin's brigade was coming up on the pike, troops of cavalry spreading out across the fields, riding hard.

But the horses were blown, moving slowly. Hard days of campaigning, the fight yesterday, were telling now. Cavalry could move quickly when need be, but then horses had to be rested. Push too hard and your entire command is on foot. That's why he had requested the pullback to the rear, to give the mounts a day or two to feed on the rich pastures, get reshod after nearly two hundred miles of marching in the last two weeks, and even more importantly, resupply his command with ammunition and rations.

And now this, a battle that was never supposed to happen, a dozen miles to the flank and rear, with me in the way, taking a break at Taneytown when a scout brought the word in that Rebs were on the road to the west.

From the bluff overlooking the river, he could see the bridge below, a solid affair, stone foundation, wide enough for two wagons to pass. Ten more minutes, and the Rebs would have had it. Only a hard ride, a flat-out gallop of five miles by his lead regiment, the Eighth New York, a ride that had killed at least a dozen mounts and blown the rest, could secure the crossing, even as the Rebs were racing in from the other side.

Now the damn affair was spreading out. This wasn't a raiding force probing the army's flank; it was a full-out attack. As his regiments came up from Taneytown, the Rebs were pouring their men in as well, rapidly extending to either side of the bridge, looking for places to cross and envelop him.

The Rebs had at least a division on the other side of the river, the trooper who was killed having just reported that they had taken a man who claimed to be with Law's brigade, Hood's division.

Damn, if I'm facing Hood down here, a dozen miles south of Gettysburg, that must mean all of Longstreet is behind him. They wouldn't just send a lone division this far off the flank. No, this was like Second Manassas all over again, with Longstreet again on the other side. Fix our attention in one direction, then slip around to the flank or rear. It was always the same with the Army of the Potomac. We focus on Lee, then he weaves like a boxer, dodging off in another direction, and our damn generals sit there dumbfounded. Once, just once, why couldn't it be the other way around?

The opposite bank of the creek was a shadowland of smoke and flickering gunfire. The air was still, humid, the smoke clinging to the ground, hanging in choking clouds beneath the trees that lined the banks of the stream. His men were giving back, rifle fire echoing in the shallow valley, but doing so slowly, with measured pace. Ammunition was low; every shot had to count.

He turned about and drew back a hundred yards, coming back out at the crest on the east side of the creek. Heat shimmers were rising off the pike to Taneytown, distorting the column of troopers coming up to reinforce the line.

"Should I tell Devin to put his men in on the right?" Gamble asked.

John raised his field glasses, scanning the opposite slope on the far side of the river. He caught glimpses of an infantry column a half mile away heading to his right. A second artillery battery was swinging into line. *I don't have a single damn field piece, Calef won't be up for another half hour, and now there are two batteries on the other side, most likely more coming up.*

I held the good ground for the army yesterday, did my duty, pulled back to refit, and now this. How the hell did Hood get around to the rear?

John looked over at Gamble, who was still awaiting orders. "We've got to hold them here, right here. Lose this line and there is no defendable position between here and the far side of Taneytown" he hesitated for a second trying to remember the name "— along Pipe Creek.

"On the right, Gamble; put whatever we've got in there."

"Reserve?"

John shook his head. "We don't have any now."

Hood was a good player; he knew what to do. Yesterday, Harry Heth was impetuous, came on too fast; Hood though, John was different. Aggressive as all hell, but he'd get a full division up and then come storming in with everything at once. Just keep extending the line until he finds a place to get across and turns us. That and some of my men have gone in with cartridge boxes half-empty. The few precious companies armed with repeating Spencer rifles were just about empty, having poured out nearly everything they had up at Gettysburg yesterday.

This was going to get bad real quick.

"Find a trooper with a damn good horse and get him over here now," John announced.

Dismounting in front of a farmhouse on the crest of the hill, he walked up to the porch. A woman with two children behind her stood in the doorway.

"I'd suggest you get your family down into the cellar," Buford said.

The woman turned, pushing the children inside, but returned a moment later, bearing of all things an earthen mug filled with foaming buttermilk.

In spite of his concern for her safety, he gratefully took the offering and downed it. It was cool, delicious. He drank it so fast his head ached for a moment.

"Ma'am, please find some shelter."

"You're wounded, sir," and she pointed to his left arm. He glanced down, saw the torn sleeve, and for the first time felt the pain. The last shell burst must have nicked him.

"I'll be fine. Now please go with your children."

"Have your wounded brought in here where it's safe."

Safe? He couldn't help but smile. This house, on the crossroads, would be a target for the guns deploying on the other side.

"Down to the cellar with you, ma'am. I'll send one of my men to stay with you."

Gamble came up, leading a trooper riding a fine-looking stallion, which had obviously just "joined" the army.

Buford pulled out his dispatch book, folded it open, and addressed a note to Meade.

2:00 PM, July 2, 1863

Monocacy Creek,
Five Miles West of Taneytown

My command, while proceeding through Taneytown, was informed by a scout that Confederate forces, in at least brigade strength, were approaching from Emmitsburg. I have moved my entire command up, securing the east bank of Monocacy Creek at the stone bridge on the Emmitsburg-Taneytown Pike. I am facing Hood's division, having directly observed at least two brigades so far and believe that Longstreet's corps is behind him.

He paused for a moment, then added the next line.

I believe Longstreet's intent is to turn the left flank of our army.

I intend to hold this position at whatever cost, though my ammunition supply is limited and many of my mounts are worn. I believe you should move sufficient forces here with all possible dispatch to secure this position; otherwise Taneytown and Westminster will be threatened.

Pulling out his pocket watch, he checked the time and handed the dispatch up.

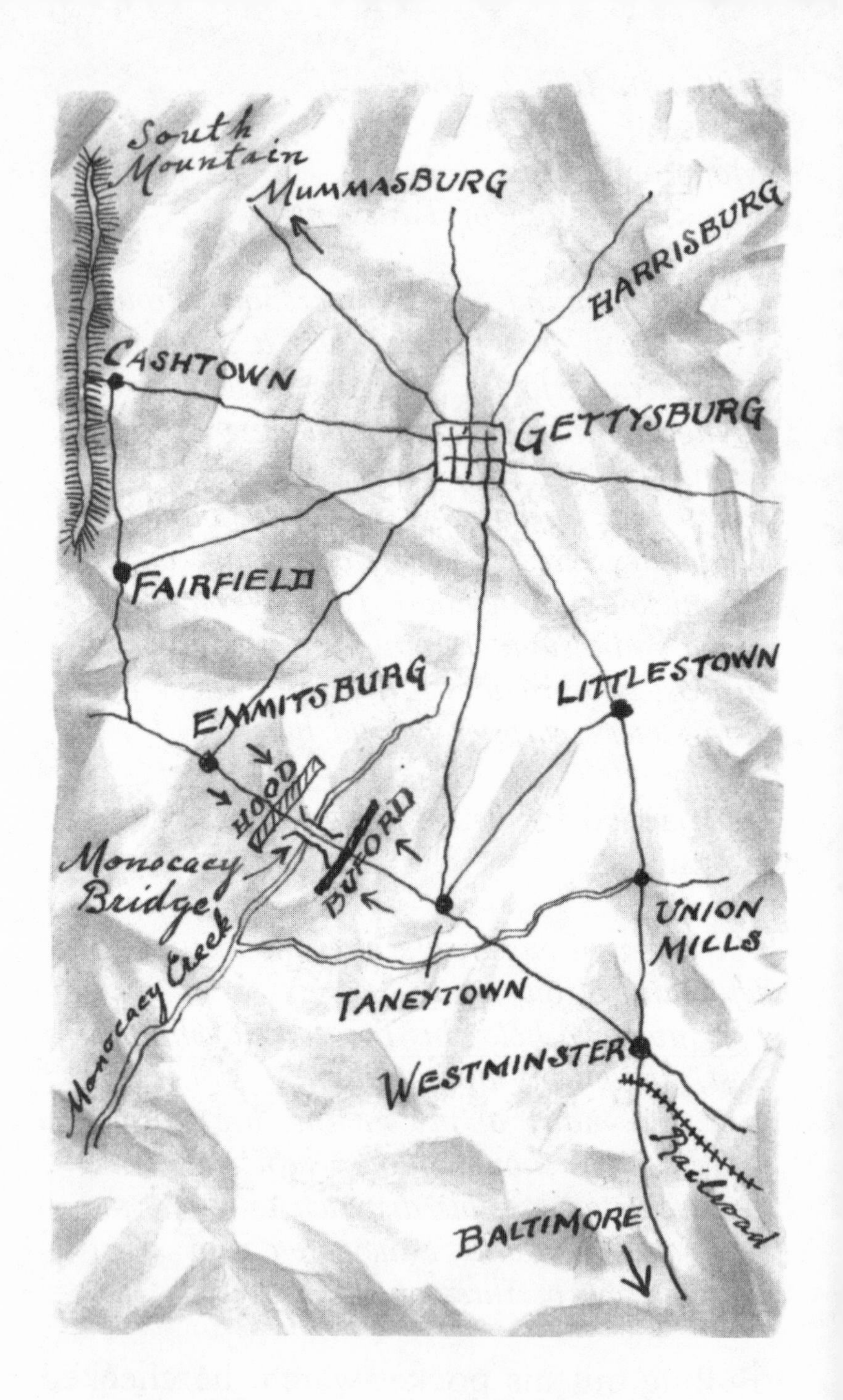
South Mountain
MUMMASBURG
HARRISBURG
CASHTOWN
GETTYSBURG
FAIRFIELD
EMMITSBURG
LITTLESTOWN
HOOD
BUFORD
Monocacy Bridge
UNION MILLS
Monocacy Creek
TANEYTOWN
WESTMINSTER
Railroad
BALTIMORE

"Ride back toward Taneytown," Buford ordered. "Take the road north to Harney, the one we came down this morning, then proceed directly to Gettysburg. Stop for nothing. I want this personally delivered to General Meade. To Meade and no one else. Do you understand me?"

The trooper, obviously pleased with the importance of his role, nodded eagerly and saluted.

"Go!"

The trooper was off with a clattering of hooves, leaning far forward, crouched down on the neck of his mount.

Buford looked back at the woman, who was still standing in the doorway of her house. "This road here" — and he pointed to the farm lane that intersected the pike at a right angle and headed north, disappearing as it turned down toward the river — "where does it lead?"

"That's Bullfrog Road," she replied. "It heads down to a ford across the river, about a mile north of here."

John nodded. Gamble had heard what she said and didn't need to be told.

"Get a regiment down to that ford. That's where he'll try and turn us. I'm staying here for right now. It's yesterday all over again, Gamble. We've got to hold. We've got to hold."

Gamble casually saluted and started to

turn. As Buford watched, a shell screamed in, bursting in the front yard. He looked back at the open doorway, the woman standing there unflinching. Another shell roared in . . . and then he was down.

There was a glimpse of sky, torn rafters of the porch, cedar shingles smoking, no noise, just a sense of floating. He caught a glimpse of white. It was the woman, kneeling by his side.

"You all right?"

He wasn't sure if he had actually spoken or not, but she nodded in reply, taking his hand. Gamble was by her side, features pale, cradling an arm. He knelt down, grimacing as he reached out, touching John on the shoulder. There were tears in Gamble's eyes.

"You've got to hold . . . ," John Buford tried to whisper, "for God's sake, please hold."

2:05 PM, July 2, 1863

Monocacy Creek

Coming to the edge of the woodlot, Longstreet reined in. Bullets were snicking through the trees, leaves fluttering down around him.

"Right down there," Hood announced, pointing.

He was right. A ford, the river shallow to the right of the crossing for a good hundred yards. The banks were a bit steep. It'd be tough getting up on the far side, but it was better than trying to force the bridge with a frontal charge against men armed with breechloaders.

Two batteries were already in place, shelling the crest behind the bridge. He raised his field glasses and focused on a plume of smoke. It looked like a farmhouse at the crest was on fire. Now that would be a signal that could be seen for miles.

The entire river valley for nearly half a mile was an inferno, stabs of light flickering in the smoke, the high crack of Sharps rifles, the tearing roar of volleys from his side. Behind him, weaving down a farm lane, a column approached, George Anderson's brigade, running at the double, men staggering with exhaustion in the ninety-degree heat, having marched nearly twenty miles and now going into this.

From the opposite side of the creek, he saw an open line of Union cavalry coming down the hill, cutting across the field, stopping a hundred yards from the riverbank, troopers dismounting, pulling carbines from saddle holsters, units of five men, four dismounting, the fifth staying mounted and grabbing the reins of the other horses.

The troopers raced down to the banks of the narrow stream, sliding down into the high grass, nestling in behind trees. No artillery though, not a single gun, thank God. One field piece, loaded with canister, would murder the men about to sprint to the ford.

Hood came up by his side.

"Almost in place."

Pete took out his pocket watch and shook his head. This had been going on for well over an hour and a half. If the signal station back in Emmitsburg had indeed warned Meade, reinforcements could already be approaching Taneytown.

"Send them in now."

"Twenty more minutes, and I'll have the entire brigade up."

"Now!"

Hood looked over at him, saluted.

"And John."

"Sir?"

"You stay here with me."

"General?"

"I need you for a lot more . . . John, after this. I don't want you getting hurt now. Give the order then come back here."

"Sir."

John galloped off. Pete continued to scan the approach to the ford. It was a steep bank down for the last fifty yards. He could see the Yankee cavalry deploying along the stream, crouching down low, getting ready. His artillery, halfway back toward the main bridge, was now up to three batteries, all of them pounding the slopes on the other side with case shot. The third battery, as ordered, was deploying out to enfilade this ford, the first shot already winging in, kicking up a geyser of water twenty feet high.

The long roll of a drum stuttered behind him, a bugle picking up the call. The first two regiments of Anderson's brigade started down the road, on the double, racing around a bend in the road. In another minute they'd be in sight of the troopers defending the ford.

Hood, his horse lathered and panting, came up to Longstreet's side, reining in.

"It's going to get tough. I've ordered the next regiment to fall in on the right. They will be going straight down to the stream in open order."

Pete nodded, saying nothing, lowering his glasses to watch the battle unfold.

The charge, advancing in columns of four, came around the final bend in the road. They were now in view. He could see Yankee troopers standing up, raising carbines, beginning to fire.

The charge pressed in, men dropping, sprawling in the roadway, staggering to either side. The head of the column hit the stream, men losing their footing on the large slippery rock that some farmer had laboriously put into place at the bank of the river.

Men jumped into the stream, rifles held high, bullets smacking the water around them. They were in thigh deep, desperately struggling to get across, churning the water into a muddy foam. The column stalled at the middle, breaking apart, men going down, bodies floating, wounded fleeing back to the shore.

The road was packed with men who started to spread out, falling in to either side of the ford, dodging into the high grass and trees, opening fire. The attack stalled.

He waited, Hood softly cursing by his side. A hundred men or more were down, littering the road, the riverbank, floating in the slow-moving current. Shells arced in, detonating along the far bank and in the field beyond, where mounted troopers struggled to control the horses of those who were fighting on foot.

Anderson's third regiment came out of the woodlot to Pete's right, deployed in heavy skirmish order, moving fast, rifles poised as they went down into the narrow valley. Long minutes passed as they pushed to the edge of the stream, adding their weight of fire to the two regiments that had gone to ground at the ford.

"Now, damn it, now!" Hood shouted, and he started to go forward, Pete reaching out to grab his reins.

Only thirty yards of thigh-deep water separated the two sides. Hood would be dead in minutes if he went down there.

A surge finally built up. A couple of dozen men leapt into the stream, fifty yards below the ford, and tried to storm across. Only three or four made it, slamming in against the muddy slope and then pushing up, going hand to hand with the troopers who had drawn revolvers to face them.

That small charge seemed to set off a fuse. A wolflike shriek began to echo, build, sending corkscrews down Pete's back.

"That's it!" Hood roared. "Go! Go!"

Anderson's men stood up, swarming by the hundreds into the stream, running with high, exaggerated steps as they splashed through the water.

The charge stormed across the stream, scores of men falling, but more and more gaining the opposite shore. From out of the thin band of trees, a scattering of Yankees emerged, running back to their mounts, followed seconds later by a gray-and-butternut swarm. Most of the troopers gained their mounts, leaping into saddles, spurring horses, but more than one fell in the excitement, or jumped astride a horse that was so worn it could barely get up to a canter before its rider was dropped.

"Let's go," Pete announced and he came out of the woodlot, Hood by his side, and raced down the slope, avoiding the road, which was littered with the wounded, dead, and dying.

Reaching the stream, he let his horse drink for a moment. It was a grim landscape. A couple of hundred casualties at the very least. Bodies floated in the stream, plumes of pink spreading from them. Exhausted men lay on both shores, pushed to the limit by the long march, the heat, and this short but deadly fight. He crossed the stream, his mount slipping as it struggled to get up the muddy bank.

The battle was sweeping up the gentle slope ahead, a strange sight, exhausted infantry pursuing equally exhausted cavalry. If he had but one regiment of fresh mounted troopers, he could bag the whole lot in front of him.

He pushed on, following the skirmishers advancing up the slope and onto the high footing beyond. Atop the crest the ragged line had halted and were blazing away, men shouting, loading frantically. Gaining the line, he saw their target. Hundreds of Yankee troopers were falling back, crowding the pike, all semblance of order gone, streaming toward the rear now that they were outflanked.

The volume of fighting down at the main bridge was beginning to drop off. They were giving up, pulling back. The sight filled him with frustration. They were getting away, damn it. But he could sense that this unit was beaten.

Long minutes passed, his skirmishers engaging at a range of several hundred yards, not feeling strong enough to try and push forward and close. Finally another regiment came up, men staggering as they deployed into a heavy battle line and at last began to squeeze in on the pike.

A final determined band came up the road when they were less than a hundred yards away from the burning farmhouse. A volley dropped several men as the last of the troopers veered off, cutting out into the open fields beyond.

His skirmishers finally closed on the main road, and a hoarse cheer rose up as they greeted troops from McLaws's brigade coming up from the main bridge.

Anderson, who had been on the skirmish line, came back, features pale, obviously on the edge of dropping from heat exhaustion. "Sir, you'd better come over here."

Pete followed the brigade commander over to the burning farmhouse. Half a hundred wounded and dead troopers were on the front lawn. A surgeon, aided by a lone woman, with two small children clinging to her side, stood at the busted gate.

The surgeon looked up coldly at Pete, who stiffened and saluted.

"My surgeons will be up shortly. We'll establish our hospital here, and your men will be tended to also, Doctor."

The surgeon said nothing.

Anderson motioned to one of the bodies. "Sir, that's Buford," Anderson announced.

Pete sighed, dismounted, went up to his old comrade, and knelt down. He wasn't sure if John was alive or not. The wound was ghastly, through the lungs.

He wasn't good at moments like this. Bad enough when it was your own men. Harder though when it was someone from long ago, now on the other side, and it was you who'd done it to him.

John opened his eyes. "We have to hold," John whispered.

"You did, John. You did just fine."

"Pete? Is that you?"

"Yes, John, it's Pete."

Buford sighed, closed his eyes.

"I'm sorry, John; it had to be done."

But Buford was gone.

General Longstreet stood up, catching the cold gaze of the woman standing protectively over the body.

"Your house, ma'am?"
"Yes."
"My apologies, ma'am. My quartermaster will give you a voucher for payment. I pray that you and your family are safe."
"My husband isn't. He died at Gaines Mills," she paused, "fighting on your side."
There was nothing he could say.
He turned away, walking back out to the road. Men from Law's and Anderson's brigades were forming up, gathering beneath their standards on the far side of the road. They were finished for now, played out, and needed several hours' rest before he could push them again.
He saw Anderson, leaning against the fence, doubled over. The man vomited. It wasn't fear; it was just the exhaustion after a tough fight. Pete waited until the brigade commander, spitting and coughing, stood back up, features pale.
"You had two regiments that didn't engage?"
"Yes, sir."
"I want them on the road in fifteen minutes."
Anderson hesitated, then saluted and walked off, his legs rubbery.
Pete drew out his pocket watch. It was nearly four in the afternoon. Too long. Too damn long.

He looked back at John Buford's body.

Maybe you did buy enough time, Pete thought, but God I hope not.

Remounting, he turned east, and continued on toward Taneytown as the roof of the burning farmhouse collapsed, sending up a pillar of flame and smoke.

Chapter Eleven

4:00 PM, July 2, 1863

Northeast of Gettysburg

It was hard to conceal his delight as the light battery of horse artillery galloped into position, guns bouncing and careening behind their caissons, mounted gunners yelling with delight.

Stuart snapped off a salute as the unit raced past him, deploying out into an open field to the northeast of the wooded hill flanking the cemetery held by the Army of the Potomac. The range was extreme. The fire would be nothing more than a nuisance, but that was not the main intent.

For the last hour he had been running the brigade of infantry ragged. They had marched five miles, swinging far north of the town, cutting across fields and down lanes beyond the sight of the Yankees, finally to emerge into view along a stretch of the road leading back to York. After marching in plain sight for several hundred yards, the column dipped out of view, heading to the east, then countermarched back around by a concealed lane, only to reemerge and do the march in sight yet again.

Farther afield small troops of cavalry simply galloped back and forth along roads and farm lanes, dragging brush, kicking up dust, while the bulk of his command concentrated east of town skirmished with the Union cavalry that was beginning to come up and probed down around the right flank of the Union lines.

It reminded him of the stories of Magruder down on the Peninsula the year before. A passionate devotee of amateur theater, Magruder had hoodwinked McClellan into believing that two thousand men before Yorktown were actually twenty to thirty thousand.

Though still smarting from the rebuke and the clear threat from Lee, he had to admit that this afternoon he was beginning to enjoy his work.

4:15 PM, July 2, 1863

Headquarters, Army of the Potomac
Gettysburg, Pennsylvania

US

Hunt saw the courier galloping up the Taneytown Road. He was astride a magnificent stallion, the animal stretching out, running hard, as its rider guided the horse around the clutter of ammunition wagons slowly moving along the road.

Henry stepped down from the porch of the small house below Cemetery Hill that was now the headquarters of the Army of the Potomac. Staff officers, who had been clustered about, nervously looking to the northeast, where the sound of gunfire was rapidly increasing, barely noticed the arrival of a courier storming up the road from Taneytown. The courier was a cavalryman, hat gone, uniform so coated with dust that he almost looked like a rebel in dark butternut. The man reined in hard, swinging down from his saddle.

"General Meade!"

Several of the staff moved toward the rider, one of them extending his hand, asking for any dispatches.

"My orders from General Buford are to present this directly to General Meade!" the courier shouted, obviously agitated.

Henry felt a cold chill. Buford was supposed to be on his way to Westminster. He moved into the group. "I'll take you to him."

Leading the way, Henry stepped into the small parlor, where Meade stood at a table hunched over a map, while Warren was tracing out a position.

"Based on the Confederate movements

against our right flank, I think we have to extend to the right," Warren said, looking around the room.

"General, a dispatch rider," Henry announced. "He says the message must be given to you personally."

Meade looked up, slightly annoyed at the cavalryman standing in the doorway. "Who are you?" Meade snapped.

"Sergeant Malady, Eighth New York Cavalry, Buford's division, sir."

Meade came erect, extending his hand, while the trooper fumbled in his breast pocket and pulled out the note.

Meade unfolded it, started to read, and Henry could instantly tell that the news was bad. Meade finished reading and then seemed to go over the note a second time. All in the room were silent. Meade finally passed it to Dan Butterfield, his chief of staff, and turned away for a moment.

"What the hell is it?"

General Hancock, who had been standing on the front porch as the courier came in, was now behind the trooper, pushing his way into the room.

"General Buford reports that he is engaged with Hood's division on Monocacy Creek along the Emmitsburg to Taneytown Road," Butterfield announced.

"Jesus Christ Almighty," Hancock cried, stepping up to a map pinned to the wall and after several seconds stabbing his finger at a spot on the lower left corner.

Meade turned, looking back at the trooper. "Did you see this?" he asked sharply.

"Yes, sir. We were in Taneytown. It was around one. I remember that because one of the church clocks struck as we rode in. A scout came in from the west, and we were ordered to horse. It was a hard ride; a lot of the horses were about ready to drop."

"Yours looks pretty good," Hancock interjected.

"Well, sir, I sort of arranged a swap with a civilian when we got to Taneytown," and the trooper dropped his eyes as he spoke.

"Go on," Meade snapped.

"By the time we got up to the bridge, Gamble's brigade was really into it. A lot of heavy fire. I could see rebel troops on the far side, columns of them just beginning to deploy. My regiment was ordered in on the right to cover a ford; at least that's what I heard. It was then that General Gamble came up, spotted me, and ordered me to report to General Buford to carry that dispatch."

"And you took it personally from General Buford."

"Yes, sir."

"And he said he believed all of

Longstreet's corp was behind the attack?"
"Yes, sir."
"Did you see that? Other divisions?"
"No sir, not exactly. But I tell you, sir, we were getting hit as hard as we were over by the seminary yesterday. They had three batteries up. There was a hell of a lot of shooting. When I got back to Taneytown, I could still hear the gunfire."
"The condition of your men going in?" Hancock interjected.
"Well, sir, to be honest, not so good. The horses were pretty worn; a lot of us were short on ammunition. I heard the troopers who had Spencer repeaters were all but empty. But we'll make a good fight of it."
Hancock looked over at Meade, who stood silent, arms folded, eyes fixed on the map.
"We'd better get people down there now," Hancock said.
"That will take four hours or more," Meade replied, eyes still fixed on the map.
Warren stepped up to the map.
"That report from the Round Top signal station that came in a half hour ago of smoke being seen to the south. It fits. Also, losing contact with Emmitsburg. Sir, this doesn't look good."
Meade was still silent.
"Maybe Sickles was right," Butterfield

interjected, and Meade turned, fixing him with his sharp gaze.

Henry said nothing for the moment. Butterfield had been the previous commander's chief of staff. Meade had kept him on simply because the man clearly knew the routine. No one in this inner circle had any real love for Sickles, but Henry knew that Butterfield's comment showed remarkably bad timing since Meade was still fuming about the incident earlier in the day.

And yet, if Hood was indeed on the flank, then Sickles had been right. How absurd, Henry thought, the foul-mouthed amateur showing up, at least for the moment, all the professionals.

"Butterfield, I want a meeting of all corps commanders within an hour. Get the staff out to round them up."

Hancock, an incredulous look on his face, turned toward Meade.

"A staff meeting? That will take hours. We've got to act now."

Meade shook his head.

"All seven corps are up, and we are deployed for battle here. Sedgwick's men are coming in even now after marching thirty-five miles."

He then pointed toward the north.

"General Slocum is reporting at least a division of Confederate infantry, supported by Stuart, moving on our right. You can hear the fire coming from over there."

All were silent for a moment, the steady thump of artillery echoing, growing louder as several batteries up on Cemetery Hill began to reply.

"Goddamn it, I have reports now of infantry moving on my right flank, something I can see with my own eyes, and now this courier reporting Longstreet to my rear a dozen miles away, something I can't see.

"I want my corps commanders' opinions before we move this army again," Meade said firmly.

"Pulling the corps commanders in just isn't wise. If Lee does hit us here in the next hour, you want the corps commanders with their units. And besides, you don't need them to make this decision. You are in command. *You* are."

"And you want me to do what?" Meade responded.

"Sixth Corps is exhausted. But Fifth is camped right along the Taneytown Road. You could have them marching within the hour," Hancock pleaded.

Again Meade shook his head. "Marching where? To my right or to the rear?"

"The rear of course. Send Fifth Corps down to Taneytown now, sir."

Meade sighed wearily and shook his head. Again the thumping of gunfire rattled the windows of the small farmhouse.

"That's our active reserve for the moment. Sixth Corps is just too worn out from the march to be of much use now. I'm not going to detach an entire corps based on one report from a courier."

"Sergeant, tell him!" Hancock shouted, looking back at the cavalry trooper. "Tell him what Buford said!"

The sergeant stood there gape-mouthed, unable to reply.

Meade put his hand up, beckoning for silence.

Henry caught the eye of the trooper and nodded toward the door. The cavalryman stepped outside, Henry following, along with Warren, as the two generals within exploded at each other.

Henry led the trooper down to the fence bordering the Taneytown Road and, reaching into his pocket, he pulled out a flask and offered it.

"God bless you, sir."

The trooper tilted his head back and took a long swallow.

"You said that you saw what was going on at that bridge?" Henry asked.

"Yes, sir, I did, but only for a minute or so while General Buford wrote out the note."

"How long have you been in the army?"

"Since we signed up back in sixty-one. I've been in every campaign since, sir."

Henry nodded.

"You know we get a lot of couriers galloping in here," Warren interjected, "claiming they've seen the whole rebel army."

"I didn't say that, sir," and there was a slightly indignant tone to his voice. "I saw at least two brigades over there, sir. Well, not exactly saw, but down around the bridge, the width of the firing, sir, you know the sound, it was wide, a front of half a mile maybe."

As he spoke the trooper extended his hands wide, and Warren nodded.

"I saw another column moving to flank our right"; the trooper continued, "that's where my regiment went off to cover. It was just like yesterday when we fought Heth and Pender. You could just tell that there was a whole hell of a lot behind them, building up, pushing in. Sir, General Buford ain't prone to exaggerating, sir. If he said that Longstreet's entire corps was coming down that road, by God, I'd believe him."

Henry nodded. The trooper was right; Buford was a good man. Yesterday John Reynolds had marched to Buford's rescue, not waiting for the nicety of formal orders properly countersigned.

"One of my batteries is parked over there," and Henry pointed across the road. "Go down there; get some water and fodder for your horse and some food for yourself. Wait there."

"Thank you, sir."

"And, trooper, did that civilian willingly trade you horses? That is one beautiful mount you got there."

The man grinned, saying nothing, as he handed Henry his flask and saluted.

Henry turned to go back into the fray.

"Sir?"

It was the trooper.

"Yes?"

"For God's sake, don't let the generals screw this one up. We can lick those bastards any day of the week, if only they'd give us some good ground and let us fight."

Henry fixed the trooper with his gaze. He understood the sentiment, but still it bothered him, even though he knew the man was right.

Without comment, Henry turned and walked back toward the small, white-washed house.

"Henry, what do you think?" Warren asked, falling in by his side.

"I think Longstreet is flanking us, that's what I think."

"What's in front of us then?" and Warren nodded toward the sound of gunfire.

"I don't know, but I'm willing to bet it's a diversion," Henry offered. "We've only seen what appears to be one division of infantry over there, just a couple of batteries, no massed battalions of guns, so where the hell is the rest of Lee's army? It's either hidden behind the seminary or it's marching to the south."

"You and I rode that ground around Westminster yesterday morning, along Pipe Creek."

Yesterday morning? God, was it really just a day ago?

"It's damn good ground, Henry. Damn good. High land, open fields of fire for anyone dug in along the south bank, and Westminster as the primary base directly behind it. My God, if Longstreet seizes that, he'll cut us off from the railroad and our supplies and be between us and Washington."

As they walked back to the house, couriers were already dashing off, heading to the various corps headquarters to fetch the generals in.

Hancock was out on the porch, face red. He caught Henry's eye. "We wait,"

Hancock snarled. "Goddamn it, we wait."

Henry, unable to believe what Hancock was saying, walked into the small, whitewashed house. Meade was leaning over the map table, fist balled up, Butterfield by his side. The room was boiling hot. It gave Henry a claustrophobic feeling. Meade looked up with a cold eye. "Well?" Meade snapped.

"I didn't say anything, sir."

"But you're thinking it."

"That trooper, I talked with him outside. General, he's a good soldier, been in the army since the start of the war and not some naive kid straight from the farm. And Buford is a damn good cavalryman. If John is telling us Longstreet is on our flank, we'd better believe him."

Meade sighed. Stepping back from the table, he picked up a tin cup of coffee and sipped on it, turning to look at the map of southern Pennsylvania and northern Maryland pinned to the wall.

Warren came in and stood silently by Henry's side.

"You two surveyed that Pipe Creek line, didn't you?"

"Yes sir, we did," Warren replied. "An army on defense would have a huge advantage at Pipe Creek and an especially big advantage if they were defending the south side of that valley. If Pete

Longstreet slides into that position, he'll be astride our line of communications."

Meade said nothing for a moment, the room silent except for the annoying buzz of horseflies, and the distant boom of artillery coming from the right flank.

"Stuart is on our right with at least a division of infantry, maybe more. You can see him out there from the top of the cemetery. Reb infantry and artillery are deployed from the seminary clear down to opposite the ridge in our center, and there're still Reb skirmishers in the town. What the hell is that?"

"Diversion," Warren replied.

Meade finally looked back at the two. For a moment the combative, dyspeptic look was gone, replaced by an infinite weariness. Henry knew that Meade had not had a moment's sleep since yesterday, had only been in command of this army for five days. It was one thing to command a corps, to receive the orders to take or hold a position; it was an entirely different game to make those orders, orders upon which the fate of this army and the Republic might hang.

"At least send a division down there," Warren said softly. "Fifth Corps is astride the road back to Taneytown. Get a division on the road now, and they can be in Taneytown before dark. If Buford is indeed holding Longstreet at Monocacy Creek, the division can reinforce. If Longstreet is into the town, it will stall his advance. I'll go down with them and send back a report."

Meade did not reply, attention focused back on the map.

"Turning this army around, marching it south, will be a bloody nightmare."

He paused for a moment.

"John reported contact with two brigades only. He surmised that Longstreet was behind the attack, but he didn't see it. It could be a diversion. Lee hit us hard last night, and we gave him a bloody nose. Maybe he thinks he can't push us off this ground, so he's trying to scare us off instead. We start marching south, then he hits us, storming out from behind that ridge behind the town with us strung out on the roads. It could be that, you know."

Warren nodded in agreement. "But I don't think it is."

"Listen to me," Meade said coldly, "it's fine for all of you to guess, to think, but if I make one mistake, just one goddamn mistake, I can lose this war."

Don't make the right decision, and we can lose this war as well, Henry thought.

"A division," Meade finally said, "Fifth Corps. Crawford's men are rested. Get them on the road, Warren. You go with them. Henry, detach a couple of batteries from the reserve and send them along."

Warren was out the door in seconds.

Meade caught Henry's eye.

"You want me to go with them?" Henry asked. "If it's a fight for Taneytown, I should scout out the artillery positions."

Meade hesitated.

"My job here is done for the moment. All our guns are in position. I've surveyed the line from one end to the other twice. If we are going to shift south, I need to be down there."

"Go."

Henry followed Warren out the door, calling for a horse. Even as he mounted, the sound of guns, again from the right, thundered. Ignoring them, he spurred onto the road, orderly following, racing to catch up to Warren, who was already off at a gallop.

4:30 PM, July 2, 1863

Gettysburg — Herr's Ridge

General Lee reined in, turning to look back toward the seminary on the ridge to the east. The ground before it was still littered with dead Union soldiers and horses. It was a grim sight, the air thick with that sickly, cloying scent.

He pulled out his pocket watch . . . four-thirty.

If we had stayed here, it would be happening now, hitting them on both flanks, the wooded hill next to the cemetery, the place the locals called the Round Tops on the other flank. He had observed the strange movement down on the flank at noon, an entire Union corps advancing, and it had caused a heart-stopping moment. He had ordered a division from Hill's corps off the line of march, deploying them out in response behind the crest next to the tavern. And then, strangely, the movement had stopped, and they had turned about and marched back to the Round Tops.

Curious, some confusion in orders most likely. It had been a tempting moment though. If that corps, a scout reported it to be the Third, had stayed there, it would have been vulnerable on its left.

But no, this was no longer the place. That decision had already been made.

A deep rumbling, Stuart's light artillery continuing their demonstration to the flank of the wooded hill, hopefully fixing the attention of the Union forces. Doctrine always was to have cavalry securing the flank along the intended line of advance. One of

Ewell's divisions was still deployed in the open ground north of town, plainly visible, his other two divisions occupying the seminary and the ridge to the south, giving every indication possible that they were preparing to attack. Once darkness settled, they'd pull out, attempting to reach Fairfield before falling out to rest for several hours.

Pickett, who was still on the far side of the mountains, would move, along with the supply wagons, pulling back down the main road from Chambersburg to Greencastle. From there Pickett was to advance over the mountain and come into Emmitsburg, to fall in on the rear of Ewell tomorrow morning.

How far Longstreet had advanced, he wasn't sure. The last dispatch rider, coming in a half hour ago, reported fighting along the creek that bisected the road between Taneytown and Emmitsburg.

This was the vulnerable moment, one that if he contemplated it too much, would freeze up his nerves. Longstreet, with two divisions, might be as far as Taneytown. Hill, so sick he could barely keep in the saddle, was now on the road, the head of his column down to Emmitsburg, the last of the troops now streaming toward Fairfield. Ewell and Stuart were here, and Pickett was still twenty-five miles away.

We are spread out all over the map, and if now, at this moment, Meade should stir and come storming down from those hills, and at the same time dispatch a corps to move on Emmitsburg, the Army of Northern Virginia would be cut to ribbons.

How many times have I courted disaster like this? Chancellorsville, everyone talks about it now, the audacity of Jackson's march; but that was an act of desperation. The Second Manassas campaign, that was a calculated move; but I knew the character of Pope, the bitterness between him and McClellan, and acted accordingly. That was nearly a year ago. If someone on the other side realizes I'm doing it again, this time they just might strike first and catch me on the roads. McClellan almost achieved that last September when one of my couriers lost our campaign plan, and we barely got the army back together in time to stop the Union forces at Sharpsburg. That was so close I spent half the day thinking they might just break through and split our forces. Let's hope Pipe Creek doesn't turn into another Antietam Creek if Meade figures out what I am doing.

An artillery battery, one of Hill's units that had been in yesterday's fight and waited hours for the infantry to pass, came clattering in from a field on the north side of the pike, a staff officer leading the way, motioning for the gunners to start south. The artillerymen silently saluted as they passed; orders had been repeatedly given to all the men that there would be no demonstrations, no cheering.

"Going around 'em again, ain't we, General?" one of the gunners shouted as he rode by, astride the lead trace horse of a three-inch rifled piece.

Lee said nothing, just nodding in reply, and the man grinned, offering a proud, almost exaggerated salute.

"It's going smoothly," Walter Taylor offered.

"As long as they don't stir over there," Lee replied, nodding back toward Gettysburg.

"They won't."

"How do you know that?"

"They never have."

"Someday they just might," Lee said softly. "Remember, this army is all we have, Walter. It's got one more good fight in it, and we came too close to using up that fight here. I came too close. I realize now that I was trying to match our blood against the ground those people over there held.

"General Longstreet was right. But even if we seize the land south of here, and force those people over there to come at us, they will do it with a fury. We'll finally be between them and Washington, and the cost will be high. When that time comes, and it might be as early as tomorrow, It has to be decisive, not just another hollow victory."

He sighed, gaze still fixed back toward Gettysburg.

"Keep a sharp eye on things here, Walter. Ewell is in command on this front. I know that rankles Stuart, him being senior in rank, but he needs to be reined in a bit.

"If anything stirs, if the enemy starts to move on Ewell, send for me at once. If not, and once Ewell starts to pull out after dark, catch up to me; I will reach Taneytown tonight and make headquarters there."

"Sir, that's a long ride for you."

Lee fixed his adjutant with a cool gaze. "I'm not that old, Walter," Lee said softly.

Walter shifted uncomfortably. Ever since the "incident" back during the winter, which one doctor called trouble with the heart, Walter had increasingly taken on the role of monitoring how much rest Lee got and how long he spent in the saddle. There wasn't time for that now, even though Lee's stomach had been troublesome throughout the day.

"It's a wicked hot day, sir," Walter finally offered. "At least try and find a cool spot by a creek to take a few minutes."

"Walter."

"Sir?"

Lee sighed and then smiled. "Just keep an eye on things here. Make sure Ewell and Stuart keep fighting the enemy and not each other."

As if to add emphasis to Lee's words, the sound of artillery fire increased off beyond Gettysburg, Union guns along the brow of Cemetery Hill opening up, replying to the harassing fire from Stuart. What sounded like the rattle of musketry was added in as well.

Walter smiled and then offered a salute.

Lee, followed by the rest of his staff, edged down to the side of the road; and gently nudging Traveler to a trot, Lee started south, toward Emmitsburg, leaving Gettysburg behind.

6:00 PM, July 2, 1863

Taneytown

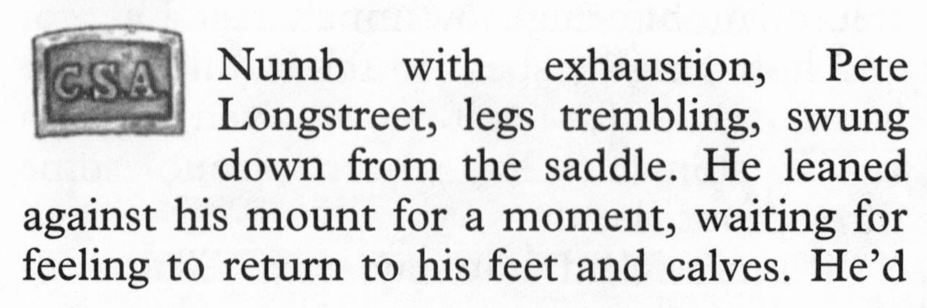

Numb with exhaustion, Pete Longstreet, legs trembling, swung down from the saddle. He leaned against his mount for a moment, waiting for feeling to return to his feet and calves. He'd been in the saddle for nearly fourteen hours, ridden over twenty-five miles, fought a battle, and been in the forefront of the pursuit of Buford's broken division. Several hundred prisoners had been rounded up on the road to Taneytown, men with blown horses that couldn't move another step.

The village was in utter chaos; dead horses littered the streets; skirmishing continued along the road to the east. Anderson's men, pushed far beyond the limit, were literally collapsing along the sidewalks. Behind them, the head of McLaws's division was coming into view. They had not been in the fight for the river crossing; but like everyone else, they had been on the road since before dawn, a long day's march in the July heat.

He finally stepped away from his horse, holding the reins, and walked slowly, grimacing as he stretched, shoulders and back aching. A staff officer came up, saluted, and said he had found a house they could use as headquarters. Pete nodded and followed the man down a bend in the road to a splendid-looking, two-story, Federalist-style mansion on the south side of town.

The lawn was torn up, bits of paper and horse droppings littering it, indicating that only a day ago a large number of troops had been here.

" 'The Antrim' locals call it," the staff

officer announced. "Nice place."

Pete nodded.

"Fine. Put someone on the main road so they can direct couriers. Send a dispatch back to General Lee telling him I am establishing headquarters here for the night."

"Then we're stopping here?" the officer asked.

Pete slowed, looking up at the captain. Hell of a day. We actually got around them. Buford's dead. Damn, John was a good man. His men, most of them, got out though, riding in every damn direction.

He sighed, coming to a stop, leaning against his horse for support.

Meade must know by now. That fight started around the bridge early in the afternoon. He must be sending something down here by now, perhaps a full corps. And to the east. Prisoners were saying there were a hell of a lot supplies already stockpiled at Westminster, but that was still another ten miles away.

We stop tonight. Meade could pull out, start moving down that road, maybe even get troops into Westminster by dawn.

Everything was so damn confusing. He was exhausted, needed food, needed to just relieve himself, to then sit and think.

"Get into that house; see if you can rustle up some food, a place to sit down; get the maps out. I want McLaws and

Hood in here, and see if one of our boys can find a few locals who are on our side."

The captain looked at him, confused.

"Well?"

"Which do you want me to do first, sir?"

"Let's start with the food." Pete sighed. "Now get moving."

The captain nodded and turned, trotting off, heading to the mansion still a hundred yards away, Pete walking stiffly, leading his exhausted mount.

He heard another rider coming up and, looking back, saw that it was McLaws, trailing a few staff officers, all of them covered in the white chalky dust kicked up from the crushed limestone paving of the road.

"My God, what a march," McLaws announced, taking off his hat and wiping the sweat from his brow.

Pete nodded, saying nothing.

"We camping here, sir? My boys are beat."

Pete stopped, lowering his head. That's what I should do, he realized. We're into their rear, a good march, in spite of the incident back at the bridge. But there's still Westminster. Meade might even be moving toward it now. If he gets there first, he can slip around our right and fall back to Washington without a fight . . . then what?

McLaws looked at him expectantly.

"Behind you? What's going on?"

"Hood's boys are blown, still forming up back at the bridge. A rider just came up reporting that the head of Hill's corps is just coming into Emmitsburg."

"Our corps artillery?"

"Between Emmitsburg and the bridge."

Pete looked back up at McLaws. "My men did over twenty-five miles, general. Even old Jack would be proud of what we did today."

That rankled him slightly. Always it was Old Jack.

He exhaled noisily, looking back down at the ground, kicking at the dust. "One hour here. Get your men fed, get water. Then I want you back on the road."

"Sir?"

"On the road. It'll cool off a bit at dusk. On the road by dusk. You should have good moonlight. I want you to push to Westminster."

"Sir, that's kinda risky to my way of thinking."

"Go on."

"Hood here. Me heading off to God knows where? Sir, I'll bet at least ten percent of my men are dropped somewhere between here and Emmitsburg. You push us through the night, and I won't have a thousand left standing under their colors come dawn."

"I don't push you now, and we have to attack there tomorrow, you won't have a thousand left come sunset," Pete whispered. "It's the good ground. It's always about the good ground. Who gets it first, holds it, and makes the other man attack. I'd rather have your men half-dead from exhaustion, than dead forever up here in Maryland."

McLaws lowered his head. "What about the road north of here, the one going straight to Gettysburg."

"There's nothing on it yet. As Hood comes up, I'll have him cover that approach."

"Three hours, at least give 'em that. Chance to cook up a decent meal, find clean water, sleep a little bit."

Pete shook his head. "Give 'em three hours, and they'll stiffen up and be useless. An hour then march. I want you on the road by dusk."

"Why then?"

"I want those retreating Yankee cavalry to see you. I don't know what they have in Westminster, but I'm willing to bet it will be like Second Manassas, maybe a couple of good regiments, but the rest of 'em units assigned to guard detail because their commanders feel they can spare them. Hell, we do the same thing. We pick the unit we feel is used up or can't be relied on anymore to guard the wagon trains. It'll be a scratch command down there, and it will fall apart the moment you push it.

"You on the road, heading straight at them" — Pete forced a smile — "it just might spook them."

"And suppose those Yankee cavalry are waiting?"

"You'll have a hundred or so mounted in front to feel out any traps. But I think they're played out. John Buford is dead."

"Damn," McLaws whispered. "I didn't know that."

"You marched past his body back at the bridge. We captured Gamble; looks like he'll lose an arm. The fight is out of them. They'll give back, falling into Westminster, and, General, I want you in there by dawn."

McLaws finally nodded in agreement.

"Good. My headquarters will be here until General Lee comes up. I'll try and come up to you in the morning. Take the town; block the roads coming down from the north."

"The north?"

"That road that heads north, goes straight through the village of Harney and then on to Gettysburg. Apparently a fair part of the Union army moved up it yesterday. They just might turn around and come straight back down. If so, Hood will have to block it until the rest of the army comes in and can be passed along to you. So until that happens, you sir, will be the lead on the right, while Hood holds the center here.

"Sooner or later Meade will wake up. And when he does, General, I want you on there, dug in and ready."

McLaws saluted and started to turn.

"They just might be on the edge of a panic," Longstreet said. "If so, fuel it, get them running. Get them running."

7:45 PM, July 2, 1863

Taneytown-Harney Road,
Three Miles North of Taneytown

He let his horse gulp down water for a minute, dismounting with Warren, kneeling down into the cool stream to splash his face with water, then taking a canteen, filling it, and half draining it.

Even as he did so, Henry looked around warily. It was the same place he had stopped only the day before, riding north to Gettysburg. He knew that for certain because the dead trooper, who had been in the back of the ambulance when he had stopped here on the way to Gettysburg, was lying by the side of the stream. He tried not to notice him, though the scent of his body hung heavy in the evening air.

They had begun to pass cavalrymen from Buford's command a half hour ago, small scattered detachments from half a dozen regiments, the men moving slowly, dejected, talking of a terrible fight along the road half a dozen miles away. He had let most of them go, telling them to stay the hell off the road and let the infantry pass. A dozen or so, who still seemed game, he had drafted as an escort. The men were on the far side of the creek, obviously nervous, carbines unsheathed.

A broken unit always made a minor setback sound like a defeat and a defeat a disastrous rout. These men were talking about thousands of Rebs. Whether it was true or not, he sensed they'd know in a few more minutes, and his gut instinct was to be ready.

Standing up, he pulled out his revolver, half-cocked it, checked the spin, making sure percussion caps were in place, then gently let the hammer back down. He mounted, looking over at Warren, who was already mounted and waiting.

He followed Warren's lead, splashing up the opposite bank. The waiting troopers, led by a grim-faced lieutenant with a cheek laid open by a shell fragment or bullet, spread out as they went down the road. They were very good, moving cautiously, a couple of men on the road, the rest filtering into the trees, meadows, and cornfields to either side of the lane. Several of them would move forward a hundred yards, pause, look around, then motion the rest up, who would leapfrog forward. And then the ritual would be repeated again.

Twilight was setting in, the western sky a dull, shimmering red, a dark, haze-shrouded sun slipping below the horizon; flashes of heat lightning, or was it gunfire, sparkled to the east.

They reached a broad, open plateau. Henry remembered it. Taneytown was just a mile or so off. The lead trooper out ahead stopped, leaned forward slightly, then held his hand up.

Henry nudged his mount, the poor beast breathing hard as it slowly went up to a trot, Warren by his side. They came up to the trooper's side. The lieutenant already had his field glasses out. Henry looked over at him in the twilight. The glasses were high quality, beautiful brass trim work, the man dressed in what was obviously a tailored uniform. Dandy or not, he at least was here rather than safely back home in some countinghouse or law office in New York, angry about the retreat, glad to have fallen in with someone from headquarters who wanted to find out what the hell was going on.

"There, sir," the lieutenant whispered, and he pointed, even as he passed over his field glasses.

There was no need for them though. Clouds of dust were boiling up from a road, most likely the main pike between Taneytown and Emmitsburg. In the fields north of town hundreds of campfires sparkled, troops swarming around them.

Far closer though, not a quarter mile away, a skirmish line of Reb infantry was deployed, advancing toward them.

A flash of gunfire, the report of the rifle echoing even as a bullet hummed overhead.

"Infantry, lots of it," Warren announced.

"As we told you," the lieutenant replied, a bit of a sarcastic edge to his voice.

"Son, we had to see it for ourselves," Warren replied soothingly. "Those were Meade's orders. I never doubted you."

A couple of the troopers escorting them dismounted. Drawing his Sharps carbine, one of the troopers levered up his rear sight, squatted down in the middle of the road, and took careful aim.

"Not yet," Henry said.

Annoyed, the man looked up at him.

It was getting dark, but the field glasses revealed a lot. Troops were marching through the town, visible through side alleys and where the road they were on finally intersected with the main road in the middle of the village. He caught a glimpse of what looked to be a field piece crossing the intersection.

Another bullet snicked past and then another, this one kicking up a plume of dust in the middle of the road, Warren's horse snorting and backing up.

"Damn it, sir, they're getting close," the lieutenant announced.

"Open up on them," Henry replied.

The trooper sitting in the middle of the road fired first, followed a few seconds later by several more, one of the men catching Henry's eye, silhouetted by the western twilight, poised in the saddle, horse absolutely still as the man took careful aim, a bright flash of light erupting as he squeezed the trigger. He watched for several seconds, cursed under his breath, and then levered the breech open, reaching into his cartridge box for another round.

"A division at least," Warren said, "and looks like they're continuing east, toward Westminster."

"Can't see their colors though," Henry replied. He looked back to the lieutenant. "You said you were fighting Hood?"

"Yes, sir. We caught a couple of them

before we got flanked. It was Hood's division."

"Wonder if that's them in the town?" Warren muttered.

"You want me to go down and ask?" the lieutenant interjected.

Henry looked over at him. The youth wasn't being sarcastic; he was trying to make a joke, and Henry nodded.

"It's more than Hood," Henry offered. "The battle with you at the river was mid-afternoon. Take a couple of hours to get everyone reorganized and on the road. What's down there now is the next division, pushed through, continuing on. Hood will come up later. Or maybe the next division has already moved on, and that's Hood coming in to occupy Taneytown."

"We're being flanked," Warren interjected. "By God, he's done it to us again. Longstreet's corps, and I'm willing to bet Hill is right behind him. Back at Gettysburg Ewell is just demonstrating to keep our attention. As soon as it gets dark, he'll pull out as well."

"I could have told you three hours ago we were facing the head of their army," the lieutenant offered, and this time there was a bitterness to his voice. "Just like yesterday, but we didn't have Reynolds this time to come in as support. Damn, if we'd had the ammunition, a brigade of infantry, and a couple of batteries, we could have held that bridge till hell froze over."

The skirmishing was picking up. A ball slapped dangerously close, passing between Henry and Warren.

Warren turned his horse.

"The line we surveyed yesterday, Henry. Do you think they know about it?"

"If not, Longstreet will figure it out real quick. He has a damn good eye for ground."

"I'm figuring the same."

"Lieutenant, pull back slowly, keep an eye on things. You've got a division of infantry coming up. They should be approaching in another hour or so. I'll tell them to deploy on the far side of the creek, but there isn't anything they can do tonight. You help them get a feel for things. General Hunt and I are going back to headquarters."

"I got maybe a hundred rounds left for the men with me," the lieutenant replied.

"Then use them wisely," Warren replied.

The two started off, moving at not much more than a steady trot.

"Do you think Meade's already moving?" Henry asked. "By God, if they're advancing on Westminster, we've got to get troops in there by dawn."

"Sedgwick just marched his entire corps up from there, thirty miles straight. If he pulled the rest of Fifth off the line while we were coming down here, he just might make it by dawn."

"Do you think he did that?"

Warren said nothing.

As they crossed back over the stream, Henry looked again at the dead trooper lying in the shadows. He wondered if someone would finally get around to burying him. Behind them, the lieutenant, with a dozen men and a hundred rounds, slowly gave ground in the opening shots of the battle for Taneytown.

11:00 PM, July 2, 1863

Westminster

"Are you certain about this, Major?"

Gen. Hermann Haupt, commander of the U.S. Military Railroads, looked up at the begrimed officer standing before him. The flickering of the coal oil lamp hanging from the ceiling of the tavern made the cavalryman look deathly pale.

"I'm certain of it, sir. There's Confederate infantry on the road not five miles from here. I saw them with my own eyes. Column of infantry, moving slow but moving, skirmishers deployed forward. I was up in a barn about a hundred yards off the road. We'd pulled in there to look for some fodder for our horses and rest a bit. Next thing I know, the road is swarming with Rebs."

"A brigade, a division, a corps?"

"I didn't stay around to count them, sir. I took my men and we got the hell out of there."

Haupt nodded, looking back down at the map traced on a scrap a paper spread out on the bar.

The first word that trouble was brewing had come in just before six, a lone trooper, absolutely panic-stricken, riding down the main street shouting that the Rebs were coming. He had the man arrested, given a drink to calm him down, and the shaken boy claimed that there had been a vicious fight west of Taneytown. Buford was dead, Gamble dead, and the entire division routed.

By eight, more troopers were coming in, enough information forming that Haupt had finally sent a dispatch rider back to Baltimore bearing a report that there had been an action of at least division-level strength. He then called an officers' meeting, which had proven to be chaotic. There was no real system of unified command here, with units from seven different corps assigned to guard duty. He had over ten thousand men here, including the heavy artillery units sent up from Washington, but each of them answered to a different commander; and they were not all that enthusiastic about taking orders from him, an unknown. Several of the regimental commanders openly called for an immediate evacuation. The meeting ended with him ordering them to get their troops ready for a fight and deploy to the west side of town.

Now more and more defeated cavalry troopers were coming in, singly, in small bands, and this major with a hundred or so men.

He looked out the window and could feel the beginnings of panic. Civilians were again out in the street; men were gathered in small knots talking, obviously agitated. It wasn't looking good.

Until this hit, everything had been going according to plan. The third convoy of trains had come up early in the evening, been unloaded, and sent back. Another convoy was due at two in the morning. So far he had unloaded over fifty carloads of rations, rifle and artillery ammunition, shoes, medical supplies, including dozens of oversized hospital tents. Wood was stockpiled, the bucket brigade to water the engines was working, and several hundred laborers had built a fairly adequate platform for unloading and half a dozen roughshod, open-sided sheds to store ammunition and rations.

Now what?

I have no orders to evacuate. In fact, I can't. If I do that, it will leave the army dangling twenty-five miles away at Gettysburg, cut off, with only the supplies in their haversacks and the field ammunition trains to support them. I've got nearly five thousand wagons here, waiting to start the convoying of supplies up to the front, once the order is given. Try to pull those out now in the middle of the night and it will trigger a panic.

He looked back down at the map. Lose this and the army is cut off. He looked back up at the major. "Get some rest, but report back to me at dawn."

"Where, sir?"

"Why here of course."

"Didn't you hear me, sir? You got Rebs, thousands of them, not three hours' march away."

"I know that. I believe your report."

"And what's to stop them?"

"You, Major, for one. The troops I have here in town. Besides, Meade will have a corps down here by morning."

"Really?"

"Of course."

He fixed the major with his best poker gaze. He had sent two dispatches up to

Meade this evening, the last one going out an hour ago with the report that Westminster was threatened. All that had come back so far were reports dated from late in the afternoon, reporting back to the War Department, routine dispatches that said precious little other than that Lee seemed to be skirmishing but not yet fully attacking at Gettysburg.

He could only hope that by now Meade had stirred himself and was sending something down this way by force march. But to say anything different . . . not now.

The major nodded and wearily left the tavern. Henry watched him go, then called for an orderly to go back out and round up all the unit commanders yet again. Troops had to be deployed, dug in, streets barricaded, supply wagons moved to the east side of town.

Even as he started to give orders, the cavalry major was back out on the street, getting on his mount. A sergeant, holding the bridle, looked up. "So what did he say, Major?"

"Darn fool plans to defend the town rather than evacuate."

"Our orders, sir?"

"Find a place to camp. We report to him at dawn."

"Shit, sir. The whole Reb army will be here by morning."

"I know, Sergeant. Let's get the men rested, then find some ammunition. There's gonna be one hell of a battle here come dawn."

"For what? So we can get killed come dawn? Goddamn generals have done it to us again."

"Enough, Sergeant. Enough."

The two rode off.

Dick Hansen, a mule driver with Third Corps, his wagon loaded with thirty boxes of .58-cal. rifle cartridges, was leaning against the side of the tavern soaking up every word. He had slipped into town after dark, dodging around the provost guards and laborers, looking for a drink, just a single damn drink. It had been three long days since he had tasted a drop. The tavern, of course, had been a draw, even though such places were always lousy with officers. And now this.

Rumors had been drifting through the vast wagon parks since midafternoon. Meade was dead, the army defeated yet again; then someone reported he had climbed a church steeple and seen smoke off to the west. Now those cavalry boys riding in, all lathered up, scared half to death.

So now he knew . . . and he'd be damned if he got killed just because some goddamn general wanted to make a name for himself. He'd seen battle once, at Fair Oaks. The humiliation of being drummed through the camp, the sign declaring that he was a coward hung around his neck, the taunts of the bastards for his having excused himself from certain suicide by running away, didn't bother him all that much. Let them get killed. In fact, he later heard most of them *had* gotten killed at Antietam.

Lousy bastards deserved it. Service with the supply trains, which his captain had sent him to, that's where a man of intelligence should be anyhow. Good rations in the wagons, always a chance for a bottle, even for the girls who trailed along behind the army, though such pleasures did eat up most of the pay of twelve damn greenbacks a month.

And twelve dollars a month wasn't enough to stay here. Not with those wolves coming this way. He'd seen them once, not much better than animals the way the Rebs came charging in. And by God, that's what they would do here come dawn.

Dick Hansen slipped away into the dark, dodging through back alleyways, finally reaching his wagon. The mules, stinking lousy beasts, were hitched up. Let the others unhitch theirs, but not

Dick Hansen. Something told him it was going to get hot, so he had left them in their harnesses throughout the day, ready to go at a moment's notice.

He climbed up onto the rough seat and untied the reins.

"Come on, you sons of bitches," he hissed.

"Hey, Hansen, what the hell are you doing?"

It was Ben Fredericks, another driver with First Corps, his wagon parked next to Dick's. Ben, sleepy-eyed, was peeking out from the tailgate.

"We're ordered back to Baltimore," Dick announced.

"What?"

"Whole goddamn rebel army is coming this way!" Dick shouted. "I was down at headquarters. Orders are coming out now for us to get the hell outta here."

"What the hell you say, Hansen?"

Shit. It was Sergeant Vernon, supposedly in charge of their detachment, coming out from behind his wagon parked behind Fredericks's.

"You heard me, Sergeant. A whole rebel corps is marching right this way."

"From where, damn it?"

"That road going west. Taneytown, I heard. They've licked the army, and we're ordered out of here."

"I ain't heard nothing."

"Well, you just heard it from me, Sarge, and I'm following orders!

"Come on, you sons of bitches!"

He cracked the whip over the ears of the lead mule, and the six whip-scarred beasts lurched forward, squeezing between two parked wagons, heading out across the field, weaving their way around hundreds of other wagons.

"What the hell are you doing?"

The cry echoed and reechoed across the field.

"Army's beat, Rebs are coming here by dawn, and we're pulling back to Baltimore. You all better get moving right now!"

And the panic began.

11:30 PM, July 2, 1863

The Antrim, Taneytown

"General Longstreet, it's General Lee."

Sprawled out on a sofa in the front parlor, Longstreet came awake. Someone had draped a comforter over his body, and he pushed it back. Embarrassed, he sat up.

I wasn't supposed to do this, Pete

thought. Not with men still on the march. All he could remember was coming into the house, speaking to the owner for a moment, assuring him that his property would be respected and all that was needed was the parlor.

He had sat down, just to take a moment to collect his thoughts.

"How long have I been asleep?" Pete asked.

"About four hours, sir. We kind of figured you needed a bit of a rest."

"You shouldn't have done that."

"Sir, you needed it."

It was Alexander, his young acting chief of corps artillery, leaning against a table brought into the middle of the parlor, several of his staff gathered around the maps spread out on it. There was the smell of coffee in the air and fresh baked bread.

"Good hosts," Alexander said, coming over, offering Longstreet a fine china cup filled to the brim with coffee and a piece of buttered bread.

Pete nodded thanks, drank down a mouthful of the scalding brew, and then consumed the bread.

"Where's General Lee?"

"He's in the town, sir. Someone just rode in to report. I sent an orderly up to guide him here."

Pete nodded, standing up, suppressing a

groan from the ache in his back and lower legs.

"What happened while I was asleep?" Pete asked.

"Nothing to worry about, sir. A rider came in from McLaws about a half hour ago. He's halfway to Westminster, reports no resistance. Hood's division is here; they're deployed out north of town blocking the road from Gettysburg. A bit of skirmishing there a couple of hours ago, a few cavalry stragglers. A report that some Yankee infantry is on that road on the other side of a creek a couple of miles north of town."

"Infantry? How much. Who?"

"Not sure, sir. It was dark. But they're there."

"Hill?"

"Head of his column is coming in now. Pettigrew, he's commanding Heth's division. They're filling in on the right of Hood and going into camp. Pender is behind them."

A commotion outside stilled their conversation. Pete looked out the window. It was General Lee, staff trailing behind him, dismounting.

Pete stepped out of the parlor. The wide double doors of the mansion were open, torchlight outside casting a warm light on Lee, who stiffly dismounted, patting Traveler on the neck before letting an orderly take his beloved mount away.

Pete went out onto the porch and saluted as Lee ever so slowly came up the steps.

"General, it does my heart good to see you," Lee said.

The way he said it caused a flood of emotion inside of Pete. He had always respected Lee, admired his audacity, even though he had not agreed, at times, with how that audacity was played out. But the way he said, "It does my heart good," touched him. He knew it was real.

Pete extended his hand, helping Lee up the last step. The clasp held for a second. Lee, several inches shorter, looked up into Pete's eyes. "You should be proud, sir, in fact the entire South will be proud of what your boys did today."

"You were the one who gave the orders," Pete replied, suddenly embarrassed.

"A day ago, at just about this time, I was ready to attack at Gettysburg yet again. I realized, though, that your words, your advice, were correct. If ever someone writes a history of this army, they will cite this march as one of the great feats of this war, sir."

"Ewell and Stuart?" Pete asked, features red, wishing to change the subject.

"I received a report an hour ago from

Taylor. Two of Ewell's divisions were on the road after dark. The last is to pull out by midnight. Stuart will stay in the Gettysburg area through tomorrow, demonstrating to their front and right."

"We need to concentrate our army now, sir," Longstreet said. "We are in a dangerous position at the moment. Those people are concentrated and rested. We are strung out yet along thirty miles of road and tired. We must bring everything together tomorrow."

As they spoke, the two walked into the parlor, Pete's staff respectfully coming to attention. Lee gazed at the map for a moment, nodding approvingly, asking about the Union deployment north of Taneytown and the latest report from McLaws.

Finally he went over to the sofa that Longstreet had been dozing on and sat down.

Nothing needed to be said. The staff withdrew out into the corridor, the last man out extinguishing the coal-oil lamp on the table. Before they had even closed the door, General Lee was asleep.

The men looked at Pete, and he could see they were gazing at him in "that way," the look usually reserved for Lee or for Old Jack.

Longstreet nervously cleared his throat and walked back out on to the veranda.

Fishing in his breast pocket, he pulled out a cigar and struck a Lucifer, puffing the cigar, exhaling softly.

The almost full moon was high in the Southern sky. It was a good night, a very good night.

11:45 PM, July 2, 1863

Headquarters, Army of the Potomac
Gettysburg

"We move starting at four in the morning," Meade repeated, looking up bleary-eyed at Henry and Warren.

"But, sir, by then they'll be in Westminster."

"I just got the latest dispatch from there sent up by Haupt. It gives no indication of that, other than some cavalry from Buford drifting in, reporting the action at Monocacy Creek."

"And that dispatch was dated three hours ago, about the same time we were in front of Taneytown. A lot can happen in those three hours."

Meade sat back in his chair, taking another sip of coffee. "Sedgwick's men are in no shape to march. They covered damn near thirty-five miles today. The only other unit in reserve is Fifth Corps. I've already dispatched one division; the other two will join them by seven in the morning.

"We're leaving First and Eleventh here. They're fought out anyhow, and besides, there're over five thousand wounded here to cover. And someone has to watch Stuart and Ewell, our own cavalry is in such disarray. That leaves Second, Third, and Twelfth Corps, which I'm sending down the Baltimore Pike toward Westminster, and they have to be pulled off the line and shifted over. Try to do that in the middle of the night, and it will be chaos."

He looked down again at the map. "No, no, we try to move them now, they'll be exhausted come dawn and not more than five miles on the road anyhow, with twenty more to go. Let them rest; they'll need it."

Henry could almost feel a sense of pity for this man. He knew that something inside was tearing at him, the realization that if he had reacted immediately, when that first courier had come in, an entire corps could already be approaching Westminster, with Fifth Corps hitting Taneytown.

What would history say of those lost six hours? Wasted, wasted on a damn staff meeting that had dragged on for over two hours of bitter arguing. One of Hancock's orderlies had filled him in on it. Hancock shouting that they should move now, Sickles arguing that his corps should storm straight across that ridge he had been obsessed with all day, Howard saying it was a trap for them to stay put, and Sedgwick so exhausted he had fallen asleep in the corner.

By the end of the meeting, a couple of dozen stragglers from Buford had come in, grim evidence of what was going on to the south. At that point it was already getting dark, and yet, in spite of the evidence, Howard kept pointing to Seminary Ridge, the hundreds of campfires flaring to life, and there had been more hesitation.

Finally he had decided, at nine, that the army would move, its primary axis dropping back on Westminster, with a secondary thrust toward Taneytown, but to do so at first light. Seventy-five thousand men, hundreds of wagons, over two hundred artillery pieces were concentrated on just a few square miles of ground. Moving that in the dark would be madness; starting it six hours ago, it could have been done.

And those six hours were gone forever, wasted, and Meade knew it.

"If they take Westminster, we're cut off from Washington," Meade whispered. "They'll go insane down there. Halleck, Stanton, the president, all of them will be screaming for me to attack."

"Lee won't turn on Washington," Warren offered, "not with us in his rear.

He'll have to face us."

"Will he?"

"He wouldn't dare make that move. We've still got over twenty thousand troops garrisoned in Washington behind the heaviest fortification system in the world. He'd never go up against that, not with us coming down behind him."

"So he'll dig in along Westminster?" Meade asked.

The tone caught Henry off guard. He was not used to Meade asking for advice, for support. He was obviously rattled, ready to drop with exhaustion, suddenly frightened by the prospect of all that was unfolding. It frightened Henry. That kind of mood is contagious. It starts with the commander, and then spreads like a plague down the line. It was like that at Chancellorsville and at Second Manassas, the last hours when Pope fell into a panic.

"It's a tough position," Henry offered. "There're two things to hope for though."

"And that is?"

"Get there fast, sir. They most likely will attack Westminster by dawn."

Meade lowered his head.

"Hermann Haupt is in command down there," Warren offered. "He's got somewhere around ten thousand men. He might very well put up a hell of a fight. If he does and the lead column pushes hard enough, it can still be retrieved."

"Put Hancock in the lead," Henry offered. "His troops are almost astride the Baltimore Road. Get them moving now."

"That will leave the center open," Meade replied.

"It's no longer the center," Warren responded forcefully. "Put Hancock on the road now, then Sickles as planned, followed by Twelfth Corps; Sixth in reserve ready to move either toward Westminster or Taneytown. The Fifth hits Taneytown, perhaps severing their line of advance."

"And if Haupt can't hold Westminster?"

"The second hope," Henry interjected, "is that if they have taken Westminster; it will most likely only be a division at most. They'll be exhausted, troops strung out from Emmitsburg to Westminster, with the head at Westminster. They might not have time to survey the ground up around Pipe Creek. Hancock forces the creek and deploys. We cut off their head at Westminster. We'll then be astride our base of supplies, with Lee strung out. We then start pushing west, rolling him up, and meeting the Fifth Corps in Taneytown."

"You think we can do that?"

Meade was indeed exhausted, Henry realized. No sleep for two days, suddenly overwhelmed by the full realization that

Lee had again done the unexpected. He needed sleep.

I do too, Henry thought. I can barely stand.

Worn down and demoralized, Meade could only nod.

"Fine then. All right, send someone up to Hancock. It's almost midnight now. Tell him I want his corps to quietly pack it up, to start moving at two in the morning. Tell Howard to then detach a brigade, push them down to fill in along Hancock's line."

Warren and Hunt looked at each other. They'd won their point.

"Get some sleep, sir," Warren offered.

There was no need to give the advice though. Meade's head was resting on the table. He was out.

The two stepped out onto the porch and spotted a young orderly sitting on the steps. It was Meade's son, new to the staff.

"Your father," Henry said softly, "get him into bed and make sure he gets at least four hours' rest."

The boy, who had been dozing, came awake, nodded, and went inside.

Henry pulled out his watch. By the light of the moon, he could read it . . . midnight.

"I'll take the orders up to Hancock," Warren offered. "Get some sleep, Henry. Tomorrow's going to be a tough day."

Henry didn't need to be told. He stepped off the porch. His orderly had unsaddled Henry's horse and spread out a blanket, the saddle as a pillow.

Henry nodded his thanks and collapsed on the ground.

The last minutes of July 2, 1863, ticked down for Henry; and in a few minutes he was fast asleep, falling into an exhausted, dreamless sleep.

11:50 PM, July 2, 1863

Near Taneytown

John Williamson sat down on the cool, damp ground with a stifled groan, leaning back against the trunk of an ancient oak. The campfires around him were beginning to flicker down. The men had been given a few hours to cook a hurried dinner, a short rest, and then orders to be ready to march long before dawn.

Hazner was by his side, curled up on the bare ground, a tattered quilt his blanket, haversack a pillow. He was snoring away contentedly, and John envied him his oblivion.

The march had been grueling, John and Hazner assigned to the rear of the regimental column to prod the men along, and when necessary to sign off permission for men too exhausted, or sick, to fall out of the line of march. Between yesterday's battle and the stragglers, the regiment was down to less than half of what it had been only three days ago.

He tried to close his eyes, to sleep as Hazner did, but couldn't. Finally he reached into his haversack and pulled out a small leather-bound volume. Elizabeth had given it to him on the day he left for the war, and the mere touch of it made him smile, remembering how she had kissed the book before handing it to him, asking him to write often, that it would be the way in which they could still touch each other. She had fancied him to be a writer, and the thought of it made him smile. She who loved Scott, Hugo, and Dickens fancied that perhaps he would become such as well.

He opened the volume up and skimmed through it. The first months of his journal were filled with pages of neatly written notes, vignettes when the world still seemed so young and innocent . . . a snowfall in camp and how the boys from the hot bottomlands of Carolina had frolicked . . . the first shock of battle before Richmond . . . the strange night after Fredericksburg when the Northern Lights appeared — a sign of the Norse gods gathering in the souls of the slain — and then long weeks of nothing, just blank pages.

He fumbled for a pencil in his haversack and rested the volume in his lap, looking off across the fields, the shadows of men covering the ground, the warm, pleasant smell of wood smoke and coffee, so reminiscent of a world of long ago.

"My dearest Elizabeth," he wrote, hesitated, then scratched the line out. No, this is just for myself.

"I am in Maryland tonight," he began again, now writing for himself. "At least I think that is where we are. It gets confusing at times with all the marching. A long one today, twenty miles or more. Tomorrow there will be another fight; if not tomorrow, then the day after.

"Why I am here I can no longer say with any certainty. There was a time, long ago, when I believed, but in what I can no longer say. All I long for is for this to end, to go home, and to somehow leave behind all that I have seen, to forget all that I have felt. I feel a shadow walking beside me, filling my nights with coldness. If I live, perhaps there will be a day when we will speak of these times with pride, but will I be there? And if not, what will be then said of me? What will you say, Elizabeth, if I do not return? Will you remember me? Will you wait for me across the long years of your life, or will memory fade and one day you will seek warmth, seek love with another?"

He stopped for a moment, pencil raised, ready to scratch out the last line. What if I die, and she reads that?

No, let her. Fine for others to hide their fears with noble sentiments, but this is my life, the only one I shall ever have. There is no romance in this agony, and those who speak of glory rarely have seen the truth of it.

He looked back down at the page.

"I wish I could fool myself into believing that what I do matters," he wrote. "But does it? Why did this war have to come into my life? Why now? Elizabeth, I would trade, in an instant, all of this for just a day, a night, as it once was, as it should have been for us. I care not for what others speak of, of all the things we now say caused this war. I just long to go home . . . but I cannot . . . and I fear I never will.

"I just want to live. If I should survive this, all I ask is for you to stay by my side, for us to grow old together in peace."

"Writing in that book again, sir?"

John nervously looked up. It was Hazner, half sitting up, looking over at him. John hurriedly closed the book.

"Yeah."

"Ruin your eyes, John, writing by moonlight."

John laughed shyly but said nothing.

"Writing to her?"

"Not really."
"Why don't you get some rest, Major. We're goin' to need it come morning."
"Can't get to sleep."
George sat up, stretched, and looked around. "Everything quiet?"
"Yup."
"John, you shouldn't think so much."
"Can't help it."
"Like I always said, if your name's on the bullet, your name's on the bullet. Nothing can change that."
"Wish I had your Presbyterian view of life."
"What? You know I'm Baptist."
John laughed softly and shook his head.
George grinned softly.
"Do you think we'll ever get home?" John asked, and then instantly regretted the question. Though they had been friends since childhood, still, out here the social division between officer and sergeant should have stopped him from ever asking that. And yet, though surrounded by these thousands of men, never had he felt so lonely and haunted.
"I guess most soldiers wonder that," George offered. "Even them fellas that marched with Pharaoh against Moses, as you read about in the Bible. Just before they got to the Red Sea, I bet one of them asked the man next to him, 'Hey, think

we'll get home for dinner tonight after killing that Moses?' "

George laughed softly at his own joke. "Worrying ain't gonna change it."

John said nothing, but he could not help but wonder, were they indeed like Pharoah's army? Was God, and dare he think it, if there is a God, does He stand against us or with us. John stuffed the book back into his haversack and slid down, resting his head against a root of the oak tree.

"Something changed today. I could of sworn we'd go straight into that town," John whispered. "I wonder about that. How a general looks at a map, ponders on it, then says, 'No, let us go here rather than there.' You could sense that from Walter Taylor. I wonder if that means that you and I will now live, or . . ." His question trailed off.

"We're here, John. Just let it go at that. You did good yesterday. I heard the men talking about it."

"About what?"

"How you led that charge. They believe in you."

"Do you?"

George chuckled. "Course I do; otherwise I wouldn't scrounge up coffee and borrow money from you. Of course I do. Just that you think too much at times."

John was silent for a moment. "George,

if something does happen to me."

"I know," George whispered, "but it won't. I got a feeling for these things. You'll go home when this is done. Be a judge like your poppa, maybe even a congressman someday, and have lots of children."

John looked at the cold, uncaring heavens. To think of that dream was too painful to bear, and he pushed it away. He wanted to say more, but a moment later he heard Hazner snoring. His friend had drifted back off.

Alone, John looked at the low-hanging moon as it crossed the midnight sky.

Chapter Twelve

4:15 AM, July 3, 1863

Taneytown, Antrim

"General Longstreet." A hand was on his shoulder, shaking him awake. He opened his eyes, disoriented for a moment. It was Alexander, his artillery chief.

"General Lee is awake. He wants you, sir."

Pete sat up on the blanket that he had spread out on the floor and stood up, stockinged feet hitting the cool, polished wood. All was quiet in the house, the pale glow of moonlight shining in through the high windows, casting soft blue shadows across the room.

Alexander motioned toward the parlor, across the hallway, where the gentle glow of a coal-oil lamp flickered. Whispered voices echoed. Leaving his corner of the dining room, where he had fallen asleep on the floor, Longstreet stepped out into the main corridor that ran down the length of the house. A dozen or more men were sprawled out, several snoring loudly. A private quietly tiptoed down the hallway, carrying an empty coffeepot, heading to the kitchen.

The old man had a firm and fast rule. If they occupied a house, try not to intrude too much. The upstairs was off-limits, the fine feathered beds being used even now by the owner and his family. It was amazing the number of men in the house, the hundred or more camped outside, and how quiet it was. The sleep of exhaustion, Pete realized. How the old man had the energy to be up now was beyond him. He pulled out his pocket watch and flipped it open. By the reflected moonlight, he saw it was a little after four. Lee had grabbed only three or four hours at most.

He ran a hand through his hair and half buttoned his uniform jacket. His mouth felt gummy, sour tasting. How long since I bathed? He couldn't remember. A cool stream, a bar of soap, how nice that would be right now. And fresh clothes, a white boiled shirt, clean socks. God, how I must smell. He had left his boots back in the room, thought about putting them on, and then decided not to.

He crossed over to the parlor.

Lee, jacket off, shirtsleeves rolled up, was leaning over a table, map spread out. Walter Taylor was with him and several staff. They looked up at Pete, and he could see the exhaustion in their eyes.

"You sent for me, General?" Pete asked. "What is it? Problems with Ewell?" and he looked over at Taylor. The young man was obviously on the point of collapse, and Pete sensed he had just come in from Gettysburg.

"No, sir," Taylor replied. "I left Gettysburg a little after ten at night. The last of Ewell's divisions, Johnson's, was starting to file onto the road. Stuart was demonstrating hard, and the Yankees still seemed to be in place."

"Then what is it?"

"A courier just came in from McLaws," Lee announced. "They've yet to take Westminster. He's stopped on the outskirts."

Pete said nothing.

"I understand you ordered him to take the town by dawn."

"Yes, sir, I did. If he stopped, there must be a reason."

"The courier from McLaws reports that a civilian came into McLaws's lines from Union Mills." As he spoke, he pointed to the map, and Pete leaned over to study the position.

"This civilian's report, we have to give it the most serious consideration," Lee reported. "He claimed Stuart slept in his house on June thirtieth and agreed to stay in our camp, under guard, until Stuart would verify his veracity. He claims Sedgwick's entire corps force-marched through, heading to Gettysburg on the morning of the second."

"That's good news at least," Pete offered. "It means Sedgwick must have marched twenty, maybe even thirty miles yesterday. His men are exhausted and now in Gettysburg. That accounts for all their corps."

"But Hancock is moving back down the road to Westminster," Lee replied.

Pete nodded.

"We had to expect they'd move sometime."

"I was hoping for eight to twelve more hours, but then again we were lucky to get this far without interference."

"Meade is no Burnside or McClellan," Pete said. "He's cautious, but he will react correctly once he's sure of the threat."

"This civilian reports that a courier came into Union Mills shortly after one in the morning. He reined in, asked for directions, and this civilian claims that he overhead the courier saying that the Union army was pulling back from Gettysburg, with Hancock in the lead, heading toward Westminster."

Pete nodded. It usually wasn't like Lee to kick up a fuss over the report of a lone civilian, especially one who was not a Virginian. But at this moment, it had to be accepted.

"McLaws believed the report and sent it by fast rider back to me. He's asking for orders, afraid that he'll get tangled into a fight in Westminster. He reports thousands of troops there, including cavalry and some heavy artillery. He's concerned that he'll get engaged, and then Hancock will hit on the flank."

Pete shook his head.

"Hancock won't be there until well after dawn, if at all."

"We must assume they are stirring, General Longstreet. That had to be expected all along, and in fact we want them to."

"Yes, sir, once we've seized a good position."

"I want you to go up and straighten things out yourself."

"Yes, sir."

"McLaws also reports a vast supply train in Westminster. I want that seized. Then we can leave our wagon trains west of the mountains. We can send them back as far as Falling Waters on the Potomac River for safety. That will free us up to move much more quickly. We will defeat the Union army using their own supplies."

"I'll leave at once."

"And another thing, General."

"Sir?"

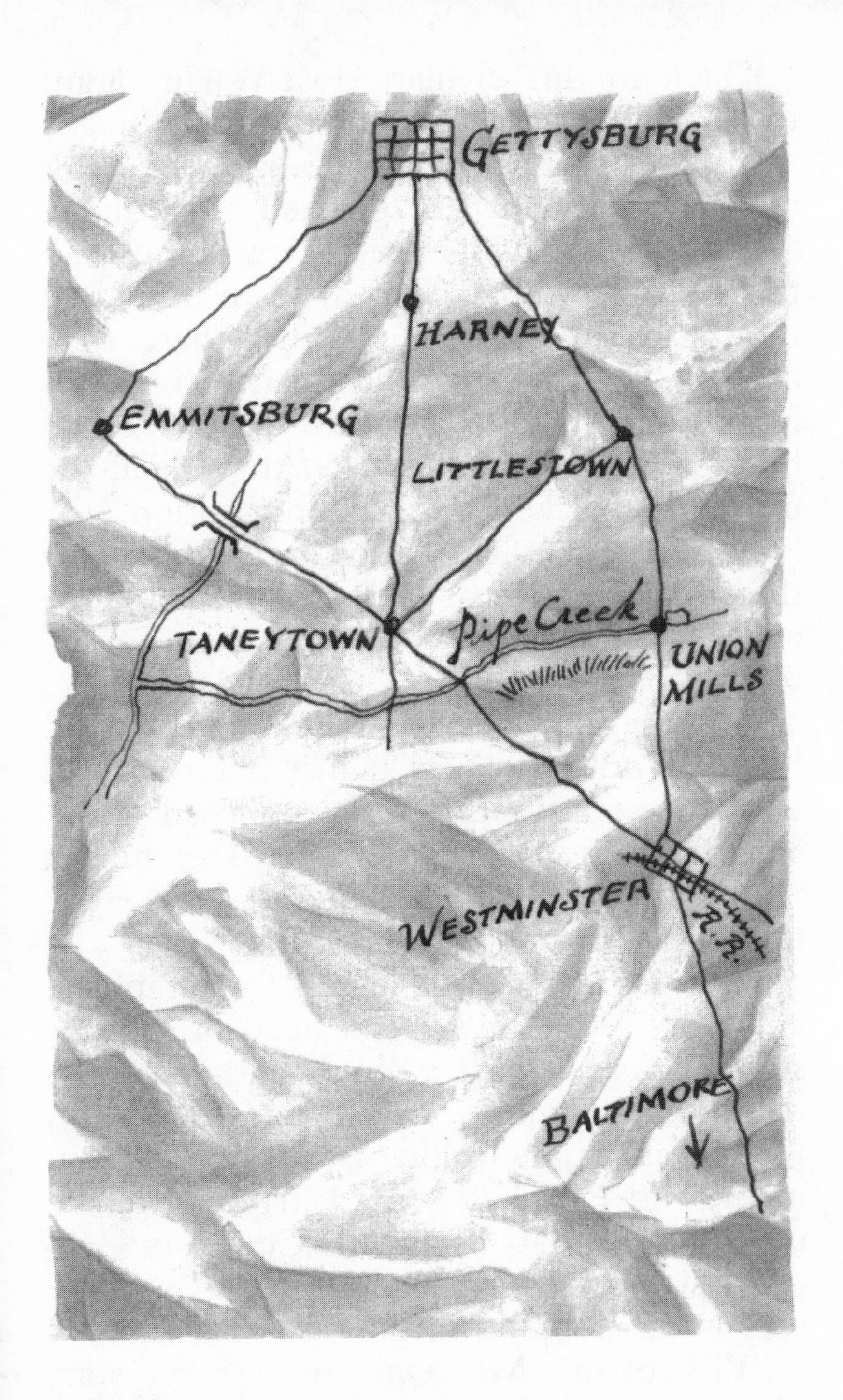
GETTYSBURG
HARNEY
EMMITSBURG
LITTLESTOWN
TANEYTOWN
Pipe Creek
UNION MILLS
WESTMINSTER
R.R.
BALTIMORE

"Talk to this civilian closely. He claims to know the area. The report is that Meade was considering a defensive line along this creek," and again Lee pointed at the map. "Pipe Creek is its name. Several of my staff talked with sympathizers in town here, and they said the same thing, that there were rumors, or they had overheard conversations, that Meade wanted to draw us down here to fight. If that is true, that meant he must have picked out a good position."

As he spoke, Lee traced out the creek that flowed north of Westminster and then curved south, just to the east of Taneytown.

"Apparently Meade sent Warren and Henry Hunt to survey it just before things started at Gettysburg. Our supposed friend stated that he watched Warren sketching a map and overheard a statement by Hunt talking about good fields of fire."

Pete nodded. The chief topographical engineer for the army and head of artillery surveying a defensive line? Both of those men knew ground. Given the right spot, Hunt was usually brilliant with gun deployment, and Pete had sensed his hand in the defense of that accursed Cemetery Hill only two days ago. Any ground *they* liked was worth looking into.

"I'll push McLaws in, then start moving people here," and Pete traced his finger over the map toward Union Mills. "I'll try and take a look myself, and then send a message back if this is the defensive line we want. What reinforcements can I expect?"

"I'm keeping Hood here," Lee announced. "He's deployed north of town here, and there's been some skirmishing reported. It looks like Fifth Corps is approaching."

"That splits my command to pieces," Pete said. "McLaws on the right flank, Hood here in the center, and Pickett still twenty or more miles away."

"I know, but it can't be helped. I'm passing Hill's corps up to you. You will take direct command. I've already sent an order to that effect. Hill is too sick to continue."

"The entire corps?"

"Yes, that will give you at least four divisions to secure the right. I think Meade will make his main thrust coming down the road to Baltimore. It's the shortest route back to their lines around Washington. They will look to turn our flank there, then slip around and into position. We must not allow that to happen.

"Ewell will file in here by midday, though his men will not be in shape to fight until rested, having marched all night. If possible, I will forward up additional troops from him as well. I'll be in direct control here for now."

Pete looked back down at the map. Things were getting a little unorthodox. All three corps were jumbled up and split apart. The last time they had tried a maneuver of this scale was Second Manassas, and both corps had remained intact.

What Lee was suggesting here was an ad hoc division of command, Lee directly controlling the center and left, and Longstreet the right.

"A long front, ten miles or more between Taneytown and Westminster," Longstreet offered.

"I know. Their response will be toward one flank or the other. If aggressive, they'll try and cut us in half here. If more concerned about regaining their base of supplies and protecting Washington, it will be toward Westminster. I suspect it will be the latter. Take that town; get Hill's men in position; see if that civilian's report is accurate.

"While you attend to that, I'll have people out surveying the land in between along the south side of this creek.

"If all is secure here, I'll pass Ewell's command down to you as well, or at least give you Pickett by the end of the day. If their main assault comes in this direction,

I want you to hold Westminster nevertheless, and I'll send down what I can."

Pete said nothing for a moment and just studied the map. The first hard stage of marching was over. Now it was time to secure the base and then find a good place to hold. If Warren and Hunt had been out exploring this ground, they had found it and would know it. He had to get it first.

Saluting, Pete left the room and then paused to look back. Lee was still leaning over the map. He caught Taylor's eye. "Get him to sleep," Pete whispered, almost mouthing the words, and Taylor nodded.

Alexander was out in the corridor, holding Pete's boots and a cup of coffee. "Let me help you get these on, sir."

Pete nodded his thanks and sat down, cradling the china cup filled to the brim with the warm brew as Alexander knelt to help him.

"Guess I'm coming with you?" Alexander asked hopefully.

"That you are, young sir. Get outside and round up the rest of the staff; they're going too. I want to move within ten minutes."

Alexander grinned. "I've already called to have our horses saddled."

At forty-two, Pete felt very old. Sighing,

he stood up and walked out the door. The horizon to the east revealed the first faint glimmer of dawn of July 3, 1863.

5:45 AM, July 3, 1863

Westminster

US Chaos.

Never had he seen such wild insanity. The main street of Westminster was packed solid with hundreds of wagons, tangled together so tightly that nothing could move. Several wagons were upended, mules still tangled up in their harnesses frantically kicking at each other in their desperate struggle to escape. Most of the wagons were abandoned, drivers having run off, joining in the uncontrollable stampede heading east.

He edged his mount along the narrow sidewalk, his horse nervously stepping over a body sprawled in front of a tavern that had been looted. The man had been shot in the back, a broken bottle of whiskey by his side. A civilian stood in the doorway, an old shotgun cradled in his arms.

Haupt nodded and said nothing. The civilian ignored him.

All order, all control had broken down during the night. How and why it had started he still didn't know. Suddenly hundreds of wagons had begun jockeying to get on the Baltimore Pike, drivers screaming that the Rebs were attacking. He had tried to send a scraped-up detail of men to stem the tide; but it was far too much, and most of them had simply joined the stampede.

Then the wagons still parked to the west side of the town had come pouring in, a wagon loaded with cartridge rounds upending and igniting. The thousands of rounds going off had truly enhanced the terror, flames leaping to a second wagon loaded with artillery shells and several hundred pounds of powder. That had exploded in a massive fireball. Several houses had caught on fire and burned, casting a lurid light on the mad scene.

The houses were still smoldering, a detail of civilians wearily carrying buckets to keep it from spreading. They looked at him coldly as he rode past.

In the early light of dawn, he surveyed the madness: the carnage, burned-out wagons, dead animals, another dead man, this one a cavalry trooper.

To the west he could hear the steady rattle of musketry growing closer.

A mule driver, terrorized, was still with his wagon, stuck in the middle of the street behind an upended load of rations, hemmed in on both sides and to the rear by more wagons, all of them abandoned. In his madness the driver was lashing out with his whip. There was no place for the poor tormented mules to go, and they screamed pitifully as their driver continued to lash them, crying out for them to move.

Hermann drew his revolver, disgusted with the spectacle. "Goddamn you, stop that!"

The mule driver looked at him, eyes filled with fear, and continued to lash the bloody backs of the mules.

Hermann cocked the revolver, aimed it over the head of the driver, and fired. He recocked the pistol and now pointed it straight at the driver's head.

The driver stopped the whipping, looking at Hermann with a blank stare.

"Drop that whip, you damn coward."

The man did as ordered.

"Get down off that wagon and do one of two things: either find a rifle and get up on the line or go join the rest of your friends and get the hell out of here. But so help me, you raise that whip again and I'll blow your brains out."

The driver was off the wagon and, uttering a strange animal-like moan, he started to run, heading east, away from the fight.

The mules looked over at Hermann,

their backs lashed open. He was tempted to put them out of their misery but couldn't bring himself to do it. He rode on, heading up the slope, the rattle of musketry growing louder.

As he rode he turned and looked back. The street was choked, impassable. He shifted in the saddle, reached into his breast pocket, and pulled out the message that had come in an hour ago.

Headquarters, Second Corps,
Army of the Potomac
Near Gettysburg 2:00 AM, July 3, 1863

To the commander of the garrison at Westminster

Sir, my corps is now on the march, having departed Gettysburg shortly after one this morning, and shall approach Westminster via the road to Baltimore.

I implore you to hold your position regardless of loss. I shall come to you with all possible speed.

Hancock

If anyone would come with "all possible speed," it was Winfield. If he had been in command of this army, there would have been no delay yesterday afternoon and evening.

But where was the cavalry? One good division right now could make all the difference. Instead, there was nothing but this scratch command and thousands of mule drivers running like madmen in every direction.

As he looked at the nearly impenetrable pileup of wagons clogging the street, a cold voice within told him it was over, to round up a crew, send them down the street, shoot the mules, and start setting the wagons on fire — and try to get out with what he could.

And yet Hancock had said he was coming.

He hesitated to leave his headquarters down at the depot, hoping that somehow, just behind the message that was over three hours old, perhaps Hancock himself just might come riding in with an advance guard.

No, it was twenty-five miles to Gettysburg, a ten-hour march for a corps moving fast, very fast.

To the west the sound of fire was picking up. So they were pushing in at last. Hell, a guard of old ladies armed with brooms could have swept them out of there during the worst of the panic.

With dawn breaking, the Rebs had to feel confident now, could see what was ahead, the mad confusion in the town, and would push straight in. He could imagine them over there. The sight of thousands of wagons, the piles of supplies stacked up around the depot, these would whip the rebels into a frenzy.

A wounded cavalry trooper came limping down the street, blood squishing out of his boot.

"How is it up there?" Henry asked.

"Won't hold much longer, sir. Goddamn infantry with us, they're just melting away. If we still had Buford, all the ammunition down here, we'd give 'em a hell of a fight, but not now."

Hermann nodded, reached into his breast pocket, pulled out a notepad, and hurriedly scribbled on it.

"This is a pass for the last train out. Get yourself on board."

He passed the note down to the cavalryman, who forced a weak grin and saluted. "Didn't relish the thought of winding up in Libby Prison."

"Trooper, you're worth saving," and Hermann looked back with disgust at the pileup clogging the street.

He nudged his horse and rode to the crest of the hill at the west end of town.

A mix of cavalry troopers, infantry, and at least a few wagon drivers was drawn out in a rough line, crouched down behind trees, pressed up against the sides of the last houses in town, some of the men up in the buildings, firing from the second floors. Bullets were snicking in, bits of clapboard exploding in splinters, fragments of brick puffing out. A shell screamed in, breaking the window of a house, detonating inside with a flash.

He had ordered up the heavy four-and-a-half-inch guns, two batteries, twelve beautiful heavy guns, posting them to hold this crest, and finally he spotted them, gunners working feverishly, one of the guns recoiling with a throaty roar.

He rode toward the batteries, and as he did so he crested the hill.

The sight was a shock. Barely 250 yards off was a heavy battle line of Rebs, emerging out of the smoke and early morning fog. These weren't skirmishers probing and fumbling in the dark. With the light of dawn they were no longer hesitating. They smelled victory; they saw the prize ahead.

"Sir, will you get the hell off that horse!"

He saw the battery commander coming toward him, crouched low.

Hermann didn't argue and dismounted, the battery commander grabbing him by the arm, pulling him behind a limber wagon. The protection chosen didn't give him much confidence. There were several hundred pounds of powder in the limber.

Five guns of the first battery fired a

salvo, followed seconds later by six more guns, positioned a hundred yards to the right, a cheer bursting from the gunners as the deadly spray of canister tore into the advancing rebel line, dropping dozens of the enemy.

The enemy advance slowed, came to a stop, and hundreds of rifles suddenly rose up and then dropped down level.

"Get down!"

The volley ignited. It sounded like a swarm of angry bees rushing overhead, around them, a ball ricocheting off the wheel of the limber. Half a dozen horses, still harnessed to the battery's limber wagons, started to kick and scream or just collapsed.

Ramrods were withdrawn all along the rebel line, men working to reload. Gunners were back up around Hermann, scrambling to load as well. The Rebs went into independent fire at will, and within a minute a storm of .58-cal. minie balls was whistling in. It seemed as if the entire rebel brigade out there was concentrating on this one position. The men with the guns began to drop.

A rebel battery was revealed by the puffs of smoke, the flashes of light barely visible in the fog, shells streaking in.

"I could use some more infantry support," the battery commander cried, even as his six guns recoiled sharply, sending another storm of canister into the enemy line. More canister went downrange from the second battery. They were doing it right, not engaging in counterbattery, but working to keep the infantry back instead.

"I don't have any more."

"A couple of the regiments up here, they're doing their job, but most of the rest are melting away or already disappeared with those goddamn wagon drivers."

"How long can you hold?"

The major stood up straight, slowly scanning the enemy line, ignoring a spray of splinters that tore up from the top of the limber wagon as it was scored by a bullet.

"They'll finally go for the flanks, lap around us. Half hour, maybe an hour. They won't come straight in against my guns, damn them."

Hermann actually smiled. This man and his heavy artillery, which threw twice the weight of the lighter field pieces, were actually itching for a fight. He most likely had been stuck in a garrison around Washington since the start of the war and been moved up here only because someone back at the War Department liked the idea of some heavy artillery posted somewhere else.

As luck would have it, the last convoy of trains that had come up at two in the morning actually had a few hundred rounds of 4.5-in. canister rounds on board, the battery commander sending down fifty men to haul the rounds up by hand, since it was impossible to move a caisson through the streets.

"Where's the rest of the army?"

Hermann told him of Hancock's urgent appeal.

The major shook his head.

"It'll be damn near noon before they get in. You're asking the impossible. We'll be flanked within the hour."

"Then we fall back into the town, fight them house to house. Your men have hand weapons. There's no way we'll be able to move your guns out. So when it finally hits, spike your weapons, smash or take the rammers with you, and then fall back into town. I'm passing the same order to the infantry. We hold the town."

The major shook his head but smiled. "You're not a line officer, are you, sir?"

"Railroad man."

"Goddamn. Wish we had more railroaders running this army."

"McClellan was a railroader."

The major spit on the ground. "Well, every business has some bad apples."

"Just hold as long as you can, Major. I'm going to see the other officers on this line to pass the word."

Leading his horse and trying not to crouch too low and thus look absurd, Hermann started to walk away, then looked back. "Major."

"Sir?"

"If it falls apart, get yourself back to the depot. I'm taking the trains out, if we can't hold. I want as many of your men as possible, and you, to go with me."

The major forced a smile. "Sir, I have a bad feeling about today, a dream last night, you know the kind. But thanks."

Hermann left him to his work and his nightmares and started down the line, shouting encouragement to the small detachments of Buford's cavalry who were still game, having rallied during the night around a sergeant, captain, and even the colonel of the Eighth Illinois, whose arm was wrapped up in a bloody sling. The half a hundred men gathered round him were mostly armed with the precious Spencer repeating rifle. A supply of ammunition had been found, boxes of it were stacked up behind an overturned wagon, and the men were pouring it in, fifty troopers with the firepower of an entire regiment. They were fighting like true professionals, hunkered down low, taking careful aim.

The weapon in their hands wasn't a carbine; only now was the factory starting to make the lighter weapon. These men had purchased, with their own money, the standard long-barreled weapon and now were putting it to damn good use.

One of the troopers looked back at Haupt. "Just keep the ammunition coming, and we'll hold them all day, sir!"

Hermann nodded and continued on.

"Hold until they flank, then into the town," he kept repeating.

We've got to hold. Hancock is coming.

6:15 AM, July 3

Dunkard Church near Westminster

"General, why have you not taken that town?"

It was obvious to all the staff gathered around General McLaws that Longstreet, who had just ridden up, was about to explode. They edged back from the confrontation.

McLaws stepped down from the entry to a small Dunkard church facing the main road from Taneytown. The sight of the building caused a flash of memory for Pete. A Dunkard church had been the center of fighting at Sharpsburg. They were a pacifist sect. Ironic, we keep bringing battles to their doorstep.

"Sir," McLaws said, obviously taken

aback by Longstreet's sudden appearance. "As I tried to tell you last night, my men are exhausted. We had no good maps, there were bands of Yankee cavalry all up and down the road, but we're getting a grip on it now."

"Show me," Pete said coldly.

Together they moved along the edge of the road, which was packed with infantry still in column, the men slowly shuffling forward, the brigade shifting from column to line of battle just back from the top of the hill. Two batteries were atop the crest, hard at work as Pete and McLaws rode into position.

Morning fog and smoke cloaked the open valley. Just beyond the next ridge he could see several church spires and a column of smoke slowly rising straight up in the still morning air. Flashes of gunfire rippled along the next ridge, suddenly counterpointed by nearly a dozen flashes of light. Seconds later a deep rumbling thump rolled over them.

Pete cocked his head; the sound was a bit different.

"I know," McLaws said. "Looks like two batteries of twenty pounders dug in as tight as ticks on a dog along that ridge."

"Their support?"

"Dismounted cavalry, what's left of Buford's men. There're a knot of them armed with those damn repeating rifles. Playing hell with us. They also have some infantry."

"Infantry? Who?"

"Not sure yet, but seem disorganized. Prisoners we picked up during the night; some were from Sixth Corps, some from the First and Second."

"Second? How many?" Pete asked, now anxious.

"Just a few. Said they were part of the wagon guard detail."

"You certain?"

"Just telling you what was reported to me, sir."

"Alexander?"

"Here, sir," and his chief of corps artillery came up.

"Get the map out."

As Alexander reached into his map case, Pete carefully surveyed the line ahead. A single brigade was advancing, spread out across a quarter mile of front. Stalled in front of the guns, beginning to lap around the flanks. But there wasn't enough weight.

"You should be hitting him with everything, damn it. This is what Heth did two days ago. If he'd gone in all at once, he'd of taken Gettysburg before Reynolds came up."

"Sorry, sir. But like I said, it was damnable confusion on that road. Brigades, regiments all tangled up. It took half the night to straighten everything out."

"It was damnable confusion for them, too!" Pete snapped, pointing toward the town.

"I've got a second brigade deploying now behind us, Semmes's brigade. That's Kershaw up on the line."

"And the rest of your men?"

"I have Wofford's brigade deploying out to flank the town to the south. He's reporting back that you can barely see what's ahead; it's thick with wagons as far as you can see. And, sir, I ordered Barksdale to swing his brigade around to north of the town. Cut across that road to Baltimore."

"What?"

"The road north of town, sir. I have men moving on it," and McLaws hesitated. "Isn't that what you wanted, sir?"

Pete grunted and nodded even as Alexander unfolded the map and handed it over to him.

"You did something right," Pete offered coolly.

"There're supposed to be thousands of wagons down there, trains, too," McLaws interjected.

"I want that road, I need to find ground we can hold, and I want that damn town. If we get the wagons with the supplies, so much the better."

Don't get diverted the way Stuart did when it comes to supply wagons, he thought. Lee wants the supplies, so do I, but getting the defensible ground is the important thing.

He studied the map for a few seconds.

"You have someone who can guide me to the Baltimore Road?"

"That civilian," and McLaws nodded to his staff officers. A lone civilian, middle-aged, prosperous looking, with a good horse, was sitting among them, chatting amiably.

"What do you think about him?" Pete asked.

"Everything he's saying seems to hit center. Described Stuart to perfection, his staff, and willing to wait here till Stuart comes in. Says we can shoot him if he's lying."

Pete studied the man for a moment. As if sensing he was being watched, the civilian looked up and nodded.

"Detail off a couple of your staff to ride with us and keep an eye on that man. Give me some of the men from your company of cavalry as well. If he leads us astray, or makes a dash for it," Pete hesitated, "well, I'm not saying shoot him, but make it damn uncomfortable for him."

McLaws went over to his staff, and Pete looked at Alexander and then back at the rest of his staff, who were easing their way through and around the brigade that was forming up behind them.

"I think General McLaws has things in hand here," Pete said, his voice low. "I want to go north and east. Look at that road, see the land up by Union Mills. If Hancock is coming down, that might very well be the place to meet him. Not here. This town is flanked by hills. It's a trap."

McLaws came back with several of his staff and the civilian.

"Mr. William Shriver, this is General Longstreet."

The civilian bowed slightly, though in the saddle. "I recognized you, sir."

"How?"

"Why from the illustrated papers of course."

"The report you gave. About seeing two Union officers around Union Mills two days ago."

"Yes, sir. A General Warren and a General Hunt, I believe, sir."

"Describe them, please."

Shriver offered a quick description and Pete nodded. It seemed close enough.

"Why are you helping us?" Pete asked.

"I have six sons serving with the Confederacy, sir. They're with the First Maryland, Johnson's division, and with the First Maryland Artillery. We of Maryland are behind the Cause, sir."

"Didn't seem that way last time we came up here to Sharpsburg."

"I'm sorry, sir, if some of my neighbors reacted thus. But I can assure you of the truth of my report."

"For your sake, let's hope so."

The man did not seem to be insulted by this questioning of his honesty.

"I understand your need for caution, sir," he replied.

"The quickest way to Union Mills without getting too near this town?"

"I know a way."

"If we wander into Yankees, sir," Alexander interjected sharply, "I will make it a point of holding you responsible." He casually let his hand drift down to his holster.

The civilian laughed, though it was forced and a bit nervous.

"There're Yankees wandering all over here, most of them cowards and running away. The roads east and south of here are supposed to be packed with them. I can't promise you, sir, but if we do meet Yankees, toss me that revolver, and you'll see me make a fight of it as well."

Pete smiled slightly. "Fine then. Now let's move."

Pete looked back at McLaws and motioned him over.

"Next time, General," Pete said softly,

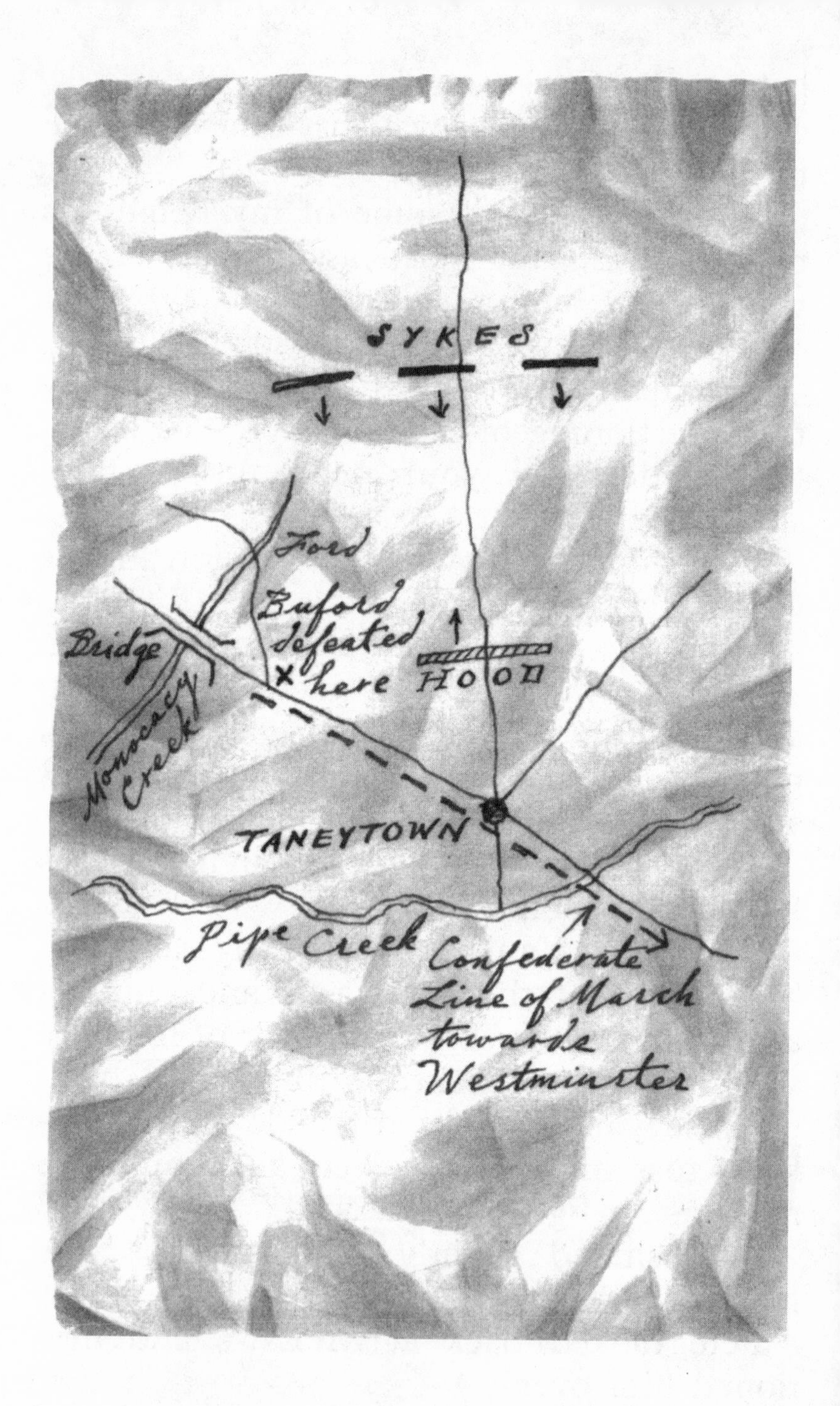
SYKES
Ford
Buford defeated here
Bridge
HOOD
Monocacy Creek
TANEYTOWN
Pipe Creek
Confederate Line of March towards Westminster

so that no one, and especially the civilian, could hear, "when I say I want something taken by dawn, I expect it to be taken by dawn and not two hours later. Do we understand each other?"

McLaws nodded nervously and saluted.

"Now get in there and take that town. Once you do, send another brigade up the road toward Union Mills. I'll most likely be there."

With staff and the small cavalry escort, they now numbered several dozen, and as the cavalcade started off Pete looked back. The Second Brigade, which had been forming up, was sweeping up the slope, battle flags held high, heading straight toward Westminster. McLaws, sword drawn, was out front, urging them on.

6:40 AM, July 3, 1863

Near Harney on the
Gettysburg-Taneytown Road

Gen. George Sykes, new commander of the Fifth Corps, who had taken over the corps after Meade's elevation, surveyed the map spread out on the table before him. Raising his field glasses, he again tried to examine the ground ahead that was cloaked in morning mist.

He looked over at Warren and shook his head. "I can't see a damn thing."

General Crawford, the divisional commander who had led the probing assault at dawn, nodded his head in agreement.

"We came up out of the low ground just ahead and got hit on front and flanks. They're out there, sir. A division at the very least."

Sykes looked back down at the map. He was an old professional, a graduate of the class of 1842 from the Point, a veteran of Mexico, and most recently in command of the division of regular army troops that was part of Fifth Corps. On the road behind him that same division was now filing in from Gettysburg after a hard, six-hour march through the night.

He studied the map sketched out by Warren, and then fixed his gaze on a cavalry captain, one of the survivors of Buford's command who had fallen back into the lines of Fifth Corps after yesterday's bitter defeat at the bridge.

"The ground around that bridge," Sykes asked, and as he spoke he pointed to its position on the map. "Defendable, if we seize it?"

"Yes, sir. If we had been fresh, backed by artillery, and with sufficient ammunition, we could have held it all day."

Sykes looked back at Warren. "What do you think?"

"We can't do both," Warren replied, shaking his head.

"I agree," Sykes said. "Our orders are to take back Taneytown. But that was given last night, and Meade is now at least twelve miles away. If I thought the bridge was more practical, I'd go for it."

The cavalry captain stirred, clearing his throat nervously. Sykes looked up at him. "Go on, Captain."

"Sir, the ground around Taneytown, it's wide open, almost a flat plateau. In fact, the town is down in a bit of a valley."

"Meaning it would be hard to defend except in a stand-up fight."

"Sir, once you take it, then what? Yesterday that road was packed with Rebs clear back beyond Emmitsburg. It most likely still is. Take the bridge, and you plug 'em up that way."

"In other words, go for the bridge rather than the town," Sykes replied.

"I'm just a captain, sir," the cavalryman said cautiously.

Sykes smiled. "Appreciate the comment, captain. The question is, what is our mission here?"

"Take Taneytown."

"No, it's to cut Lee's column off from Westminster or at the very least delay it."

He looked up and pointed to the distant cloud of smoke that was visible above the early morning haze.

"It's obvious the head of their column has seized Westminster," Sykes continued. "The fires are most likely our supplies burning, gentlemen. We all know Meade. He commanded this corps before I did. He's going to focus everything he has on taking that town back."

As he spoke he traced a line on the map from Gettysburg to Littlestown and from there on to Union Mills. His finger paused over Union Mills.

"That's the ground you surveyed, isn't it, Warren."

"Yes, sir."

"From what you've told me, it's an ideal position to cover Westminster, but it's ground that starts east of Taneytown and then arches northeast to Union Mills."

Warren nodded.

"That's why we move on Taneytown rather than the bridge. We are now Meade's flank and not an independent command," Sykes announced.

He was silent for a moment, looking back down at the map again as if meditating. All around him were quiet, the only sound the steady tramp of the column marching along the road beside them, and from ahead the final sputtering of fire as the last of Crawford's men fell back across the creek after their dawn repulse.

"His whole army might already have passed," Sykes said, "but I doubt that. Lee's goal is Westminster. If we swing to the southwest and cut the bridge, we'll be advancing at a right angle to where we should be going, which is straight at Taneytown. If I were Lee, I'd let me do it. The troops beyond the bridge, if there are any, engage and hold us while the rest of his army continues eastward. We'll cut off only part of the tail. I want to cut him right down the middle, and that means Taneytown. That's what will really help Meade in this situation.

"If we hit Taneytown, he's going to have to make a fight of it. The report is that Hood is in front of us. We hit him hard enough, whatever is in that town will have to turn to fight us. And yes, whatever is on the far side of the bridge will hit us as well. We might tie up three, perhaps four divisions of theirs in the process."

"A tall order," Warren whispered.

Sykes looked around at the division and brigade commanders who had come in to receive their orders and were standing silent, some of them obviously nervous with the way the conversation was going.

"Gentlemen, this campaign might very well decide the fate of the Union," and as he spoke he pointed toward the smoke over Westminster, which was beginning to expand and spread out.

"Lee has Westminster. The Army of the Potomac has been flanked, and we are cut off from our line of communication and supplies. Meade will be forced to attack, maybe as early as this afternoon, most definitely by morning tomorrow."

No one spoke.

"I want a concentrated attack on Taneytown, straight into the town. That will draw the rear of Lee's army back to us. It has to. Two, maybe three of his divisions will be tied up by us. It will tie them up for most of the day, and we might even bleed some of them out. It could very well delay Lee and give General Meade his chance."

He hesitated for a moment. "The fate of the Union rests here now. I am prepared to risk losing this corps if by doing so we give Meade a chance and thus save the Union."

The men around him nodded gravely.

"There'll be no glory in this, gentlemen. It will be a bloody stand-up fight. Crawford will be on the left, Ayres with my old division of regulars, you're in the center, and Barnes on the right. Get your staffs moving to lay out the deployment and try to keep it concealed as much as possible from the Rebs."

He pulled out his pocket watch and snapped it open. "It's a little after seven. It will take at least two hours more for the rest of the corps and our artillery to come up. An hour beyond that to deploy, so we go in no later than ten. The massed batteries will fire two salvos; that will be the signal to begin.

"Advance on a two-brigade front, one brigade in reserve for each division, and aim straight for the town. Once in, fully expect to be overlapped on the flanks as Lee pushes in what he has. That's what your reserve brigades are for. Once we get into Taneytown, we dig in and hold on, and make 'em pay for it."

A couple of men grinned.

"If anyone can do it, we can," Romeyn Ayres, who was in command now of Sykes's old division of regulars, announced proudly.

"Get back to your commands."

The men saluted and started to mount up, leaving Sykes and Warren alone for the moment.

"You don't like it, do you?" Sykes asked.

"It's that bridge to the west. Suppose they still have another division over there, maybe even two. Your right will be wide open, and they'll turn your line."

"Send a brigade down there and they'll get flanked same as Buford. And I can't afford a division. I want my command concentrated for this attack. I don't have enough to do two things at once. It's a risk we have to take for the Union."

"So your plan is to just draw them in on you and slug it out."

"Something like that."

Warren shook his head and smiled. "Mind if I stick around."

Sykes forced a smile in return. "Thank you. I'll need you, the corps will need you, before the day is done."

6:45 AM, July 3, 1863

Near Union Mills on the Baltimore Pike

US Gen. Winfield Scott Hancock reined in, glaring coldly at the cavalry lieutenant who had cut in front of him, and then skidded his horse to a stop.

"Damn it, sir, I'm asking you to stop!" the lieutenant cried.

"Out of my way, lieutenant."

"Sir, I am responsible for you. That's the job of the cavalry company assigned to your headquarters. At least let me scout down to that mill below before you proceed."

"There is no time for that now."

"Sir, if you get yourself killed, then I guess I'm going to have to get killed, too. Because if I don't, my captain will most assuredly kill me if I come back without you."

The young lieutenant tried to meet Hancock's wrathful gaze, but couldn't hold it. He started to blush and lowered his eyes.

"Please, sir," the lieutenant asked, and there was a bit of a quaking to his voice. "We're six miles, maybe more, away from the head of your corps. It's just you, me, ten of my men, and your aides out here alone."

Hancock spared a quick glance back over his shoulder. The rest of the men, not as well mounted, were just rounding the bend of the road at a full gallop.

Hancock nodded, and the lieutenant sighed with relief.

"Hear that?" Hancock asked, turning slightly.

The lieutenant nodded. It was artillery . . . distant, maybe two miles, maybe four or five. Hard to tell.

The valley below was lush, covered in a heavy mist; the treetops on the opposite slope a half mile away were poking up out of the fog, illuminated by the long, slanting light of the morning sun. The air was rich with the heady scent of a summer meadow at dawn, a mixture of wildflowers, grass, warm water.

It was quiet, peaceful, except for that distant thunder.

The staff finally caught up, reining in, the lieutenant shouting for his troopers to head down to the mill, its roof a sharp, dark line standing out in the morning mists.

The men set off at a trot, the lieutenant in the lead.

Hancock smiled. The boy had guts to stand up to him like that. And he was right. Get cut off by some Reb cavalry out here, my corps still miles away. Goddamn stupid way to get oneself killed or captured.

If I'm going to die in this, let it be with my men, out in front, leading a charge, damn it! And as he looked out across the valley below, he wondered for a moment, Might this be the ground where we finally decide it?

This had to be Union Mills and Pipe Creek. Warren had described it to him just before he left. High ground on both sides. Mill on the east side of the road with a good bridge beside it. Stream dammed to the east; ground marshy to the west. Hills nearly bare except for occasional woodlots, the wood having all been harvested off long ago for lumber to be cut by the mill and as charcoal for the smithy. Farmhouse about a half mile to the west down by the creek.

He looked carefully, and in the mists could just see it, a coil of smoke rising from the chimney.

Good fields of fire, Henry had said. Damn, this had to be it.

"Sir, we're getting the all clear."

Hancock looked up. A shadowy figure was up on the opposite slope, just above the slowly undulating wisps of fog coiling up from the damp bottomland, waving his hat back and forth.

Hancock spurred his mount and started down the road, which curved across the face of the slope and then leveled out. They clattered over the bridge, mill on their left. All was still. No one was working this morning.

The road pitched up sharply, and Hancock eased back on his horse, letting it slow to a trot. No sense in winding him out now.

The lieutenant and his men were at the crest of the hill, reined in, one of the men pointing. Hancock came up to their side.

Thick columns of smoke filled the sky to the southwest. The thumping was louder. Half a dozen civilians were out, standing by the side of the road, and Winfield rode up to them. "Is that Westminster?" he asked.

"It was burning during the night; you

could see the flames!" a young boy shouted.

"Is that Westminster?" and this time he was a bit more insistent, focused on a middle-aged woman wearing a plain dress of dark gray.

"Yes, sir. It's Westminster."

"The sound of gunfire, how long has that been going on?"

"All night long. A couple of big explosions and then the fire. Just about an hour ago, it started getting louder."

"How far is it to the town?"

"About four miles, maybe five."

Winfield looked over at the lieutenant. "Think you can get through?"

"Well, sir, that does depend on whether the Rebs are to the north side of the town or not."

"Supposedly General Haupt is down there in command. I want him to know we're coming up."

"Look! Is them Rebs?" the boy shouted, pointing off to the west.

The lieutenant turned in his saddle. Hancock looked to where the boy was pointing.

A small troop was cutting across a field about half a mile away.

"That's Grandpa on the white horse!" the boy cried.

Hancock looked back over at the woman. She said nothing, but lowered her eyes.

"Your granddaddy with the rebel army, son?" Hancock asked.

"Sure is! My pa and all my uncles joined the army a year ago. My grandpa went out to warn them last night. He said you Yankees were going to get whipped. General Stuart himself visited our house, and Grandpa went to fetch him back along with the whole rebel army."

The woman looked back up, eyes cold, her arms going protectively around her grandson, pulling him in tight against her side.

"Madam, you and your boy have nothing to fear from me," Winfield said coolly, almost insulted by her reaction.

"It's Rebs, sir," the lieutenant announced. "Looks like some staff, a few troopers."

The approaching group had obviously spotted them, slowed, and were spreading out. He caught a glint of reflected sunlight, someone with field glasses raised.

Winfield took out his own field glasses and raised them, focusing.

The rebel officer with field glasses raised slowly lowered them.

"Longstreet," Winfield whispered. "It's Pete Longstreet."

"Want to try for them, sir?" the lieutenant asked. "We've got about the same numbers."

He stayed focused on Pete. Several of the troopers with him had revolvers and carbines drawn.

Now that would be something, wouldn't it? Hancock thought. Two generals charge each other and have it out, like princes of old jousting in front of their armies. Certainly would make the cover of *Harper's Weekly*. The thought almost had a romantic appeal.

He chuckled sadly and shook his head.

"Those days are gone forever, Lieutenant. They'd drop half of us before we got across that field. Your dreams of a cavalry charge and dueling knights are long finished."

He lowered his glasses for a moment and looked over at the lieutenant, who was obviously upset by the put-down of the cavalry.

"No offense, son. Several of them boys have carbines. If I was Pete, I'd just pull back and lead us into them woods. For all we know, a whole brigade of Reb infantry is in there. Then where would we be? Dead or on our way to Libby Prison."

"Yes, sir."

He raised his glasses again. Pete's glasses were up as well. Unable to resist the impulse, Hancock waved, and a second later Pete responded with a wave.

"Damn war," Hancock sighed, and he

lowered his glasses, putting them back in their case.

"You're right about the infantry in the woods, General," the lieutenant announced in a whisper and pointed.

A hill beyond where Longstreet was, a mile or so farther back, a dark smudge was moving, a column of infantry.

"Damn all to hell!" Hancock snapped. He looked over at the woman, realizing he was swearing in front of a female, but he didn't offer an apology.

The rumble of gunfire from the town was increasing. Suddenly there was a deep rolling boom and a second later a spreading cloud of smoke appeared beyond the hills.

"Something blew," one of the troopers whispered, "and it was damn big."

"They're taking the town," Hancock sighed.

"Still want me to try and get through?" the lieutenant asked.

What good would it do now? Winfield thought. Tell them we're too late? Tell Washington the army was now cut off?

"No, son, stay with me."

"Then I advise, sir, that we pull back to the other side of the creek. I've got only ten men, but we could give them a fuss if they try and come over the bridge."

"He won't come over the bridge."

"Sir?"

"That's General Longstreet, Lieutenant. He'll dig in right here, right where we are standing. And then it will be we who will have to come back over that bridge.

"He's got the good ground now."

Winfield turned his mount and looked down at the woman and boy. "My compliments to your husband, madam. He guided General Longstreet well this day."

She said nothing, her arms still around her grandson.

"Remember this day, son. When you're an old man, you can tell your grandchildren about it. Now take care of your grandmother."

He looked back at the woman. "I advise that you leave your home."

"Why? Are you going to burn us out?" she asked defiantly.

"No, madam. We don't do that; at least not yet. You're going to be in the middle of a battlefield though before too long, and it's going to get very hot around here."

He started back down the road and turned to the young lieutenant. "Ride like hell, Lieutenant. Get back up to my corps and tell them to move on the double. We are now in a race with Longstreet."

The boy galloped off. Winfield looked back one last time at Longstreet and waved. Spurring his mount, General Hancock headed back across the bridge.

7:15 AM, July 3

Union Mills

Pete watched as Hancock disappeared around the bend in the road.

"My family, sir, I'd like to get to them," Shriver said, for the first time showing real fear.

"Don't rush. Let them get back across the river."

"My family is in jeopardy, sir. Do something. I've helped you; now do something."

"That was General Hancock, Mr. Shriver. And I can assure you, sir, he is a gentleman."

Pete fell silent for a moment. Yes, so many over there were gentlemen. Reynolds was. So was Buford. Will I be killing Hancock now? How would Armistead, who commanded a brigade in Pickett's division, react to that. Armistead talked often of Hancock, their friendship before the war when stationed together out on the coast of California.

Damn war!

Shriver was still obviously concerned.

"Sir, General Hancock would lay down his life to protect your wife and family, even knowing the invaluable service you've just given us this day. So please relax. Let's wait for our infantry support to come up, and then we'll go forward."

"Are you certain?"

Pete looked over at the man, and the civilian fell silent and lowered his head.

"My apologies, General."

"None needed. You don't know the army, our old army. We trained together at West Point, and we live by the code of honor taught there. We might be fighting against each other now, but we still live by that code."

"Look at that place!" Alexander exclaimed, interrupting the two.

Pete turned his attention back to the task at hand. Alexander was pointing to the north.

"Looks like those hills slope down nicely to the creek. Ground on the far side might be a bit higher, but far enough back and not too much higher to give them an advantage if we dig in first."

"These ridges," Pete asked, looking back to Shriver. "Do they flank this creek like this in both directions?"

"Yes, sir. For miles to the west. You

can't see it yet, but down where those Yankees just rode, there's a mill owned by my cousin, a fairly big pond backed up behind it. Then the stream curves a bit to the south, with a very high ridge on this side facing it."

"Natural flank," Alexander offered, "with a good physical barrier with the pond."

"Over there," one of McLaws's staff announced. "I see them."

Hancock and his small cavalcade were a mile away now, up on the distant slope on the north side of the creek.

Pete smiled. For a minute there he had half expected Winfield to do something rash, a charge. That would have been devilish to deal with. Foolish, medieval-type thinking. Stuart still had it in spades. The men around me, though, they'd expect me to respond in kind and not simply pull back, whispering I lacked stomach if I didn't draw a saber and ride out to meet him. Damn, war certainly brings out the stupidity in man.

He shaded his eyes. The morning sunlight was burning through the haze, making it hard to see.

Hancock had reined in, his small escort dismounting.

So you wait there, Winfield. Wait and watch. Now, who can get the most here first?

Pete looked back over his shoulder and caught a glimpse of Barksdale's brigade coming on hard, at the double. He had put the fire into them when riding past a half hour ago.

We get a brigade in here first and start digging in.

"Damn all, sir, this is good ground. Best I've seen since Fredericksburg."

"Better," Pete replied.

"How's that, sir?"

"They didn't have to attack at Fredericksburg; it was just Burnside being bullheaded. But once we take that town, cut them off from Washington, they'll have to attack."

The question now, Pete thought, looking back toward the town and then to the approaching column of his infantry who had bypassed the battle, the question is, do we get enough men here first. Hancock knows it, and by God he will push it. We're still spread out, all the way back to Emmitsburg. If they hit us hard enough in the middle, they could break our lines. Or Hancock has a corps just behind that bend in the road and could storm across it in the next hour or two.

Too many ifs. Focus on now. Get that brigade up and barricade the crest. Seize the town, and get those precious supplies.

A series of explosions rumbled across the

fields. Longstreet looked back toward the town and the rising columns of smoke that seemed to be spreading out.

"My God," Shriver whispered, "it looks as if all of Westminster is burning."

"Most likely is." Pete sighed. I don't have the time to worry about that now, he thought coldly. "Come on, Mr. Shriver," Pete said, "let's get you home to your family."

7:15 AM, July 3, 1863

Westminster

US "Burn it!"

Hermann Haupt stood with arms folded, watching as a detachment of men from his railroad command began to upend cans of coal oil on the stacks of boxes piled up under the open-sided sheds that he had so laboriously built only the day before.

The main street of Westminster, which passed directly in front of his makeshift depot, was still jammed with abandoned wagons. The last remnants of his command were falling back, running between the wagons, shouting that the Rebs were closing in.

He spotted several gunners, red trim on

their hats and trousers, coming around from behind some wagons and then sprinting toward the trains. Hermann shouted for them to come over.

"How far away are they?"

"Not a hundred yards, sir. Them cavalry troopers are dying game. Holed up in houses with their repeating rifles, but the Rebs are pouring in fast."

"Get on the trains; we're clearing out."

The men saluted and started to run down the track.

"Where's your battery commander?" Hermann shouted.

"Dead, sir. Shot in the head," one of the men shouted back, even as he continued to run.

A sergeant lit a torch with a match and looked over at Hermann. "Sir, this fire might spread to those wagons in the street. We got ammunition here. It's gonna be a hell of a mess; might burn down half the town."

"I know," Hermann said coldly.

"All right then, sir, but suggest we start the train the hell out of here before I light this."

Hermann climbed up onto the cab of the locomotive and nodded to the engineer. The other three trains behind him had already pulled out a half hour ago. Ten flatcars were behind the train. Exhausted infantry, artillerymen, and a few cavalry piled on board.

"Let's go!" Hermann shouted.

The engineer opened the throttle, letting the steam rush into the locomotive's pistons. Pressure started to build.

The sergeant threw his flaming torch, the last of the railroad men running out from the sheds, tossing aside the empty cans of coal oil. The fire caught, flames dancing across the boxes of rations, piles of shoes, ponchos, tents, barrels of whiskey, barrels of salted beef, barrels of axle grease, boxes of ammunition for Springfields, Sharps, and Spencer rifles, and limber chests filled with canister, case shot, solid shot, and serge bags filled with powder.

The wheels of the locomotive spun, grabbed, and the train lurched, starting to back out of the station, pushing the flatcars. A few more troopers came running from the main street, cavalrymen, one pausing to take a final shot, and as he did so, he spun around and collapsed. One last man appeared, arm in a sling, Major Beveridge, commander of the Eighth Illinois.

Hermann leaned out of the cab, offering a hand. The major took it with his good hand, and Hermann pulled him up into the cab, the major gasping, leaned over, gagging, shaking like a leaf.

He looked back up at Hermann and nodded his thanks. The engineer of the locomotive leaned over, offering a half-empty bottle of whiskey. Hermann said nothing about this breech of discipline, and the major gratefully took the bottle and finally handed it back after draining off one hell of a long gulp.

"You'll see 'em any second," the major announced, still shaking.

They were a hundred yards back from the depot, slowly picking up speed.

The open-sided warehouses were engulfed now in flames. Hermann saw butternut, a lone rebel soldier, step out onto the track and, within seconds, dozens more. They stood watching the fire, several advanced toward the flames, as if getting set to try and put them out, and then they scattered, the engineer chuckling at the sight.

A second later the engineer doubled over with a grunt. Startled, Hermann looked to his left. Rebs were out in the field flanking the track, not fifty yards away. Looking back, he saw places where they were already over the track, swarming around the wagons jamming the open fields.

He eased the wounded engineer aside, grabbed the throttle, and opened it up full, carefully feeding a bit more water into the boiler to keep the steam up. Now they started to pick up speed.

"Hey, you damn Yankee, stop that train!"

Amazingly, a Reb officer, on horseback, was galloping alongside the locomotive, pistol raised.

For a few seconds they were only a couple of feet apart. And then the Reb reined in hard as the train passed over a culvert. The Reb raised his pistol and then simply lowered it and waved a salute.

But this didn't stop the infantry out in the fields from taking potshots. Rifle balls sparked off the side of the engine, another round passing through the cab. Some of the troopers on the flatcars were firing back, but most of the men were simply sprawled out flat, cursing.

And then it let go.

Just as they rounded the curve, a flash ignited in a pile of burning supplies, then another, bags of powder flaring up. There was no real explosion, for there was nothing to contain the rapid expansion of gasses, just a dull whoosh, but the eruptions were sufficient to upend other boxes, tearing them open, exposing more powder, and like a string of firecrackers going off, the detonations spread and then truly started to build in power. Later, when he looked over the shipping manifests, he might be able to give an exact number, but it was safe to guess that at least six to eight tons of powder were going off. The roof of one of the sheds lifted up, peeling back. The sound washed over him, building. And then it just simply flashed, a continual rolling explosion that soared up and out, windows across Westminster shattering, wagons in the street catching fire, and the poor beasts harnessed to the wagons dying.

A dark pillar of smoke rose to the heavens.

Hermann said nothing, the major next to him watching it all in silence as well. Even the Rebs shooting at them lowered their weapons, turning to look at the apocalyptic devastation.

The supply depot for the Army of the Potomac went up in flames, but the wagons not caught in the devastation, thousands of them outside of the town, trapped in the panic and then abandoned by their drivers, were now in the hands of the Army of Northern Virginia.

Rounding the curve, Hermann left the throttle wide open. He had to get back to Baltimore and from there to Washington.

Somewhere, somehow, a new line of supply, a new depot had to be set up and opened. Millions of dollars in supplies had just been lost, but this was a modern war, a war of railroads, and the factories up north would make it good, replace it, and, he hoped, continue to press the fight . . .

even if it meant creating an entire new army as well.

7:45 AM, July 3, 1863

Treasury Office
Washington, D.C.

"Is there anyone here who can give me a clear indication of what is going on?" Abraham Lincoln asked, as he dropped the latest telegram from Baltimore and turned to face Halleck and Stanton.

He had been awakened at five in the morning by one of his staff bearing a copy of the dispatch from General Haupt to Halleck that the Confederate army was in the rear of the Army of the Potomac and advancing on Westminster. Dressing quickly, he had come over to the Treasury Office across the street from the White House. It acted as a nerve center, the vast web of telegraph lines linking Washington to the rest of the world, terminating in an office of clattering keys and bustling messengers.

As he spoke, the telegraphers behind him continued at their work, though more than one was looking over at him with nervous, sidelong glances.

Stanton, always jumpy about secrecy, motioned that they should retire to a small side office, and Lincoln followed, first scooping up the pile of messages and nodding a thanks to the operators.

Stanton closed the door and sighed. He was suffering from another asthma attack, his breath coming in short, wheezing gasps. He looked over at Halleck. "Well?"

Halleck was silent for a moment. "I think Meade might have been embarrassed."

"Embarrassed?" Lincoln asked, a sharp edge to his voice. "You sound like he was caught with his britches down, and the parson's wife has just walked by with the church choir. Embarrassed?"

"For the moment only, sir."

"Only for the moment?" and in frustration Lincoln held up the sheaf of telegrams and started to scan through them. "Report from Haupt of an enemy division, perhaps a corps or more advancing on Westminster. Report from Baltimore, dated one hour ago, of panic, that Confederate cavalry is on the edge of the city, and that Westminster has fallen. Report from Philadelphia that rebel cavalry is across the Susquehanna and moving east. And from General Meade, a report now close to half a day old that there are indications of Lee moving to his left and yet also demonstrating on his right before Gettysburg."

Lincoln let the papers drop on the table that separated him from Halleck. "What are you going to do, General?"

Halleck looked at him, blankly.

There was a long, drawn-out moment of silence, broken at last by a rap on the door. Stanton pulled it open. A rather nervous-looking telegrapher was standing there, holding a slip of foolscap. Stanton snatched it from him and slammed the door shut. He scanned the paper, wheezing noisily, shoulders hunched over as he struggled for breath, then handed the paper to Lincoln.

"A newspaper in Baltimore has just reported that smoke from the direction of Westminster has been observed from atop several church steeples. They claim a distant explosion was heard a few minutes ago."

Stanton coughed noisily, handkerchief over his mouth.

"It might mean our supply depot is burning," Stanton offered between gasps for air.

"If that is the case, then what are we going to do?" Lincoln asked.

"There is the good news from Vicksburg at least," Halleck offered. "It should be finished there within the next couple of days."

"That is a thousand miles away," Lincoln replied, his voice soft but filled with frustration. The mere fact that Halleck had mentioned it caught Lincoln by surprise, for there was no love lost between Halleck and Grant. It showed to him that Halleck was desperate, grasping for anything to divert attention from what was happening literally at their back door.

"We have to wait to hear from Meade," Stanton interjected. "We shouldn't react until we have clear and certain intelligence from the commander in the field. We've seen this type of thing before and have survived, discovering later it was not as bad as was at first thought."

"What about Couch in Harrisburg?" Lincoln asked. "Could he advance?"

"Militia," Halleck interjected. "They would be worse than useless against the Army of Northern Virginia."

"Our garrison here in Washington?"

Both Halleck and Stanton shook their heads no.

"That is our final reserve," Stanton announced.

"So you are saying we can do nothing but wait. Is that it?"

Halleck reluctantly nodded. Lincoln looked to Stanton, who nodded as well.

"My God." Lincoln sighed. "I fear we

are heading toward a debacle. The Army of the Potomac cut off from Washington, its supply base gone, and all we can do is sit here and wave telegrams at each other."

He lowered his head and turned away.

Chapter Thirteen

8:00 AM, July 3, 1863

In Front of Taneytown

US Ignoring the hum of minie balls clipping through the trees, Col. Joshua Lawrence Chamberlain carefully scanned the enemy position half a mile to the south.

"Over there, to the right, about two miles away, is where Buford was killed yesterday," Strong Vincent, Joshua's brigade commander, pointed out.

Joshua and the other regimental commanders around him said nothing. Several cavalry troopers from that fight, who had fallen back into the advancing regiments of First Division, Fifth Corps, and were now acting as guides, nodded.

"Goddamn bastards!" one of them growled and spit a stream of tobacco juice near Joshua's feet.

"So we're back in Maryland, gentlemen," Strong said.

Joshua looked over at him. He liked Strong, newly promoted to brigade command. Strange, he remembered a comment by Strong a couple of days earlier, about dying under the colors in Pennsylvania. He half suspected it was a prophecy, for men were indeed allowed, at times, a glimpse of the fate ahead.

He was tired, feeling a bit shaky, the regiments having been rousted out at two in the morning and sent back down the very same road they had come up only the day before. A countermarch always sapped morale, especially when done at night. Rumors were flying that the army had been flanked yet again.

The distant pillar of smoke, off to the southeast, was troubling as well. It looked like a great conflagration, and rumors were spreading it was the main supply depot at Westminster.

"Gentlemen, we're the right wing of this attack," Strong announced. "Crawford's division, which positioned itself here last night, attempted a drive on Taneytown at dawn and was repulsed. General Sykes has decided that in this next attack the entire corps will go in at once."

Joshua listened, raising his field glasses to scan the ground. A couple of hundred yards to the right, it sloped down sharply to Monocacy Creek. Directly ahead was a small tributary, locals called it Piney Creek, again the land dropping down, marshy terrain, then up a slope to the other side . . . where he could see Reb skirmishers waiting.

"The First and Second Brigades of this division will open the assault," Strong continued. "Our brigade will be in echelon on the right as the reserve. The objective of the attack is to cut straight into Taneytown. Once over the creek, we move across the open plateau and envelop the town. Our brigade will advance covering the flank."

Joshua lowered his glasses and looked at the sketch map Strong was holding up against the trunk of a tree.

"Confederate forces on our right?" Joshua asked.

"Supposedly nothing."

Joshua said nothing for a moment. "Are we certain of that, sir?"

Strong sighed and looked over at one of the cavalry troopers, a lieutenant who simply shrugged his shoulders and shook his head.

"We're not certain, Colonel Chamberlain, but General Sykes believes that the bulk of the rebel army has passed and is now deployed between Taneytown and Westminster."

"Whether they are or not, sir, why not move on the bridge, the one Buford tried to hold yesterday? That would be the natural barrier for the right to secure our flank as we advance. If we go charging straight into Taneytown and our right is totally exposed, we could be shattered just like Jackson rolling up the Eleventh Corps at Chancellorsville. It makes me uneasy."

Strong nodded.

"General Sykes says there's only this one corps, Colonel Chamberlain, and if we try to advance on a front from the bridge to the town, we'll be spread out across four miles or more. He wants a concentrated attack. Besides, the town is most likely where they are basing supplies."

Joshua did not reply. If Sykes had given that order, there was no sense in troubling Strong about it now. Colonels don't countermand corps commanders.

Vincent pulled his watch out, opened it, and then muttered a curse as he started to wind the stem.

"We're already late. We were supposed to go in at approximately ten o'clock. Get your men in formation as I've outlined. The signal will be the massed firing of the batteries now going into position at the center of our line."

The other regimental commanders saluted and started back to their troops, who were resting in columns on the far side of the village of Harney. Joshua lingered for a moment, and Strong looked over at him.

There was a close bond between the two.

Only a short while ago Strong was a regimental commander like Joshua, more experienced and gladly willing to share what he knew with Joshua. "What are you thinking?" Strong asked.

"Don't like it. We're just asking to get hit from the flank. Being vulnerable against Bobbie Lee just makes my stomach ache."

Strong chuckled softly. "That's what this war is like."

"I have no idea what is going on with this army, how we got flanked, if we're being supported, or not. Do you?"

Vincent said nothing.

"So we are alone out here?"

"Looks that way. I heard most of the army is moving toward Westminster. We're the right flank."

"Strong, if they have not completed their march, which seems likely when you consider the amount of men and the time involved, we'll be flanked in turn."

"I know that," Strong replied.

Joshua smiled.

"You figure, then, that we will wind up holding the flank. Is that it?"

"Something like that."

"Can't we send out a recon."

Strong shook his head.

"Sykes tried after his first probe was turned back. They have a heavy screen of skirmishers out from here clear back to

Emmitsburg that can't be penetrated. Also, with Sykes I talked to a couple of staff. They said that around three this morning, headquarters was in a damn panic. Joshua, they're between us and Washington now. You know what that means."

"We attack no matter what."

Strong said nothing, but the look he gave said it all.

Another bullet zipped through the trees, clipping a branch over their heads. Amusingly a squirrel, which had been sitting on the branch, jumped off, chattering loudly. The two watched it race up the trunk and disappear into the top of the oak.

They could see the skirmisher who had fired across the creek, just a couple of hundred yards off. One of the cavalry troopers, who had stayed behind, drew a bead with his carbine, fired, and the Reb scurried back up the bank of the creek and into the tangle of brush.

Vincent, without saying a word, stepped back slightly, putting the trunk of the oak between himself and the other side. He caught Joshua's glance and grinned. "Stupid way to die, the two of us standing out here gabbing."

Joshua joined him.

"You hear about Adelbert?" Vincent asked.

"General Ames?" and Joshua felt a cold chill.

"Killed the first night in front of the cemetery."

Joshua lowered his head and looked away. Ames had been the commander of the Twentieth Maine who had greeted Joshua to the regiment with the comment, "Just what the hell am I supposed to do with a book-learning professor?" Word of that one got around and was now something of a joke, one that Vincent appreciated.

Ames had taught Joshua nearly everything he knew about soldiering, and he had transformed the Twentieth from a rabble of farmers, loggers, fishermen, and clerks to a fine-edged killing machine. Ames had then moved up to brigade command with Eleventh Corps and Joshua had taken over the Twentieth.

And now Ames was dead.

A couple of more bullets slapped pass, one scoring the bark off of the oak only inches from Joshua's head.

"Ah, sirs, if all you're doing is chatting, maybe you'd better get back," a trooper announced, firing a reply. "Them bastards have seen you. And they sure love killin' officers."

Joshua looked over at the trooper and nodded a thanks. Together, he and Strong walked back through the woods and the line of Union skirmishers, who were lying down on the thick mat of leaves and green ferns with orders to not engage until the attack went in.

As they cleared the woods, the open field around the village of Harney was swarming with troops forming into lines of battle.

This was a moment Joshua both loved and hated. The sight of thousands of men falling into the long, double ranks, muskets flashing in the hazy light, blue uniforms almost like a black wall as the line stretched out across hundreds of yards, colors getting unfurled, bronze barrels of Napoleon twelve-pounders flashing in the sunlight, swinging into position; it set his heart racing.

And it always took too damn long. Crawford had been down here the evening before, made a halfhearted attack at dawn, came back across the creek, and now the other two divisions, men who had been up since shortly after midnight, were wearily deploying out.

A lone regiment could be shifted from column of march to battle line in a matter of a few minutes. An entire corps with more than forty regiments filling half a dozen miles of road could take three hours or more.

Three hours of waiting, your stomach

knotting, men standing, sweltering in the heat, some so nervous that they'd suddenly turn, stagger back a few feet and vomit, or suffer the embarrassment of a sudden onset of diarrhea, and even the bravest could succumb. "Old soldier's heart," would strike many, palpitations so fierce that it felt as if your chest would explode. It had hit Joshua once, and for a few minutes he actually feared his heart was exploding and he would die.

Every man had his ritual; some prayed, with pocket Bible out, reading their favorite verses, lips moving silently. Some prayed loudly, calling on God to watch over them, their voices pitched to a near hysteria. If allowed to sit, many would pull out a pencil, find a scrap of paper, and try to pen a farewell sentiment. Others would try to show a complete indifference, playing cards, telling jokes, or making ribald jests about others who were praying or crying . . . though even that was an act.

It was the waiting that was wearing. Once it started, then came the rush, the exultation, and, yes, the terror, but at last you were in it. It was the waiting that exhausted you and made you wonder, as well, just what in God's name were the generals doing?

And that is what Joshua wondered now: What were they doing?

10:00 AM, July 3, 1863

Headquarters, Army of the Potomac in the Field Near Littlestown

US Henry Hunt slowed, head cocked, listening carefully. Artillery, felt more than actually heard, a distant echoing thumping, almost like the sound when a woman at a neighboring farm was beating carpets for spring cleaning.

The long, swaying column of men, filling the road ahead and behind, most not hearing; the "feel" of gunfire was drowned out by the rhythmic tramping of feet, banging of tin cups on canteens, the myriad of sounds of an army on the march.

He pushed up from the road, riding to a low rise, and reined in. Again the thumping. It rose for a moment, dropped away.

Taneytown? Was Fifth Corps going in?

It was silent again, except for the steady rumble of troops passing on the road below. The pike, which ran from Gettysburg to Westminster and Baltimore beyond, was packed with men, an entire army on the march, dust kicking up and hanging over the road in a low, choking cloud, the morning air heavy, humid.

The men were quiet, marching with heads bent, muskets slung over shoulders, the side of the road already littered with blanket rolls and packs shed as the slow, weary miles passed. Stragglers were falling out, collapsing in exhaustion, provost guards trailing to the rear of each brigade checking the men, giving out passes when it was obvious the soldier was played out, prodding back into line with a sword tip those who were malingering.

The sky was hazy, promising a day of stifling heat. The village of Littlestown was directly ahead, the column of troops pressing through it and continuing on toward Westminster.

The smoke from the fire ahead was spreading out on the horizon, a dull, dark cloud staining the gray sky. All the men could see it, and they figured it out soon enough; the army's main supply depot was burning. More than one of the veterans in the dark, swaying columns were saying it was Second Bull Run all over again.

No, it's worse, Henry thought. Far worse. At Second Bull Run only part of the army had been cut off, and if need be the depot at Manassas could indeed be bypassed, with a single day's march bringing the troops back into Washington and its fortifications. Now they were seventy miles out from Washington. Now the enemy was holding ground that he and Warren had surveyed only two days ago, and he more than anyone else knew how good a spot that was for the defending side.

Henry nudged his mount, weaving around torn-down fences, trampled crops, and empty pastureland. Stuart's men had passed up this road on June 30th, followed then by the Union's Sixth Corps only yesterday, and now four more corps of the Union army were passing down it yet again in the opposite direction. The macadamized paving was disintegrating under the stress; farm wells had been drunk dry. Fences were used as firewood, chickens, pigs, cows, and horses disappearing. The campaign was exhausting the land, just as the ceaseless marching and countermarching were exhausting the men.

Hunt entered the town, the long column of troops standing still while a mule that had collapsed was cut away from the traces of an ammunition wagon and dragged to the side of the road. Muskets grounded, the men leaned against their weapons for support. Some looked up as he passed; others stood with heads hung low, leaning against their muskets, too exhausted to note his passing. Nothing was said. He could sense that sullenness, their anger and confusion over this turn of events.

The flag of the army commander hung limp over the entryway of a church just beyond the center of town. Headquarters was always easy enough to spot even without a flag. Staff, couriers, and reporters were always clustered about.

Hunt dismounted and slowly walked up the steps into the cool darkness of the church, ignoring the shouted questions of several reporters who tried to intercept him. They knew a major story was developing and were begging for a comment that they could then chop up as they saw fit. He avoided them as he always did.

Meade was in the cool darkness of the church, leaning against a pew, surrounded by staff, bent over a map spread out on a table dragged into the main aisle of the church. Butterfield, chief of staff, was leaning over the map, drawing a line with a pencil.

General Slocum, commander of Twelfth Corps, which was now passing through the town, stood by Meade's side; Sickles was sitting in a pew with arms folded, gazing off, his body tense with controlled fury and frustration, surrounded by his staff.

Meade looked up at Henry's approach and motioned him to approach.

"What's the situation?" Butterfield asked.

"As ordered, I stayed behind to ensure the proper withdrawal of artillery," Henry said. "The Artillery Reserve should be getting on the road by now. When I left Gettysburg," he paused, trying to remember the time exactly, "at seven-thirty this morning, Sixth Corps was just starting to file out.

"Third Corps," and he looked over at Sickles, "was moving in good order; I passed the head of their column about two miles above the town."

Henry moved to an opening around the table; Meade looked up at him. The map was hand-sketched, and he realized it was based on the survey done by Warren and himself of the Pipe Creek line.

"They're moving into the line," Meade said, "my line, the one I selected."

Henry could detect the hint of weariness and desperation in Meade's voice. Not a good sign.

"Hancock reports Longstreet has taken Union Mills."

"They have Westminster," Butterfield interjected.

"I could see it on the road; that fire could be nothing else but Westminster," Henry replied.

"The situation back in Gettysburg?" Meade asked.

"Still some skirmishing north of town with Stuart. Howard sent a brigade out just after dawn and pushed up to the Lutheran Seminary. Ewell is gone."

Henry paused. He had ridden up to take

a look before turning about to head south. Union dead carpeted the landscape, many of them the old Iron Brigade, which had made the last-ditch stand around the seminary. The building was a hospital, packed with Union wounded who had been left behind, along with Confederate wounded too critical to move. The air reeked of death and torn flesh.

"I talked with one of our surgeons," Henry continued. "He'd been captured on the first day and then left behind as the Rebs pulled out. He said the Confederate army started moving before dawn yesterday, the last of their infantry abandoning the line before midnight. All of them were heading west, and then it looked to be south. He overheard several rebel officers talking about getting around our left."

Henry almost wanted to add that Sickles's assumption had indeed been right, but knew that would only make the situation worse.

"The road to Fairfield, as I said," Sickles interjected, looking back at Henry.

Henry ignored him.

"So the only thing they have left up around Gettysburg is cavalry?" Meade asked.

"Yes, sir."

Meade nodded, looking back at Butterfield.

"Our cavalry will have to focus on Stuart," Meade said, "but if their infantry is gone, I think it's safe to pull either First or Eleventh Corps down here."

"It's a nightmare up there," Henry said. "From what I saw, there must be six to seven thousand wounded in the town and surrounding area, a couple of thousand of them rebels. The area has to be secured and help brought in."

"I'd suggest Eleventh Corps stays behind, and we put First Corps on the road down here later in the day," Butterfield replied, and Henry nodded in agreement.

The First and Eleventh had sustained over 50 percent casualties, but the old First still had a fighting edge to it. The morale of the Eleventh was totally gone after the rout at Chancellorsville and the brutal first day's fight at Gettysburg, the few good units left in that formation having been annihilated in the battle for Cemetery Hill.

"Did you say that this surgeon reported the last rebel infantry left Gettysburg around midnight?" Sickles interjected, now standing up and joining the group around the map.

"Yes, sir."

Sickles looked over significantly at Meade. "Then what we talked about before," Sickles said. "I'd like to press that case again."

Meade lowered his head.

"We know Longstreet is at Westminster," Sickles continued. "We're almost certain Hill is down there as well. So where is Ewell? Still on the road, most likely."

Sickles pulled out his pocket watch and opened it.

"It's shortly after ten in the morning. If his corps left Gettysburg around midnight and then did a night march, they've covered fifteen, twenty miles at most. That would put them between Emmitsburg and Taneytown. You only have Fifth Corps attacking there."

"That's all that *will* be there," Meade replied stiffly.

"My corps will be coming into this town within the hour," Sickles continued.

From the look on Meade's face, Henry sensed that this argument had been going on for some time.

"All they have to do is turn off on to the road between here and Taneytown. Let me support the attack on the right. Do that and we can cut off the tail of Lee's advance and put ourselves between his army and their line of supplies and communication."

"General Sickles, he doesn't need a line of supply now," Butterfield interjected. "He has ours."

"But . . ." and before he could get another word out, Meade exploded. "God-damn it, Sickles, it is our line of supply and communications that's the issue now! They are between us and Washington."

"To hell with Washington," Sickles muttered. "They've got enough men behind the fortifications to hold. We're dancing to Lee's tune; let's make him dance to ours for once."

"To hell with Washington?" Meade gasped. "Good God, man, they are bound to be in a panic down there. If Stanton can find a way, he'll get a message to me and it will be one word, just one word . . . 'Attack!' "

Meade looked back at the map and shook his head. "They're running around down there like headless chickens. Every newspaper will be screaming panic. Where's the army, Washington surrounded, Meade lost. You're a Goddamn politician, Sickles. You know it even better than I do how they'll react."

"I'm a general now," Sickles said coldly.

"For the moment," Meade snapped.

"Are you threatening my command?" Sickles retorted.

Meade looked up at him a dark fire in his eyes.

"I warned you about this yesterday," Sickles pressed, and Henry turned away.

Goddamn, now was not the time to bring that up.

"Do you want me to put it in writing?" Meade shouted. "General Sickles guessed right. Then when you run for president you can claim you could have won the battle at Gettysburg? Is that what you want?"

"I want us to win," Henry said, his voice pitched even, leaning over the table, wondering if his interruption would bring the wrath of both generals down on him. Damn all, now was not the time to argue; it was a time to make decisions and carry them through.

The two looked over at him. There was a flicker of a smile on Butterfield's face.

Meade exhaled noisily and nodded.

Sickles, still fuming, leaned back against the pew across from Meade.

"General Sickles, by the time your corps marched from here down to Taneytown, it will be mid to late afternoon," Henry said. "If your assumption is correct, that Ewell is on the road, it won't matter by then; they'll have moved down to here."

He looked up at Sickles as he spoke, but there was no response. Yet again, the irony of it, Henry thought. Sickles was right yesterday morning, even yesterday afternoon when he pressed to move straight down on Emmitsburg or support Sykes toward Taneytown. But that was too late now. Meade wanted the concentration on Westminster, a natural instinct, hoping to get the bulk of his troops there before Lee. It was obvious, though, that Meade had just lost the race, maybe by not more than an hour or two, but lost it all the same. That would haunt him. Sickles was positioning himself to be the ghost who did the haunting.

The question now, however, was what to do. By the end of the day, Meade could bring four corps into position across from Union Mills. If First Corps came down from Gettysburg, it'd be up to five corps. Then what?

Meade, as if reading Henry's mind, looked back down at the map. "Hunt, you're the only one here who's seen the entire line along Pipe Creek."

"It's a natural defensive position," Henry said, tracing the position out on the map.

"The area around Union Mills has an open ridge rising up a hundred and fifty feet or more from the flat, open land flanking the stream. Our side is slightly higher, which could give us a small advantage with artillery.

"Their right flank is guarded by a millpond and a very steep slope, which turns to the south, offering a natural anchor point."

"What about their left flank at Union Mills?" Butterfield asked. "Maybe we can go around them?"

Meade shook his head.

"We shift to the right, toward Fifth Corps, that takes us even farther away from Washington. It's Washington, damn it. We must reestablish contact with it."

"Then shifting to the left?" Butterfield offered.

"The roads just don't work for us," Henry replied. "There's a high ridge they can deploy along for half a dozen miles to the east. It'll take another day to even try to reposition to the left. In turn, that will draw the rebel army straight into Baltimore, which will cut Washington off by rail and telegraph from the North."

"It might already be cut," Butterfield said.

Meade shook his head.

"Not yet. Lee is concentrating. He knows he can't turn and move on Washington or Baltimore with us at his back."

The room was silent for a moment.

"What about waiting him out?" Butterfield offered.

"We can't," Meade replied bitterly. "They have the supplies now, and we don't. In three to five days, we'll be near starving. The only reserve ammunition we have is what we brought up with us to Gettysburg; Lee now has the rest. We can't disperse with Lee there and with that damn Stuart wandering around behind us. Lee has the line, and he's begging us to attack.

"And Washington, they'll all be screaming bloody murder. I have to attack; I have to! Once we bring the four corps on this road into line we go in. That will be nearly fifty thousand men, supported by all of Hunt's guns, two hundred pieces. One hard assault and I think we can batter our way through. We take Westminster back, reestablish contact with Washington, and Lee will be forced then to either attack us or withdraw."

Henry was silent, looking at the map. A momentum was developing, like a train that had lost its breaks and was rolling downhill. The army was moving south; Lee was in the way. There was no way to turn it around yet again, to perhaps fall back on Harrisburg. Do that and every anti-administration paper in the country would be screaming about cowardice and defeat. Stanton would hang Meade. Then who would get the army? Sedgwick, who was notorious for being slow, maybe even Sickles as a compromise to his Democratic party cronies?

Meade looked up wearily at Henry. "Go down to Union Mills. You already know the ground. Start picking out your positions. I want the artillery concentrated the way you keep talking about."

Henry nodded and tried to suppress the slight flicker of a smile.

"Knowing Hancock, he's most likely trying to force the position even now. Perhaps we'll get lucky, but if Longstreet is there already, I doubt if one corps can do the job."

"Pick your spot well, Hunt. I want every gun you've got on the line. Tomorrow morning we punch a way through. I'll come along shortly."

Henry saluted and left the church, yet again ignoring the reporters shouting questions as he mounted up, motioning for his staff to follow.

The troops in the street were moving again, wearily shuffling along; the morning heat was already trapped in the street by the buildings, everything and everybody coated in a choking cloud of dust.

Off to the right he could hear the thunder building. Fifth Corps was going in.

10:30 AM, July 3, 1863

Taneytown, Antrim

Leaning against the railing of the "widow's walk," of the Antrim mansion, four stories above the surrounding countryside, Robert E. Lee trained his field glasses on the roiling clouds of smoke billowing up just to the north of town. The battlefront was spreading out, the sound growing wider, the high crackling of musketry punctuated by the deeper thump of massed artillery.

Another courier came galloping down the street from the north, and a minute later he heard the heavy clump of boots racing up the stairs. The young lieutenant stopped beneath the ladder up to the widow's walk and Lee nodded, motioning for him to come up.

The boy saluted and handed the dispatch over.

10 AM, July 3
North of Taneytown

Sir,

I believe that I am now facing the entire Fifth Corps of the Union army. My ability to hold the forward position assigned is rapidly being compromised by flanking forces both to the east and west. Prisoners indicate that the entire Union army is moving in this direction. I request additional support.

J.B. Hood

Lee handed the note to Walter Taylor. As Walter read the note, Lee gazed back to the north and then west, the road to Emmitsburg. Rhodes's division was wearily marching past, dust swirling up, the men staggering after a twelve-hour march. Behind them Johnson's division, which had been so badly mauled at Gettysburg, should be coming up, followed at last by Pickett. At last report he was approaching Emmitsburg from over the mountains to the west.

He balanced the odds. McLaws had two brigades in Westminster, the other two going into position at Union Mills. The three divisions of Hill's corps were moving toward Union Mills and Westminster, all three of them having suffered some loss at Gettysburg, especially Heth's, which was now commanded by Pettigrew.

If I really thought about this risk, Lee thought, I'd freeze. Part of one division holding the forward flank of the line, another division here barely securing our main road of advance, and three divisions badly hit two days ago maneuvering to get into line in front of Westminster. Ewell's men were exhausted after an all-night march, all three of his divisions having been engaged the day before. They needed to rest; at best they'll be ready tomorrow for a fight, but not today, and the same stood true of Hill's men.

If indeed Hood was right, and the prisoner reports were true, in two hours the Union army could be through my line of march, cutting off two divisions to the west, throwing the whole plan into chaos.

The goal of this campaign is Westminster, but to secure it, we must hold Taneytown until the army has passed. Every man cut off, or tied up here, might be the crucial difference. If need be, Johnson can be used to support Hood, though the men of that division were badly fought out from the doomed assault at Gettysburg.

But if I don't reinforce Longstreet, and Meade is driving not here, but to Westminster, I lose that; they slip around my right, slide into the defenses around Washington, and this madness continues.

Washington, just what is Meade getting from Washington right now? That was easy to surmise, remembering the panic of only a year ago when it looked as if McClellan would indeed gain Richmond. Few politicians can see beyond the moment, to the broader strategies that can win a war, tying the hands of those who, in the next breath, they berate for having followed their orders and then lose as a result.

Stanton, Lincoln, and every politician in that town will pressure the Army of the Potomac to attack. And the quickest path to attack is Westminster. That is where he'll concentrate and drive for.

Lee looked back to the courier.

"Tell General Hood that I appreciate his concern, but at this moment can spare no reserves; I must push every available man toward Westminster. I know General Hood will do his utmost to hold the line assigned. Tell him I expect that he shall be careful of his own well-being and to keep me appraised."

The courier nodded, obviously disappointed by the orders. He repeated them dutifully then descended the ladder.

Walter looked at Lee, who smiled. "Our nerve, Walter. We must keep our nerve. Hood must hold, and we must shift the army to the right. If we get tangled up in a fight here, we could lose everywhere. Hood must hold."

11:45 AM, July 3, 1863

Union Mills

"He's going to do it," Porter Alexander, Longstreet's corps artillery commander, shouted, pointing across the valley to the north side of Pipe Creek.

Longstreet, intent on watching as the men of Barksdale's brigade furiously dug in, looked up.

Along the crest of the ridge, twelve hundred yards to the north, a line of skirmishers was in view, followed a moment later by a battle line of Union troops, a quarter of a mile wide.

He raised his glasses, scanning the advancing troops.

"A division at least," he remarked to Alexander.

Some of Barksdale's men stopped in their backbreaking labor and looked up. "Keep at it!" Longstreet shouted. "They won't be here for fifteen minutes. Keep at it!"

The men reluctantly stooped back over. Across the crest of the hill looking down on the mill, Barksdale's boys were digging in. Dirt was flying as men dug away with bayonets, canteens split in half, and the few precious shovels that someone had thrown into an ammunition wagon.

Saplings and low brush down along the slope, which flattened out into the bottomland of the creek, were being cut back to deny cover, and several hundred men were swarming over the mill, tearing off planks, clearing out the stacked-up lumber alongside the mill, and dragging the loot uphill to reinforce the trench.

The artillery batteries were better equipped for this kind of work, the crews laboring to build up lunettes, crescent-shaped earthworks around each gun, which Alexander had personally set in place.

The few scattered trees were going down as well, dropped by men who had an ax or hatchet with them. Sharpened stakes were being cut to drive into the ground, branches dragged into place and then tied to the stakes to act as a barrier to slow down a charge.

But his men, arriving exhausted, had only been at work a couple of hours. A day here, with fresh troops, Longstreet thought wistfully, even twelve hours, and I could turn this into a fortress that could stop ten times their numbers. The earthwork was barely knee-high in places, the ground hard and flinty.

Wofford's brigade had fallen in on the left of Barksdale only an hour ago, their line barely traced out. The four batteries assigned to McLaws were up, positioned between the two brigades, but short of ammunition after the action in front of Westminster. The Confederate army might have stumbled onto the biggest bonanza of the war in Westminster, but the town was still burning, reports indicating that it was utter chaos, McLaws's remaining two brigades struggling to round up prisoners, sort out some supplies to send up to Union Mills, and fight the fire sweeping the town.

Barksdale came up to Longstreet, white hair hanging limp, covered in sweat from the heat. "Should I get the boys formed?"

"Five more minutes."

The minutes slowly ticked by.

Longstreet finally turned and nodded. "Order your men to arms."

Barksdale let out a whoop and took off at a gallop, shouting for his men to form. Bugles echoed, drummers picking up the long roll, and the men of his command eagerly scrambled out of the dusty trench to where weapons and uniform jackets were stacked twenty yards to the rear.

The Yankee line was less than a thousand yards off, and now a second battle line emerged, this one moving on the oblique to the right.

Alexander waited quietly by Longstreet's side. The young artilleryman was calm, not begging for orders, knowing that he had to go with what little ammunition he had.

A Union battery crested the hill, six pieces, moving fast, guns skidding around as they swung into line abreast. A second battery came up and then a third. The infantry advance slowed and then halted, standing roughly eight hundred yards off, left flank into the edge of the small village on the other side.

Longstreet nodded to himself. Hancock knew he had to take this place, that he was most likely only facing two brigades. He wasn't going to make the mistake of feeding his men in piecemeal, the way it had been done too often by the Yankees. He would bring up every man and gun he had and then throw it all in at once.

The first gun on the other side fired; six seconds later the shot roared in, plowing up a furrow of earth in front of the First North Carolina Artillery. The gunners from Carolina hooted derisively. Seconds later the other guns of the battery opened, and a minute later another battery joined in.

The Tarheel gunners were soon down on the ground, hugging the earth behind the lunettes, as solid shot plowed in and case shot began to detonate around them.

Barksdale's men, now armed, were back into their shallow trench, some standing to watch the show, others hunkered down to wait out the storm, a few continuing to dig away.

The Yankees soon had five batteries up on the crest, thirty guns banging away, and Longstreet could tell that Alexander was getting edgy, especially when a solid shot hit one of the guns from North Carolina, smashing a wheel, the piece collapsing, a wounded gunner staggering out from behind the lunette, screaming, a jagged splinter the length of his arm transfixing him through the stomach. Several of his comrades came out, ducking low, grabbing the man, who, seconds later, collapsed dead.

The bombardment continued, and off to the left Longstreet saw a third line emerging, this one clearly overlapping Wofford's position.

He reined his mount around and trotted down the line, ignoring the shells winging in. An airburst detonated over the trench to his right, dropping several men. He pushed on, reaching Wofford's line. Looking back over the Union forces, he saw they were preparing to overlap him by at least a quarter mile or more.

There was only one thing to do, and he passed the order for Wofford to extend to the left, doubling the width of front covered by the unit, and sent Alexander galloping back to the North Carolina battery with orders to pull out of their position and move down to the left flank.

Minutes later the five surviving guns of the battery thundered by at the gallop, dismounted gunners running to keep up.

The Union artillery fire shifted, now dropping down on Wofford's men, who were spread out along the crest, exposed, lying down in the high grass of the pasture.

Longstreet, ignoring the shot humming in, slowly rode the line, letting the men see him.

"Here they come!"

The cry went up along the line, some of the men standing up to see. Longstreet looked to his right and saw them, the left wing of the Yankee line starting to advance, coming down the sloping hill, the two divisions on their center and left holding their ground.

This was going to get dicey. Hancock wasn't coming straight in; he was trying to stretch the line out, overlap it, pull off Barksdale from the position overlooking the mill, without having to charge straight in. Smart move. Though Hancock had three-to-one odds in his favor, the flat, open ground in the vicinity of the mill would be murder to cross in a direct frontal attack.

Alexander, without waiting for orders, finally unleashed his guns, dropping shell and case shot into the flank of the advancing division. Wofford's men tensed, waiting, as the range closed to six hundred yards, then four hundred, the Yankees hitting the shallow creek, slowing as they stumbled through the marshy ground.

Longstreet watched them, scanning the advancing line with his field glasses. The ground was wet and would soon get churned up. If I get another chance at this, he thought, I should push a line forward, down near the base of the ridge to tear into them when they hit the marshy ground.

The North Carolina battery was in place; and though the range was long, it opened with canister.

The second Yankee division now started forward, a classic attack in echelon, aiming for the center of Wofford's line and the artillery.

Longstreet grabbed a courier, sending him off to Barksdale, ordering the release of a regiment to extend into Wofford's line and provide close support for the guns.

The range was less than three hundred yards; with the field glasses Longstreet could pick out individual faces. The men were holding formation, sloughing through the marsh grass and damp meadows, the land beginning to slope up under their feet.

"Make ready!"

The cry raced down Wofford's line, men

standing up, holding rifles high.

"Take aim!"

Longstreet felt a frightful cold chill streak down his spine. It was horrifying to watch and yet beautiful as well, fifteen hundred rifles leveling across a front of four hundred yards, the hot noonday sun sparkling off the barrels.

"Fire!"

The volley roared, tearing across the crest of the ridge. Seconds later fifteen hundred ramrods were withdrawn, men emptying cartridges, pushing down loads, raising their rifles up, cocking, putting on a percussion cap, taking aim, and firing again, a continual roar as fifteen hundred rifles were discharged every twenty seconds.

The smoke eddied and boiled around him. He rode down the line, standing in the stirrups trying to see above the yellow-gray clouds. No one was falling along the line; the Yankees must still be coming on, pushing up the slope.

He reached the battery at the far end of the line, two guns aiming straight ahead, three angled to the left, hitting into a regiment that was beyond their flank and coming up fast. They were less than 150 yards out, charging, bent over low, a regimental flag out front, a mounted officer leading the way.

The small troop of cavalry that had ridden with Longstreet was out on the flank, individuals armed with carbines, a few with revolvers, spreading wider to try and contain the threat.

Another blast of canister ripped into the Union charge, dropping the mounted officer and the flag bearer. The men slowed; some came to a stop, raised their rifles, and fired. Longstreet felt something tug at his shoulder, and he turned slightly.

"You're hit!" It was Wofford, on horseback, coming up to Longstreet's side.

He looked down and saw the torn fabric, but there was no pain.

He looked at Wofford and forced a grin, though his heart was now thumping hard, shaking his head.

"I'll hold them here, sir," Wofford cried. "I'd prefer it if you got back a bit, sir."

Longstreet nodded. There was no telling what was going on at the center or right. He was the commander of a corps, not a brigade. Wofford was ambitious as all hell and could control things well enough.

He turned, another bullet clipping the mane of his horse so that it danced for several seconds on the edge of bolting until he reined in hard. He finally eased up and rode at a swift canter down the length of the line. It was hard to see with the smoke, but the line appeared to be holding. Men were dropping, indicating that the charge had come to a stop, the Union forces firing back rather than advancing.

Now it would be a question of volley against volley. Hitting men on a crest was far more difficult than troops deployed in the open and downslope. Once the troops out in the open stopped their charge and began standing and firing, they were sapping the momentum of their attack by the minute. The longer they reloaded and fired, the less likely they were to ever again be able to move forward. The ground might negate the three-to-one odds, but then again a determined charge just might break through. However, with this kind of firing, a new charge was less and less likely.

Reaching Alexander, he slowed for a moment. A fair amount of rifle fire was coming in on the guns, the Union artillery continuing to hit the position as well. Gunners worked their pieces, drenched in sweat, each discharge cloaking the field in smoke.

He heard a tearing volley from the right, Barksdale's men. So Hancock was wagering it all, hitting along the entire line.

Riding to the right of center, he saw the mill, blue coats swarming around it, Yankees hiding around the building and in the miller's house. A column of troops was storming across the bridge, ignoring the horrific casualties from the canister sweeping down from the heights, coming on at the double.

The charge continued on the road, a couple of regiments, running hard, colors bobbing up and down, men dropping. One of Barksdale's regiments stopped firing, waiting, men loading and holding rifles at the ready. The charge was coming up the slope, and he felt a surge of pride for those men. They had guts.

The range was less than a hundred yards, and still Barksdale held, another regiment falling silent, loading and waiting.

The range was at seventy-five yards, and the cry went up.

"Take aim!"

Five hundred rifles aimed downslope. The seconds dragged out, the hoarse cries of the Union troops rising up.

"Fire!"

He watched, features fixed, trying not to feel anything as the charge disintegrated, dozens of men going down, collapsing, their cries clearly heard.

Twenty seconds later another volley tore in and the charge broke apart, the men running back, a taunting yell rising from the Confederate lines, some of the men coming up out of their shallow trench, beginning to charge, officers screaming for them to stand in place.

And then it was over, like the passing of a summer storm that in one minute had been blinding in its intensity and now began to drift away to distant thunder and clearing skies. The smoke slowly lifted, drifting in great dark clouds, stirring and parting as the occasional hot breath of wind wafted across the crest.

The land below was littered with hundreds of bodies, some still, others crawling or twisting about in agony, their comrades falling back into the marshy ground, bugles calling for the retreat.

He watched it, curious, for a moment. They had pulled back without a real fight, not pushing in hard. That wasn't like Second Corps, which had stood defiant for hours, charging again and again at Fredericksburg.

No, that was Hancock. He's doing what I would do. Make a stab at it, hope you can break through in one quick rush; but if you can't, don't bleed yourself out. He might very well have been able to take this ridge, but his corps would be a shambles by the time they were atop it. Hancock could see that. And as always, there was the element of doubt. Hancock did not know what I might have or not have concealed just beyond this ridge. Take the crest with nothing left in reserve and then get torn apart by a counterattack.

Pete smiled.

He'll maneuver now, most likely to our left, and come in again on ground he hopes is clear. And he will soon have a lot of friends to help him if the rest of the Union army is now on the way to recapture Westminster and reestablish a line of communication with Washington. This was only the first bloody probe of what could be a long couple of days. The rest of our army had better get here if we are to hold this line against the entire Union army.

Several of the men were up and out of the trench, one of them waving a dirty handkerchief in one hand, a canteen in the other, heading down to help the tangle of bleeding men in the road.

We kill each other and then turn right around and risk our lives to save each other. A strange war, Pete thought.

The Yankees in the mill began to fire, not at the good Samaritans, but aiming to the crest, at Longstreet and the men around him.

He raised his glasses and for a moment thought he caught a glimpse of Hancock on the other side of the bridge.

You'll be back, Pete thought, next time on my flank and with more guns. Always you'll have more guns than we do. So we dig in and pray for reinforcements.

He looked to the west. Hill's divisions were still not in view, and beyond, from over by Taneytown, the gunfire echoed.

Chapter Fourteen

1:50 PM, July 3, 1863

Baltimore

Hermann Haupt set the brake on the engine and wearily leaned over a moment, head resting on the side of the cab. He looked back at Major Beveridge, who was slumped over in the wood tender, cradling his wounded arm.

"Major, could you please see to the wounded aboard? Roust someone out at the station to get ambulances."

Beveridge nodded.

"And take care of my friend there," Haupt added, nodding toward the body of the engineer. The man had died only minutes before, his last moments unnerving as he lapsed into delirium and kept calling for his wife.

His legs shaky, Haupt stepped down from the cab and started across the rail yard toward the signal station. All around him was chaos. The engines he had sent back down from Westminster were parked in a row, some with wounded still on board, a sight that angered him since they had most likely been here for at least a half hour. A dozen more engines were lined up, loaded down with supplies, barrels of rations, crates of ammunition, half a dozen guns on flatcars, and now with no place to go. Men of his command, spotting their leader, came running up, shouting questions, asking for orders, and he waved them aside, the men falling in behind him, trailing along as he stepped into the Signal Office, the lone telegrapher hunched over, writing down a message as it came in. Henry waited patiently. There was nothing ruder than to start talking to a telegrapher at work; it was a protocol that anyone in the railroad business learned rather quickly. You might be the president of the company, or a general; but when a message was coming in, you were silent.

The key stopped clattering, and the operator looked up. "Thank God you are here, sir," the boy gasped. "I've been getting queries from the War Office every fifteen minutes demanding to know where you are."

"Clear the line for a priority," Haupt said.

The telegrapher rested his fingers on the keys and started to tap out the signal ordering all other operators to stay off the line.

A moment later he looked up at Haupt and nodded.

Haupt was already writing the message down, and he handed the sheet over.

To General Halleck
War Department, Washington

Sir. At seven this morning Westminster fell to Confederate forces of at least division strength. Supplies set afire, but must assume significant amount will be captured, enough for the enemy to sustain operations for at least a week or more. Hundreds, perhaps thousand or more wagons, fully loaded, captured as well. Believe attack is supported by Longstreet's entire corps.

Last communication with Army of Potomac received shortly after dawn, from Hancock, reporting army was moving from Gettysburg to Westminster.

I am proceeding to Washington and will report on arrival.

Haupt

The message went out, and Haupt turned to the men gathered round him.

"Sir, it's a mad panic in town," a captain announced. "Damn mule drivers came storming in here at dawn, screaming the Rebs were right behind them. Pro-Union civilians are already clamoring to get on trains to get out, while others are supposedly hanging out rebel flags. Hundreds of drunks and copperheads are tearing up downtown. Several have been shot. Sir, is Lee coming here like they say?"

Haupt shook his head. "I saw no cavalry up at Westminster. I think Lee will hold there."

"Why, sir? He could have all this, if he wanted it. There ain't an organized regiment in the entire city at the moment."

"First, the Army of the Potomac. That's what Lee will go for. He will want to destroy it before he turns toward us, and that's what we have to get ready for next."

Haupt turned and looked at the rail-line map pinned to the wall of the station. It was most likely overstepping his bounds, but he sensed he had better act and do it now. To simply leave these trains here in Baltimore was a waste.

He looked back at his men.

"I want the line cleared up to Philadelphia. Get ready to move everything we have up there."

"Philadelphia, sir?"

"From there to Harrisburg. I think that is where we'll be needed most."

The men saluted and started to scramble. He saw a pot of coffee sitting on a small wood stove. The fire was out, the day far too hot to have the brew warming. He took a tin cup from the windowsill, poured it full, and drank the black syrup down cold, the drink jolting him awake.

"Get me an express down to Washington," Haupt snapped.

2:00 PM, July 3, 1863

Taneytown

"We're going in!"

The cry was like a shock from a galvanic battery. Joshua Chamberlain, half dozing in the midday heat, back against a lone elm tree in the corner of a field, was instantly awake and standing up, as one of Vincent's staff officers galloped through their ranks, waving his hat.

The struggle for Taneytown, less than half a mile away, continued to rage, the battle lines that had surged into the edge of town wreathed in smoke, soaring pillars of smoke and fire marking where part of the town, including a church, burned. The air pulsed with the roar of battle; and yet amazingly, here in reserve, only hundreds of yards away, he had actually dozed off, ignorant of the occasional bullets slapping into the tree branches over his head, the men of his command hunkered down behind a low barrier made from a split-rail fence. It wouldn't stop the random shells that winged overhead, but it could at least absorb the stray bullet.

The staff officer raced down the line of four regiments, men standing up as he passed.

"Is this it, Lawrence?"

Joshua looked over at his brother, Tom, now a company commander. The boy was all eagerness, nervously fumbling to button his uniform up so that he looked "proper" for what was to come.

"We wait for Colonel Vincent," Joshua replied calmly.

The men of his command looked over anxiously at Joshua. He extended one hand in almost a soothing gesture. Several of the men sat back down.

The heat was oppressive, the air thick with humidity made worse by the choking clouds of smoke, which slowly twisted and coiled on the field. The place they were resting had been hotly contested only a couple of hours ago, and the field around them was littered with the dead. In the area where they had halted, at least half a hundred wounded of both sides were piled around the broken-down fence.

Joshua had ordered the dead moved to one side and laid out in a row, the regimental surgeon coming up to help with the wounded, both Union and Confederates from Johnson's division.

That bit of intelligence had been disquieting. They were supposed to be facing

Hood. He had talked briefly with a captain from the Twenty-seventh Virginia, the old Stonewall Brigade. The poor man was gut shot, obviously dying, and yet still game, boasting that this time Lee had the ground and then begging for a drink of water, which Joshua gave him before stretcher bearers from his regiment carried the casualties to the hospital area in the rear.

"Here comes Strong!" Tom cried.

Joshua fixed Tom with a chilling gaze. "Officers do not get excited in front of their men, Tom," Joshua said coolly.

"Sorry, Lawrence."

"Just go to your company, Tom. I think we're moving out now."

"Yes, Law . . . yes, sir."

"And, Tom."

His brother looked at him carefully, caught off guard by the suddenly solemn tone in his brother's voice.

"Keep back from me today."

"Why?"

"A shell. Well, if we both got hit, it'd be a hard day for Mother."

Tom hesitated then extended his hand.

"Luck to you, Lawrence."

"God be with you, Tom."

Strong rode up to the edge of the fence farther down the line, shouting orders; and within seconds the other regiments started to fall in, forming a column by companies.

Without waiting for Vincent, Joshua shouted the command. His men, coming out from the shelter of the low fence, raced to fall in. Company A, in two lines, led the way with the colors out front, Company B behind them, and so on back through the ten companies of the regiment. Three-hundred-odd men forming a column fifteen-men wide and twenty ranks deep. It was a formation that in less than a minute could go from column into line of battle facing any direction.

Joshua, mounting, rode down the length of the column, saying nothing, ignoring the inferno ahead, the tearing thunder of volleys, the steady stream of walking wounded heading to the rear and the killing heat that made him feel light-headed.

"Twentieth Maine!"

Joshua turned and saluted as Strong came up to his side.

"Hell of a fight in the center. They're into the town, and it's hand-to-hand in places, but ammunition is running low. We're ordered in on the right. Warren came in a few minutes ago. Reports that Confederate troops are deploying on the flank."

"How many?"

"Don't know. He tried to go forward, heard he almost got killed, lost most of his cavalry escort."

Joshua nodded.

"We advance by column; Warren will show us where to deploy. You're last in the line, Chamberlain, so you'll be on the right flank."

Joshua nodded again.

"Nothing beyond you. You're the end of the line. Do you understand that?"

"Yes, sir."

"Let's go then."

Vincent reined his mount around and galloped off, waving for the brigade to follow. First off was the Sixteenth Michigan, followed a moment later by the Fourty-fourth New York and then the Eighty-third Pennsylvania. Joshua ordered his small column to move out on the double. The men surged over the low wall and started across the open field, the inferno of battle engulfing Taneytown now on their left as they raced on the oblique to the right.

Men from the column ahead started to drop, falling out of the ranks, in most cases hit by random shots that plucked into the field. Joshua spared a quick glance over his shoulder. So far, at least, discipline was holding. The shirkers had been weeded out long ago; all that was left now was the solid core of steel.

A massive explosion thundered across the field. To his left he caught a glimpse of a battery, a caisson going up in flames, gunners scattering.

They dropped down into a shallow valley, the stream simply a dirty rivulet in the summer heat. The land was carpeted with the wounded of both sides, seeking shelter from the storm, desperate for a drop of moisture so that the muddy trickle of water was tinged with pink from the blood of men who had crawled into the cooling bottomland and then died.

Imploring hands reached out, men crying out for water, accents of New York, Midwestern twang, and deep Louisiana bayou blended together in one hideous howl of pain and anguish.

The column crested up out of the nightmare dell. They were beyond the town, and there ahead and to his left he could see the main pike, the road from Taneytown back to Emmitsburg. The heavy post-and-rail fences bordering the road were still up in most places, festooned with bodies dangling over the rails. A line of Union infantry crouched behind the fence on the south side of the road, ghostlike in the smoke, shooting at unseen targets beyond.

The men running with Joshua were bent over, chins tucked in against throats, the instinctive pose, it seemed, of troops going into a storm, or a battle. The regiment was beginning to take casualties, fire coming in on their flank as they advanced. A bad moment. Troops hated to be caught thus, without a chance to strike back.

Joshua moved from his position on the flank of the column straight up to the front, swinging in before the colors, trailing a couple of dozen yards behind the column of the Eighty-third Pennsylvania.

The march at double time continued, running across the fields two hundred yards to the north of the road. He saw Vincent again, stopped now, sword out, pointing. The head of the column swerved, swinging down to the road, shifting from march into line of battle. Warren suddenly appeared, as if rising up out of the ground. The road ahead, Joshua realized, dropped down into another creek bed.

Joshua spurred forward, passing around the men of the Eighty-third coming up to join the two.

"It's not good!" Warren announced. "A division down by the bridge, just as I feared."

Vincent looked back at Joshua. "On the right, Chamberlain. We're forming a right angle here to the main line!"

Joshua offered a quick salute, turned about, and, waving his sword, he caught the eye of the lead company, motioning for them to follow.

They swung out from behind the Eighty-third.

The ground ahead sloped down gently into marsh and yet another muddy creek, most likely the same one they had crossed minutes before, Joshua realized.

He spurred up to a swift canter and rode along the bank for a couple of hundred yards. The creek bed curved back, turning from a north-south to an east-west direction.

This was the place, he realized. Chance to refuse the right. He watched as the Eighty-third fell in on his left. Good. They were occupying enough of the ground so he could concentrate on the bend here.

The men rapidly fell out from column into line, Joshua directing the company commanders to their places, with A Company and the colors in the center.

The men were near to exhaustion, breathing hard, several obviously on the edge of sunstroke.

Looking around, he wasn't impressed. The shallow valley did drop down forty feet or so, the land open, marshy, obviously a place where cattle would loll on hot summer days. The only animals down there now, though, were several dead horses from yesterday's fight, swelling up in the heat.

He looked to the opposite side. The

ground rose up higher, by at least thirty to forty feet more, about four hundred yards away. Not enough for an infantry advantage, but if they got artillery up there it would be hell.

The land below would be hard to traverse, but that was all. He thought of yesterday, where they were camped, the hill he had climbed shortly before dusk, the position held by Sickles. That was good ground. A regiment could hold up an entire brigade atop that hill. This would be different, a damn sight different. No great advantage to the defense here.

He turned and looked back at his men, who were now in double line, deployed in a shallow curve following the bend of the creek.

"Dig in! Get fence rails; get some men into that woodlot behind us; drag out anything that will stop a bullet. Company commanders, get water details together."

He looked down at the creek and grimaced, blocking out the thought of the bodies piled into it a half mile back.

"Just find a clear spot above the dead horses and do it quick!"

The men sprang to work even as Vincent came up and dismounted.

"Hot day, Lawrence."

"Damn hot."

The rare use of a profanity caused Vincent to smile. "Wish you were back at Bowdoin?"

Joshua forced a smile and shook his head.

"Nor I to my law office. Lawrence, you know your position here."

Joshua nodded. "I was at the staff meeting this morning. Sykes said that if need be we would sacrifice this corps, if by so doing we could save the Union."

"Sounds nice as a speech," Joshua offered dryly.

Vincent looked past Joshua and pointed. "You can see them stirring."

Joshua followed his gaze. The low crest ahead blocked the view, but the rising plumes of dust were evidence enough that something was coming.

"They get past you, Chamberlain, the entire corps gets rolled up."

"I know."

Vincent hesitated, and then lowered his head. "I think this is our place today, Chamberlain. For a while I thought it would be yesterday, back up where we were at Little Round Top. Fate decided differently."

He smiled awkwardly.

"I'll see you at the end of the day, Lawrence."

Joshua grasped his hand.

He could feel the nervous tremble, the

clammy coolness of Vincent's grip. The man before him outwardly showed no fear, but Joshua could well imagine the turmoil within, for he felt it as well. Not so much the fear for self — he had settled that with God long ago — it was for all the others, the men of the command, the fate of the corps as Vincent now said, not to make a mistake, not to waver, not to doubt. That was the thing that was frightening: not death but dishonor was the compelling fear.

"God be with you," Joshua replied. Vincent's hand slipped away. He mounted and was gone.

Joshua turned back, the swirls of dust building on the horizon.

3:00 PM, July 3, 1863

Taneytown

"Texans! Are you Hood's Texans?"

General Lee blocked the middle of the road heading south out of Taneytown as a stream of soldiers swarmed toward him. The town was a cauldron of battle, buildings on fire, artillery fired at near point-blank range sending hot blasts of canister down the street, terrified civilians fleeing, the hospital area set up in front of his headquarters at the Antrim, now under direct fire.

The heat, as well, was oppressive, so much so that he felt dizzy, weak, after two hard days with little sleep and the endless stress of this campaign. And now the center of the line was giving way, peeling back, hundreds of exhausted troops staggering from the fight, some without weapons.

The leaderless mob pouring down the road slowed at the sight of Lee advancing toward them.

"Texans? I do not believe this!"

One of the men, a sergeant, a bloody bandage wrapped round his head, stepped in front of Traveler, reaching up to grab the horse's bridle.

"Sir, General Lee! You'll get killed!"

He was near hysteria, voice high-pitched, cracking.

Lee jerked Traveler's reins, his horse shying away from the man.

"Men, my men, you must not run from those people."

"Sir, get back!"

As if to add emphasis to the sergeant's words, a corporal by his side doubled over, shot in the back, sprawling into the middle of the road. His death set off a panic, dozens of men breaking into a run.

"I am ashamed of you!" Lee cried.

Many of them slowed, looking back, lowering their heads like schoolboys caught by the local preacher in some sinful act.

More troops were pouring out of the town, some in rough formation following a regimental standard, others singly, in pairs and small knots of half a dozen, many of them dragging along wounded comrades.

"Rally to me. Form line here!" Lee cried.

The men directly around him looked up, incredulous.

"We're out of ammo, water," the sergeant replied, his voice shaking.

"You must hold, men. Hold just a few minutes more. Pickett's Virginians are coming up."

"Then, General, you go to the rear," the sergeant exclaimed. "We will hold, but only if you go to the rear."

The cry was picked up.

"Lee to the rear. Lee to the rear!"

He felt his heart swell, a momentary flutter that was almost frightening, wondering if something was giving out inside. If so, not now. Please, O God, not now.

The tightness lingered, and he felt as if he just might lose control, dissolve into tears at the sight of these men, and yet there was a fury of the battle within him as well. They had been pushed far beyond what mere mortals could be expected to endure. Five hours of hell, most without ammunition, most with wounds, some of which would prove mortal or crippling. Yet now they started to gather round, men and boys pushing in front, shouting for him to retire.

He looked up. The center of town was only several hundred yards away. Surely they were noticed by now. He saw flashes in the dim smoky light, sharpshooters up in buildings. Another man nearby went down.

He looked to the west. The left flank, what was left of Johnson's division, bowing back out of the town, driven from the road. Beyond them, nothing.

Where was Pickett?

A bullet snapped past. He felt a cold rush of anger.

"I am with you!" Lee cried. "Now forward. Forward!"

He started to edge up the road, pushing his way toward the town. As if a flood tide had reached its crest and now fell away, so did the rout. By the hundreds men turned, some with a fire in their eyes, many with reluctance, but determined nevertheless. Their throats so parched they could no longer break forth with the eerie shriek of their battle cry, they went back in to the fight.

Lee tried to force his way forward, but

the sergeant and half a dozen others blocked his path.

"Out of my way."

"No, sir."

"Out of my way. That is an order, Sergeant!"

The sergeant held Lee's gaze.

"You can shoot me after this is over, General Lee," the sergeant cried, his voice breaking with emotion. "But I ain't gonna see you killed this day. The boys will hold."

"Out of my way, Sergeant. Do it now!"

"Sir, you're the spirit of this army. You die and we lose. I'll die making sure you live to carry on."

The men with the sergeant gathered round, hemming Traveler in, silent, looking up at him.

"General Lee!"

He looked back. His staff was coming up, riding hard, obviously frightened that he had slipped from their grasp.

The few hundred who were left of Hood's old Texan Brigade were back into the town as the staff swarmed around Lee, putting themselves between him and the line of fire.

The sergeant who had so defiantly stood against Lee now seemed to shrink as one of the staff angrily shouted for the sergeant to let go of Traveler.

Lee, tears in his eyes, shook his head.

The sergeant let the reins drop and bracing his shoulders looked up at Lee. Their gaze held for a minute, and it shook Lee to the core. The man was true to his word. He expected to be shot for insubordination, an insubordination of trying to save his general from a foolish act. It was one thing to ride along a volley line wreathed in smoke, another to lead a charge into a town. If the sergeant had not intervened, Lee realized, he'd most likely be wounded or dead by now. He looked back up, and the Texans who had turned about were dropping by the dozens as they pushed back into the town.

"Your name, Sergeant?"

"Sgt. Lee Robinson, sir, Third Texas."

Lee, in an uncharacteristic gesture, leaned over and extended his hand. The sergeant nervously took it, holding the grasp for just a second before stepping back as if the touch of a god might scorch his hand to the bone.

"I shall pray that you return safely to your family when this is over, Sergeant Robinson. God be with you."

The sergeant saluted, then lowered his head.

Lee looked back to the west. Where was Pickett?

3:10 PM, July 3, 1863

West of Taneytown

"Virginians! This is our moment! Forward for Virginia!"

Standing in the stirrups, George Pickett raced in front of his advancing line, a battlefront three brigades wide, from left to right half a mile, six thousand rifles flashing and gleaming in the hot, murky, afternoon sun. Four batteries of artillery advanced with him, bronze Napoleons glinting, gunners running alongside their pieces. Red battle flags, the square Saint Andrew's cross of the Army of Northern Virginia, held high, marking the advance.

He wept with joy at the sight of it. The chance, at last, to lead a charge across a sunlit field of glory, battlefront sweeping forward relentlessly, marching to the sound of the guns. It might have taken an extra half hour to form everyone into line of battle, but by God, it was worth it for this moment. We are ready. We are doing it in style, Pickett thought. It was good, so good to be alive on this afternoon in July, the dream of all things possible before him.

3:20 PM, July 3, 1863

West of Taneytown

"They're coming."

The cry raced down the line.

Joshua, intent on strengthening his front, urging the men to dig in, pile up logs and fence rails, anything that could offer shelter on this bare slope, paused and looked to where many were now pointing.

His heart swelled at the sight of it. The flags were visible, held up high, materializing beyond the shallow crest, now rifle tips, and then the men. He gasped at the sight of it. A division advancing as if on the parade ground, line of butternut and gray, their right flank overlapping the road, the left arcing far beyond his own right.

Skirmishers, who had been visible for several minutes, darted forward, coming into long rifle range. From out of the center of the advance, he saw something that he had often read about but never witnessed on the field, a battalion of their artillery advancing with the attack, as in the days of Napoleon, one battery of guns actually galloping ahead of the line and then swinging into position atop the low crest four hundred yards away.

He looked back. The corps artillery was enmeshed in a fight for the town. There was not a single piece here to reply. He knew where that fire would be focused: It would be a cauldron of hot iron against human flesh, and it would be his men who bore the brunt.

Unsheathing his sword, Joshua stepped to the center of the line. He was not one for dramatics but felt that if there was a time for it, it had to be now.

He climbed atop a small boulder that studded up out of the thick pasture grass. "Men of Maine!" he cried. "We are the right of the line. We must hold."

The men looked at him. They were veterans. They did not need the false theatrics that some officers indulged in, and they knew better than to expect it of him.

"The fate of the Republic might rest on what we do now," he said, with a passionate, heartfelt intensity. "Let us resolve to stand and, if need be, die for the Union."

The men were silent, but he could see the glint in their eyes, the nods coming from a few. He stepped back down and turned to face the approaching attack.

Rifles that had been stacked while the men dug in were snatched up, uniform jackets put on, the regiment hunkering down behind the flimsy barrier thrown up in the few precious minutes given to them prior to the attack. The watering party came running up from the creek, twenty men burdened down with the canteens of the regiment. Most were still empty, the others covered with mud and green slime. The men grabbed for them anyway.

A lone wagon came up behind Joshua, a welcome sight as half a dozen boxes were offloaded, six thousand more rounds of ammunition. The driver, seeing the rebel advance, lashed his mules, continuing down the line.

The boxes were torn open, packages of cartridges passed down the line, men stuffing the packets of ten into pockets and haversacks.

The first shell screamed in, air bursting just behind the line, shrapnel lashing into the grass. Another shot, then another, and in a couple of minutes it was a virtual storm as four batteries concentrated their shot on the Twentieth.

The rebel battlefront came relentlessly in, the center brigade breaking to the south of the batteries, the other brigade to the north. Once sufficiently downslope and below the muzzles of the artillery, they started to edge back in to form a solid front.

Joshua watched, impressed by their cool, steady advance, their relentless professionalism. It was obvious the enemy brigade to his right would outflank him by several hundred yards. He looked down his line. There was not much he could do other than refuse the right. He passed the word.

The gunners had found the range. Several times he was washed with clods of dirt and scorched grass from shell bursts; men were collapsing, wounded beginning to stagger back.

It was down to two hundred yards, the Confederates now coming down the slope into the shallow valley of death.

Joshua stood up tall, raising his sword high. "Volley fire present!"

The men stood up, rifles rising up, held high.

"Take aim!"

The three hundred rifles of the Twentieth Maine were lowered. The Confederate advance did not falter, a defiant cry bursting from their ranks.

"Fire!"

The explosion of smoke cloaked the view. To his left the other three regiments were already engaged, tearing volleys ripping across the line.

"Independent fire at will!"

He started to pace the line, crouching down low at times, trying to see what was happening. The charge was still advancing, slowed by the marshy ground but coming on hard. The artillery fire slackened, and he caught a glimpse of their guns, moving up, coming in closer to extreme canister range.

A volley suddenly tore through his line, men to either side pitching down. The sergeant holding the National Colors aloft staggered backward, collapsing, a color guard prying the staff loose from dying hands and hoisting it back up.

His men were down now, crouched behind their cover. Shooting, tearing cartridge, kneeling up to pour the powder in and push the bullet down into the muzzle, charge rammed down, then sliding behind their cover again while capping the nipple, taking aim, and firing.

Flash moments stood out, a man endlessly chanting the first line of the Lord's Prayer while loading and firing, a young soldier screaming hysterically while cradling the body of his brother, an older sergeant laughing, cursing as he coolly loaded and took careful aim, all wreathed in smoke, fire, sections of piled-up fence rails disintegrating, the men behind torn apart with splinters as a solid shot smashed in.

The smoke eddied and swirled, parting momentarily to reveal a surge of rebel troops coming up the slope, stopping and firing a single volley, men in gray and butternut dropping, then slowly falling back . . . and then surging forward again.

He heard wild shouting, looked to his

left and saw a red flag right in the midst of the Eighty-third, a mad melee of clubbed muskets, men clawing at each other, the charge falling back.

To his right the enemy attack had already overlapped, a couple of regiments across the creek angling up the slope into his rear. Grabbing Tom, he sent him down to the end of the line, ordering him to refuse the right yet again, to turn a thin line back at a right angle. He lost sight of his brother.

How long it had gone on it was hard to tell. The sun shone red, dimly through the smoke. Men were standing up, pouring precious water from their canteens down their barrels, the water hissing, boiling, then running a quick swab through in a vain effort to clean out the bore enough so they could continue to fight. Some were tossing aside their rifles, clogged with burnt powder, picking up the weapons of the fallen.

The Confederate artillery relentlessly pounded away. In several places the dry pasture grass was burning, adding to the smoke.

"Chamberlain!" He looked up. To his amazement, it was Sykes in plain view, his mount bleeding from several wounds.

"Are you Chamberlain?"

Joshua instinctively saluted. "Yes, sir."

"I'm retiring the corps!" Sykes shouted,

voice drowned out for a moment as a shell exploded directly above them. For a second he thought Sykes had been hit; the man seemed to reel from the shock and then recovered.

"Chamberlain," and Sykes's voice was low-pitched, the general leaning over, staring straight into Joshua's eyes.

"Sir."

"I need twenty minutes, Colonel. Your regiment is staying behind."

"Sir?"

"The corps is flanked here. They're counterattacking in the town. The Fifth is fought out. I have to save what is left, Colonel. As this brigade begins to fall back, you are to retire, slowly forming a defensive line. Then, sir, you must hold. You must give me twenty minutes to save what is left."

Joshua nodded. The world seemed to be floating. He felt a strange distant detachment from it all. This man was ordering the annihilation of his regiment, and all he could do was nod in agreement.

"You understand what I am ordering, Chamberlain. No retreat. You stand until overrun. You must stop this charge."

"Yes, sir."

Sykes sat back up in the saddle, his staff gathered nervously around him, ducking low as a shot screamed past.

"Strong is dead, Chamberlain. So are

Barnes and Crawford."

The words seemed to float through him. He knew he should feel remorse, anguish over the death of a trusted comrade. But he found himself still trying to fully comprehend Sykes's order.

Sykes extended his hand, and Joshua took it.

"God be with you. I hope we meet again someday."

"Thank you, sir."

Sykes spurred his mount and galloped off.

Joshua dwelled for a moment on the absurdity. That man had just ordered him to near certain death, and he had thanked him for it. The madness of war.

"Company officers!"

The men came in, only half a dozen; the rest were down, or did not hear the order. One of them, thank God, was Tom.

He squatted down, the men crouching around him.

"The Eighty-third is falling back!" one of them cried, half standing and pointing.

"I know; that doesn't matter."

They looked at him, focused, some already sensing what their corps commander had just ordered.

"We're staying behind. The corps is pulling back. We're the sacrifice to buy time."

"Goddamn!"

Joshua fixed the swearing captain with a sharp gaze. Embarrassed, the man lowered his head.

"We start to fall back, slowly, spreading out to fill the line and try to draw that entire division in on us. Don't lie to the men. Tell them what we must do. We hold until overrun. I'm not ordering any of you to die. You feel you can't hold anymore, that it is meaningless, then try and get out with what you can."

"Lawrence, you're staying, though?" Tom asked.

Joshua nodded.

"Begging your pardon, sir, but I'll be goddamned if I run," the profane officer announced.

Joshua smiled and slapped him on the shoulder. "Good luck to you."

He stood back up. "Twentieth Maine. Form skirmish line. Guide on me!"

The company officers raced down the narrowing front, passing the word. Several men looked at Joshua, incredulous; one of them stood up, threw aside his rifle, and ran. A sergeant started after him, but Joshua called him back.

"I want volunteers this day!" Joshua cried. " 'The rest of you who have not the stomach for this fight, let him depart.' "

The men looked one to the other, several of the more literate grinning at his theft of a good line from Shakespeare.

The men began to spread out into open skirmish order, extending their front as the other regiments gave way.

To either flank, the enemy division surged forward, wild exuberant shouts marking their advance.

Joshua continued to back the line up slowly, men firing, loading as they fell back a dozen paces, firing yet again. The flanks were overlapped, some of the Rebs surging on, particularly along the road that was too far away for him to cover, but in the center, and on the right, the Confederate charge curled in on this last defiant regiment.

Several minutes passed, and then a blizzard of shot began to sweep the line as entire regiments fired volleys into this final knot of defiance. He had a moment of grim satisfaction, realizing that in the smoke and confusion shots that were missing his men were slamming into the opposite flank of the enemy.

Joshua, bent low, came up to the flag bearer.

"I don't want our flag captured. Cut it up!" he shouted.

The men nodded, grounding the staff. One pulled out a bowie knife, and tears streaming down his powder-blackened face, he cut the national colors from the staff and with violent slashes began to tear the flag to ribbons. Several of the color guard gathered around protectively, the men tearing off parts of the stripes, cutting away the stars; and then racing down the volley line, they paused by each comrade, slapping a piece of the precious fabric, so proudly borne in battle, into the hands of those who had stood beneath the symbol of all that they fought for.

This action triggered a final, convulsive ringing in, like an animal trapped in a fire, which finally, in its agony, begins to curl up on itself to die. The men came in around the bare staff, fragments of flag passing to outstretched hands, many of which were trembling, covered with blood.

Joshua reached out. The color bearer, weeping unashamedly, handed him a small patch of blue emblazoned with a gold star. Putting the fragment of flag in his breast pocket, then with sword in his left hand, Joshua drew a revolver with his right.

He began to dissolve into tears as well. They were down to less than a hundred men, the regiment, now almost in a circle, firing to nearly every point of the compass. Thousands of Confederates swarmed around them, closing in.

He saw an officer coming toward him, sword held high, shouting something, a wall of men behind him, coming on at the double.

Joshua raised his pistol, lowered it to take aim. . . .The blow staggered him. He slammed the point of his sword into the ground, to act as a crutch. He felt numbed from the waist down, his legs uncontrollable. He dropped the pistol and, reaching out with right hand, grabbed the flag staff. The color bearer stared at him, and a second later the boy silently collapsed, the life gone from his eyes.

That final volley seemed to drop half of those who were left. For a moment there was no sound, only the terrible blow against his hip, the fear then of falling, of failing now in front of his men.

"Lawrence!"

It was Tom. Cheek torn open, blood streaming down on to his chest, wrapping an arm around him.

"Cease fire! Hold your fire!"

He had not given the order. Incredulous, Joshua looked around.

"Who gave that order!" He tried to speak the words, but they wouldn't come, only a soft groan of terrible anguish from the pain.

An officer was before him, Confederate, with hat jammed strangely down on to the hilt of his sword.

"For God's sake, sir," the Confederate said, "please surrender."

Joshua looked around. They were

hemmed in tightly, the few men still standing in a knot around the empty flag staffs.

"How much time?" Joshua asked woodenly.

"Sir?"

"How much time did I buy?"

"More than enough," the Confederate whispered. "Now let me help you."

The man extended his hand. Joshua tried to reach out, but couldn't. The world was growing dim, the rebel officer standing a great and terrible distance away. There was a moment of darkness, and then he was on the ground, looking up.

"Can you help my brother?"

It was Tom, voice that again of a boy.

"My brigade surgeon is one of the best; I'm having an ambulance brought up."

"Thank you," Tom gasped.

Focus returned. He was looking up at someone kneeling by his side. Others were gathered around, his own men and Confederates mixed in.

"You are my prisoner, sir. And, by God, sir, I will see that you survive this."

Joshua could only nod.

"Two hundred of you defying a division. My God, I wanted it to stop before you all got killed, but you wouldn't stop!" the Confederate exclaimed. "This damn war! I'm sorry for what we did to you here. You

have the soul of a lion, Colonel."

Joshua smiled and tried to reach up.

The Confederate took his hand.

"I don't believe we have been introduced," Joshua whispered. "I am Colonel Chamberlain, Twentieth Maine."

"Gen. Lo Armistead at your service, Colonel."

"My brother, my men," Joshua whispered, "don't send them to Libby Prison. All that I ask."

"You have my word."

Joshua fumbled at his breast pocket, touching the torn fragment of blue and gold.

"Then I can sleep now," Joshua sighed, and he slipped into darkness.

Chapter Fifteen

4:00 PM, July 3, 1863

The White House

The heat in the room was oppressive as Lincoln came in and nodded an acknowledgment to the men standing; he motioned for all of them to sit down. Directly across the table from him was Stanton, still struggling with his asthma attack, face ashen. By Stanton's side was Secretary of State Seward, on the other side Gideon Welles, Secretary of the Navy, and finally General Halleck.

Before Lincoln even spoke, Stanton pushed over the latest telegrams, and Lincoln scanned through them.

"This one from General Haupt," Lincoln said. "That confirms it. The Confederates have seized our base of supplies at Westminster."

"Yes, sir," Stanton replied.

"I want to see Haupt."

"He's trying to get down here now," Halleck interjected, "but the situation in Baltimore is difficult."

Lincoln nodded, adjusting his glasses as

he went through the messages that reported rioting, a wrecked switch blocking the line that might be the act of Confederate cavalry, and now a report from New York that there were threats of a riot over the draft, which had just been instituted.

"I have a delegation of congressmen and senators waiting downstairs," Lincoln finally said. "What am I to tell them?"

"That Meade is reacting in an appropriate manner," Halleck replied. "The military can handle this."

"Can it?" Lincoln asked sharply, fixing Halleck with his gaze. "Do you know, at this moment, what General Meade is doing?"

Halleck's features went flush, and he cleared his throat. "Mr. President, you have the same communications that I do."

"And they tell me nothing," Lincoln replied. "So, may I ask how do you know that Meade is acting in, as you say, 'an appropriate manner'?"

"Sir, he is a good officer, well trained. He will know what to do."

"And that is?"

"To move on Lee and block him from advancing on Washington."

"He won't advance on Washington," Gideon Welles interjected.

"May I ask how the navy is aware of this?" Stanton retorted.

"Because he can't; that's how I know."

"Pray, enlighten me," Stanton snapped.

Lincoln extended his hand in a calming gesture as Welles, bristling, leaned forward, ready to take the bait.

"Go on, Mr. Secretary," Lincoln said softly, "I want to hear your reasoning."

"Thank you, sir," Welles replied, turning away from Stanton as if he didn't exist. "The Army of the Potomac is still a viable force, even if they have been surprised, flanked, and cut off."

"We don't know if they were surprised," Halleck interjected.

"General, please let the secretary speak," Lincoln said, and Halleck fell quiet.

"Simple logic dictates that Lee cannot march south on us with such a potent threat in what will now be his rear. Second, it is fair to assume that though he has seized Westminster, it will take hours, perhaps days, to sort out all the supplies taken there, if he has indeed seized those supplies intact, though reports from Haupt and from Baltimore indicate a vast conflagration is consuming that town."

Halleck raised his head as if to speak, but a glance from Lincoln silenced him.

"Finally, you have two forces here in Washington. A garrison of over twenty thousand men behind heavy fortifications, and my own forces as well, several ironclad ships and more available by tomorrow morning, which can be brought up from Fortress Monroe, along with the garrison there, and the naval yards at Hampton Roads."

"What good is a navy for Washington?" Stanton snapped.

"If the government has to be evacuated, you'll thank God one of my ships is here to take you off," Welles replied sharply. "But beyond that last extremity, the guns available can, if need be, sweep all of this city. Lee will know that. He knows, as well, that it is the Army of the Potomac that must be his first goal. That should be our focus now, and frankly, sir, you can tell the members of Congress that if they are truly afraid, they can go to the navy yard and my men will protect them tonight."

Lincoln could not help but smile, and he nodded his thanks.

"Mr. Seward, you have been quiet, sir," Lincoln said, now turning to the man who he knew, even after two years, still felt that the presidency should be in his own hands rather than that of a Midwestern lawyer.

"I agree with Gideon, sir, but there are other considerations, political and international ones."

"Go on."

"If General Lee can achieve a true triumph of arms on Northern soil, the destruction of the Army of the Potomac, the threat or even the seizure of Washington might be moot. We have to be concerned about the potential for major riots over the draft in New York and Philadelphia. The combination of those factors might embolden Napoleon III to do something rash."

"Such as?"

"An attempt to break the blockade."

"I'd like to see him try," Welles interjected.

"We are not dealing with someone who is totally rational here," Seward replied calmly. "The emperor of France is caught up in Mexico with this absurd attempt to put a Hapsburg on the throne there, to create a dream of a Catholic empire, as he puts it."

"He's half-insane," Stanton snarled.

"Precisely the point," Seward replied. "We are not dealing with someone rational. Oh, the English will make noises, but they will not act, knowing we could sweep Canada off the map if we so desired. Besides, Parliament will not support an effort that also includes supporting slavery. But Napoleon may think he has little to lose. Up to now he would not recognize the Confederacy unless Britain did so as well, but a victory by Lee could change that. He won't try for Charleston or Wilmington, but Texas, being on the border with his war in Mexico, that might be different. I could see him attempting to force the blockade at Brownsville and thus triggering a fight.

"He knows that if and when we win our struggle here, we will indeed move to oust the regime he is setting up in Mexico. He is counting on a Confederate victory. If at this moment he can create a debt from the Confederate government by recognizing them and offering much-needed supplies, it will serve his purpose. All he is waiting for is an excuse."

"And a victory against Meade might do that?" Lincoln asked.

"I think so."

Lincoln nodded and looked back down at the telegrams. "What you raise needs to be seriously considered, but I think we should focus now on the moment and not a potential that might not develop for months, if at all."

Lincoln looked back at Stanton. "Do you concur that, for the moment, Washington will not be threatened?"

Stanton coughed, struggled for breath, and all were silent. "In general, yes. But that is not to say that Stuart might not be here soon. He could ride from Westminster to Baltimore in half a day, from there to here in just one more day."

"We don't know Stuart is there," Lincoln replied. "Haupt reports only infantry."

"I can't imagine Lee leading his attack only with infantry," Halleck said. "It's against all standard doctrine."

"Perhaps Lee is ignoring doctrine. He has done so before."

"Lee is a professional, sir. We of the military spend years studying so that it is done right."

Lincoln sensed a veiled rebuke from Halleck. Like so many of the generals of his army, they were ready to blame any failure on civilian interference.

"Well, apparently Lee did it right today," Lincoln replied softly, "with or without cavalry in the lead. But I am not interested in a debate over your doctrine, General Halleck; I want a clear understanding of what orders should be issued to Meade, if any."

Stanton and Halleck looked at each other, and Lincoln could easily tell that these two had been talking long and hard about this prior to the meeting.

"He has to attack Lee at Westminster," Stanton announced. "He must cut through and reestablish contact with Washington, to impose his forces as a barrier against attack on Baltimore and Washington."

"But I just heard a fairly cogent argument from Secretary Welles that Lee will not march on Washington first."

"Are you suggesting then, sir, that Meade do nothing?"

"No."

"Then what, sir?"

Lincoln shook his head wearily and looked out the window for a moment. "He must preserve his force at all cost but then, at the same time, so threaten Lee as to prevent him from maintaining a prolonged operation in the North."

"Then that means attack, sir," Stanton replied sharply. "With luck, Lee is not yet concentrated at Westminster. He might be able to cut off the head of Lee's advance, then swing into a favorable position closer to us."

"Is the Army of the Potomac the imperial guard of Washington or is it an army intended to fight and destroy Lee?"

"Sir?"

"Answer me that, please."

"It is the main army of our efforts in the East, sir."

"Then it must be used wisely and not sent into a headlong attack simply to get back here. Gentlemen, I pushed for that attack at Fredericksburg, and I will live with the price of that, the terrible memory of that tragedy and those unnecessarily lost young men to my dying day. I think the order to Meade should be one of latitude, to make offensive actions as deemed necessary, but not to rush headlong into an assault solely to regain contact here."

He paused for a moment.

"If need be he can even fall back on to the Susquehanna, there to reestablish supplies. His presence there will prevent Lee from moving on us and also prevent Lee from threatening Philadelphia or Harrisburg."

Stanton looked at Halleck, and the two were silent.

"Are we in agreement then, gentlemen?"

Welles and Seward nodded.

Lincoln took a sheet of paper and quickly jotted down a note, which he then pushed over to Stanton.

"I am ordering General Meade to act on his discretion, but to ensure, above all else, the cohesiveness of his forces, to threaten Lee, but not to seek a headlong assault unless certain of its outcome."

"To be certain in anything, sir," Stanton replied, "that, sir, is impossible in war."

"You know what I mean," Lincoln replied. "I do not want him to act rashly at this moment. He must be off balance. He might assume that we are here screaming for him to counterattack. I want him to understand our thinking, to move with some prudence and judgment."

"Yes, sir."

"Anything else, gentlemen? I must attend to that delegation from Congress."

"None, sir," Stanton replied, and the others nodded.

"Then if you will excuse me."

All stood as he left the room. Seward and Welles quickly followed, leaving Stanton and Halleck alone.

"You'll take this over to the Treasury Department," Stanton said, passing the note to Halleck. "Send it to Baltimore. See that it gets routed to a courier who has a reasonable chance of getting through, perhaps up to Hanover."

"Anything else, sir?"

Stanton sat silent for a moment, a shudder passing through him as he fought to draw in a breath of air. He took another sheet of paper and started to write then passed it over to Halleck.

"Send this as well," he said, "and make sure it is postdated after the president's."

Stanton left the room, and once the door was closed Halleck scanned the second message.

From Secretary of War Stanton

Sir,

In accordance with the president's orders I am adding as well that while the preservation of your forces is of the first and fore-

most concern, I must still strongly urge you to act by any means possible to ensure the safety of Washington and Baltimore, using whatever means at your disposal to prevent the advance of General Lee's forces in this direction.

Stanton

6:30 PM, July 3, 1863

Union Mills

The evening was hot, oppressive. Henry Hunt looked to the west, shading his eyes against the blood red sun. Thunderheads were building to the southwest, the clouds of heaven mingled in with the haze of smoke from over toward Taneytown.

Word was filtering in of a brutal fight, most of Fifth Corps annihilated, tangling with three divisions of the Army of Northern Virginia. Strange, though, two of the divisions were Longstreet's corps, yet Hancock had sworn that old Pete was directly across from them.

Raising his field glasses, he scanned the Confederate line under construction along the south bank of Pipe Creek. It was a chilling sight, watching an enemy army dig in, thousands of puffs of dirt popping up, then falling, as troops labored away using bayonets, canteen halves, shovels if they could find them, even their bare hands.

The entrenchment rimmed the crest of the hill, the new fortification line a raw slash of earth across pastures, corn and wheat fields, following the contour of the hills and ridges facing Pipe Creek.

A second line was beginning to form farther down the slope, an advance position that would protect troops firing straight across the open ground over which the Army of the Potomac would have to advance before hitting the base of the opposite slope. The only disadvantage, it was a hundred feet or more lower than where he'd planned to place his guns. He could fire down into it, and perhaps break it apart, if they did not dig in deep enough during the night.

The lumber mill, blacksmith shop, outbuildings, and the miller's house alongside the main road to Westminster were still burning. The compound had been hotly contested ever since Hancock's midday assault, the issue finally being resolved when a rebel battery put a couple of dozen shells into them. The civilities, of course, were first observed, with a flag of truce offered to get the miller and his family evacuated. They chose to come across the creek and into the Union lines. The irony was that one of their kin across the road, whose house had been torn apart for lumber by the Confederates, had supposedly acted as a guide for Longstreet.

"How are you, Henry?"

Henry turned and offered a weary salute as Hancock rode up, trailed by several staff. With a groan, Hancock dismounted. Henry noted that for once the dapper general's shirt was stained and dirty, his blue jacket open, vest gone. The heat, the exhaustion of the day, were obviously getting to Hancock as well as his men.

"General, how are you?" Henry asked, offering a salute.

"A bad day, Henry," Hancock sighed. His chipper attitude was gone. He had fought a hard fight and didn't like to lose. He knew, as well, there'd be an even grimmer fight come tomorrow.

Union infantry directly in front of where the two stood were half-heartedly digging in, their officers not pressing them too hard. They had, after all, marched nearly twenty miles, gone into a failed assault, and were suffering now in the early evening heat. They knew, as well, that short of some insane miracle, the Rebs would not be so courteous as to attack, so the digging in struck many as busywork without purpose or profit.

Hancock, without waiting for permission

from Meade, had asked for a truce an hour ago in order to clear the wounded and dead from the field. The truce would end at sunset, and the last of the ambulances that had lined the road were coming back through the lines, bearing their grisly cargo to the hospital area set up on the far side of the ridge behind them.

Henry looked again at Hancock and saw that what he had first taken to be dirt on Hancock's shirt was, in fact, dried blood, as if someone had grabbed hold of him and then let go.

Hancock, noticing Henry's gaze, looked down. "One of my brigade commanders — Webb. Held him as he died." Hancock's voice trailed off.

Henry looked over his shoulder to one of his staff and motioned. The boy reached into his pocket and pulled out a flask, tossing it over. Henry handed it to Winfield, who took a long drink.

"Thanks, Henry."

"Losses?" Henry asked.

"Fifteen hundred dead and wounded," Hancock sighed. "I wonder now if I should have pressed it. We might have been able to flank them."

His voice was edged, pitched a little too high. Exhaustion and shock were hitting him, Henry realized.

"It was at least an hour after I called it

off before we saw more of their troops come up. If I'd had another division in reserve to exploit the break, I think I'd of continued the assault regardless of loss. It was just that I had no reserves. I needed all three divisions to try and turn the flank."

He lowered his head.

"Damn. Fifteen hundred men. Goddamn, what a waste."

"You didn't know that then."

"I do now, Henry. I do now. Looking at them over there, now, digging in like that, it puts a knot in my gut when I think my boys will have to go in against that tomorrow."

Henry did not reply. Whoever was directing the buildup on the other side of the creek knew his business. Henry had been surveying the position for over two hours, and nowhere could he see a weak spot, a fault, some uncovered defilade for advancing troops to exploit. Across two miles, it was a covered front. Throughout the night they'd most likely extend it farther in both directions. This line was beginning to look just as tough as he thought several days earlier when he had surveyed it from the other side. Except now it was Confederate troops digging in on the good ground, and Union soldiers who would be going down into that wet valley and climbing the hill. Exactly the opposite of what he had envisioned when first he had surveyed this valley for Meade. "How many guns you bringing up?" Hancock asked.

"Every one. I plan to have two hundred and fifty pieces in place by tomorrow morning. A massed battery here with a hundred and twenty rifled pieces, the Napoleons farther down the slope, and to the right a quarter mile for close-in support. Meade's authorized me to have control of corps artillery as well in terms of initial placement."

Hancock shook his head.

"Sickles for certain won't like that."

Henry wanted to say the hell with him, but knew better.

"Once it gets dark I'll start moving my pieces into place. Some of them are still halfway back to Gettysburg though and might not be up here till dawn."

Hancock nodded wearily, gaze still locked on the opposite slope. "Goddamn, they're digging in hard," he whispered.

Henry left him to his thoughts, mounting up to ride on, carefully picking the spot for tomorrow's fight.

7:30 PM, July 3, 1863

Frizzelburg (Five Miles West of Westminster on the Taneytown Road)

"Sir? General, sir, we're here."

Startled by the gentle touch on his shoulder, General Lee sat up, momentarily confused.

He saw Walter Taylor, silhouetted by the twilight to the west, leaning over him.

"Where?"

"I think it's called Frizzelburg, sir," and Walter chuckled softly. "If someone tries to pin that name on this battle, sir . . . well, I hope you call it something else."

Lee smiled and stifled a yawn. The canvas sides of the ambulance had been pulled down in order to give him some privacy on the ride down from Taneytown. He barely remembered leaving the burning town after sending a swift courier ahead to arrange a meeting with Longstreet.

"Are you feeling all right, sir?" Walter asked.

"Fine, Walter, just fine."

It was a lie of course. What happened after the Texans had rallied and then, moments later, Pickett had come crashing in on the flank was a blur. He remembered Walter riding up, triumphal, exclaiming that hundreds of prisoners had been taken and the Union troops were falling back in disorder.

Shortly after that he passed out. He remembered awaking on the broad veranda of the Antrim, anxious staff gathered round, a doctor leaning over him, listening to his heart through a hollow wooden tube. For a moment there had been a sense of panic, that the attack he had suffered during the winter had come back.

"Heat and exhaustion," was the doctor's prognosis, along with an order for a day of bed rest in a cool room.

Absurd.

He agreed to two hours of rest, a sofa being dragged out of the Antrim and set up on the porch so that he might have a cooling breeze. A drink of cool lemonade made him nauseous, but he managed to keep it down, and then reluctantly took a glass of Madeira on the doctor's orders to settle his nerves.

The battle was turned over to Ewell, who pressed the enemy back onto the road to Littlestown before the fight simply gave out, both sides equally exhausted after a six-hour struggle in the boiling heat.

Yet another half victory, he thought. We should have completely enveloped the Fifth; now they will have the night to dig in, perhaps be reinforced. Yet again he sensed that Ewell had not pushed when he should have.

The doctor and Walter had strongly objected to his desire to come down to Westminster to meet with Longstreet, but it had to be done, though he was glad for the compromise of riding in an ambulance and the suggestion that Longstreet come part of the way to meet him here.

Walter unlatched the back gate of the ambulance and offered a helping hand, which Lee refused. He must not let the men think he was weak. Before sliding out, he buttoned his uniform, wiped the sweat from his brow, and put on his hat, a straw flattop with a broad brim, the one concession he had publicly made to the heat.

As he stood up, the vertigo returned and he swayed for a few seconds, reaching out to rest a hand on the wheel of the ambulance and then withdrawing it. Too many were watching. The men must not have the slightest doubt, the slightest fear as to his well-being. Too many men had died back at Taneytown to protect him, and too much now depended on the men believing in him. They drew their strength from his strength, and there could be no doubts in a battle like this.

Staff and some cavalry were setting up a large wall tent on the front lawn of a small church. Several pews had been brought out and set in a horseshoe around the front of the tent. Smoke was curling up from a blacksmith shop alongside the church, a team of artillerymen working to reset the rim on a wheel. At the sight of Lee, they stopped their work and stood in respectful silence.

Lee recognized Porter Alexander, Longstreet's chief of artillery, and Porter saluted.

"I came on ahead, sir," Porter said. "General Longstreet is coming here as fast as he can."

"Thank you, Colonel. And all is well with you?"

"Yes, sir. A tough fight today, but we did well."

"I am glad to see you are well."

Porter nodded. Looking into Lee's eyes, he started to say something and then just simply smiled awkwardly.

A black cook was already tending the fire burning before the tent and circle of pews. As Lee approached, he stood up, offering a cup of tea in an earthenware mug, which Lee gratefully took, nodding his thanks.

He sat down on one of the pews and then caught the attention of a cavalry captain, who seemed to be in charge of the detail setting up camp.

"Captain, did you get permission to borrow these pews and tables?"

"Sir?"

"Permission from the minister or sexton?"

"Sir, ahh, I couldn't find them."

"Then please do so and at once. Otherwise, take them back in. We do not steal from churches."

The captain looked around exasperated, then sharply motioned for a sergeant and a couple of privates to find the minister. They ran off.

Lee stood up and walked over to the blacksmith shop. The artillerymen came to rigid attention at his approach.

"Stand at ease, men."

The artillerymen drew back, looking nervously at each other.

"Were you in action today?" Lee asked.

"Yes, sir," a corporal replied, his skin so fair that it was blistered and peeling from the harsh sun.

"Where?"

"Sir, in front of Westminster. One of our guns got this here wheel knocked off by a shell. Cap'n sent us back here to get it fixed since we can't find our forge wagon."

Lee, half listening, nodded.

The smell of the forge was somehow comforting, clean charcoal, hot iron; it triggered a memory, but he wasn't sure what of; of childhood perhaps. It was soothing somehow.

He could see that he was making the men uncomfortable by his presence, and saying, "Carry on," he turned away, walking, sipping the tea that was flavored with honey, breathing in the clean air of a hot summer evening, rich with the smells of pasture, fields, and woods.

Twilight was deepening. All was quiet except for the movement of a column of troops on the road nearby. The men moved slowly, no banter or high spirits. They were exhausted, staggering on, turning north to move up toward the front line.

Since he was standing in the shadows, they did not notice him. He was grateful for that. It gave him a moment to be alone, to clear his thoughts.

What I did today bordered on madness. It was madness, he realized. If I had led that charge, I most likely would have been killed. If I die now, in battle, or from something else, such as my heart, it might doom our cause. The burden of that realization was always something that struck a chord of fear within: the frightful responsibility of all this.

For I am a man under authority, having soldiers under me: and I say to this man,

Go, and he goeth, and to another, Come, and he cometh. . . .

As a boy I thrilled to hear the stories of Washington, my father beside him, he thought. I never realized the burden, the weight bearing down on Washington's soul that if but one mistake was made the dream of the Republic would die.

And the men, merciful God, the men. That sergeant. I could have drawn my revolver, pointed it at his head, and still, for my sake, he would have hung onto the bridle, letting me kill him before he would let go, doing that to protect me.

He lowered his head. "Do not let me fail them, O Lord," he whispered. "For their sake, not mine, let me not lead them astray."

A pot clattered behind him, and he looked over his shoulder. The black servant had accidentally spilled a coffeepot. A couple of the men laughed, one in a whisper vilely swore at the cook, and the poor man lowered his head.

And what of him? Is this the reason we fight? To keep him in bondage? If so, what would God say of our cause?

He pushed that thought aside. He had reasoned it out long before; at least he thought he had. When this war is over, then perhaps this scourge upon our souls can be addressed. Those around him at headquarters knew it was a subject not to be discussed; the higher ideal of fighting for the Constitution, for the right of states against the usurpation of the central government, was the cause. Yet in his heart he knew that for some, especially the wealthy planters and men of ignorance who could only feel superior when another was suppressed, slavery was indeed their root cause; and in the end that root would have to be torn out.

He shook his head. He had to stay focused; to ponder on such imponderables would take what little strength he had, divert him for all that must be done; otherwise, yet again this sacrifice of the last three days, on both sides, would be in vain.

He looked eastward. There was a glow in the darkening sky. The reports of what had happened in Westminster were frightful. Half of the village had burned to the ground, dozens of civilians dead or injured in the conflagration. Burning along with it, he was told, were millions of dollars of precious supplies. Yet even then, in spite of the destruction, millions more had been captured. The Union army was so well supplied that even the leftovers seemed amazing to the men of the Army of Northern Virginia.

Two of McLaws's brigades were still

sorting it out, but reports were that over two thousand wagons had been captured along with their teams and the contents within those wagons, limbers, ambulances, and carts. A quartermaster with McLaws had sent up a written report that Taylor had read off to him just before they had left Taneytown: a pontoon train; 50 wagons loaded with precious shovels, picks, and other tools; 250 wagons of rifle ammunition; 200 limber chests of artillery ammunition; wagons loaded with boots, uniforms, champagne, medical supplies, canned milk, tobacco, cartridge boxes, belts, socks, a virtual cornucopia for his army, which just three months back was on the edge of starvation because less than half a dozen trainloads of food a day could be delivered to the front lines at Fredericksburg.

To think of all that was destroyed and yet so much remained to be taken, a treasure trove far exceeding what Jackson had taken the summer before at Manassas.

And they will replace it, he thought. The only question left, the only way he knew he could win, was to break their resolve here, to deal them so shattering a defeat that though they could make the weapons of war, there would be no one left with the moral strength and will to wield them. That was the only way victory could be achieved, though it would mean that many a boy on the other side of the stream dividing them that night would be dead by tomorrow.

He thought of the week before Chancellorsville, a cool spring evening, and how a Yankee band serenaded his men, until both sides stood along the banks of the Rappahannock, laughing, sharing songs, and then all together singing "Home Sweet Home," most of them dissolving into tears.

We must win the war, but in so doing we cannot shatter the peace, so poisoning the common well of our shared heritage that the hatred on both sides will burn for a hundred years. Win or lose, if this war continues, that might happen nevertheless. That is yet another reason it has to end here, he thought.

Win it here. I must steel myself for that, even if it kills me a day later, as I thought it might this afternoon. Defeat them and in so doing save lives and bring this brutality to a close before it consumes us all, North and South.

The twilight deepened. Flashes of light on the western horizon caught his attention. He stiffened and focused toward the west, and then he relaxed; thunderstorms, not gunfire.

A first hint of coolness wafted around him, drifting across the fields, a gentle breath of wind carrying the scent of fresh-mown hay. He sighed, letting the moment settle his nerves.

"General Lee?"

It was Walter, coming out of the shadows.

"Yes."

"General Longstreet is coming in."

"Yes. Thank you, Walter."

He headed back toward the tent. The cavalry captain stepped before him and saluted. "Sir, the minister for this church; we found him."

Lee nodded.

"And?"

"He gave us permission, sir. Said he was a Southern man and would be honored."

"Thank you, Captain, and in the future, always check first. When we are finished here, make sure everything is returned to its proper place."

"Yes, sir."

That detail taken care of, Lee went back to the fire in front of the tent and settled down on one of the pews. The straight hard back of it was somehow comforting, a reminder of more peaceful times.

He caught the eye of the cook and handed back his earthen mug.

"It was very good. Could you please

pour another cup? And I think General Longstreet will want one as well."

As he spoke softly, he looked sharply at the trooper who had sworn at the cook. The trooper dropped his gaze and turned away.

Taking the refilled mug, Lee stood up as Longstreet approached, trailed by his staff, all of them dust-covered, hollow eyed. The two exchanged salutes, Longstreet taking the mug offered by the cook, who nervously withdrew.

"Tell me everything, General," Lee said, motioning for the two of them to sit down on one of the pews by the fire.

Longstreet all but collapsed and leaned back for a moment, stretching, looking up at the sky. "Hancock attacked at midday. Almost overran our position, then withdrew. If he had pressed harder, he might have taken it. I only had two brigades up at that point; he hit with all three of his divisions."

"Winning with those odds; then it must be an excellent position," Lee interjected.

Longstreet nodded.

"It seems that a couple of officers with Meade's staff had surveyed the ground on the morning of the first. Meade was thinking of establishing his line there before he got drawn into Gettysburg."

"Which officers?"

"Gouvenor Warren and Henry Hunt."

Lee smiled sadly.

"I remember Hunt from New York. Very good man."

He fell silent. Yes, Hunt knew good ground. Malvern Hill a year ago was proof of that.

"I've had my people out examining the south bank of the stream all day. Before coming here I rode most of it myself. Sir, it's highly defensible. The creek, locals call it Pipe Creek, is open bottomland, in some places a quarter-mile wide and flat. The land slopes up sharply on our side. The right flank is very secure. There's a millpond blocking the approach, and then the creek curves back to the south and southeast, with a very high ridge looking down on it. Most all of the countryside is clear cut to feed several mills and forges along the creek. Open fields of fire along most of the front.

"The other side, they have some advantage. At a number of points the land on their side is higher, fine positions for massed batteries."

"The range?"

"Eight hundred to twelve hundred yards at a couple of points."

Lee nodded.

"I didn't get across the creek, but locals tell me that there's a fairly decent road behind the ridge, perfect for them to shift troops to one flank or the other and to keep men concealed until they attack."

"And you believe they will attack?"

Longstreet took a sip of the tea and set the mug down on the ground. He leaned over, hands clasped, gazing at the fire. "They have to."

"I have my reasons to believe so, General," Lee said. "Tell me yours."

"Meade will be forced to. We trumped him these last two days. He's new in command. Communications with Washington are most likely still down for him, though a courier might have slipped past Stuart by now and gotten in. If so, that courier will describe what is most likely a mad panic in Baltimore and Washington."

Longstreet chuckled sadly and, lifting up the mug, took another drink.

"First off, he'll be ordered to break through at any cost, an order he cannot deny or refuse. Second, he is new in command. If he allows us to achieve what we did without a fight, he'll be branded an incompetent and a coward. If he turns back, retreats toward York or Harrisburg, he will definitely be branded a coward and relieved of command. Therefore he will attack."

"What would you do if you were

Meade?" Lee asked.

Again the sad chuckle. "I'd retreat."

What would I do? Lee wondered. There was a flash of arrogance, a sense that he never would have allowed this to happen in the first place. Then again, I did attack frontally at Gettysburg two days ago and was within a hairsbreadth of doing it again the following morning, until Pete talked me out of it. Don't be so quick to judge.

"I believe he will attack come dawn," Lee said.

"I do too."

"What will he have?"

"I know that Second Corps is there. Additional troops were spotted on the flank of Second, a skirmisher reporting he recognized Slocum commanding the Twelfth Corps riding along the line."

"The Fifth attacked in front of Taneytown today," Lee interjected.

"I heard."

Longstreet looked at him, and he flushed slightly. Most likely word of the incident with the Texans had spread.

"I understand Pickett did it right this time."

"Masterful," Lee replied. "If it hadn't been for one regiment holding out, diverting Armistead, we might of bagged the lot."

"Sir, that still leaves four of their corps unaccounted for."

"Where you are, the road toward Westminster, that's where you will see them next."

"You mean Union Mills."

"Yes, where the road crosses Pipe Creek. That's what he'll drive for."

"You expect everything then on that flank?" Longstreet asked, cradling the mug of tea and then taking another sip.

"Yes."

"What about Taneytown?"

"If his intent had truly been to try and cut our flanking march, the time to act was this time yesterday. Meade sent down only one corps, and I suspect that the commander of that corps took upon himself the responsibility of hitting as hard as he did. If he had been backed up by another corps, he'd of cut us apart today.

"No," Lee continued, "Taneytown is not his focus. It's Union Mills."

"Tomorrow then?"

"Five corps most likely. Maybe one in reserve or back even at Gettysburg. The last report from Stuart, dated at noon today, reported a mass movement of troops on the road from Gettysburg toward Westminster. But some infantry, Stuart identified it as Eleventh Corps, remains at Gettysburg and still holds the high ground there."

"And what of Stuart, sir?"

"He's doing his tasks as ordered. He continues to shadow Gettysburg, but reports, as well, that he has heavily engaged the Union cavalry on the road from Gettysburg to Hanover. The results are not conclusive, but at least he is keeping them occupied, which is all he need do at the moment."

Lee turned and looked off.

"At dawn," Lee said, his voice now cool, eyes half-closed as if he were looking off into some distant land, "they'll open with a barrage, every gun they have. Under cover of that, they'll advance. It won't be piecemeal, as at Fredericksburg. I suspect Meade is still bitter about that fight, how he almost broke through when commanding his division there but wasn't backed up. Meade will have time to think about this, and he will come in with everything at once. His goal will be to overwhelm with sheer numbers."

Lee fell silent and like Longstreet he sipped at his tea.

"We've lost fifteen thousand men so far in this campaign," Lee whispered. "Johnson's division is shattered almost beyond repair. Hood has taken heavy losses as well. We can't afford another day of losses like the last three."

"I know that, sir. But we're dug in now."

"You'll finally have that defensive battle you've talked about so much," Lee offered.

Longstreet looked over at his commander, not sure if there was a touch of reproach in the last comment.

"Your placement of men?" Lee asked.

"Two brigades of McLaws's astride the road and to the left. Next is Anderson, then Pender, Pettigrew, and Early on the left. Rhodes is the reserve, with one of his brigades to the right of McLaws.

"Our front is about four miles, the left extending to a bend in the creek, which again refuses the flank; the land below is marshy. It's not as dense a line as I would like, roughly one rifle per foot."

"Artillery?"

"Alexander has done an excellent job," and Longstreet nodded toward his artillery chief, who was gathered with the staff over by the blacksmith shop.

"He's warned me, though, that if Hunt brings up all his reserves, it will be hard going with counterbattery. We'll have somewhere around a hundred and twenty guns on the line."

"Supplies?"

"That's the good news, sir. McLaws is

overseeing the movement of captured supplies up from Westminster. I believe he sent a list up to you."

Lee nodded.

"We're moving up every captured round we can lay our hands on," Longstreet continued. "Wagons loaded with shovels and entrenching tools are getting the highest priority at the moment. There's plenty of rations as well. We can stay here for a week, fighting a pitched battle throughout, and still have supplies left over. In fact, we would have more supplies than we have ever had before. The Union army does have its supply system mastered."

"Have one of your people draw up a detailed map for me, then have them go over it with Walter. I want place names clearly marked so there is no confusion. Major topographical features to be shown and the placement of troops indicated.

"Copies are to then go to each division commander. Communicate to McLaws as well that I want the tightest security on Westminster. Property of civilians is to be protected and aid given to those displaced and injured. Any soldier who violates the law will be dealt with harshly, swiftly, and publicly before the citizens of that town."

Longstreet nodded in agreement.

"I want a list of those civilians who

died. Personal letters of regret signed by me will be sent to each of their families, along with offers of compensation. I'll not have the Northern press blame us for that tragedy or lay accusations of abuse on us."

"The Yankees started that fire, sir."

"Yes, but it is we who now hold that town."

"Yes, sir."

"I'm establishing my headquarters here. That will put me equidistant between the two wings of the army."

"Sir, regarding the arrangement of troops."

"Yes?"

"Two of the divisions of my corps are on the left. I have units from Hill and Ewell mixed in together on the right. The placement was haphazard in a way without regard to unit designations."

"You filled them in as needed," Lee replied.

"Yes, sir. There's no way to sort it out now. Its just that . . ." and his voice trailed off.

In the darkness he took another long sip on the mug of tea, nearly draining it.

Lee sighed.

"General Longstreet, though it is not official, I have decided, at least for this moment, to relieve General Hill of his responsibilities without relieving him of his command."

"Sir?"

"He is sick."

Lee said nothing more, but his distaste for the origin of the illness was obvious in his tone of voice.

"For the remainder of this campaign, you shall command the right wing centered at Union Mills comprised of the divisions just described. Ewell will command the left centered on Taneytown, and Stuart will command the forces north of the Union army."

"Early might not like it," Longstreet offered.

The dislike between Longstreet and Early was a barely concealed secret. Several of the division commanders who had served under Jackson looked upon Longstreet as a slow plodder.

Lee slapped the side of the pew with an open hand. "I don't care who likes or dislikes it!" he snapped. "We are here to win this battle. Everything else, likes, dislikes, vanity, and pride, are to be left behind. If someone disagrees with that, I will hand them their discharge and they can go home. Do I make myself clear, General?"

"Yes, sir."

The outburst was loud enough that the staff who had been standing at a respectful distance stiffened, hearing every word. Good, it was theatrics, but at times a general needed to resort to that.

"I give you authority to relieve any division commander who does not comply with your orders" — he hesitated for a moment — "as I would relieve you as well, General Longstreet, if you did not comply with mine."

"Yes, sir."

He caught the sense of surprise and even a touch of resentment in Longstreet's "Yes, sir." Good, let everyone standing in the shadows hear this exchange as well.

It was something he had realized back in Chambersburg less than a week ago. If this campaign was to be won, ultimately it would be on his shoulders whether it was indeed won or lost. He must seize firm control. There could be no moment of hesitation, no questioning, no confusion. An army must have a single sense of purpose and mission, deriving from its commander clear down to the lowest mule driver or cook. If not, when the crisis came, someone would shrink back and in so doing ten thousand would die for yet another hollow victory, or worse, a bitter defeat.

"Then we understand each other, General?"

"Yes, sir."

"Fine then." Lee slowly stood up, indicating that the interview was finishing.

"Ewell will command the left wing of Pickett, Johnson, and Hood. Johnson's division is fought out; Hood took a rough beating as well. Therefore, Pickett will be the vanguard of maneuvers when the time comes."

"Your intentions with him, sir?"

Lee smiled. "I'll decide that in due course, and I may go with him when the time comes. The left is the element of maneuver, and you are the base of maneuver. You must hold and defeat the vast bulk of the Union army when it attacks. After that, we will flank it and force its collapse. Then Stuart will round up the remnants as they flee from us.

"They must not be allowed to reform," Lee said, with a sharp emphasis.

He said no more. He had learned something from Jackson, who was infamous for his sense of security. Ever since the lost orders before Sharpsburg, dropped by either a courier, or perhaps even a general, and recovered by a Union soldier, he was learning to be more cautious. An overheard word, a staff officer boasting in front of a civilian, upon such things battles often turned, as it had, indeed, at Sharpsburg.

"Come tomorrow," Lee said. "Now, General, a suggestion for both of us that I know my young Colonel Taylor would approve of, and that is sleep. We both need our strength for tomorrow."

Longstreet nodded in agreement.

"I'll leave Alexander and Venable here to review the map with Taylor," Longstreet announced. "My headquarters will be on the lines above Union Mills."

"God be with you, General," Lee said.

The two saluted and Longstreet disappeared into the shadows.

Walter came up and Lee quickly reviewed what needed to be done. "I'm sorry, Walter; I know you are even more weary than I."

Walter smiled. "Sir, to be frank, and no disrespect intended, but I am half your age. All of us wish that you would just get some sleep."

Lee nodded; again the weariness.

Without comment he retired to the privacy of his tent. His cot was already set up within. He removed his jacket and hat and sat down on the cot with a muffled groan. He tried to struggle with his boots but then gave up, not wishing to call for someone to help. Slipping off the cot, he knelt, offering his evening prayer, thinking of his boy in a Union prison, his wife in Richmond, his daughter lost and in the warm clay of North Carolina, and all the boys he had seen fall this day, July 3, 1863.

Did I do the right thing today? he thought. *Dear God, I hope so. It could have been more, far more, but then I must know it could have been different, an ending of dreams rather than a hope that it might soon end in victory.*

Lying back, he stared at the ceiling of the tent. On the outside of the canvas several fireflies had alighted, their soft, golden green glow winking on and off. Katydids and crickets chirped outside, mingling with the sound of whispered talking, a horse snickering, a banjo in the distance, and surprisingly, some laughter.

Tomorrow, tomorrow is the Fourth of July, he thought. I hope that is not a bad omen. We break the Union on the birthday of its founding. God grant us strength.

A moment later there was a gentle knock on the tent pole.

"Sir. General, sir?" It was the black cook, bearing a plate with dinner.

Lee was asleep, and the old man quietly withdrew.

8:45 PM, July 3, 1863

Headquarters, Army of the Potomac, Near Union Mills

It had been a very long day. Henry slowly dismounted, letting the reins of his horse drop, one of the staff taking the horse and leading it away. Headquarters had been pitched off the pike a mile or so north of Union Mills, half a dozen tents with sides rolled up, coal-oil lamps gleaming. The scent of rain was in the air, a brief shower having dampened the field minutes before.

They were gathered here, Meade, Hancock, Sickles, Slocum, Sedgwick, along with dozens of staff, orderlies, cooks, cavalry guards, provost guards, reporters, even Sullivan the photographer.

Henry was barely noticed as he stepped into the largest tent, where the generals were gathered around a table, maps spread out, the air thick with cigar smoke and the scent of whiskey, sweat, and unwashed bodies.

Meade looked up and nodded a recognition. His eyes were deep set, hollow, obviously half-closed with exhaustion.

"Your report, Hunt," Meade snapped.

"Sir, nearly all the guns will be in place by six A.M. Four batteries, however, will definitely not arrive from Gettysburg until later in the morning. The road is a shambles, and it looks like rain, which will make it worse getting them through."

"What can we count on?"

"I'll have nearly forty batteries in place, including those batteries nominally under corps command. A grand battery of a hundred and twenty guns on the heights just above Union Mills, a secondary battery of sixty Napoleons downslope a third of a mile to the right, and then other batteries positioned farther down the line.

"We have an average of two hundred rounds per gun; that's everything, solid shot, case and shrapnel, canister. We have no real reserve anymore."

"I know that," Meade snapped.

"Sir, it means I can offer, at best, two hours of sustained fire, at which point we will be getting dangerously close to depletion, except for canister."

"Can you put enough fire into the point of attack to support a breakthrough?"

Henry did not reply for a moment.

"Can you?"

"Sir, I can't promise."

"Damn it, Hunt, just give me a straight answer."

"Sir, there are too many variables. I plan to put upward of twenty thousand rounds of fire into a front less than a mile wide. I think that will have a serious impact. That's all I can promise, sir."

Meade grunted. He sat back, striking a match on the table leg, and puffing a half-smoked cigar back to life.

"Then that's it," Meade said. "Any questions?"

Henry looked around at the four corps commanders standing about the table. Hancock seemed to have recovered from his shock of earlier and was sitting quietly, eyes intent on the map, sipping whiskey from a tin cup. Slocum and Sedgwick were whispering softly to each other to one side, while Sickles stood alone.

Henry could sense the disquiet, a terrible sense that this was not what any of them had dreamed possible only four days ago.

"Hunt, is it possible to get more guns on my flank?" Sickles asked.

"I want everything massed," Meade said, before Henry could reply.

Sickles was uncharacteristically quiet and simply nodded.

The gathering was silent, and Henry looked back at Meade. "Sir, if there is nothing else, to be honest I'd like to get a little sleep. It's going to be a long day tomorrow."

"Yes, Hunt, a very long day. You're dismissed."

Henry stepped out of the tent, glad to be

back in the open. He looked around, trying to spot where his own staff had gathered, and then saw them alongside a house adjoining the field where headquarters was pitched. He started toward them.

"Hunt."

He almost wanted to ignore the summons. It was Sickles.

"Hunt, a moment of your time."

Henry turned slowly, offering a salute as Dan approached out of the shadow, tip of his cigar glowing.

"What do you think of this?" Sickles asked.

"Sir, my job is to follow orders. I was to position my guns to support a grand assault come dawn, and that is what I've done."

Sickles, hands in his pockets, looked down. "Hancock's badly shaken. It will be his corps that starts the assault. Meade has already given him a direct order that he can't go forward with them. The man is heartsick."

Henry was surprised by the note of sympathy in Sickles's voice.

"Hunt, it's going to be bloody, very bloody. Second and Twelfth Corps advancing side by side, then Sixth Corps coming in behind as the breakthrough force, with First Corps arriving before dawn as additional support. We both know that the old Second and the Twelfth are decimated."

Henry said nothing. He had heard the plan earlier, the argument by Sickles to strike to the right, if need be to slice down toward Frederick, Maryland, the suggestion sent down by Howard to retreat back to Harrisburg. He had heard all the arguments, the endless damn arguments. And now they had settled on this, a full-out frontal assault come dawn.

If there was a hope, any hope, it was that Lee's men were just as exhausted from their grueling march, the two days of running battles, and the casualties inflicted on them. Combine that with a massive bombardment at dawn, the greatest of the war from the way things were developing, and maybe, just maybe they would break through.

"Hunt, it will be a frontal assault across twelve hundred yards of open ground. As bad as Fredericksburg."

"Burnside fed it in piecemeal there. Meade at least knows to do it all at once," Henry replied.

Sickles shook his head. "Goddamn. I looked at the land around Gettysburg. Maybe this is it, I thought. Maybe just for once it is us on the high ground and them coming at us. I could see it from atop Rocky Hill, imagine them coming across those open fields with our guns bellowing in their faces. Now, yet again, it's us."

Henry nodded.

"Meade can't do anything else," Henry finally offered.

"I know! There's been no word yet from Washington, but we both know what those damn politicians will scream for."

Henry couldn't help but smile. Sickles, a politician, denouncing his own.

"But it doesn't have to be tomorrow," Sickles said softly.

"That will give them another day to dig in."

"And maybe another day for us to think, to think and then try and maneuver."

"What about Washington?" Henry asked.

"As I said before, the hell with Washington. Lee can't take it; anyone with a brain knows that. We slide to the west and break off the action. Lee can't get across the Susquehanna; all the bridges are down, and Couch has twenty thousand men up in Harrisburg."

"They're militia, not worth a damn in a real fight," Henry said.

"Enough, though, to keep Lee from trying to force a crossing. Let him take Baltimore, if he wants the damn place.

We slide around to the west, cross the Potomac, and start marching on Richmond if need be. Do that and in the end Lee will have to bow to the same pressures that are on Meade right now. He'll have to break off and come after us."

"It will never happen," Hunt said wearily. "The attack goes in at dawn."

"And do you think it will succeed?"

Henry sighed. "I have to believe it will. Give me enough ammunition, and I can suppress their guns. Do that and there's a fair chance with a full assault of three corps; forty thousand men, hitting all at once, just might break through."

Sickles dropped his cigar and snuffed it out with the toe of his boot. "Fine, Hunt," he said dejectedly. "Just keep enough ammunition in reserve to cover the retreat. You'll need it."

Henry watched as Sickles turned and went back to the command tent.

What more could he say? That he felt sick to his stomach, that he wished the hell he could just go to sleep and not wake up for a week? Sickles was a corps commander looking to him for advice.

Then again, he could almost feel sympathy for a man who prior to this campaign he had viewed with outright distaste. Sickles was outside the mold. He was vain, self-serving, glory hunting, and yet he loved his men and had the guts to stand on the front line. If there was to be a sacrifice tomorrow, he wanted it to mean something, and not just be another mad exercise in futility. There was nothing for him to offer though.

Henry slowly walked over to where his staff was camped. The boys were all asleep; he could not blame them. They had tied his horse off, brushed it down, and by the soft, glowing fire left a plate with some salted beef and hardtack. He didn't have the stomach for it.

Finding his blanket roll, Henry opened it up. Looking up at the sky, he decided to put the rubber poncho on top and lying down on the cool, damp grass felt good, comforting.

A light rain began to fall, but Henry didn't notice. He was fast asleep.

Across the fields to either side of Pipe Creek ten thousand campfires flickered, glowed, and then slowly guttered out as the cool blanket of a summer's night rain drifted down from the heavens. It was not enough to wash away the blood in the pastures around Taneytown or to still the smoldering embers of Westminster, but for the moment it was a comfort after the long days of heat and dust and misery.

Some were still awake. Armistead,

looking up at the sky, thinking of the colonel he had tried to save, wondered if that gallant soldier was still alive. At least I am still alive this evening, he thought and curling up under a horse blanket, he drifted off into a dreamless sleep.

Winfield Scott Hancock did not sleep, gazing out from under his tent, watching the droplets fall, watching the night slowly pass, wondering what this day of July 3rd had brought and why it could not have been different.

George Pickett, lost in dreams of glory won and the embrace of a fair lass, slept the sleep of the victorious.

Major Williamson, sitting on the bluffs overlooking Pipe Creek, was wrapped in silence, comrades asleep about him, wondering what the morning would bring and would the day to come be his last.

Wesley Culp, a private with Johnson's division, lay curled up on his side near the Taneytown-Emmitsburg Road, clutching his torn stomach, crying softly, as his life trickled out. Only the day before he had crept through the lines to visit his family home at Gettysburg, a Northern boy who had somehow wound up in the Southern ranks. Now he was dying here. At least I could have died on my own land, he thought.

John Bell Hood, arms folded, walked

slowly through the camps of his division, nodding, offering a few words of congratulations, as men looked up at him. Finally he walked out into the fields, alone, looking north toward the fires burning on the other side. His arm hurt, scratched by a ball. It could have been worse though, he realized.

Porter Alexander crawled under a limber wagon, stretching out, calculating the numbers in his head, glad for once that there was more than enough ammunition to go around, in fact more ammunition than he could fire in a long battle; glad as well that the day was over as he closed his eyes.

And thousands more drifted in and out of sleep. Those who were still alive, who might have been dead, and those who were alive and would be dead come morning. From the far reaches of a nation or from just down the lane they had come, these 160,000 boys and men, filled with tragic dreams of glory or with no dream at all other than a realization that they had to be here.

They had flowed over the roads, cresting mountains, leaping rivers, a tidal flow of a nation that still had not resolved if it could, indeed, be a nation. They were unlike any armies in history. Few of them truly hated; none had dreams of conquest, of pillage and rape and destruction. Both armies fought mostly for an ideal, ironically the same ideal in the minds of many, and a few fought for a greater vision of all that could be, a dream that transcended the moment and the age they lived in. If they prayed, both prayed to the same vision of God, and even at this moment thousands had that same book open to favorite passages, most of them turning to the Psalms, silently reading while comrades and enemies slept.

Some now wandered the fields near Taneytown, lanterns bobbing up and down in the night mists. And when a comrade was found, more than one sat in silent grief, wondering why, wondering as well if fate had been different, might that smiling friend be alive this evening, rather than cold and ready to go back into the earth.

The campfires guttered out. All was still except for the muffled calls of sentries, the snoring of exhausted men, the steady patter of rain, and the distant, muffled sobs of the wounded. Occasionally a man asleep would cry out, stir, and sit up. Looking around, he'd remember that it was but a dream, and then silently lie back down. The nervous who could not sleep sat by the dying fires, staring off into the night, pondering, as all soldiers have pondered, the meanings behind all things, the reasons why, the dreams yet to be lived, the fears of what might be.

And so, four score and seven years after the founding of the Republic, July 4, 1863, began.

Chapter Sixteen

5:30 AM, July 4, 1863

Union Mills

A steady cool rain fell from the early morning sky, the first light of dawn revealing the dark gray overcast blanketing.

Coiling mists rose up from the bottomland of Pipe Creek, blanketing the earth in a dull, impenetrable gloom. Clouds above turned into fog in the valley. Everyone in the valley labored in virtual blindness. Above its fogged-in floor, gunners, who had been up most of the night, continued to labor on the barricades protecting the grand battery of 120 rifled guns. Tarpaulins were spread above caissons to protect the precious ammunition loads from moisture.

Henry paced slowly along the battery front, trailed by his dejected, wet staff. He kept looking to the south but it was still too dark; nothing could be seen of the opposite slope. All was gray and black.

The guns were spaced at fifteen-foot intervals, far too close for field operations, but he wanted a maximum concentration of firepower. Hopefully, multiple damage against his own guns from a single hit would be at a minimum. He had seized on the idea of using one caisson to provide ammunition for each two-gun section, thereby keeping the area directly behind the guns a little less crowded. The sixty caissons in place ten yards behind the guns were loaded almost exclusively with solid shot and case shot, with only a couple of rounds of canister. Once depleted, the caisson would be sent to the rear and a fresh load brought up. His orders were to keep up a sustained, rapid bombardment for two hours, set to begin at six in the morning.

The minutes ticked by as he continued to pace the line. Gunners were beginning to drop their entrenching tools, falling in around their pieces. Men looked expectantly at him. He said nothing, lost in thought, pacing the line, and now silently cursing . . . the mist and ground fog blanketing the valley and opposite slope. Nothing was visible.

"General Meade," one of his staff hissed.

Henry turned and saw Meade riding up, headquarters' flag hanging limp in the rain, a cavalcade of several dozen staff and hangers-on following.

Henry saluted as Meade approached.

"Goddamn it all, Hunt, what do you think?"

"Sir, I won't fire unless I can see what I'm shooting at."

"I know that, but what do you think?" Meade leaned forward in his saddle, as if by drawing a few inches closer he might penetrate the gloom.

"Sir, you know, maybe we should go in now." It was Butterfield.

Meade turned and for a moment said nothing.

"They won't expect it. With luck we'll have men on the opposite slope before they open up."

Meade half nodded, his gaze shifting to Hunt. "What do you think?"

"About going in now sir?"

"Yes, now."

Henry was caught by surprise on that one. Ever since yesterday morning he had been preparing for this moment. And now Meade himself was proposing a departure from the plan. But then again, it did have some merit. A surprise assault, out of the mists, might turn things. But were the men ready for it? They had been told there would be the bombardment first to suppress the rebel lines.

"I think it might have merit," Henry finally replied.

"This from my artilleryman?" Meade asked.

"Sir, guns against entrenched positions . . . well, you saw the effect at Fredericksburg. We pounded them for hours with little effect. Artillery against prepared positions is a tough job."

"The range was twice as far then."

"I know, sir."

Meade was silent again, and then finally shook his head. "Except for a few officers, none of our men have seen the layout. They'll get tangled up, lost in that mist. Besides, the Rebs will hear us anyhow. I don't like the thought of them getting lost out there in the fog with the Rebs pouring it in."

Meade looked back at Hunt. "Don't you have confidence in this, Hunt?"

"I'll do the best I can, sir. Just that the element of surprise might work."

"Surprise?" Meade barked out a gruff laugh. "Goddamn, what surprise? He knows we're coming just as sure as I do. No, I want a clear field. I want every gun pouring in on them to shake them loose. I want every man to see where it is he's going. I did that at Fredericksburg. My division was the only one that got into their lines, and I would have broken them if that damned ass Burnside had supported me."

He fixed Hunt with an angry gaze. "If I could do it at Fredericksburg with a division, I'll do it here today with four corps going in. You open up, Hunt, when you can see the bastards. I'll leave that up to you. And you tell me as well when it is time to go in."

"Sir?"

"Do you have any problems with that?"

"Sir, it's not for me to judge when to go in. I can only advise as to the effect of my bombardment. But the order to go in or not, well, sir, that's up to you."

"Just do what I order you to do, Hunt," Meade snapped, and without comment he rode on.

Henry shook his head. There was no sense in arguing about protocol now.

Leaning against the wheel of a ten-pound Parrott gun, he waited for the mist to clear.

6:15 AM, July 4, 1863

Headquarters, Army of Northern Virginia
Frizzelburg

"General Lee?"

It was a courier from Ewell, his inquiry a whisper.

Walter, who had fallen asleep on one of

the pews in front of the tent, half opened his eyes and sat up, putting a finger to his lips.

"He's asleep," Walter whispered, pointing to the tent behind him.

"I've got a dispatch from Ewell."

"I'll take it."

"I was told to bring a reply."

"He needs his sleep," Walter hissed softly. "Now wait over there."

He pointed toward the blacksmith shop, where many of the staff had sought shelter during the night. His own orders had been strict and without compromise. Unless the entire operation was going to hell, Lee was not to be disturbed. Sentries had been posted along the road ordering strict silence for everyone who passed during the night.

He then posted himself in front of Lee's tent, the cook first helping him to set up a tarp over the pews to at least give him some shelter.

He unfolded the dispatch. Ewell was reporting that the road back from Taneytown had been cut, a brigade of Union cavalry from the south taking Emmitsburg.

Walter thought about it for the moment. Their supply trains were parked over the mountain at Greencastle, protected by two brigades of cavalry, and would now retire back to Falling Waters on the banks of the

Potomac River. That should be sufficient; besides, the captured supplies at Westminster made our own reserves look miniscule in comparison. The only drawback, communications back down to Virginia were cut. Ironic, both armies were now cut off from their capitals.

Walter actually smiled. Would this trigger a panic in Richmond as well? Probably not. Davis was not used to the kind of telegraphic leash Lincoln could keep his generals on. And Richmond had far more faith in General Lee's ability to bring a miracle forth than the Union had in all its generals combined. No, Richmond would be anxious and curious but not panicked or desperate. Well, at least there will be no dispatches to trouble Lee.

Let him sleep.

Walter stood up. All around was cloaked in fog, rain slashing down. All was silent. Good. Let him sleep a few more minutes.

Lee heard the soft exchange outside his tent. He'd been awake for nearly an hour, quietly going over the plan, eyes half closed, listening to the drumming of rain on the canvas.

They love me. That thought struck him with a sharp intensity. Walter keeping watch outside throughout the rainy night, the stage-whispered commands from the road for those passing by to keep quiet because "Lee is sleeping."

Today is the Fourth of July. He had a memory of childhood. Old men gathering at the house while he sat quietly to one side, listening as they talked of Washington, of the cold of Valley Forge, the heat of Monmouth, the triumph of Yorktown. I thought them to be giants, men who had shaped the world to their vision and desires.

What would they say of me now, leading this war to divide the nation they created?

He had settled that argument long ago, at least he thought he had. It is not us, but they, those people on the other side who had drifted from the intent of the Fathers. We are now defending that heritage, not they. We represent the Founding Fathers' intent of a nation of states, not a centralized dictatorship of one government.

And yet what would they say then to all of us squabbling children, tearing apart the dream they had created. I cannot change that now. I am on the path set before me and cannot waver from it. Afterward, perhaps afterward we can find some way to sit down, to talk, perhaps to heal.

He thought of his boy in prison. Even now old friends will look out for him, while I, here this day, shall kill the comrades of those friends.

How many will die this day? How many a boy stirring in camp at this moment is awakening to his final day?

He swung his legs off the cot, moving quietly so Walter would not hear, stifling a groan, his legs and back stiff. He knelt on the damp ground and lowered his head, hands clasped in prayer.

7:30 AM, July 4, 1863

Union Mills

Exasperated, Winfield Scott Hancock looked to the heavens. It seemed as if the rain was easing slightly, the uniform flat dull gray beginning to shift, a cloud parting for a second, revealing a gunmetal blue patch of sky before closing over again. Occasional spits of rain fell for a few minutes then drifted away.

His men, deployed out in the open fields behind Union Mills, sat on the ground, hunched over, heads bowed. They had begun to file into position at dawn. There was no enthusiasm, but then again these were veterans, not green boys excited about going to see "The Elephant" for the first time. They knew what was coming, what to expect.

The two-division front stretched for

nearly half a mile, Caldwell's men forming the first wave on the left, a division of Twelfth Corps to his right, then Hays's the second wave, and Gibbon's — whose boys had taken the brunt of yesterday's assault — the third.

He rode slowly along the line, motioning for the men not to stand up, offering words of encouragement, trying above all else not to reveal the heavy sickness in his heart as he looked at them, his men, his boys.

Most of the men of Kelly's brigade were saying the rosary, kneeling together in a semicircle, prayer beads out, chanting together . . . *"Hail Mary, full of grace, the Lord is with thee . . ."*

He had been their division commander from the banks of Antietam Creek to Chancellorsville and knew many of them by name, never forgetting the sight of them going up the slope at Fredericksburg chanting "Erin GA Braugh!"

He respectfully edged around the circle, not wishing to disturb them, taking off his hat as he passed.

He looked up the slope to where scores of limber wagons were parked. What had been dull shadows only minutes before were now visible, wisps of steam rising off the backs of horses.

All was silent.

8:10 AM

Pete Longstreet, sitting on a camp chair, nursed his fourth cup of coffee of the morning, gaze fixed northward. The coffee was excellent, several wagon loads of the beans having been found in Westminster and brought up during the night. Someone back there was thinking. Many of the men had not had a real cup in months, and as it was distributed along the line in the early morning men awoke to the smell of kettles full of the brew boiling on smoldering campfires. Several dozen head of cattle and pigs were driven up as well and slaughtered just behind the line. His men were going into this one well fed for once, and he could sense the effect as men chewed on half-cooked steaks or fried pork. There was even real sugar for the coffee. He knew that McLaws was most likely chafing at being stuck back at Westminster, but the man was doing his job, knowing what the boys would need this day. Along with the food had come the entrenching tools and ammunition, extra boxes stacked with each regiment, covered over in the trenches, and extra limber loads for the artillery kept a mile to the rear.

Most had slept only four or five hours,

the work details for digging in finally told to stand down shortly before midnight, if for no other reason than the fact that the men were literally collapsing from exhaustion. Most had simply gone to sleep in the mud. Tents had been left behind long ago. Almost to a man the troops were filthy beyond belief, having marched for days on dusty roads and then labored like madmen for upward of twelve hours digging in. In some cases you literally could not tell who was behind the encrusted dirt.

Still, no time to stop digging and clean up. The fortifications were still not up to his liking. In most places the trenches were only three feet deep, with the dirt piled up forward to form a parapet. The battery positions had been fortified with whatever trees or lumber could be found for additional protection.

The artillery battalion bastions, positioned above the mill and then spaced at intervals of two hundred yards or so down the length of the line, were the strong points, fallback positions for infantry as well if the line broke. These points were fully enclosed on all four sides, with earthen walls four-to-five-feet high, strengthened on the inside with logs and cut lumber.

Unfortunately, there was no reserve line

to the rear, nor traverses; not enough time for that. Extra supplies moving up and wounded heading to the rear would have to run the open gauntlet behind the lines.

A forward line, down at the bottom of the slope, was little more than a shallow cutout, able to protect men lying down, but not designed for a hard, stand-up fight. There were no covered access ways down to the forward line. The men stationed forward would have to simply hold as long as possible then, if need be, run like hell up the slope to gain the protection of the main line. But if they did their job right, they would slow down and break up the coherence of the Union charge. That could be worth everything.

The scattering of trees, saplings, and brush bordering the flat bottomland had been cut down to provide a clear field of fire.

A faint breeze stirred, and he noticed that the steady drumming of the rain had eased, almost come to a stop. Mists still blanketed the valley.

The shadows of the hills to the north, only moments before a dim outline, began to take shape, coming into focus. The men who had been up out of their trenches, gathered round smoky fires, drinking coffee, wolfing down strips of meat with singed fingers, fell silent, all looking to the north.

Now he could see them; all could see them. The crown of the opposite ridge was a raw slash of earth across more than a quarter mile; the guns lining the brow were a dark menace. Another great battery, farther down the slope and to his left, positioned near a farmhouse that had been torn apart during the night, was composed of Napoleons, their bronze barrels dull in the diffused gray light.

Longstreet looked over at Porter. Nothing needed to be said. Porter nodded and then, strangely, he came to formal attention and saluted before mounting up to ride down the line.

Pete took another long sip on his coffee and braced himself for what was to come.

8:50 AM, July 4, 1863

US "Battalions, on my command!"

All up and down the line 120 gun crews stood to attention, battery commanders standing back from their pieces, looking in the direction of Henry Hunt, each crew sergeant standing with lanyard taut, layers, rammers, loaders, fuse setters, runners all poised, ready to spring into action.

A shaft of sunlight poked through the clouds for a second, fingers of light illuminating the ground below and the opposite slope. The air was still, not as hot as yesterday, but thick with humidity. He knew that within minutes smoke would obscure the target, and the battery commanders had been given careful orders to ensure that their guns were properly laid after every shot.

He raised a clenched fist heavenward and held it poised for a moment.

All were silent and he felt as if he were on a stage, the culmination of all that he had ever lived and trained for narrowing down to this moment.

Dear God, please let this work, he thought, and even as he muttered the prayer, he knew the irony, the obscenity of it, praying that he could successfully kill hundreds on the opposite slope with what he was about to do.

His arm started to tremble. There was no reason to wait, to drag it out. Let it begin. He let his arm drop.

"Fire!"

The cry echoed down the line, battery commanders mimicking the downward sweep of his arm. The salvo ripped down the length of the line, 120 guns recoiling, more than three hundred pounds of powder igniting, twelve hundred pounds of solid and case shot splitting the silence apart as the bolts shrieked across the valley.

Henry, ducking low, raced between two pieces, crouching, trying to watch the impact, all the shot aimed at three rebel batteries dug in along the crest. Five seconds later, the first bolts hit, thin geysers of earth kicking up, airbursts detonating. He caught a glimpse of at least one rebel piece upending from a direct hit.

The valley echoed and reechoed from the concussive blast. Dimly, to his right, he heard the battery of sixty Napoleon smoothbores firing in unison, their round shot aimed to strike the forward line directly across the valley and only eight hundred yards away. Though he could not hear it, he had to assume that the other sixty guns, positioned farther down the line, on Sickles's front, had opened as well.

Looking over his shoulder, he saw that rammers had already sponged their tubes; loaders stood poised with powder bag and shot.

He stepped back, weaving through the organized dance of gunners at work. A shot screamed overhead, clearing the crest, a second later detonating beyond the slope, high enough that the shrapnel raining down on the vast columns would be relatively harmless.

Gun sergeants were hooking lanyards into friction primers set into the breeches, stepping back, carefully bringing the lanyard taut, raising a left hand indicating their piece was ready, shouting for the rest of their crew to stand clear.

More bolts were beginning to come back across the valley, ripping the air overhead, casting up clods of muddy earth from the front of the parapet.

When each unit of six guns was loaded, their commanders raised clenched fists in the air, then brought them down. It was impossible to command 120 guns to fire at once, except on the first shot, too cumbersome and wasteful of precious time. First one battery fired, and within seconds the rest fired as well, guns recoiling violently. A few batteries had managed to pave their gun positions with heavy boards torn off the sides of barns; most were working on the muddy ground, the recoil already tearing into the earth, the men responsible for rolling their pieces forward straining and slipping on the wet ground.

Loaders ran past Henry, bringing up the next charge of powder and bolt, while rammers again sponged the bores clean. The thunder of the battery salvos came rolling back across the meadows, seeming to pitch the volume to a higher level. The clap of the rebel guns on the far slope washed over him as well.

There was a flash and then a staggering explosion to Henry's right, a caisson going up, bodies tumbling through the air, horses tied to the traces shrieking in agony as splinters, burning powder, and parts of human bodies slammed into them. One poor beast, most of its hind-quarters gone, screamed pitifully until a gunner ran up with drawn revolver and systematically put a shot into the head of each of the dying animals.

Another well-placed shot came in, this a solid bolt, striking the trunion of a three-inch Parrott gun, dismounting the tube, the piece collapsing onto a gunner who died without making a sound.

Splinters exploded as another round struck a wheel of a neighboring gun, parts of the fennel and spokes scything across the field, the fennel literally tearing a man in half at the middle.

He started to ride down the line, ig-noring the scream of incoming shells, carefully examining each crew at work, chewing out a battery commander for not taking the time to try and aim. The smoke was beginning to build up into a billowing cloud that cloaked the entire ridge, the occasional puff of breeze driving it along the slope. At times it was so thick he could barely see twenty feet, the men working around him looking like fiends in some infernal nightmare as they ran back and forth, brilliant flashes of light marking the discharge of each gun.

It was getting hot, the heat radiating off the barrels, the choking sulfurous smoke, the damp air, the gutted ruins of a caisson burning, shells bursting overhead.

He spared a quick glance back across the open fields on the reverse slope. The infantry, close to forty thousand men, were down, lying in the tall grass, trampled corn and wheat fields, their dark lines spread across dozens of acres. They were starting to take the brunt of it now. Typical of rebel gunners, they were shooting high, trying to hit the narrow silhouette of a target along a higher crest. Off by even a fraction of a degree and the shot winged by, ten, twenty feet overhead, only to plunge down into the fields a quarter, even a half mile away. The men, in general, were protected by the reverse slope, but enough shells were detonating, or coming down on a high-enough arc, to hit the lines.

It was all becoming silent to him; the continual crack of artillery was deafening him. He couldn't hear their screams, but he could see the stretcher bearers running back and forth, carrying their bloody burdens to the rear.

He looked back toward the roiling clouds of yellow-green smoke, so thick that it would eddy and swirl as shot shrieked back and forth through it. I only hope they're getting hit far worse, he thought grimly. My God, this has to do it.

9:30 AM

Longstreet finally accepted the inevitable and went into the trench, his staff pushing in after him. There was no sense in getting killed in this, he realized. Two of his orderlies were already wounded, one with a leg blown off.

The infantry around him nodded in recognition, one of them grinning. "Too hot out there for ya, General?"

Pete said nothing, just offered a grin. Leaning up against the parapet, he trained his field glasses on the area below. It was hard to see. Everything was cloaked in smoke every bit as thick as the morning mist.

The noise was beyond anything he had ever experienced. His own batteries were pouring it back, unmindful of ammunition spent. The captured Union supplies at Westminster guaranteed that, for the first time in the war, the Confederate artillery could fire more intensely and longer than its Union counterpart. Alexander finally had a chance to fight an artillery duel without rationing out each round and counting each minute of the engagement against a dwindling supply of ammunition. The effect was amazing to Confederate soldiers used to absorbing more than they hit with the artillery arm. The opposite slope was barely visible in the gloom. The only way to mark the battery position was by the continual ripple of flashes racing along the crest of the slope.

A shot came screaming in, men ducking, a spray of mud and dirt washing into the trench, covering Pete. Spitting, he stood up, pulling out a handkerchief to wipe the lenses of his field glasses.

Another shot tore past, and he heard anguished cries. From the corner of his eye he saw a body collapsing, the man decapitated, comrades crying out in fear and anger.

Looking beyond the dead man, he saw Porter emerging from the smoke, on foot, crouched and running low. Venable stood up, shouting for Porter to come over. The artilleryman slid into the trench, breathing hard.

"How goes it?" Pete asked.

"Twelve guns with Cabell and Poague's battalions are wrecks, sir, guns dismounted, a couple of hundred horses dead; casualties with those batteries are high. Looks like they had every gun aimed at them first. Should I get them out?"

Pete shook his head.

"I want them to stay," his words cut short by an airburst exploding nearly straight overhead.

"Sir?"

"I want them to stay."

Porter looked at him, as if ready to voice an objection.

"All this smoke, they can barely see. Tell the surviving gunners they must keep firing."

"It will be a slaughter," Porter objected.

"It will be a slaughter wherever their fire is directed. That's Hunt over there, Porter. He knows counterbattery. You pull out and he'll shift fire to the next target. I want you to keep those men at it."

"Yes, sir."

"Ammunition?"

"More than enough. I have reserve caissons and an ammunition train a mile back. I'll begin to move them up when we need them."

"Just make sure you have plenty of canister in reserve."

"We will."

"Keep at it, Porter."

The gunner wearily stood up and ran back down the line into the middle of the storm.

The fire continued to thunder and roll, reverberating off the hills, the earth beneath Pete shaking and trembling.

9:50 AM, July 4, 1863

Washington, D.C.
The White House

Abraham Lincoln stood alone, looking out the window. The traffic on Pennsylvania Avenue was still this morning. It was, after all, a day of observation and celebration. Word had just been publicly announced confirming that this day Vicksburg was surrendering to Grant. A great salute was planned for this evening, a discharge of a hundred blank rounds of artillery at Lafayette Square.

No one's mind was on that now. A runner from the War Department had just come in bearing a telegram from Baltimore, declaring that heavy gunfire was clearly audible to the northwest, toward Westminster.

There was no need for that report. Putting his hand on the windowpane, Lincoln could feel the vibration from over sixty miles away.

10:15 AM

Union Mills

"Hunt, is there any sign this is achieving anything?"

Henry, ears ringing, did not know what to say.

Meade stood expectant, hands on hips, both instinctively ducking as a round, one with a high-piercing scream, snapped past. Several gunners nearby looking up, exclaiming that it was a Whitworth bolt.

"I cannot say, sir. The smoke. You can't see."

Henry waved toward the south. The swirling, eddying canopy completely obscured the valley and the slopes of the hill, mingling in with pillars of smoke rising from burning caissons, wagons, and several of the houses in the town hit by the Confederate counterfire.

The gunners moved like men seized with a terrible palsy, convulsively, gesturing wildly, typical of men who had been delivering a sustained barrage for well over a hour, crews manhandling the one-ton pieces back into place after each shot, rammers covered in black filth, loaders gasping for air in the thick fumes. A hundred or more dead horses littered the ground behind the pieces, cut down by solid shot, shrapnel, splinters from exploding caissons, and shattered field pieces.

Everything around the guns was churned to mud, the recoil from firing each piece eighty times or more having dug the earth up into a sticky mess.

Injuries were mounting, men hit by shell and explosions, caught momentarily unaware and crushed as a gun recoiled, kicked by panic-stricken horses, impaled by splinters bursting from limbers shattered by solid bolts.

Behind the lines, the infantry continued to endure, curled up on the open slope, but staying in place. If anything they were far safer than trying to make a run for the rear because the shot skimming the ridge was plunging down behind the lines.

"How much longer, Hunt?" Meade shouted.

"Sir, as I said before, I can sustain this for roughly two hours. We must keep a reserve, sir . . ." and his voice trailed off.

He did not want to add the final words, . . . "in case we lose."

"I will not commit my men in until you have suppressed their batteries, Hunt. You will tell me when the time is ready."

"Sir, I can only advise you on that."

A round shot clipped the parapet nearby, moving slow enough that Henry could see it go careening off, cutting into a team of horses, dropping two of them in a bloody heap.

"I can't wait here all day, Hunt."

Henry turned away for a moment. Meade was trying to shift it onto him, to have him make the decision. He started to move toward a gun. It was obviously too high, someone letting the elevation screw at the breech wind down. He stopped. I can't walk off from this.

He looked back at Meade. "Sir, at this moment I can't see a damn thing. All I know for certain is that they are still firing back."

A distant thunderclap echoed across the field, most likely a caisson going up on the other side.

"If you can't see, then how the hell will you know?" Meade shouted.

"Let me cease fire for a few minutes," Henry replied. "Perhaps this smoke will lift enough so that we can judge the results. I can then redirect fire as needed."

"Then do it, damn it!" Meade shouted.

10:30 AM, July 4, 1863

Headquarters, Army of Northern Virginia

Lee cocked his head. All around him were silent, looking toward the north, expectant, wondering.

Yes, the volume of fire was dropping, intervals of half a minute or more between distant peals of thunder.

He looked over at Walter. The young colonel was actually asleep, stretched out on a pew, snoring lightly.

"I'm going up," Lee announced to no one in particular.

The gathered staff nodded; they were eager to see what was going on; the inactivity of sitting here, half a dozen miles from the action, was chafing on their nerves.

One of them started toward Walter to shake him awake. "No, no, let him sleep," Lee said, with an indulgent smile. "He can act as liaison here. If word comes from Ewell, forward it up to me immediately."

A groom brought up Traveler, and Lee

swung up into the saddle, several men approaching to help him, but a sharp glance made them step back.

He was feeling better; the long night of sleep had been a blessing, some strength returning for all that was needed this day.

He started north toward the fight, the world around him so quiet that he could hear the chirping of birds, the sigh of a gentle breeze in the trees.

10:40 AM, July 4, 1863

Union Mills

It had taken fifteen minutes for the smoke to slowly clear, fifteen minutes of agonizing frustration. Even the slightest of breezes would have lifted the curtain, the thick humid air holding the clouds in place.

The rebel lines were now visible. They were continuing to fire back, a slow measured pace, but with the lifting of the smoke it was regaining accuracy, another of his guns dismounted by a direct hit as they waited for the air to clear.

He carefully scanned the line with his field glasses, Meade by his side.

The shooting looked fairly good in places. The parapet overlooking the mill was torn, busted down in places, four, maybe five guns definitely out of action. The grand battery of Napoleons to the right was continuing to fire slowly, shot impacting along the lower line. But the enemy was still in place, a fact that did not surprise him at all. It was one thing for guns to engage an enemy out in the open, another to try and force them out of a prepared position.

He looked over at Meade. Hancock had come up as well, remaining on his black horse, which fidgeted nervously as a shot screamed overhead.

"Keep at it," Meade announced, "I want those batteries suppressed."

Behind them fresh caissons were coming up, crews struggling to back them into place, maneuvering gingerly around wrecked equipment and dead horses. Gunners were leaning on their pieces, speaking in loud voices, everyone's hearing stunned by the pounding of the last hour and a half.

Word was already going down the line to aim carefully and be prepared to resume fire.

"I have enough for one more hour," Henry announced. "That's it, sir; beyond that and we run the risk of totally depleting our reserves."

"I want those guns over there knocked

out," Meade replied, his voice shaky with weariness and nervous strain.

"I've passed the order to slow the rate of fire, gunners not to fire until they can clearly sight a target," Hunt replied.

"Then do it. Resume fire."

Henry nodded and, stepping back, he raised his fist up.

10:50 AM

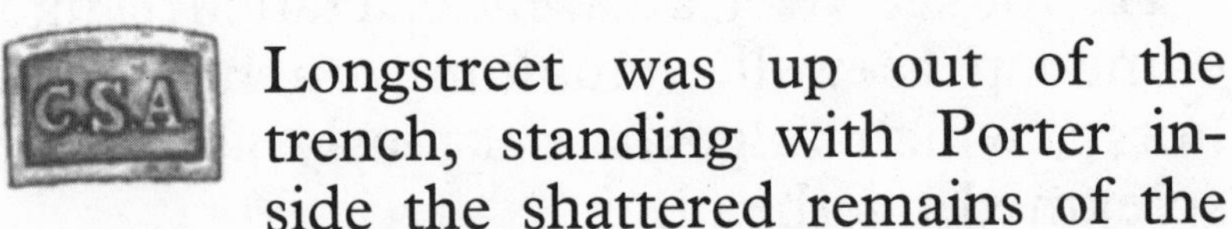

Longstreet was up out of the trench, standing with Porter inside the shattered remains of the earthen fort occupied by what was left of Cabell's battalion. Over half the pieces were destroyed, the gunners all but collapsing from shock and exhaustion. The brief respite allowed them a few minutes to sink to the ground, oblivious to the blood, the dead horses, the dead men dragged to one side. The wounded who could not walk were being run out by stretcher bearers taking advantage of the interlude.

"I think he's about to open up again," Porter announced.

Pete, standing beside him with field glasses raised, nodded in agreement.

"They're good, damn good," Porter offered.

"So are we," Pete snapped. "Your gunners are pretty damn good, too."

He lowered his glasses, looking to the left and right. Some of the infantry were up out of the trenches, walking about, examining the damage, like boys who had taken shelter from a violent storm and were now looking at the destruction wrought.

The position was still relatively intact, casualties about what he had expected. The long bitter hours of work yesterday and through the night were now paying off. If the men had been caught in an open field under this barrage, he doubted if they could have held.

The men suddenly began to scatter, diving back into their trenches. He looked back and saw the flash of fire racing down the front of the grand battery, like firecrackers igniting on a long string.

The sound finally hit, a sustained rolling boom, followed a little more than a second later by the scream of more shells coming in. Dignity forgotten, he flung himself down against the parapet, Porter by his side, as dozens of shells and solid shot plowed into the battery position. Screams echoed as the concussion of detonations washed over him.

Porter grunted, cursing. Pete looked over. The man was grimacing, holding his arm, the sleeve of his uniform sliced open, blood already welling out.

Behind them a caisson blew, jagged splinters spraying the position.

Pete stood up, knowing that it'd be a minute or more before the next salvo came in.

Porter, shaking, face pale, stood up, clutching his arm.

"Let me see it," Pete shouted.

"I'm all right," and he gingerly held out his arm, flexing his hand, the gesture indicating that a bone was not broken. A gunner, seeing the situation, came up to Porter, pulling out a handkerchief, which he deftly wrapped around the arm, pulling it tight so that Porter cursed softly under his breath.

"Another one!" somebody shouted.

Again they were down, the blizzard of shot raining down on the position.

"Damn all, General, my men can't take this much longer."

Pete nodded, standing back up again. Two of the guns with the battalion finally responded, lone shots going back in defiant response.

He realized that his staying at this exposed point served no logical purpose. Lee was right on such things; the potential loss of a general through reckless exposure was nothing more than a foolish waste. Save yourself for the key moment, not now. I get hit and things here might begin to fall apart.

Reluctantly he scrambled up over the side of the parapet, motioning for Porter to follow, blocking out the stares of the gunners watching him leave, hoping they did not see it as cowardice that he was leaving them to stand the hurricane alone.

Porter moved slowly, favoring his arm.

"Can you stay in command?" Pete asked.

"Yes, sir, I can manage. They will not drive me off this battlefield."

The curtain of smoke on the opposite slope began to part again, and seconds later more shots came screaming in.

"He's measuring it out now," Pete announced. "They must be running low on ammunition. We have their supplies, and it is beginning to limit their rate of fire."

He stood silent for a moment, staff that had been trailing the two trying to act poised, but obviously nervous as a solid bolt came far too close to the group, killing the horse of a courier, who jumped off as the dying creature reared up screaming and then went down on its side.

Suppose they don't come in? he thought. Then what?

"Porter, how is the ammunition supply?"

"More than enough left, sir. I have

more than a hundred rounds per gun stockpiled back there," and Porter gestured toward the rear area, where the park of limber wagons was clearly visible and safely out of range. "And then there are the additional supplies at Westminster. The Union army has provided for all our ammunition needs."

The group ducked as yet another salvo impacted, dirt flying. Another secondary explosion ignited from within Cabell's position. Part of a broken wheel came spiraling out of the battery position and plowed into Longstreet's staff.

A staff officer was down, trying to stifle a scream, leg torn off below the knee; another man had been hit in the chest by a wooden splinter as thick around as a man's wrist, blood washing over him.

Pete, stunned, came up to the first man's side, grabbing him by the shoulders, holding him as someone struggled to wrap a tourniquet around the knee.

Stretcher bearers came running up, lifting the wounded captain up, and then turning to run off. Longstreet stood up, trying to wipe the blood off on his trouser legs.

He looked around at the carnage and destruction. Porter was right. Cabell's men, and beyond him the redoubt held by Poague's battalion, were played out, shattered by the thousands of shells that had poured in on them.

"Order Cabell to pull out now, also Poague's battalion. Have them retire to the rear."

"Sir?"

"Order them to retire now!" Longstreet shouted.

"And bring up the reserve?"

Pete shook his head. "No."

He turned away, catching the eye of Wofford, the brigade commander holding the heights above the mill.

"Come here, Wofford."

Wofford, as ever, stepped smartly forward and saluted, looking a bit absurd since his uniform, which had been all brightness and shiny trim the day before, was completely soaked in half-dry mud.

Wofford stared at Longstreet as the order was given.

"Are you sure, sir?"

"Just do it," Longstreet snapped. "Do it now."

11:15 AM, July 4, 1863

"Are you seeing this?" Meade asked, riding up to where Henry stood at the center of his grand battery.

Henry nodded, lowering his glasses. The rebels were abandoning their two main bastions facing the ground over which Second and Twelfth Corps were supposed to advance.

"Are they pulling back, Hunt?"

"I can't tell yet, sir."

Now he could see infantry getting out of the trenches, not many, but still a significant number, breaking, heading to the rear. His ears were ringing; sound was distorted. It was hard to see, not because of the smoke, but because of his own eyes, which were red, stinging, tears clouding them.

He looked at Meade.

"Hunt, have you done it?"

"Sir," and he paused to rub his eyes with blackened hands, "Sir, I can't tell you that. I see two battalions of their guns withdrawing. Some infantry breaking. I know we gave them a rough going-over, but I can't speak for anything beyond that."

Even as they spoke, Hancock came up, followed only a minute or so later by Slocum and Sickles riding side by side.

"Are they breaking, Hunt?" Hancock cried.

Henry felt his chest tighten. He knew that here, now at this moment, whether he wanted to or not, the decision was devolving into his hands. If he said no, if he told Meade flat out that the sustained bombardment by every gun of the Army of the Potomac had failed, perhaps this assault would be called off.

And then what? Follow Sickles's wild scheme? Meade would never do that. Fall back on Harrisburg? Impossible. Just as impossible as trying to flank to the left. Washington would hang all of them because surely Lee would finally move toward the capital, even if just to occupy the outskirts, to bring the place under siege and trigger a panic.

No. Fate was drawing them in. The web, whether created by us, by Lee, or ordained long ago, had come to this moment. He looked back at the long lines of troops. Some were standing up, many of them looking straight at this knot of officers, obviously the high command of the Army of the Potomac, who were about to make the decision.

A light shower opened up, the cool rain drifting down.

"If you are going to do it, sir," Henry replied, voice trembling, near to breaking, "then do it now. I have to break off this barrage to keep enough rounds left to provide minimal cover once you go in. Once the columns are into the valley, I'll open back up with measured support."

Meade said nothing; the corps commanders were silent; Hancock was stock-still, gazing across the open ground.

"Now is the time, gentlemen," Meade announced, voice steady. "To your posts. Remember my orders. No corps commanders are to go forward. My headquarters is here, and I expect you to report back here. Hunt, in ten minutes, fire one salvo from all your guns; that will be the signal to go in."

Henry nodded, unable to respond.

"God save our Republic," Sickles whispered, taking off his hat and lowering his head.

Henry, startled, looked up at the normally profane general.

The corps commanders rode off at a gallop; the sight of them moving thus, followed by their flag bearers, set up a rippling cheer from the tens of thousands assembled behind the ridge. Drums began to roll, bugles echoing, calling the men to arms.

Henry lowered his head and prayed, letting the minutes slowly tick out.

He finally looked back up and saw Hancock, dismounted, kneeling in the wet grass with Kelly's Irishmen, a priest standing atop a small boulder, making the sign of the cross. Battle flags were uncased; a hundred or more American flags, each one marking a regiment, were held up, a faint breeze stirring them to life.

The sight of them made his heart constrict, his throat going tight, tears coming to his eyes. Today is the Fourth of July, he thought yet again. Dear God, let there be reason to celebrate another come next year.

Kelly's Irishmen were back on their feet, their battle chant beginning to echo, "Erin GA Braugh."

Other regiments began to cry out as well, "The Union, the Union, the Union!"

His gunners were poised, at their pieces, looking toward Henry.

Hat still off, he looked straight up, letting the light rain wash his face for a moment.

Henry raised his hat up over his head, and cleared his throat. "Battalions, at my command!"

The cry was picked up, racing down the line yet again.

He looked across the field, gaze fixed on a small knot of mounted officers atop the distant crest. He closed his eyes and slapped his arm down. "Fire!"

For over eighty thousand men, Union or Confederate, it was a moment unlike any seen before, a moment all would carry to their dying hour, whether that was but minutes away or destined to be four score years into the future.

Hancock, tears streaming down his face, saluted as the Irish Brigade started up the slope, falling in to ride by their side.

Sickles, not yet back into his own lines, turned, mesmerized by the sight of two full corps, the 22,000 men of the first waves, going up the slope, line after line, flags held high, a breeze snapping them out.

Henry, arms at his side, turned, watching the vast phalanx approach. As the first battle line drew near, he shouted for his gunners to stand clear, trace riders to hold their teams. Many of the gunners came to attention, saluting; others cheered, their cry picking up, echoing down the lines . . .

"The Union!"

For most of the men, there was no grand sight. If in the first line, just the slope of the ground ahead, dead horses littering the field, dead artillerymen, now the guns coming into view, gunners blackened standing, saluting, some cheering.

For those in the second rank, the third rank, or those with Sedgwick's corps moving forward to occupy the ground just vacated, all that could be seen was the man in front, haversack and canteen over left hip, sky blue trousers caked with mud, trampled grass, occasional stains of blood, and bodies where those caught in the barrage had stayed behind. File closers kept shouting the same litany, "Close it up. Guide on the colors, boys. Close it up."

Some prayed; some, caught in the grandeur of the moment, stared about. Men with the Twentieth Massachusetts, Hall's brigade, of Gibbon's division of the Second Corps, led by a grandson of Paul Revere, heard an officer reciting from *Henry V*. Some scoffed; more than a few recited along, knowing the words by heart . . . " 'we few, we happy few, we band of brothers . . .' "

Along the far slope, twelve hundred yards away, men were up and out of the trench. A teenage boy from North Carolina, one of the "pets" of the company, disemboweled by a fragment, was surrounded by weeping comrades as he penned a farewell note to his mother with trembling hand, then accepted the draught of morphine from a doctor who knew the amount he was giving to him was not murder, but a merciful blessing.

Others stood silent, voices whispering in awe, "Here they come; my God, here they come."

John Williamson, with Sergeant Hazner

by his side, was silent, watching as first the tips of flags, then muskets, appeared along the crest of the ridge; and then, finally, the first rank was in view, a solid wall half a mile across, followed by another rank, and then another.

It was terrifying, and yet it held him with its frightful grandeur, its pageantry, the sheer power of what was unfolding before him, coming straight at him.

John looked over nervously at Hazner, who gave him a tight-lipped grin. Standing to the rear of the trench, they slowly paced the line together. The regiment had taken a couple of dozen casualties so far, one shell detonating inside the trench, killing several men and horribly wounding half a dozen more. The wounded were being carried to the rear in the lull, the dead pulled out of the trench. John stepped around one of the bodies, swallowing hard as he looked down. It was Mark Arnson, one of the boys from home, a cousin to Elizabeth. Same hair, pale blond. He looked away.

One of the men had a Bible out and was standing, reading it aloud.

" 'A thousand shall fall at thy side, and ten thousand at thy right hand; but it shall not come nigh thee . . .' "

He felt cold, empty, the words bringing no comfort. Thousands would fall in the next few minutes. If all of them pray this same prayer, then whose trust will be betrayed?

If only I could believe, take comfort in that. As he paced the line, he looked at the men, their expressions, wondering who would still be alive an hour from now, who would be silenced forever.

The vast, undulating line of blue was atop the opposite crest, coming on relentlessly.

"My God," Hazner whispered, "I'm glad it's them rather than us."

John said nothing. Hand absently slipping into his haversack, touching the leather volume, wondering if he would ever write in it again.

General Longstreet stood with arms folded and for a moment he felt doubt, hesitation. Such power, line after line cresting that distant ridge, coming on as if they would never stop, feeling as if behind them came a million more. Can I hold them now? Even if we do stop them today, can we hold them?

A cheer began, rippling down his line, building in intensity, the rebel yell. He sensed, though, that it was not given in the lust of battle, as his men so often did when going into a charge. It was a salute, an acknowledgment that those coming to

ward them had created a moment never to be forgotten, a moment that, win or lose, would be remembered across history.

They most likely would have given the same cheer for us, Pete thought.

Drums rolled, calling the men to the ranks, forming up along the length of the trench. From out in the field, the men of Wofford's command who had feigned retreat now came about, running at the double, piling back into their trench, while from a mile back ten batteries, the replacements for Cabell and Poague, came forward at the gallop.

The trap had been sprung. Now, now it

was simply a question of holding on against what he knew would be the most vicious assault of the war. Meade might have gotten it all wrong these last four days, but at least in this he was getting it right. No hesitation. If it was necessary to go in frontally, throw every man in at the same time and come on relentlessly, regardless of loss.

"It's General Lee, sir."

Longstreet saw Lee coming up, several staff following, one bearing the guidon of the headquarters of the Army of Northern Virginia.

Longstreet saluted as Lee reined in. He could see that his general was awed as well. Lee was silent for a moment, eyes bright as he scanned the distant lines now sweeping down the slope.

" 'As terrible as an army with banners,' " Lee whispered.

Chapter Seventeen

11:45 AM, July 4, 1863

Union Mills

The first shots came from the skirmishers who had watched the barrage in relative safety, crouched down in the marsh grass lining the banks of Pipe Creek. They had gone out shortly after midnight, sent to act as an alarm if the Union should attempt a night assault or come in through the fog at first light.

More than one man, once the barrage started, had laid back, watching the shells arc overhead. An informal truce was declared between them and the Union skirmishers deployed in the pastures on the north side of the creek, men on both sides standing up, leaning on muskets, watching the grand fireworks show.

Now that the infantry battle was on again, the logic that had stilled the slaughter down along the banks of Pipe Creek was null and void. Some of the men, unable to resist the sheer size of the target coming toward them, raised their rear sights to four hundred yards, aimed even

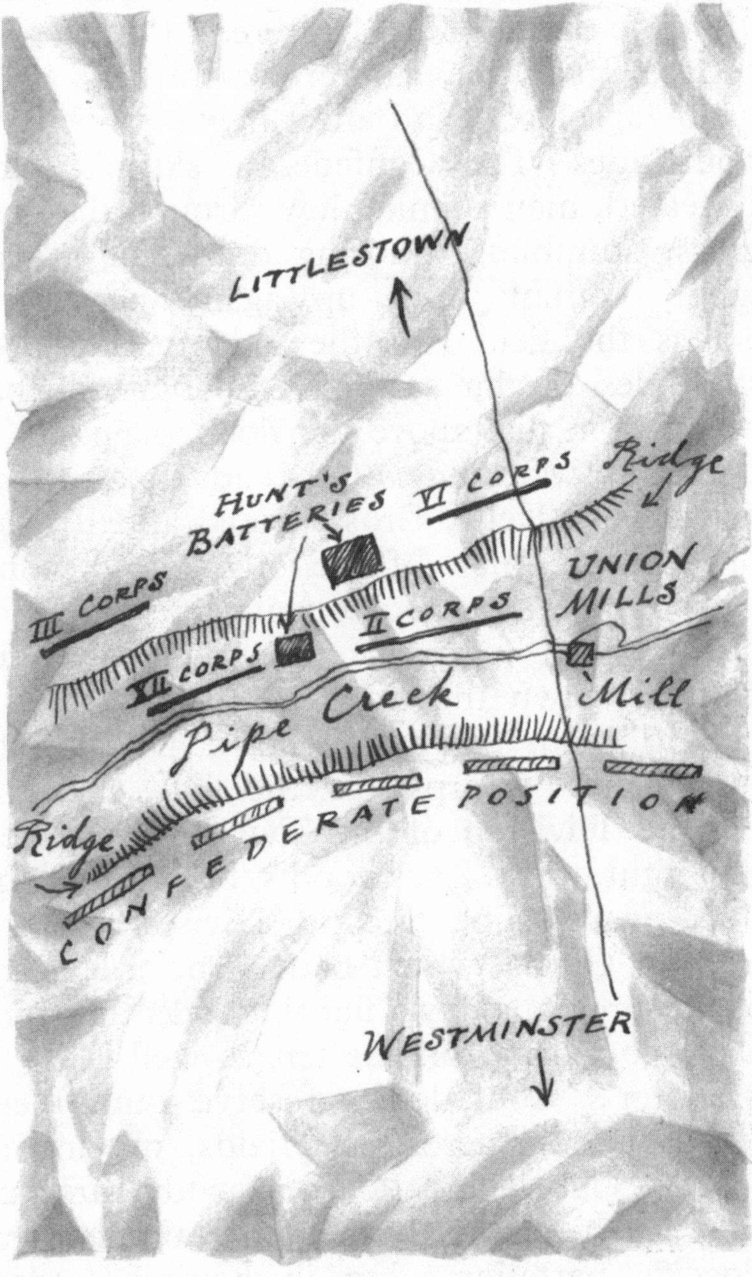

LITTLESTOWN
HUNT'S BATTERIES
VI CORPS
Ridge
III CORPS
UNION MILLS
II CORPS
XII CORPS
Pipe Creek
Mill
Ridge
CONFEDERATE POSITION
WESTMINSTER

higher, and lobbed a scattering of rifle balls into the lines. This triggered a quick response from the Union skirmishers, who were far closer, and men began to fall on both sides. The Confederate skirmish line retreated, men running low through the high grass, stumbling, ducking down for a moment, coming back up again, zigzagging across the field and then clambering over the sides of the earthen embankment that was dug in just above the flood plain.

The forward line of the advance — the brigades of Kelly, Cross, Zook, and Brooke on the left; men of the old solid Second Corps, including McDougall; and Ruger of the Twelfth Corps on the right — were halfway down the slope. A hundred yards behind them came the Third Division of the Second Corps on the left and the Second Division of the Twelfth Corps on the right, with Lockwood's brigade as the third wave. The Second Division of the Second Corps, which had borne the brunt of the previous day's fighting, was the third wave coming in on the left as well.

Porter's Confederate reserve guns were still bouncing across the fields, moving to replace Cabell and Poague, so the first artillery to fire was the next battalion down, Posey's battalion, dug in behind Anderson's division.

The guns were well placed to drive their

shot in enfilade across the front of Second Corps, and the gunners opened with a will, cutting their fuses to five seconds, and then to four seconds, and then down to three seconds. In a sense they were getting even for the battering they had taken from the Union artillery three days earlier at Gettysburg. Farther on the line to the left the battalions supporting Pender and Pettigrew were joining in as well, though the range was long, at nearly a mile, for batteries positioned with Pettigrew's to reach, and most of them turned their weapons onto the batteries deployed along the front of Third Corps, which was not yet committed to the fight. Joining them were the gunners covering the front of Early's division, which was on the far left of the Confederate line.

Onward the battle lines came, the men moving fast on the steep, downward slope, jumping over torn-down walls of split-rail fencing, which had been knocked apart in the previous day's assault. The far left of the column swept through the edge of the town, the ground to their left opening out, leading toward the still-smoldering mill and miller's house. Alignment was kept, a grim professional pride taking hold in these, the elite troops of an elite army that had only known disappointment and defeat.

If there was a hope, and nearly every officer had spoken of this, the hope was that they, the veterans of the Army of the Potomac, would sweep onward, regardless of loss.

Keep closing on the flags, men. Let that be your guide this day, your flag. Don't stop, don't slow down for anything, keep pushing forward. Forty thousand of us will be in this together; never has a charge been done like this by our army. Meade is sending us in together; Hunt and his boys will pound a way clear. Just go for the heights, and we will win.

These were not green recruits so innocent that they would believe anything said, as they themselves had once believed in a long-ago time. Many had attempted to cross this same field in the boiling heat only yesterday; they knew its slope; they knew what would happen; and yet they were going forward now without hesitation.

Those who would hesitate were gone from the ranks; they had run away or found a way to skulk off. Those going knew what was at stake and what would happen to many of them in the minutes ahead.

Just stay with the colors. Keep an eye on that flag and, by God, if it goes forward, you go forward. If it falls, every man of you should move to pick it up and keep it going.

Do not let the flag touch the ground.

They were stripped down. Blanket rolls were stacked to the rear, the cowards, or those truly too sick to advance, staying as a guard. Canteens at least were full; that had been an order passed straight down from the top. Drink your fill and runners to refill all canteens two hours before the assault goes in. Haversacks were mostly empty of rations; they had been consumed on the march south from Gettysburg; now an extra forty rounds were in most of them.

Enduring the morning showers, most of the men were wet, but it was at least comfortable for the moment, cooling after the heat of the previous three days. The shoes and wool socks, however, were heavy with moisture, walking made more difficult by the wet, tangled grass on the downslope.

By order of the commanding general, brigade and division commanders were not to advance ahead of the line, but several ignored it; Kelly, of course, for what self-respecting Irishman would not be in the lead at a moment like this; Gibbon, a professional who should have known better, was out front as well, sword held high.

As they marched down the slope, the great amphitheater of this drama was spread out before them, the open valley ahead, the meandering stream, millpond to the left, the raw slash of earth across the base of the opposite slope, the second line of torn-up earth along the crest above. Their professional eyes judged it and they knew with a terrible certainty what would come down upon them in just a few more minutes.

And yet, for a brief moment, they saw beyond it, the awe-inspiring sight of the long battle lines rolling down out of the hills, flags of over thirty regiments held high, the dark waves of blue moving on like a relentless tide.

Maybe, just maybe, we'll do it this time.

Half a prayer, half a dream, and thousands said it, looking sidelong at neighbors and friends, nods, tight grins of acknowledgment, a few weak gibes. A rabbit kicked up out of the grass in front of Ruger's brigade, dashing along a farm lane in a mad panic back and forth before it finally cut straight between the legs of the soldiers and went tearing back to the rear. Men laughed, shouting they wished they could trade places.

The Napoleons in the lower battery, whose front they had yet to cross, continued to fire, pounding the opposite line, the sharp, almost bell-like "sprang" of the guns echoing with each discharge.

The ground started to slope outward into a gentle decline. Ahead was a sharp bank that tumbled down half a dozen feet, marking the divide between hills and flood plain. Men slid down the grassy slope, some falling, comrades reaching out to help pull each other up, officers shouting to keep alignment, to keep moving.

The first wave was into the bottomland pastures, a giant undulating wave of men, one man for each foot and a half of front, two ranks deep, nearly a mile across. Behind them the second wave of two ranks was a hundred yards to their rear, behind that the third wave of Gibbon's division and Lockwood's brigade. Deployed out in heavy column, a division wide and three divisions deep, eighteen thousand men of Sedgwick's corps, just beginning to crest the ridge, poised to exploit any breakthrough that developed.

The grass in the bottomland was thicker, tangled mats in places, the ground soggy after the rain. Men began to lose their shoes, unable to stop to retrieve them, continuing on with wet wool socks sagging, peeling off.

The shells from the enfilading fire cut in across the front; men began to drop. Mercifully, the ground was damp enough that when a round ball or bolt hit, it tended to plow into the earth, the notoriously poor fuses of the Confederate artillery going out in the spray of muck. Airbursts of case shot, however, sprayed down on the lines. Here and there a man dropped, or cried out, stumbling away from the line. In Zook's brigade, one well-placed bolt came skimming in, dropping a dozen men in one bloody burst, officers shouting for the ranks to close up, to keep moving.

The first wave was a hundred yards into the pasture. Union skirmishers in the field now stood up, some sprinting back the few yards to fall in with their comrades, others waiting for the first wave to pass over them. The creek tended to favor the south bank of the valley, though in places it meandered out in its slow, wandering course, looping to midfield. The first wave was nearly upon it, men able to see its waters now, really nothing more than a shallow, muddy flow, in places so narrow that an energetic farm boy could leap it in one bound.

And then, along most of the front — in spite of the rumbling of the cannons, the shouts of their own officers, the banging of tin cups on canteens, the sloshing of wet leather — they heard it. The command racing down the Confederate front line, picked up by officers, riflemen shouting the order in response.

"Ready!"

A wall seemed to materialize out of the ground, a wall of butternut, gray, occasional splashes of sky blue trousers, rifle barrels, several thousand of them held high.

The range was in some places 300 yards, in others, such as the approach to the burning mill, less than 150.

"Take aim!"

The barrels dropped; hammers clicked back. For those in the very front rank there was the terrible moment, the strange illusion that made it look as if every rifle was aiming straight at you.

"Steady, boys! Steady!" the cry echoed across the Union line. No matter how brave, how determined they were, there was an involuntary flinch, a slowing down, as mere flesh recoiled in anticipation of what was about to be unleashed upon them.

Time distorted. Some felt as if every step taken now seemed to transcend into an eternity. Some could look only at the guns; others could not look. A few gazed heavenward beseechingly; some noticed the most trivial of things, a frightened dove kicking up out of the tall grass, a grasshopper poised on a stalk of grass, about to jump, the sidelong glance of a beloved comrade who in another second would be dead, the back of an officer, hat poised on sword blade, who had turned, looking back to shout something to his men that could not be heard.

"Fire!"

The command was barely heard by either side. As if a single hand had struck the flame, in an instant three thousand rifles discharged.

Three thousand rounds of .58-cal. slashed across the open field, muzzle velocity slow at but seven to eight hundred feet per second, but carrying a frightful punch, the conical round weighing close to an ounce, made of soft lead. Sometimes the rounds sounded like the buzz of an angry bee or the hiss of a snake, and if it passed close enough to you, you'd feel the smack of the shock wave.

If it hit human flesh, the sound was audible, like an open-handed slap. The slower speed, at that instant, that microsecond as the bullet struck, actually made the impact more deadly; the round would begin to flatten out, distort as it first penetrated cloth, striking a button, a cartridge box sling, or belt plate. Often it would begin to tumble, glancing off at a slight angle, mushrooming out as it tore into the body, and traveling so slow that it was not sterilized by the heat of its passage, dragging with it bits of black powder, tallow that had been used to grease the ball, and fragments of whatever it had struck first before entering the body.

Arteries that might have been cauterized by the passage of a high-speed jacketed round were instead torn open, the next pulse of the heart sending out the first spray of bright arterial blood. The truly frightful moment was when the round struck bone. It did not punch through a bone; rather it shattered it, the shock of the blow causing the bone to disintegrate laterally, fracture lines and fissures often running the length of that bone clear up to the joint. Here the bullet would flatten out even more, to the diameter of a quarter, at times to nearly a half dollar, tearing everything in its path. If there was enough momentum left, the hunk of lead would exit the body, pulling out fragments of broken bone, marrow, flesh, and blood with it, sometimes striking a man behind the victim, injuring him as well, or spraying him with the contents of the comrade in front.

If the ball struck between rib cage and pelvis, death was just a matter of time, be it seconds if a main artery was hit, or days of slow agony if it simply lodged in the intestine. A man shot crosswise might have his liver shattered, the stomach or small intestine punctured, the kidney torn apart. Within minutes he would begin to bloat up, as blood cascaded into his abdominal cavity.

To be shot through the lungs was almost as bad. It took time to die unless the bundle of arteries and veins linked directly to the heart was severed. The lungs would slowly fill up with blood and liquid, each breath a struggle to keep from drowning, sometimes the air wheezing in and out of the bullet hole.

If one was to be struck, and die, then the lucky shot was to the head or the heart. It would be barely felt if it was the head, just a sudden going out of the light. If in the heart, more than one man would actually stop, look down, and have a few seconds to comprehend what had just happened, perhaps enough time to even look up at a friend with that strange, quizzical look of men when they know they are dead but have yet to fall back into the earth.

For several hundred along that first line, this is what now happened. Rounds thwacked into the first line; men grunted from the blows, those who survived describing it as feeling like you had been kicked by a mule or hit with an ax handle. Some just simply collapsed, comrades to either side sprayed with blood and gray, sticky matter if the man next to them had been hit in the head. Others turned, staggering backward, dropping rifles, more than one man not being hit by a round but struck instead by a broken musket spinning through the air or from splinters kicked back as a ball tore through a gun stock.

Some paused, doubled over, and then, with iron will, staggered back up, pressing forward, dropping after a dozen feet. Those hit, but not too bad, perhaps with an arm broken, would stop, look down, and grin. Honor had been fulfilled; they could now walk back past the provost guards to the rear, who would shout the demand, "Show blood," and now blood could be shown and they were safe. Many would be in shock, not even feeling pain until they staggered into the hospital area and saw the surgeons at work.

Some simply sat down, not quite comprehending, looking down at a shattered leg, seeing the bright blood spurting out, knowing what it meant, and then quietly lying back, gaze fixed on the heavens. More than one would be found later clutching a Bible or a daguerreotype of wife and children.

"Close up! Keep moving! Guide on the colors!"

The line staggered, slowed for an instant, and then forged ahead. The front contracted slightly as regiments aligned to their centers, the first gaps opening between formations.

The first wave began to hit the creek, some jumping at the narrow points, others slipping down into the cool, muddy water, churning it up. Dozens of men, hit in the first volley, reached the bank and then collapsed, more than one of them to drown in water so shallow that a toddler could have splashed his way to safety.

Alignment of the first wave began to waver, a few stopping at the stream, ducking down behind the relative safety of the low bank, file closers slapping them across the backs with the flat of swords or musket butts, pushing them up. The flag bearers of the thirty-two lead regiments, almost to a man, pressed forward, caught up in that strange euphoria that seized men of their kind, men who fought for the privilege to carry the sacred totem of their regiment, of their Republic. Colors held high, they defiantly pressed forward.

Directly to their front, through the coiling wisps of smoke from the first volley, they could see arms moving rhythmically up and down as the rebel infantry tore open cartridges with their teeth, poured powder down barrels, pushed greased ball into the muzzle, pulled ramrods out from under the barrel, or now, in many cases, retrieved them where the long, thin steel rods had been jammed into the dirt of the earthworks. Arms rose up, then pushed down, ramrod slamming rounds down to the breech of the barrel. Rammers were then stuck back into the earthen bank, rifle raised, half cocked, percussion cap fumbled out of capbox on the belt, cap set on nipple, and then gun raised up to the vertical, signaling that all was ready. After thirty seconds nearly every gun was poised at the vertical.

"Battalions, take aim!"

Again the barrels were leveled. The advancing blue wall now seemed to hunker down, men advancing with heads lowered, leaning forward, as if going into the teeth of a gale.

"Fire!"

A couple of hundred more dropped. Not as many as from the first volley, which was always the most accurate because the field was clear of smoke, and the loading had been done more carefully. In the excitement more than one rebel had pushed the ball down first rather than the powder or had fumbled the percussion cap and now snapped the hammer down on an empty nipple, and the smoke in places obscured the view, but the range was closer as well by forty yards or so.

Men collapsed into the high, wet grass, the dirt starting to churn up, more men losing shoes, some dropping rifles when a comrade in the front rank two feet ahead came slamming back into them. Flags dropped, for always it was the flag bearers who were special targets. Within seconds, though, eager hands grabbed the colors, hoisting them back up.

"Close on the colors! Keep moving, men! For God's sake keep moving!"

To some the assault might appear to be an exercise in madness, men advancing shoulder to shoulder against a deadly fire, standing erect, out in the open . . . and yet there was a terrible cold logic to it all, the idea of bringing a maximum number of men, in a close compact line, into effective combat range, and then either charge over the opponent with fixed bayonets or drive him back by concentrated musketry. The hard part was to keep the men moving, to keep them moving forward and not let the charge grind to a halt out in the middle of the field.

"On the double, quick time . . . march!"

The pace accelerated, from 110 yards a minute to twice that. Start it too early and the men would be winded when the climatic moment came, a fine equation balanced against how many would fall getting there at the slower pace.

The forward line surged ahead, those drummer boys allowed to go in on the advance, beating out the tattoo, officers waving swords, flag bearers setting the pace, the steady rulerlike line now beginning to break apart into thirty-two inverted *V* formations, each regiment closing in on their colors with the flags at the apex, flanks lagging a bit behind.

"Take aim!"

In places the range was down to 30 yards. Over on the right, with Slocum's brigades, the men were still 150 yards short of the enemy line.

"Fire!"

More fell, the charge staggering from the blow, collapsing bodies tumbling into the second line, men tangling up, flags going down.

Finally the tension was too much, and as in nearly every charge, the momentum began to slow. The enemy was so close that in the swirling smoke individual features could be seen, an officer, filled with battle madness, standing atop the low parapet, old men with graying beards standing alongside fresh-faced boys, all of them tearing cartridges, loading.

One of Zook's regiments came to a halt, a few men raising their rifles, firing, and then in seconds the entire Union front, spread across that open plain, leveled rifles and fired, the volley an explosive tearing roar that raced up and down the line, drawn out for long seconds, the shock wave from the discharge thumping across the fields, the sound of it mingling in with Henry's cannons, which had resumed their bombardment, the artillery fire aimed high to pass over the advancing lines and strike the crest of the hill.

Another thunder was adding in as well. The first of the replacement batteries reoccupying the bastions of Poague and Cabell were swinging into action. Gunners unhooking the trail of their pieces from caissons, manhandling the one-ton weapons forward, pulling aside bodies, smashed caissons, and in more than one case simply pulling the gun up and over the prone body of a dead horse. The first of the guns recoiled, throwing case shot down into the third wave of troops, who were still on the downward slope.

The Confederates in the forward trench went into independent fire at will, men loading furiously, barely aiming, just pointing into the clouds of smoke, some trying to sight on the flash of a rifle discharging in the gloom. More than a few loaded, forgot to cap the nipple, pulling the trigger then grounding their weapon and pushing another load in. A tragic few, after doing this half a dozen times, would successfully cap and when they squeezed the trigger, the breech of the gun burst, blinding or killing the man behind it.

A searing fire raced up and down the lines, men firing individually, some officers maintaining company volleys, a couple of regiments firing all at once, these volleys of three to four hundred rifles at once a sharp crack above the rolling cacophony. Upward of twelve thousand rifle balls were crisscrossing the field every minute.

Logic would seem to dictate that after a minute no one would be left alive, and yet for each volley of a hundred fired, maybe only three or five rounds would find their target. Rifles were aimed too high or too low; smoke covered the field so that it was rare to clearly see what one was shooting at. A strange illusion was created with the high grass. Rifle balls, aimed low, would come zinging through the grass, a line of stalks leaping into the air with its passage, the streak racing straight at a man, sometimes passing between his legs, as if a deadly invisible snake were flying past.

Bodies dropped on both sides, men collapsing into the muddy bottom of the

Confederate trench, Union troops falling in the grass.

One of Brooke's regiments went into a mad charge, bayonets leveled, racing across the last hundred yards, emerging out of the gloom, Confederates to both sides pouring in a ghastly enfilade that dropped a hundred or more before the battered remnant swarmed up the low, mud slick bluff delineating the end of the flood plain, clawing their way up onto the parapet of the shallow trench. Some of the Confederates gave back a few dozen feet; others leapt down, clubbed muskets raised, men rolling down the embankment, kicking, gouging, stabbing.

The charge broke, a final melee ensuing when a dozen Rebs tried to tackle the flag bearer and drag the colors away from him. Retreating men turned, surged back, clubbing and stabbing, physically dragging the dying flag bearer out of the melee.

This action finally broke the deadlock. It was the men themselves to either flank of the dying regiment that started to scream out a single word. . . .

"Charge! Charge!"

That strange, almost indefinable moment in a battle was occurring when morale surged for some reason, and men, rooted to a spot only a minute before, knowing that to take but one step forward would mean death, began to move, as if shoved into the maelstrom by the hand of some angry god of war desiring more blood.

A wild frenzy took hold, men screaming, lowering weapons, bayonets flashing, here and there two or three beginning to go forward again, in other places entire regiments advancing, keeping formation.

The dam broke.

The Confederate infantry, deployed up on the ridge, had so far remained silent, ordered to hold their fire; but some, unable to stand the strain, stood up, aimed down into the valley, and opened up. The artillery was still aiming across the valley to strike at the second or third line or Sedgwick's heavy brigades. Eighteen-thousand men strong who were in reserve and halfway down the slope began to crank up their elevation gears, raising the breeches of their guns, dropping the muzzles in anticipation of what was coming.

The brunt of the storm hit the muddy embankment, men floundering, falling, getting back up, sergeants and corporals physically pushing men up the slope. The assault wave broke into the line three hundred yards to the west of the mill, drowning it under in a wave of blue. The breach spread, like an old rag disintegrating as it was torn asunder.

Many of the Confederates backed out of the shallow trench, turned, and started scrambling up the slope to the main line. Some stayed; many died; many others dropped weapons, holding hands high, and for some the gesture was too late as they were shot or bayoneted in the wild frenzy.

The small bastion thrown up around the ruins of the mill and miller's house continued to hold. Its eastern flank was guarded by the millpond, the regiment that made up the extreme left of the Union attack stalled by the shallow, open body of water, the soldiers there simply kneeling and lying down along the bank to pour in supporting fire. The bridge below the mill had been destroyed during the night. The stream here had banks steep enough to offer a barrier and cover, so that the men who struck it stopped on the opposite shore, trapped in the narrow defile, while from thirty yards away the rebels inside the rough-built earthworks poured out a continual blaze of fire, dropping any man who dared to try and stand up and push forward.

But beyond that, from the opposite side of the Baltimore Road, clear down to the end of Slocum's divisions, who were opposing Pettigrew, the forward Confederate line fell.

For some this was as far as they felt they could get. They had braved the impact of the first volleys, stormed across the open fields, taken an entrenchment, but above them, three hundred yards above, was the crest.

All had been told what to do; officers had gone over it again and yet again. *"Don't stop, boys. There're two trenches. Don't stop till we're over the top of the ridge. Don't stop!"*

"Come on!" The cry echoed along the line, some men, still capable of cold logic, realizing that if they pressed quick enough, right on the heels of the retreating first line, the second might not fire until they were up onto them.

"Come on! Charge, for God's sake, charge!"

The blue wave lurched forward, all semblance of formation gone, men from Massachusetts, New York, Pennsylvania, Ohio, and even Maryland, a few of them having once played and fished along this same creek an eternity ago, pouring over the breastworks and up the slope.

Behind them the second and third waves, which had stopped at midfield and at the base of the slope on the northern side, moved forward again, while Sedgwick's divisions waited for what would develop next.

The surviving Confederates from the first trench ran up the hill, arms flapping, some casting away rifles in their haste, a few loading as they ran, turning to fire a defiant shot. Their comrades on the crest were up, rifles raised high, the signal that all were loaded and just waiting for the command.

Officers were out in front of the trench, screaming for the survivors to run, to keep running. Behind them the Union charge was gaining momentum, the race now going to the strongest, old battle wisdom telling some that if they could stay on the coattails of the retreating enemy they just might make it into the next line without facing another deadly volley.

The fleetest of the retreating Confederates gained the trench, eager hands pulling them up over the parapet.

"Hold! Hold your fire!"

The command was shouted by officers and NCOs, the waiting line solid, ranks packed shoulder to shoulder.

Ever since the Union charge had crested the opposite ridge forty minutes ago, they had waited, awed, fearful, defiant, angry all in turn, emotions jumbled together. They waited a few seconds more.

The Union wave coming up the slope could see them silhouetted on the crest, rifle barrels poised high, muzzles of cannons depressed, yawning wide. That struck the first fear after the euphoria of sweeping the lower trench. The artillery was not supposed to be there; all had said they'd be swept away.

All knew what a blast of canister could do at two hundred yards, or far worse double canister at seventy-five yards.

Some of the men slowed, particularly those going up toward where Poague's and Cabell's battalions had been. The charge was now less than 150 yards from the crest. For a moment there was a strange, almost deathly silence except for the drumming of thousands of men racing up the slope, men gasping for air, a few voices crying out to keep moving.

"Take aim!"

Several hundred Confederates, now caught in front of their own comrades, dived to the ground, hugging the earth, crying out, praying not to be killed by their own men.

"Fire!"

This time it was not three thousand rifles, it was over ten thousand, many of the men in the front rank kneeling down, resting their barrels on the waist-high parapet to steady their aim.

The twenty-seven artillery pieces in place across the front opened up, each gun discharging a round of canister, the smaller three-inch rifles letting loose with a can containing forty to fifty iron balls, the wider, four-and-a-half-inch bore Napoleons firing cans holding eighty to ninety iron balls.

The blast swept down the slope, and it was if the thirty-odd regiments still in the advance had slammed into an invisible wall. In an instant the charge collapsed.

Hundreds dropped or were thrown back down the slope. Parts of bodies, shattered muskets, busted canteens, fragments of uniform soared up and rained back down twenty, thirty yards to the rear, especially along the front swept by the canister.

Nearly every flag bearer dropped. One of the green flags of the Irish Brigade was swept off its standard, the standard shattered by two canister rounds, the bearer riddled so that his body was a bloody sack.

The men of that famed unit paused for a few brief seconds until they saw Colonel Kelly, their brigade commander, holding aloft the torn green flag of one of his regiments, the 116th Pennsylvania, waving it over his head.

"Ireland!" he screamed, and he started up the slope at a run, green flag fluttering over his head.

The decimated regiments of Erin leapt forward with wild battle cries, racing up the slope straight at the guns on the heights.

It was a race that would be decided in seconds. Rammers didn't bother to sponge, calling for the fixed round of canister and powder bag to be slammed straight into the muzzle. Gunners struggled to roll their pieces forward even as the rammers slapped their loads down to the muzzle, one gun going off prematurely, blowing the rammer, his staff, and the canister out over the Irishmen, gunners working the wheels crushed by the recoil.

Gunnery sergeants fumbled with friction primers, setting them in, hooking on lanyards, shouting for crews to jump clear.

Some of the Irishmen were actually up over the parapet, Kelly on top, waving the flag.

One gun, then seven more, fired in the next few seconds, some of the rounds discharging straight into the faces of men only a few feet away. There seemed to be a horrified pause for the briefest of moments as both sides were staggered by the carnage wrought.

At nearly the same instant, Kelly

dropped, and some claimed that even as he fell, tumbling inside the parapet, he clutched the colors to his breast.

A wild hysteria seized the few men left of the brigade as they scrambled up onto the parapet, screaming for their colonel, dropping as Confederate infantry waded in around the guns to repel the charge. The surge broke at the crest and fell back, leaving a carpet of blue and red and small swatches of green flag in the mud.

Most of the rest of the line did not advance, the first volley having driven them to ground, to halt yet again along that terrible, invisible line that seems to appear on a battlefront, a line that not even the bravest will pass, knowing that to take but one more step forward is death.

Some were demoralized, clutching the ground; others, in shock, were cradling wounded, dying, and dead comrades. Most settled down to the grim task at hand. Raising rifles, taking aim up the slope, firing, grounding muskets, reloading and firing again.

In the coldest sense of military logic, this battered line was the shield, the soak off, having taken the first position and now stalling in front of the second. Their job was simply to absorb the blows, to die, to inflict some death upon those dug in until the second and third lines came up, still relatively unscathed, to push the attack closer in.

And so across the next ten minutes they gave everything they had, these volunteers turned professionals, the pride of the Army of the Potomac, the pride of the Republic. Thousands of acts of courage were committed, none to be recorded except in the memories of those who were there, the greatest courage of all simply to stand on the volley line, to fire, to reload, and all the time the litany chant in the background . . .

"Pour it in to them. Close on the colors, boys. Pour it into them!"

Two hundred yards to the rear, the next assault wave reached the south bank of the flood plain, their officers ordering a halt, letting the men catch their breath for a few minutes, to gulp down some water, while forward their comrades died.

Atop the crest the Confederate forces blazed away, some of the men, acknowledged sharpshooters, calling for others to load, to pass their guns up, making sure that every shot counted, though in the still air, now laced again by showers, the smoke quickly built to a hanging cloud of fog.

Men were falling in the trenches, though not near as many as down on the open slope. Rifle balls smacked into the loosely piled dirt, spraying the men; shots when they hit tended to strike arms raised while ramming or, far more deadly, in the chest or face.

A growing line of dead and wounded lay directly behind the trench, dragged out of the way so as to not be trampled under.

The Union artillery was again in full play, though aiming in most cases too high out of fear of striking their own battle line in the confusion. But enough shots were tearing in to do terrible damage, a shell bursting on the lip of the parapet of Williamson's South Carolina troops, sweeping away eight men by his side.

A large cauldron that had been used to boil enough coffee for a regiment was struck by a solid shot, flipping it end over end, scalding men nearby, crushing the life out of a man unfortunate enough to be caught in its path.

An ammunition wagon went galloping off, two of the mules with broken legs, the driver dead, the two mules still intact dragging the wreckage in a blind panic.

A brief burst of rain swept along the slope, hard enough that as men tore cartridges open the powder got wet and their guns then misfired. The rain, at least for the moment, cut down the clouds of smoke, opening the visibility.

The forward line of the Union assault was staggering. Men no longer able to take the sweeping blasts, many, especially in front of the batteries, beginning to drop back. A few were running; most were giving ground slowly, angry, bitter that after having come so far, they could go no farther.

Drum rolls echoed along the base of the slope; bugles sounded. The second wave, which had waited, hugging the slope along the flood plain embankment or resting in the shallow trench, stood up.

There was no cheering. These men were grim. They had marched over and through the carnage already wrought, lying alongside dead and wounded comrades and enemies in the shallow trench. More than one had given what was left of his canteen to a gut-shot rebel begging for water or a blinded lieutenant asking for someone to wash the blood from his eyes so he could see again.

As they stood up, the first wave of broken troops coming down the slope passed through them. This was always the hardest moment for the following waves in an attack. All ahead looked to be nothing but chaos and disaster, ground covered with bodies and parts of bodies, men contorted and twisted into only the poses that those who had died violently could assume, soldiers, on the edge of panic, screaming that the battle was lost, visual evidence on all sides of the fate that might be waiting just one more step ahead.

Nevertheless, the regiments rose up, heads bowed, pushing up the slope. Behind them the third wave, which had been waiting, crouched along the banks of the stream, stood up and started forward as well. The broken troops fell back. Some slid into the Confederate trench at the base of the slope, rallying around a trusted officer, or their flags, though up forward a thin line still held, the colors of several regiments now planted in the ground, marking the point of farthest advance, or lying on the ground, the entire color guard dead or wounded.

For the next two minutes, the charge going up the ridge could not slow to open fire; too many of their own men were still in front. Twenty-seven regiments stormed up the slope, men from New Jersey, two entire brigades from New York, and another from Pennsylvania, regiments from Ohio and Indiana, a lone regiment from the mountains of West Virginia, and another from the flat coastal plains of Delaware.

The lash of the hurricane descended on

them. Gone was the panicked firing of the Confederate batteries about to be overrun by Kelly's now-annihilated brigade. Gunners took a few extra seconds, sighting their weapons as barrels were swabbed out and canister charges set in.

At two hundred yards, one entire battalion of guns cut loose with a salvo.

The impact dropped the entire line across a front of nearly a hundred yards, sweeping it to the ground like toy soldiers cast down by an angry child. At that point of the mile-wide advance the charge did not simply stop, it just disappeared into the ground.

To either flank of this hole, the survivors of the two divisions coming from Second and Twelfth Corps surged onward, in many places storming over the forward edge of the line held by their comrades of the first wave, formations breaking up as men slowed to move around the bodies, which at some points seemed almost to have been laid down in perfect lines.

The charge was getting closer to the Confederate lines, the blaze of rifle fire atop the crest a continual thunder sweeping up and down the length of the parapet. On the extreme left, this second wave finally broke over the bastion built around the ruins of the mill complex, the

Confederate regiment within swarmed under in a frenzy of clubbed muskets and bayonet thrusts, the survivors scrambling out the back of the bastion and running up to the main line, their enraged attackers coming on behind them.

If someone could have hovered far above the battle and not seen the minute details, they might have assumed that this charge would indeed break over the top. Yet within the ranks of the charge, the sheer volume of fire coming down upon them was having a deadly effect. It seemed that with every step another man went down in every company of every regiment. Officers screamed themselves hoarse shouting for the men to keep closing on the colors, to follow the colors, the torn flags in many places nothing more than dim shadows in a surreal Stygian twilight of smoke and fire.

The air actually felt hot from all the fire. Men's legs felt like rubber both from fear and from exhaustion after the long run up the slope. The pace slowed and yet it was so maddeningly close, not fifty yards away in many places; one bulge, led by a couple of Ohio regiments of Carroll's brigade of Hays's division of the Second Corps, literally got up to the edge of the breastworks and there leveled their rifles, firing a scathing volley into the enemy from less than fifteen feet away. This caused a momentary breech in the line, the surviving Confederates diving down for cover, or breaking, pulling back out of the trench.

The flag bearer of one of the Ohio regiments stood atop the breastworks, waving the national colors before going down, struck by three rounds in a matter of seconds. As he fell, the colors dropped into the trench, and the Ohioans piled in, desperate to retrieve their precious colors.

In many places regimental commanders called for volley fire, slower perhaps than independent fire, but far more devastating psychologically when striking into an enemy so close that you literally could catch glimpses of the whites of their eyes.

Along the Confederate front a madness took hold as well. Gone was any sense of compassion, of admiration of the higher ideals that many spoke of. Now it was a killing frenzy, a rage at those who kept pressing in, not letting them rest, not letting them breathe just a few gulpfuls of fresh air. Men began to curse wildly, slamming charges down barrels thick with gummy residue after having fired thirty to forty rounds or more.

Ammunition carriers staggered down the line, passing out packets of ten cartridges, which men stuffed into their

pockets. A shell struck one of these carrying parties, the two men dying instantly, the thousand rounds in the heavy wooden box going off like firecrackers.

Out in the open field in front of the trench the volleys came pouring back, men loading, some trying to stagger forward a few more feet, then raising rifles to fire again. In spite of the steady rain now coming down, the blanketing fog of smoke choked the field in blindness.

And then the third wave came up the slope, men of Gibbon's division, tough professionals, men of the First Minnesota, the Nineteenth Maine, the Sixty-ninth Pennsylvania, on their right flank Lockwood's brigade.

They slammed up against the backs of the second wave, swarming in, ranks mingling, men shoving each other to step to the front to fire, others then pushing past them.

Only paces away, men of McLaws's brigades; Pender's division; and Pettigrew's, who had been so badly mauled only three days before in front of Gettysburg; Anderson's division, which had gone in on that final doomed charge up Cemetery Hill, stood in place, firing back. Both sides were screaming defiance, firing blindly, more than one man collapsing when shot in the back of the head by a comrade only a few feet in the rear. The line in front of the battery bastions was nearly swept clean; gunners struggled to swing pieces around to pour canister into the flanks, while shot from Henry's batteries continued to pour down.

A brigade of Early's division, not yet engaged, finally swarmed out of their trenches, moving to enfilade the attacking columns, an action that triggered Sickles to order one of his divisions forward to try and catch this flanking column in its flank, though it would be long minutes before Sickles's men could cross the open meadows and come up the slope to engage.

At several points, to the left of the bastion held by Cabell's gunners, and a quarter mile farther down just to the flank of Poague's old position, the Union charge gained the trench, the Confederates grimly giving the few feet of ground, now standing in the open, firing down into the trench, Union soldiers hugging the muddy ground, loading while lying on their backs, rolling up, half standing to fire, then sliding back down.

Over it all a slow but steady rain was now falling, the ground beneath the feet of the combatants churned to a thick mud, wounded falling into it, those in the bottom of the trench getting trampled under, some of them choking to death before bleeding out.

The battle hung poised; seconds were like years, minutes centuries. . . .

Chapter Eighteen

12:45 PM, July 4, 1863

Union Mills

The battle was poised on the most delicate of balances. An officer panicking, a flag bearer falling, perhaps even one man turning, screaming that all was lost, could set off a stampede on either side. In turn, a few men were determined to hang on. An officer oblivious of risk and riding forward, a man who could inspire and lead, could make the decisive difference.

For the Confederates, at that moment, there were four profound advantages, which were at that same instant distinct and terrible disadvantages for the Union. The Confederates had not been forced to advance, all they had had to do was wait, saving their already half-depleted strength for the supreme moment. They were on the high ground, with all the natural advantages that implied, and along most of the front. Except where several small breaches had been cut into their line, they were still in the trench or the battery bastions, while their foes were downslope and in the open . . . and finally, they had a commander who at that moment was inspired to lead, to make the decisions that had to be made second by second. The psychological advantage thus gained was tremendous.

The supreme moment was at hand before Union Mills.

Even as the two breakthroughs cracked into the Confederate line, Lee was galloping back to the rear, not in retreat, but with orders, his staff at least grateful that for a few minutes he was relatively out of harm's way except for the continual rain of shot arcing down from the Union batteries.

Rhodes's heavy division, minus one brigade under O'Neal, which was up on the forward line, had sat out the bombardment and first assault, lying down in a field of waist-high corn, four hundred yards away.

The first ranks could see Lee riding up, waving his straw hat, and the men were instantly up.

"Lee! Lee! Lee!"

Rhodes, mounted and at the front of his division, snapped off a salute.

"General, send your men in now!" Lee shouted. "Reclose the line and then push those people back!"

Rhodes needed no further orders. He could see where the battered brigades of McLaws and Anderson were beginning to bend under the strain.

Rhodes's First Brigade, Daniel's North Carolinians, already deployed in regimental front, leapt forward on the double, while behind them, the brigades of Dole and Ramseur shook out from column to line by regiment and began to move toward their left. Iverson's brigade, so badly shattered in the fight before Gettysburg, was held back for the moment, Rhodes having decided to personally lead the unit after Iverson's ghastly, drunken display three days earlier, which had nearly annihilated the entire unit when he let them advance into a trap, while he hid in the rear, bottle in hand.

Lee started to turn, to go in with them, but this time his staff did revolt, pushing their mounts in front of Traveler, shouting for him to stay back. Again the realization hit him, and slightly embarrassed he nodded an assent.

Meade, pacing back and forth nervously, turned yet again, raising his field glasses. It was impossible to tell. The smoke was thickening again, the rain increasing, the effect now being to mingle cloud and smoke into one impenetrable haze, all but obscuring the view.

Sedgwick was by his side. "Should I go in?" he asked.

And within Meade, at that moment, there was a terrible indecision. To speak an hour ago of forty thousand men at once sweeping forward was one thing; now he was seeing the result. Thousands of men were emerging out of the gloom, streaming back, individually, in groups of two or three, helping a wounded comrade, in several cases entire regiments, or what was left of them, moving slowly, sometimes pausing as if debating their course.

The front of the first trench was still visible in places, easy enough to pick out by the carpet of bodies spread before it.

Two entire corps were fought out, and now word had just come that Sickles, without orders, had thrown at least another division into the fight, advancing onto the open.

If that was true, then Sedgwick was now the only true reserve left, that and the small remnant of the devastated First Corps, which had marched up during the night.

"Do I go in?" Sedgwick asked yet again.

Meade was silent, gazing at the heavy columns of Sedgwick, and the ever-increasing flood of beaten men emerging out of the gloom encasing the opposite ridge.

"Sir, what do you want me to do? Should I go in now or wait?"

"Only if Hancock and Slocum break

through," Meade replied.

Meade turned, galloping down the line to see what Sickles was doing, leaving Sedgwick alone.

Longstreet stood with Porter in the shattered bastion built by Cabell and now occupied by McIntosh's valiant gunners, the Second Rockbridge Artillery posted at the right corner, pouring blast after blast of canister into the smoke, confident that canister would do its work at this distance almost without aiming.

Another of Longstreet's old West Point comrades suddenly went down less than a hundred paces away, John Gibbon struck in the stomach by a canister ball from a Rockbridge gun. John struggled back to his feet, clutching the agonizing wound, and continued to scream for his men to press forward.

Another seam in the Confederate line ruptured, as men from half a dozen regiments, all mingled together, pushed up across the road and the ruins of the Shriver house, led by the men of the old Philadelphia Brigade, yet again Irishmen under green flags. The hard-fighting Sixty-ninth Pennsylvania led the way, breaking over the trench, gaining a small inverted *V* lodgment, bending several companies back to hold either flank. It might have gained momentum, but the Seventy-first, on their right, broke apart only feet away from widening the breech, and began to fall back, their comrades of the Sixty-ninth jeering them before turning back to the fight.

Henry, shaking with exhaustion, was at a near hysterical pitch, shouting for his gunners to aim high, to keep pouring it in. He could no longer see what they were shooting at, but from the flashes of light through the gloom, and the continual roar of musketry along the crest, he knew that the top was almost gained but not yet taken.

Winfield Scott Hancock, hat off, eyes blazing, galloped at full speed down the Baltimore Road, oblivious to Meade's orders to stay back from the fight. Those were his boys up there, but that was not where he was heading first.

On his right, arrayed across the open slope that his divisions had marched down less than an hour before, were the three heavy divisions of Sedgwick, eighteen thousand men . . . and they were not moving!

Reaching the front of the Sixth Corps, which was deployed at the edge of the flat bottomland, he leapt a ditch, nearly losing his saddle, and then streaked across the field, his mount nervous, shifting and weaving to avoid trampling the dead and wounded.

At last he spotted Horatio Wright, commander of the First Division of the Sixth.

"In the name of God, why are you not advancing?" Hancock roared.

"Sir, we've yet to receive orders to go in," Wright replied, stunned by the near hysteria of Hancock. "I was ordered to stay in reserve until a breakthrough had been achieved by your men."

"Goddamn you, sir. Go in! Go in! My boys are dying up there."

"Sir, I was ordered to wait for General Sedgwick to give the final order to advance."

Hancock threw back his head and screamed the foulest of oaths against Sedgwick. Standing in his stirrups, he fixed Wright with a malignant gaze. "Look over there, man!" and he pointed toward the opposite crest. "You can see we're almost in. My men are dying up there by the thousands. All that is needed is one more push. Now give your men the order to charge, and I will go with you!"

Wright hesitated, looking to his staff, who were gazing at Hancock as if he were a madman. The seconds dragged out, and finally Wright nodded. "I will follow you, sir."

Hancock swung about, drawing sword and holding it high. "On the double, men, on the double!"

Wright's division lurched forward. At the sight of them advancing, the second division in line behind them, Russell's, believing that the order had been given, stepped forward as well, followed a minute later by the third and final division.

Wright's men still had over eight hundred yards to go before coming into effective range; at double time it would take five to seven minutes. If deployed forward, on the opposite side of the valley, it would have only taken one minute.

"Here comes Rhodes!" Longstreet cried hoarsely, thrilling at the sight of the brigade-wide front charging the last hundred yards, the Second and Third brigades advancing at the oblique to their own left, followed in the rear by the decimated remnants of Iverson's brigade, those men now eager for pay back for the slaughter endured in front of Seminary and Oak Ridges three days before.

The countercharge swept into the thinning volley line of McLaws's two brigades, hitting it like a tidal surge. The units instantly mingled together and now flooded back into their trench, in places continuing straight forward, down the slope, covering the last few paces into the men under Gibbon and Hays.

The charge hit with a vicious momentum, in many places propelling men forward who normally would have hesitated to cross those last ten to twenty feet into actual hand-to-hand combat.

An audible impact of men slamming into men, rifles against rifles, and steel into flesh was heard, the Union line staggering backward like a wall about to burst when hit by a battering ram.

Hundreds fell within seconds, many just tripping, going down in the confusion, men then backing up or pushing forward, stumbling over the fallen and going down as well.

For a moment the battle degenerated into a brawl in which all lashed out, some in rage, others in terror, kicking, stabbing, clubbing, and gouging anyone within reach. More than one man, in his terror, was slammed into by another, and whirling about stabbed a comrade by mistake, sometimes not even realizing what he had done.

And yet again, all of what was said about the "good ground" came to pass here. If the rebel charge had been met on level ground and by men not already exhausted, the line just might have held, but their backs were to a downward slope now churned up into slippery mud, all was confusion in the smoke, none could see more than ten, maybe twenty feet, and what little could be seen was a glimpse of hell.

Men began to stagger backward; some in their terror simply threw aside their rifles and ran; others, as always those around a sacred flag or trusted officer or sergeant, backed out, slashing and stabbing at those who pressed too close.

The entire Union line disintegrated as Rhodes's Second Brigade slammed in and the Third Brigade, a few minutes later, obliquely hit Lockwood's lone brigade on the Union right.

John Gibbon, defiant to the end, stood clutching his ghastly wound. Mercifully, a North Carolina boy stopped short of him, grounded his musket, and then just simply offered a hand, not saying a word. Gibbon, nodding, slowly sank to his knees.

Those still standing from the second and third waves of Hancock's and Slocum's corps poured down off the slopes above Union Mills.

"Keep moving; don't stop!"

Hancock was still out in front, weaving back and forth in front of Wright's brigades, sword held high.

Already across the stream, they had taken almost no casualties, all the Confederate fire concentrated on the annihilation of those on the slope.

Though he could not see it, so thick were the smoke and the steadily increasing curtains of rain, Sickles, a mile and a half to the west, was going in with two divisions. Sickles's charge was just now slamming into the flank of Early's brigade, which itself was on the flank of the retreating Twelfth Corps.

Hancock caught a glimpse of a courier riding straight down the middle of the Baltimore Road, swerving off, going down into the streambed, and then just disappearing. He suspected it was from Meade or Sedgwick.

To hell with them now.

From out of the maelstrom cloaking the ridge ahead, he saw a wave of men emerging, falling back, some running like madmen. Spurring forward, he waded straight into their ranks, standing high in the stirrups.

"My men. Rally to the old Sixth! Fall back in. Rally!"

At the sight of their corps commander, many of the men actually did turn about, though there was little fight in them now, exhausted as they were.

The blue wave of the Sixth Corps hit

the bottom of the slope and started the final climb up toward the blood-soaked ridge.

"My God, another one," Porter gasped. "When will they stop this?"

Rhodes had somehow managed to rein in his men charging down the slope, and they were now falling back up the slope in fairly good order, firing a volley, withdrawing a couple of dozen yards, then firing again before sliding into the trench.

Porter's guns had switched back to solid shot and case shot with fuses cut to two seconds, firing downslope into the mist, the passage of the shot visible by the twisting swirls lashed through the smoke.

"One more time!" Longstreet shouted, stepping back from the walls of the bastion, looking at the gunners. "They can't have anything behind this."

Venable and Moxley were waiting outside the bastion, holding Longstreet's horse. He left the position, pausing for a second to look back. The battlefront was emerging out of the smoke, a powerful block. He caught a glimpse of a divisional standard, the new ones that the Army of the Potomac had just instituted. He wasn't sure which division it signified, but it was obviously Sixth Corps. So, after all these days, he knew exactly where they were at last, the heaviest corps of their army, coming straight at them.

He judged the width of the line, a half mile or more across. Most likely a second division behind it. Thank God, they had not come up ten minutes earlier.

He turned to Moxley. "Ride like hell. This will hit here," and both ducked as a shell screamed in close, but failed to burst.

"Pender and Pettigrew are to leave a light screen, one brigade each to cover their lines, but then start moving everything else down here."

"Sir?" Moxley looked at him, a bit confused.

"Every regiment, every battalion, I want them here! Get a message back to General Lee as well. Tell him we've pinpointed the location of Sixth Corps. They are directly in front of us. They are not before Taneytown; they are here!"

Moxley saluted and galloped off, his horse kicking up sprays of mud.

Longstreet swung up into the saddle. The rain had closed in hard, dropping visibility to less than a hundred yards, so that for a moment the advancing lines were lost to view. There was no need to see them; one could hear them, the ground, the air vibrating from the steady trample of eighteen thousand men, coming straight at him.

* * *

Henry watched the advance, tears in his eyes, knowing that the timing was off, that they should have gone in ten minutes earlier.

Barely able to speak, he grabbed the nearest battery commander. "Pour it in. Sweep that crest. Don't stop!"

The major shook his head. "Sir, we're out. Just canister and half a dozen rounds of case shot as reserve."

"Then fire the case shot!"

Even as he spoke, Meade, who had swept past Henry twenty minutes earlier, in response to the word that Sickles was advancing, reined in.

Sedgwick, hat off, came racing up to join Meade.

"Did you order your men in?" Meade shouted.

"No."

"Then why are they going in? Did we break through?"

Sedgwick hesitated. "I'm not sure. I sent a courier down to order them to stop, but they are still going forward."

"They're going in without orders?" Meade cried.

Henry looked at the two, at first mystified, and then overwhelmed with despair.

"I did not yet order the final advance," Meade gasped.

Henry, all thought of propriety gone, stepped forward between the two. "Let them go!" Henry shouted, his voice breaking. "They still might carry it."

"It's out of control, Hunt," Meade said, his voice cold and distant. "Sickles went in without orders; it's too late to stop him; now this, my last reserve other than First Corps."

Henry wanted to ask him why, if that was the case, had he had Sedgwick move up halfway in support to start with. He sensed that at this moment Meade was losing his nerve, thinking more of a battle lost than a battle that could still be won.

"They can still carry it," Henry offered.

"Those are my men going in without my orders," Sedgwick announced stiffly.

"Then go in with them now, sir," Henry replied, his voice filled with rebuke. "Show them that you can still lead."

Sedgwick glared at him coldly. "Goddamn you, sir. I'll have you court-martialed for that."

"Go ahead," Henry said wearily, shaking his head.

The nearest battery fired, and Meade, startled, looked up.

"I thought you said we were nearly out of ammunition."

"I'm putting in what we have left,"

Henry replied, turning away from Sedgwick. "My God, those men need my support. Sir, they are our last hope. Let them go in."

Meade was silent, watching as the Sixth Corps started up the slope, disappearing into the smoke and mist.

"Go, John, see what you can still do." Meade sighed.

Sedgwick glared angrily at Henry for a moment and then, with a vicious jerk of the reins, turned his mount around and raced down the hill.

Henry said nothing, looking up at Meade, who sat astride his horse as if transfixed, not moving, almost like a statue, rain dripping from the brim of his hat.

Flashes of light danced along the ridge crest; long seconds later the rumble of a volley rolled across the valley.

"I've lost control of the battle," Meade whispered, speaking to himself.

Even as he spoke, Henry saw a rider emerging through the drifting clouds of smoke, standing tall in his stirrups, shouting for General Meade. A gunner pointed and the courier turned, seeing the flag of the commander of the army, and raced up, then reined in hard, mud splattering up from his horse.

"Sir, I've come down from Hanover,

sir," the courier gasped. "Hell of a ride. Damn near got caught twice by Reb cavalry."

As he spoke the courier fumbled with his breast pocket and finally pulled out a packet. It was sealed with wax, several large matches tucked into the edge of the envelope, so that if the courier felt he would be captured he could quickly burn it.

"Has anyone else brought this in?" the courier asked.

Meade grabbed the envelope and shook his head.

"I was told three other riders were carrying the same message, sir."

"Well, Lee is most likely reading those by now."

Meade tore the envelope open; inside were two memos. Henry, standing by his side, caught a glimpse of one, the letterhead standing out boldly THE WHITE HOUSE.

Meade read the first memo and then the second one. His shoulders slumped.

"My God," Meade whispered, and folding the letters from Lincoln and the contradictory one from Halleck back up, he tucked them into his breast pocket.

"Useful for my court-martial," he said, looking at Henry; then, turning slowly, he rode away.

★ ★ ★

Hancock continued to ride back and forth across the front of the advancing division, shouting for the men to keep moving, to close it up, to close in.

A blast of canister swept across the line, dropping Wright and a dozen or more around him. He could see them now, the final line, the ground before the entrenchment paved with bodies. "Just a few feet more!"

John Williamson, with Hazner at his side, braced for what was about to hit, the right wing of the Union advance lapping over into his division's entrenchments.

Merciful God, when will this ever end? he silently pleaded.

More than one officer, pistol ammunition expended, had picked up a rifle and stood on the firing line. Williamson held his poised, waiting for the order.

"Ready!"

He raised his rifle up, hands trembling, and then brought it straight down. It was hard to pick an individual target; all he could see was a dark blue wall emerging, coming up the slope. Time seemed distorted, the men in front of him moving woodenly, slipping on the wet grass and mud, line weaving as the Union troops stepped around and over bodies.

"Take aim!"

He pointed his rifle downrange, finger curled around the trigger. A rider crossed in front of his sights, turning, sword held high, now coming nearly straight at him.

"Fire!"

He squeezed the trigger, the heavy Springfield rifle recoiling sharply. All was again cloaked in smoke. It was impossible to see, to know, what he had done.

The blow slammed Hancock back in his saddle. At nearly the same instant, his horse reeled, screaming pitifully, half rearing up, blood cascading out of a torn neck, the round then bursting through the pommel of his saddle and into Hancock's upper thigh. For a moment Winfield was filled with a blind panic, terrified that his horse was rolling over.

Hands reached up. Someone was grabbing the reins of the horse, pulling its head down, steadying the dying animal. Others grabbed Winfield, dragging him from the saddle. The shock, the pain, struck him with such intensity that he felt the world start to spin away, drifting on the edge of passing out.

Men were storming past him. He caught glimpses of feet, mud spraying about. He looked up. A soldier was leaning over him, shouting something; he couldn't hear what the man was saying. Someone was holding a canteen, cutting off the sling and then kneeling down. Another man helped Winfield to sit up while the first soldier looped the canteen sling around his left thigh.

He wrapped the canteen sling around a discarded bayonet scabbard and began to twist it, the pressure increasing, the pain unbearable.

Sound was returning; he could hear men shouting.

"The general's dead!"

He wasn't sure if they were talking about Wright or himself.

"I must stand up," he gasped.

"Your left leg, sir." It was one of his staff, kneeling, examining the wound.

"I know it's my leg, damn it."

"You're bleeding bad."

"Get me up."

No one moved.

"Get me up!"

Several men gathered round, bracing him, hoisting him up, and for a few seconds he passed out and then vision gradually returned.

The line he had been leading was stalled, having advanced only a few more yards past the place where he had fallen. A volley erupted and men, standing in place, began to reload.

"Charge, don't stop!" Hancock gasped.

The men holding him up started to turn away. Swearing, Winfield feebly struggled to break free from their embrace, but they ignored his pleas.

"Charge them, charge!"

One of the men stumbled and then just collapsed, shot in the back of the head. Winfield fell, hitting the ground first with his injured leg.

The world went dark.

Longstreet, crouching low in the saddle, rode along the line just behind the trench. The air was thick with shot, but for the moment he was all but oblivious to it.

The charge was stalling, caught out in the open ground. Some of the men in the trench were so exhausted that they simply sat on the ground like statues of stone, incapable of moving. Rhodes's men, though, in general, were still relatively fresh, and in places ranked three and four deep, pouring a devastating fire down into the blue ranks.

The Second Division of Sedgwick's corps pushed up the slope, merging into the stalled line of the First, but this renewed surge only advanced the line a few dozen feet before it stopped yet again.

They had seen too much, the defeated troops coming down off this damnable ridge. The footing was increasingly treacherous in the rain, and the piled-up carnage before them was almost a barrier in itself, thousands of dead and wounded caught in the open between the two volley lines, men thus trapped curled up, screaming, begging for the horror to end.

Sedgwick, coming down from the grand battery across the open field, was nearly stopped several times by the sheer numbers of wounded and fleeing troops heading to the rear. At last he reached the left flank of his Third Division, which was just reaching the first trench line.

"Halt! Halt!"

He pushed through the ranks, shouting the order over and over again. Men looked up at him confused, not sure of what was happening, more than one assuming that Sedgwick had to be on the front line, leading the advance; otherwise why would they be going in?

Wheaton, commanding the division, turned on Sedgwick, mystified. "Why are we stopping?" Wheaton shouted.

"I did not order this advance."

"Sir, we are in the middle of it now. I am going to oblique to the right," and as he spoke he pointed up the slope to where one could catch glimpses of a swarm of Confederates now outside of their trenches, moving to flank the assaulting column.

"Who authorized you to advance?"

"I thought you did, sir."

"I did not."

"We can still turn this," Wheaton cried, "but we've got to move now; our boys up there are getting flanked."

Sedgwick shook his head. "It's lost," he replied. "I want you to hold here."

"Sir, it's lost if we *do* hold here."

"Hold," Sedgwick cried. "You, sir, are the last reserve division in this entire army now. Meade wants you to hold."

Wheaton hesitated, and then finally nodded his head in agreement.

"General Lee!"

Lee, who had remained behind the lines at the point where Rhodes had been deployed, saw Taylor approaching, and somehow he knew exactly what would be reported.

Taylor reined in and saluted.

"What is it, Walter?" Lee asked, trying to keep his voice calm.

"Sir, I felt I should report to you personally on this."

"Yes."

"Sir, about a half hour ago, a courier came in from General Ewell." Taylor handed the message over and Lee opened it.

> *12:00 PM*
> *Near Taneytown, on the*
> *Littlestown Road.*
>
> *Sir,*
>
> *I have heard the cannonade from our right for the last two hours, the sound of it just now diminishing. I am, at this moment, unaware of conditions along the front held by General Longstreet and have received a report that his position is about to be turned.*
>
> *Therefore, respectfully sir, I am refraining from initiating the advance ordered by you last night until such time as I can be assured that my right is secured. In addition, sir, the condition of Hood's and Johnson's divisions makes offensive operations highly problematic.*
>
> *I await your orders, sir.*
>
> *Ewell*

Lee crumpled the message in his right hand, held it in his clenched fist for several seconds, and then flung it to the ground. All about him were shocked by this display.

Lee looked at those gathered around him. He pointed at a young cavalryman who was part of his escort detail, the same one who had sworn at the black cook the night before.

"You. Ride up there," and he pointed to the battlefront. "Longstreet should be in that artillery bastion. I want an answer, and I want it now. Can he hold against this latest assault? I expect you back here within ten minutes."

The trooper saluted and galloped off.

"Where are McLaws's two brigades from Westminster?" Lee asked impatiently. "I ordered them up here nearly three hours ago."

A trooper, without waiting to be ordered, spurred his mount onto the Baltimore Pike and galloped south; but even as he did so, Lee could see the head of a column coming out of the mists, the men running flat out.

Without waiting, he turned and started to ride straight toward the front, none of his staff now daring to try and intervene.

Longstreet stood silent, unable to speak. The slaughter that was unfolding before him had simply become too much. Straggling units were now coming in from Pettigrew, pushing down on to the flank of the Union forces, pouring fire in.

The courier from Lee had been answered with a single word, and he vaguely saw, in the smoke and curtains of mist, the rider slowing, a momentary glimpse of Lee.

"They're giving way!"

The blue wall was starting to fall back, caving in. Rhodes's men were again up and out of their trenches, pushing forward.

"General Longstreet!"

Pete turned, recognizing the voice. It was Lee.

"Are you all right, sir?" Lee asked.

Pete realized that in his numbness he had failed to salute, and now did so.

"Yes, sir, I am unhurt."

"Fine then, sir. But remember, I ordered you to take care of yourself," Lee said chidingly.

"Sir, you are under fire as well." Lee forced a weak smile and nodded.

"Can you hold here, and maintain the action on this front?" he asked.

"Sir, they are falling back."

Lee stood up slightly in his stirrups and surveyed the ground ahead. His features were grim, lips tightly compressed.

"Yes, I see," he replied softly.

"General Lee, that is Sixth Corps falling back. We now know for certain where they are. I think they are out of this fight. In fact, after this slaughterhouse, I think Meade's entire army is out of the fight. They will not find the will to attack again this day."

Lee said nothing for a moment,

unmoving though random shots were still clipping the air around the two.

"General Longstreet, the orders for you are still the same."

Lee reached into his pocket and pulled out his watch. "It's nearly one-thirty. We might have just enough daylight, six hours, to finish this once and for all. I am leaving here now. You know what to do."

"Yes, sir."

Lee snapped off a salute and, calling for Taylor, he galloped off.

"Come on!"

Sergeant Hazner was scrambling up out of the trench, the men around Williamson following.

Hazner looked back at him, grinning.

"I told you you'd live through it. The battle's over." Hazner laughed.

They were the last words Williamson ever heard.

There was no pain, no fear, never a realization of how profoundly he had affected the battle, just a quiet going out, the rifle ball striking him in the left temple.

The breaking of the First and Second Divisions of Sixth Corps, there on the muddy slopes above Union Mills, precipitated a general rout all across the field. As the men swarmed back down the hill, the

Third Division of the Sixth attempted to hold on in the first trench, but within minutes gave way, John Sedgwick, still not sure of what should be done, first ordering them to fall back, then for a moment reversing himself, as the realization came, with awful intensity, of what had just occurred. But to try and push the thirteen thousand survivors of his corps back into the fight in any organized manner was now beyond the ability of any mortal man.

Hancock, slung in a blanket carried by four men, was borne across the muddy pastures, and even in that moment of disarray and panic, he was a rallying point. As word spread that their general was down, dozens of men came to his side, finally several hundred in all, forming a protective shield. Sedgwick rode past him, less than twenty yards away, not even aware of Hancock's presence.

"Cease fire."

Henry, head bowed, turned away from his batteries and walked away. All was wreckage around him, dead horses, shattered caissons, dismounted cannons, a long line of dead gunners dragged to the rear. It was a terrible fact of his chosen profession of arms that artillerymen tended to suffer far more terrifying wounds than the infantry. Men had been torn in half by shells, impaled by flying splinters, burned from bursting ammunition wagons, crushed beneath recoiling or collapsing guns. He looked up at Meade and was startled by the sight of tears in the general's eyes.

"My God, Hunt," Meade said, still holding the dispatch from Washington, "what have I done here?"

Henry looked back toward the enemy lines. Thousands of men were staggering back; the field seemed like a seething mass of floundering lost souls, coming back with heads bowed, the rain still lashing down, torn battle flags hanging limp.

"I'm going to try and rally the men," Meade announced. "Have your guns ready, Hunt."

"Rally the men? The guns ready?" Henry gasped. "For what?"

Meade said nothing and, trailing a dejected staff, he started down the hill.

"Let us go in, sir," Rhodes cried, pointing at the broken forces streaming away, covering the pasture below.

Longstreet wearily shook his head.

"No, General Lee wants us to reform here."

"We have them beaten now, sir, beaten."

"I know that."

"Then let us go in."

Longstreet held his hand out, motioning

for Rhodes to be silent.

Some of the men along the line began to cheer. A soldier came in, triumphal, holding a torn and mud-splattered national flag aloft. That set off a scramble, with dozens climbing out of the trench to run down the slope in search of trophies.

"Stop those men!" Longstreet shouted.

Venable nodded and spurred his mount, the horse so exhausted it whinnied in protest and then moved off at a slow trot, nearly falling as they tried to go down the muddy forward slope of the trench.

"Reform your division, General Rhodes. Rations should be coming up. Get your men some food; find water other than that down there," and he nodded toward the millpond, now a muddy brown with splashes of pink all along its banks.

"Why are we not attacking?"

"General Lee ordered it so. You saw what we just did to them. Broken or not, we try and cross that field now, and it will be the same for us. We have shattered them, sir, but they are angry, as angry as we would be. They will turn and fight back. I know I would. Let us get them truly running first, and then on other ground it will be finished."

Pete lowered his head. "And for God's sake, sir, get some volunteers down there to help the wounded, theirs and ours. I want prisoners taken care of. Colors taken, returned here, and not to be dragged about. They deserve some respect, sir, the same respect we would want."

Rhodes nodded.

"When this war is over," Pete whispered, pointing toward the carnage, "what will we say to each other then?"

With that he turned away, stepping around the wreckage, the chaos, pausing for a second to look at a sergeant cradling the body of a major, the sergeant rocking back and forth, telling the major over and over how sorry he was.

Longstreet walked off to be alone with his thoughts.

Of the nearly fifty thousand men who had advanced, including those men of the two divisions of Sickles who had attempted to engage Early, nearly eighteen thousand were dead, wounded, or captured. Of the roughly twenty-six thousand Confederates who had faced them, close to five thousand were down as well. The terror of the twelve hours along Antietam Creek, the horrendous losses of that bitter day, had been compressed into less than four hours.

Second Corps was forever finished as a fighting command. As Hancock was loaded into an ambulance, around him close to 70 percent of his men were casualties. All three division commanders were dead or dying. Ninety percent of the officers of colonel's rank or above were dead, wounded, or captured. Entire regiments had been swept off the roster of battle. Slocum's Twelfth Corps had fared nearly as badly. Slocum was unconscious, like Hancock disobeying orders and going forward to be with his men, knocked out by a bursting shell. Both of his divisional commanders were dead.

Dan Sickles, ever the survivor, was getting out. Breaking off the engagement in which he had briefly committed two of his divisions, one of which was badly mauled, he was even now preparing to abandon the line.

Kelly, dying, had refused to let go of his flag, respectful Confederates kneeling by his side, a son of Ireland, whom fate had cast up in Charleston rather than New York, reciting the rosary with him, then, as Catholic rite allowed, hearing his confession so that afterward as a proxy, he could carry that confession to a priest. Kelly slipped away, his confessor prying the colors from the colonel's hands, folding it up, and tucking it under his shirt with the solemn promise that one day they would be returned to his brigade.

Porter, passed out from loss of blood, was loaded onto an empty caisson to be taken to the rear by gunners.

Where terrible blood lust had ruled only minutes before, small acts of compassion now held sway . . . a shared canteen, a slip of paper torn from the back of a pocket Bible and then used to write down a few last words of a dying foe, a soggy blanket wrapped around an old man with no visible wounds, but shaking uncontrollably with shock, lips blue, heart failing.

Prisoners, heads bowed, not with shame, but sheer exhaustion, labored up the slope, carrying the wounded with them. A large hospital flag went up just behind the crest, men laid down on the ground beneath it so that the field was soon a sea of anguish, men suffering under the cooling rain that again was drifting off, faint shadows flowing across the scarred landscape as the sun struggled to emerge.

Along the banks of Pipe Creek, Meade slowly rode back and forth. "My fault," he said, repeating it over and over, "it is my fault."

No one listened. Men staggered past, some sparing an occasional glance, most not hearing, or if they did hear, not caring.

2:50 PM, July 4, 1863

On the Taneytown-Littlestown Road

C.S.A.

And ten miles away, Gen. Robert E. Lee turned off the road. He needed no directions; it was easy enough to find what he was looking for. Troops, men of Johnson's command, were spread out in an open field. Some had ponchos out, strung together, and spread atop inverted muskets, men clustered beneath. Clear-enough sign that they had not moved for some time.

The rain was picking up again. Off to his left he could see a thin coil of smoke; something in Taneytown still burning, he realized.

He rode on, his anger building as he saw no activity.

Ahead he could hear a scattering of fire. Skirmishers, an occasional thump of a field piece, but no movement. The men sitting where they had most likely been sitting for hours. As he rode past, word spread ahead, racing down the line. Men were up, some with hats off, others saluting. A few bold ones shouted questions, asking of the fight "over on the right."

He rode on.

At last he saw them. The carriage that Ewell had taken to riding in due to his missing leg, staff, Hood and Pickett together to one side, both looking up expectantly as Lee rode up to the small farmhouse.

"Where is General Ewell?" Lee asked sharply.

"Inside," Hood offered, pointing to the open door.

Without another word, Lee walked up the steps and into the front parlor. The house was modest, made of fieldstone, the ceilings low. Ewell, leaning against a table, stood up and saluted.

"How is it on the right?" Ewell asked.

"Longstreet held," Lee replied sharply. "The question is, General, why have you not advanced as ordered."

"Sir, we heard the cannonade, two hours of it. Someone came in reporting that Longstreet was falling back."

"Who, sir?"

"A soldier with Early."

"A soldier with Early? No one from my command? No one sent by Colonel Taylor or General Longstreet or me?"

Ewell was silent. From the corner of his eye, he saw Hood and Pickett standing outside the doorway.

"Why are you not advancing, sir?" and his voice was loud enough to carry outside.

"Sir, given the confusion of the situation, the report from that soldier, the intensity of the cannon fire, I realized, sir, that what I had under me was the only remaining reserve of the army. Sir, I thought it prudent to wait for further clarification before advancing north."

Lee nodded.

"General Ewell," he said, in a cold deliberate voice, "I gave you clear written orders before action was joined this morning. You were to wait until it was evident that the Union forces were fully committed and attacking at Union Mills. You were then to push north, finishing what was left of their Fifth Corps, and then advance behind their lines toward Littlestown."

He paused for a moment. Ewell was silent, staring straight at him.

"You have not done that, sir."

"General Lee, with all due respect, sir. We still do not know where Sixth Corps is. For that matter where their First and Eleventh Corps are located. I might very well be facing four corps over there, and I only have three fought-out divisions."

"You did not do as ordered, sir," Lee stated flatly.

Ewell lowered his head. "Sir, I thought it prudent not to."

"Prudent? By all that is holy, sir, it is such prudence that will lose us this war and waste the lives of our men. I did not ask you for prudence; I ordered you to show leadership."

Ewell looked down at the map and vaguely started to trace out the lines.

Lee stared at him and for a moment almost felt pity. Ewell had once been a good division commander, the right hand of Jackson. That Ewell was gone, lost with the leg shattered at Second Manassas. He had become doubtful, hesitant.

Is that what I could have become? Lee wondered. What might have happened if I had shown hesitation these last four days, a moment of doubt, a moment of deference when I could so clearly see what had to be done but could not quite face up to it . . . that the nature of this war had changed, and we must change with it if we are to win, if we are to have any chance of winning.

He turned his head slightly, saw Hood at the door, Pickett and Johnson behind him, staff gathered out on the lawn, all of them silent.

"General Ewell," and his voice was pitched cool, even.

"Sir?"

Lee took a deep breath. "General Ewell, you are relieved of command."

"Sir?"

"I am relieving you of command, sir. Kindly report to Westminster and there take over the organization and distribution of supplies."

Ewell blinked, face gone red. He opened his mouth as if to say something, but no sound came.

Lee offered a salute and turned for the door.

"You cannot do this, sir," Ewell whispered.

Lee turned and for a moment, the old courtly sense of deference almost held sway — to offer a soft word, almost an apology. And then he thought of what he had witnessed along the heights above Union Mills, the sheer magnitude of carnage, the worst he had ever seen.

If that was to mean anything, if it was to change anything, then he had to change with it, to take full moral responsibility and bring meaning out of it. To do what was necessary to find some value, some gain out of the horrid sacrifice that was tearing the country to shreds, both North and South.

It is up to me, he thought yet again.

Lee slowly came back to the table that Ewell was leaning on and fixed him with a cold gaze. "Not another word, sir," Lee said coldly. "Not another word. Now report to Westminster."

Ewell gulped and nodded, tears in his eyes.

Lee turned and headed for the door, the three division commanders nervously backing away at his approach. He could see it in their eyes, the shocked disbelief. At no time in the thirteen months of Lee's command had anyone witnessed such a moment. Always in the past, when someone had to be relieved, it was done quietly, as gentlemen, with a face-saving transfer to some out-of-the-way posting, and never in the heat of battle.

He could see the touch of fear in their eyes. And he thought of the fear in the eyes of all those lying along the slope, in the eyes of the dead gazing up lifeless, the rain pooling on their still, gray faces.

He stood silent, looking at each in turn. "I am taking direct command of this wing," Lee announced. "Longstreet has held at Union Mills and inflicted grievous losses. Meade's army is ready to collapse. We will be the decisive blow to finish him."

He closed his eyes for a moment, haunting images floating before him. Think of that later, he told himself.

He looked back at Pickett. "You will lead the assault, sir, supported by Hood and then Johnson. I want you into their rear, at Littlestown, by dark. We have four hours of daylight left. I do not want another Chancellorsville or Second Manassas, with darkness allowing them to escape.

"You are to push on regardless of losses.

You will be facing the remnant of only one corps, and they will be shaken, for surely word must be reaching them now of their failed assault at Union Mills.

"I expect you to be across the Baltimore Road by dusk. And I will be with you to the end."

"General, sir," Pickett interrupted, "thank you for the honor and glory, sir. Virginia will bring victory this day, sir."

Lee's features reddened. At this moment, all the flourishes, all the high talk that had been so much a part of all of them, now seemed to have turned to ashes.

"War is hell, gentlemen," Lee said, his voice icy. "I pray that God will forgive us all for what we have done to each other this day. And General Pickett, we will talk of victory when it is finally won, and not before."

He said nothing more, stepping off the porch, walking toward Traveler, Walter holding the horse's reins. All gathered around the small farmhouse were silent. Many stunned, more than a few nodding, features grim.

The Army of Northern Virginia had changed forever.

4:30 PM, July 4, 1863

The Grand Battery — Union Mills

US Henry walked down the battery line, glancing at each piece in turn. Occasionally he would pause and point one out.

"This one," he announced, and as he moved on, gunners would drive a spike into the breech touchhole with a mallet, the rammer then slamming his tool down the bore, bending the spike inside the barrel, effectively destroying the gun. Others attacked the wheels with axes, cutting spokes until the piece collapsed.

It was almost like shooting a beloved pet, an old companion.

There were not enough teams available to take out all the guns. Even if there were, the road heading north was clogged; chances were most of the guns tangled into the mess might wind up being abandoned anyhow before the day was done.

All had been silent for nearly an hour after Sedgwick's men crossed back over Pipe Creek. A few had hoped that the Confederates would impetuously countercharge, as they so often had done in the past. Gunners muttered about what they would now do in turn, though all they had was roughly half a dozen rounds of canister per barrel.

Henry knew they wouldn't come. There was no need to. And the logic for their waiting finally was apparent when a growing thunder, to the west and north, started to increase in volume, and ever so slowly shifting more and more to the north . . . behind their lines.

Lee was flanking yet again, this time driving to cut off the one paved and useful road out of this nightmare, the road back to the north and east. The rebels in front had barred the road back to Washington, and now the line of retreat back to York and Harrisburg was being shut as well.

Word came by courier to get the guns out. The army was retreating.

From atop the ridge he could already see the exodus, columns of troops swinging onto the road, some marching in good order, others staggering from exhaustion, especially the men of the Sixth Corps, who had marched up this road on July 2nd to Gettysburg, turned around the following day to force march all that distance back, been thrown into a doomed assault, and now turned about yet again with orders to make for Gettysburg or Hanover once more. It was too much for many to bear, and in the pouring rain, before they had moved even half a mile, the straggling was massive, hundreds, and then thousands of

men breaking column to just collapse or wander off to the side of the road, dejected, ignoring the threats and pleas of their officers.

As the batteries slowly began to work their way out of the bastion, Henry kept a close watch on the Confederate lines on the south side of the creek. He could sense that they were ready, just waiting, but would not be so foolish as to try and push in.

No, that would come later, this evening, when the road back to Littlestown, the turnoff to Hanover and York was packed with tens of thousands of exhausted, demoralized, and frightened men . . . when hundreds of ambulances and thousands of walking wounded clogged the pike. Then Longstreet would hit, and then the panic would truly begin.

Dejected, alone, Henry mounted, pulling the brim of his hat down low against the rain, and rode up the slope and over the hill, leaving Union Mills behind.

Chapter Nineteen

On the night of July 4, 1863, the old Army of the Potomac died.

The cause of death could be traced back across an illness of a year or more, incompetence of commanders, the tragically bitter politics that had divided officers against each other, but most of all the disintegration of belief in those who led them by the weary foot soldiers who had seen defeat once too often.

Never in the history of the Republic had there been such an army. An army of idealisms, of volunteers willing to lay down their lives for such abstract ideals, the belief in the Republic that had called them to arms, a visceral sense that there was a destiny to that Republic, the "city on the hill," as their puritan forefathers had called it, "the last best hope of mankind," as their current president defined it. For some there were other causes as well, a belief in a dream as defined in the Declaration, that all men were, indeed, created equal.

And never had so good an army been so ill served. Man for man, they were the equal of any soldiers in history; that had been proven in the cornfields of Antietam, before the sunken road at Fredericksburg, on Seminary Ridge in the first day of the Gettysburg campaign, and in the final closing hours, on the blood-soaked banks of Pipe Creek.

Few in those battered regiments knew even a fragment of the details that had led them to such a tragic moment, but those few fragments of knowledge were enough. They had fought with a gallantry unparalleled in history . . . it was, yet again, their commanders who had failed them. Whether it was incompetence, self-serving interests, cowardice, or ignorance, the bitter sacrifice was one that created nothing except another defeat.

Something within broke at that moment, striking into the heart of each man, of every company and regiment, brigade and division. They could still fight as individuals or small units; if any dared to try and reach out, to touch their sacred blood-stained flags, they would indeed fight for that, for that they still believed in. For their survival if cornered, they would still fight; but for the generals, that was gone, perhaps forever.

On the other side, it was a moment long dreamed of, a fulfillment of a sense that half victories, which had cost a hundred thousand men in the last twelve months, had now finally reached a climax, that on this Fourth of July all things were, indeed, still possible.

The Fifth Corps of the Army of the Potomac made its final stand in a torrential summer downpour on the outskirts of Littlestown, after being driven back four miles by the relentless onslaught of Pickett, Hood, and the hard-bitten survivors of Johnson's division, the men of the old Stonewall Brigade.

In a way this final stand was indeed their finest hour, reminiscent of the Old Guard's stand at Waterloo. The backbone of the "old Fifth" was the division of regular troops, men who had been in the army since long before the war, when no self-respecting civilian would be caught dead in army blue, and now they were the ones dying in a final bid to hold the road open in the same way they had held the road after the debacle at First Manassas.

Sykes dismounted after losing three mounts in a row, stood with the division as it was battled back, yard by yard, in the pouring rain. If hit only in the center, they most certainly would have held; but whatever position they attempted to secure was soon outflanked, the rebel hosts threatening to completely encircle them. And yet, even then, they bought time, allowing several thousand to move up the road to safety.

Forced into Littlestown, Sykes finally made the fateful decision to turn the division north, back toward Gettysburg, to get what was left of his men out. To try and hold the town would have meant encirclement; to turn south would have meant encirclement as well.

He would be remembered for that moment, for when a panic-stricken officer galloped past, screaming that the army was destroyed, Sykes watched him go then turned to his men. "Yes, the army is gone," Sykes announced sadly, "but these regiments will always remain."

For the men of the Stonewall Brigade charging into Littlestown, it was like the memory of a springtime long ago, marching on relentlessly through the rain, sweeping forward to victory. Old Jack was gone, but now there was Lee, riding at the fore, urging them on, pointing the way, promising that but one more charge would crown them with victory undreamed of.

And so they stormed into Littlestown at the point of the bayonet, rifles all but useless as sheets of rain washed across the fields, churning the road to rivers of mud. The old Fifth broke apart, its bitter survivors turning back on the road toward Gettysburg, their morale broken by the certain knowledge that the rest of their army had just been defeated behind them at Union

Mills and there was no sense of hope or rescue. A grim hopelessness set in among the men.

The back door had been sealed. It was six in the afternoon of July Fourth.

Hood, deployed across the Baltimore Road, now had to simply wait, for there was no other way back from Union Mills, except for narrow country lanes that were turning into rivers of mud. The one pike north, its pavement a sticky glue of crushed limestone, was sealed.

Their first take was the flood of broken survivors of the old Second and Twelfth Corps, coming back from the disaster, and the sight of Hood blocking that road sent them recoiling back again, word racing like an electric shock: "The rebels are in Littlestown."

The men of the First Corps, so savagely mauled in the first day's battle, formed a final defense along the ridges north of Pipe Creek, still game and defiant, but the rest of the army now began to break apart.

Sickles kept his head, both figuratively and literally, though his action, even as he undertook it, would be the source of bitter debate and acrimony. With the largest intact command, he had waited for over two hours, listening as the sound of battle from the north, the flanking march by Lee pushing back Fifth Corps, gradually receded to the northeast. Several of his officers begged for him to march to the sound of the guns, to flank Lee in turn, but he refused, announcing that the battle was already lost, and his duty was to keep his units together to form the nucleus of a new Army of the Potomac.

He ignored, as well, the garbled order that came from Meade's headquarters to fall back onto the Gettysburg-Westminster Road, saying that would take his command straight into the trap.

When he judged the time to be right, he ordered the position along Pipe Creek to be abandoned, along with all guns and wagons and those wounded who could not walk, each man to load up a hundred rounds of ammunition, and then set the corps off on a grueling march to the northwest, cutting far behind Lee's flanking force, an action that, when first reported to Lee, caused an hour of tense anxiety until it was realized that Sickles was making for Harney and the road back to Gettysburg. Lee decided to simply let this command go; to try and bring it into the net would overextend an already exhausted and far overextended command.

The march would be the most harrowing the Third Corps had ever endured, a nightmare of slogging through the mud, exhausted men by the hundreds collapsing and Dan Sickles relentlessly setting the pace and already lecturing to his staff about why Meade had lost the battle. He had misstepped every inch of the way, and if only he had listened, just listened, how different it would all be, Sickles announced with self-righteous bitterness. He would be damned if ever he would take an order from such a man ever again. His mission now was to save his men and, around the nucleus of the Third Corps, rebuild an army, this time with the right general in command. After all the failures, Lincoln would have to buckle to that; Sickles's Democrat war allies in Congress would see that Sickles now had his chance. In fact, if Lincoln had picked him instead of Meade, Lee would be defeated and his army broken, or so Sickles reasoned to himself, increasing his own anger and determination.

Sedgwick felt as angry as Sickles and as bitter at Meade. Already word was spreading that Meade was now blaming him for the failure, that Sedgwick had failed to advance when he should have, then failed to stop when he should have, thus destroying the reserve that could have been used to punch a way out. The fact that Hancock had usurped command would be an issue that Sedgwick would make sure he answered for; and, if need be, he would take it all the way to the Congressional Joint Committee on the Conduct of the War and demand a court-martial as well as a congressional investigation.

Hancock knew nothing of this. His ambulance had passed through Littlestown only minutes before the road was blocked, his escort of loyal men pushing on toward Gettysburg. The word was already out that Stuart's men were closing in on the rear, having brushed aside the disjointed efforts of the Union cavalry to contain them. At Gettysburg, there might be safety with the men of Eleventh Corps, who still occupied the town.

The death blow hit just before six in the evening. Longstreet had waited, resting his men, bringing up rations, though the meal was a cold one of soggy hardtack and salted pork, but it was rations nevertheless. Units were reorganized; dry ammunition was distributed; a dozen batteries were organized and limbered up.

He knew the plan, watching the weather, trying to calculate. No word came from Lee, but Longstreet sensed that the flanking attack had indeed gone in, the distant sound of gunfire fading northward, by then washed out by the intensity of the storm.

Finally, just after five-thirty, he ordered a

general advance all along the line. It was evident that there were still troops deployed along the opposing heights, but all could see, as well, that since the previous two hours that line was melting away, guns moving out, skirmishers bringing in prisoners who reported that the Army of the Potomac was abandoning the field.

Three divisions went in: Rhodes on the right, Pettigrew in the middle, Early on the left. Pender, McLaws, and Anderson, those who had suffered the most in the defense, were formed into marching columns and held in reserve, with Anderson's division detailed off to the task of preparing to receive the anticipated flood of prisoners. And for once there was a surplus of supplies and an order to prepare to feed these thousands of men as well.

The orders were to avoid a frontal assault at all cost, to probe, to go around the flanks, for Pete sensed that if anyone was still up there, they would fold once their flanks were turned, but would indeed fight if hit head-on.

It was as he assumed. The First Corps held for less than half an hour, with Rhodes only skirmishing at long range, until Early's men swept over the heights abandoned by Sickles. With that the First Corps of the Army of the Potomac, the "old First" — the men who boasted that they were the backbone — broke and started for the rear.

With Pender's column pushing up the road, the pursuit was on in earnest, but the advance was determined and careful. The goal was to herd the Union army north and gather up stragglers as prisoners, not to engage in a frontal fight that would force the Union army to draw itself together and cause unnecessary casualties to the already weakened Confederate forces.

A thunderstorm of frightful intensity now lashed the skies, as if reflecting the far more violent confrontation unfolding below. In the darkening gloom, the hot electric blue flashes revealed a road swarming with tens of thousands of men, all semblance of order breaking down among the Union forces, troops splitting away from the line of retreat, streaming off into nearby woods, there to simply collapse. Individual regimental commanders, those with some initiative, ordered their men to turn aside, to march cross-country, hoping to break out of the net. For word raced up and down that desperate column that Lee was now in their front on the Baltimore Pike at Littlestown, and Longstreet was closing up from the rear.

It was the worst night of the war for both sides.

For the men of the old Irish Brigade,

Second Corps, haunted by the loss of their commander, there was a vicious lashing out when a regiment of Pender's division stormed into the road expecting a quick surrender.

To a man, the Irishmen turned with clubbed rifles and bayonets. It was a brutal vicious melee, no longer a military battle; now it was a settling of scores, and men on both sides were beaten to death without mercy in the gloom, until the survivors broke from the road and spilled into the darkness, heading due east and out of the fight but leaving more than a hundred dead Confederates behind.

All organization at corps and division and even brigade level was gone.

With the road severed at Littlestown, the vast, surging column had come to a complete halt, unable to move. Some regiments just stood in line, waiting and waiting in the driving rain — a colonel or in many cases now a major or even a captain in command — for someone to tell them what to do, until the enveloping wave of gray and butternut swarmed in about them.

Here and there fires briefly flickered to light as a lantern was smashed, the coal oil poured over the regimental colors, and then burned; or like their comrades of the Twentieth Maine, the flag was cut to ribbons and pressed into hands, men weeping in rage, frustration, bitterness, and exhaustion.

Every farmhouse, every barn and outbuilding, became a refuge, filled to overflowing with the wounded and with those too exhausted or too frightened to continue.

Strange moments, only possible in this war unfolded, and acts typical of any war. A soldier with one of Pender's North Carolina divisions, coming upon an exhausted Union straggler, discovered him to be his own son who had moved to Ohio before the war, the two embracing and weeping by the side of the road, while less than a hundred yards away another North Carolinian unknowingly shot his own brother in the back when the latter tried to flee.

In nearly every case, prisoners were taken in and treated with at least some compassion, a quick bandaging of wounds, a shared drink from a canteen, though a Georgian, moved to insanity by the death of his brother earlier in the day, methodically stabbed a wounded boy from New York to death as the boy begged for mercy; and then, within seconds, the murderer was summarily executed by his own colonel, who had witnessed the crime.

An unimaginable array of equipment littered the road and fields, discarded muskets, cartridge boxes, blanket rolls, uniforms, caps, boxes of rations and ammunition, an entire collection of musical instruments dropped by a regimental band, a case of French champagne found by some boys from Mississippi, who promptly got drunk and were finally placed under arrest, books and newspapers, a paymaster's box with ten thousand in greenbacks, all mingled in with upended wagons, braying mules, burning caissons that exploded with thunderclap roars, and everywhere bodies, some dead, most just collapsed in exhaustion by the side of the road.

Some commanders broke down in the confusion, told the men to save themselves and scatter. But more than one elected to fight, pulling their regiments off the road. Some would fight clean through to the next day, others perhaps only a few minutes before being overwhelmed, but the old army did not die easily.

Vicious, frightful battles unfolded all along the road. The survivors of the First Minnesota turned about when Rhodes pressed too closely, their volley killing the hard-fighting Confederate general, dropping him into the mud. The First was swarmed under then and disappeared.

One colonel, who had survived a year in Libby Prison before being exchanged, when facing the prospect yet again, shot himself in the temple right in front of his men. Some officers wept, some raged, a few abandoned their own men, but most tried to lead as best they could; and more than one NCO and private emerged that terrible night as a leader as well.

Henry became an infantryman. He had come across two batteries of guns, stalled in the road, the way ahead blocked by a tangle of wagons, ambulances, an overturned caisson and gun, its team still tied to their harnesses, kicking and thrashing.

Behind, in the semidarkness, he could hear the dull crackle of rifle fire, flashes of light reflecting off the low-hanging clouds, a stampede of men racing by on either side of the road, crying that the Rebs were coming.

A battery commander stood before him, waiting for orders.

For a moment he was tempted to order the guns unlimbered, but in all that mad confusion, what would he shoot at? Thousands of Union soldiers were swarming across the surrounding fields, a flash of lightning revealing a compact column of Confederates already passing him in an open field to the left.

"Spike the guns!" Henry shouted.

Exhausted gunners climbed down from

limber wagons, battery blacksmiths moving along the line with mallets and the deadly spikes, iron ringing against iron. Loaders tore into almost empty limber boxes, pulling out their few remaining rounds, tearing the powder bags open, throwing them onto the road.

"Sir, should we shoot the horses?" someone cried.

Henry shook his head. Merciful God, there had been enough slaughter this day. Sacrificing the poor beasts for no reason other than the failure of their masters was beyond him.

"No," he said gently. "Those that can stand the march, cut them from the traces and ride; the rest, just leave here. They'll get picked up by some farmer or become the property of the Confederacy. They have served us well, and we can't simply slaughter them because of our failure this day."

The horses were unharnessed, some of the men swinging up on them to ride bareback, a sergeant riding one of them, bearing a battery guidon, which now served as a rallying point.

A flash of lightning revealed a wheat field to the right, a farmhouse on a low ridge beyond, a road climbing up past the house. It was as good a direction as any to go. "Follow me," he said, and pushing through a break in the fence, he led his ragged command out across the field and into the night.

10:00 PM, July 4, 1863

The White House

"General Haupt, I am grateful that you are well," Lincoln said, standing up and extending his hand as Haupt came into the office.

Hermann could see that behind the kind words the president was numb with exhaustion, eyes red rimmed, as if he had been in tears only minutes before.

"I received word, sir, that you wanted to see me before I left Washington."

"Yes, General."

"What can I do for you, sir?"

Lincoln tried to force a smile, then turned away. "I guess you know the reports are not good."

Haupt said nothing. Rumors had been sweeping the city all day of a battle being fought to the north, near Westminster. A captain, claiming to be on Sedgwick's staff, had ridden into Baltimore, stating he had broken through the Confederate cordon and that the Army of the Potomac had been soundly defeated and was reeling back in full retreat.

Lincoln finally turned to look back at Haupt, eyes shiny. "I wonder how many men we lost this day," Lincoln whispered, "this Fourth of July."

"I have no idea, sir," Haupt replied, not sure what to say.

"For several hours today you could actually feel the bombardment," and Lincoln motioned toward the window, "if you put your hand on the windowpane you could feel it. And then silence, nothing but silence."

"We should know tomorrow, sir."

"Yes, tomorrow."

Lincoln nodded and then drew a deep breath. "You know that Halleck was against your wish to go to Harrisburg to establish a new base there. He claims that the army will break through and the supplies and equipment will be needed here."

Hermann was aware of the argument; in fact, he had threatened to resign if not allowed to go. All his instincts told him that if Meade was rash enough to attack at Union Mills or Taneytown, he would be repulsed. He knew the land. He had lived in Gettysburg for several years, often ridden down to Westminster there to visit friends, and if Lee had indeed taken position along Pipe Creek the result was all but a foregone conclusion. Therefore, Harrisburg would be the new base, for Meade would have to retreat. And even if he did not engage, with which all indicators now seemed to agree, Harrisburg would still be the base; but a bridge had to be thrown across that river now, tomorrow, if there was any hope of saving the Army of the Potomac.

Apparently Lincoln had learned of the fight with Halleck and had intervened directly, overriding the General of the Armies.

"I did not wish to cause trouble, sir," Hermann finally offered.

Lincoln nodded. "Sir, I think it is all right for me to say that controversy with Halleck shall soon be a thing of the past."

"Sir?"

"Oh, nothing, sir, but that comment stays here please, at least for now."

Hermann was startled to realize what the chief executive had just shared with him. Halleck was to be relieved as nominal commander of all forces in the field.

"But that is not the purpose of this meeting. General Haupt, I just want to ask you, if the Army of the Potomac has been defeated, perhaps destroyed . . ." and his voice trailed off for a moment. When he started to speak again, his voice was tight, as if near to breaking. "Can we rebuild?"

Hermann looked into the man's eyes,

shocked by this momentary display of heartfelt anguish. His heart went out to this man who carried the burden, who in fact tomorrow could simply announce that all was over, that the killing would stop . . . but in so doing the Republic would forever be cut asunder.

"Sir, by the day after tomorrow I will have a bridge across the river at Harrisburg, supplies sufficient for fifty thousand men stockpiled, at least a battalion of fresh artillery brought up to defend the crossing. The rail network from Harrisburg is a good one. I can call in trains from New York, Pittsburgh, Reading, and Philadelphia. That, sir, is our strength, the mere fact that I can do that. As long as there is the will to fight, sir, I will provide the tools to do it."

"As long as I have the will," Lincoln said, turning away to gaze out the window.

All outside was silent. The celebration of the Fourth, the firing of the hundred-gun salute in Lafayette Square across from the White House, had been canceled, the troops on alert, those guns now deployed around government buildings, two batteries' worth on the grounds of the White House.

Lincoln finally turned and looked back at Haupt. "Good luck in Harrisburg, sir, and thank you."

"Thank you, Mr. President," and Hermann took the president's hand, Lincoln's grip warm and powerful.

"General Haupt, you provide the material, and I will provide the will."

11:00 PM, July 4, 1863

Littlestown

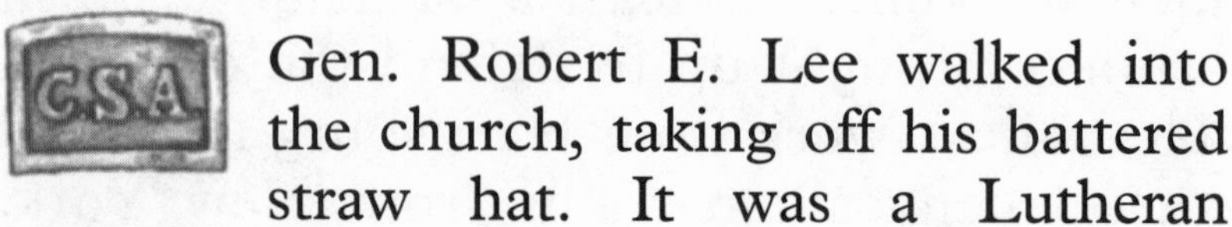

Gen. Robert E. Lee walked into the church, taking off his battered straw hat. It was a Lutheran Church, simple in its design and appointments. Flashes of light outside briefly illuminated the stained-glass windows. The distant roll of thunder and of gunfire was continuous. He tried to block the noise out of his mind.

Lee turned and looked at Walter, who had walked up to the altar and, after struggling with several damp matches, finally managed to strike a light, touching the flame to the two candles.

Lee nodded his thanks. "I'll be along in a few minutes, Walter."

"Yes, sir."

The door to the church opened, several staff coming in. Lee said nothing as they approached.

"Sir," one of them cried, "Generals

Johnson and Hood beg to report that they can no longer keep track of the number of prisoners. Pickett just sent back a report that he will push on toward Gettysburg as long as one of his men can march with him. He's taken twelve colors and more than a thousand prisoners from the Fifth Corps. General Stuart sends his compliments as well, sir, and will block every road as ordered."

"Any word from General Longstreet yet?" Lee asked.

"No, sir. But we can see the flashes of gunfire from his columns. They are pushing the Yankees straight into us."

Lee said nothing.

"Sir, are there any orders?"

Again a moment of silence.

"Sir?"

Lee looked at the three with a sense of infinite weariness. They were really nothing more than boys, filled with that strange exuberance that sometimes comes after a battle, exhaustion not yet laying them low.

"Repeat the orders I've already given," Lee said softly. "Show mercy now. The time for killing is over. Show mercy."

"Yes, sir."

Walter stepped between the messengers and Lee, gently turning them about. One of the men stopped and came up to Lee, extending his hand. "Please forgive me, sir," the lieutenant gasped, "I just want to be able to one day tell my grandchildren that I shook your hand this day, this most glorious Fourth of July."

Lee nodded and briefly extended his hand, forgiving the boy his bad manners.

Tears came to the boy's eyes. "God bless you, sir," he stammered and then, embarrassed at his impetuous act, he fled.

Walter looked back and Lee just motioned for him to leave and close the door.

Alone, Lee sat down in a pew, and leaning forward he clasped his hands, resting his forehead upon them.

Walter Taylor stood outside the church, arms folded, guarding the door. A small crowd had gathered, curious civilians, wounded soldiers, staff, even a few Union prisoners, disarmed, standing in the rain.

He waited and as the minutes passed, he finally became concerned. Throughout that long day he had watched his general almost like a child, now an adult, keeping a watchful gaze over an aging parent. Three times during that final drive into Littlestown, he had been compelled to hold the general back, for the fire was in him as he drove Pickett forward, directing the battle, reeling from exhaustion as they finally broke into the town and gained the road that cut off the Union line of retreat.

Finally, after a half hour of waiting, he felt a flicker of fear. Motioning for the cavalry escort to block the door, he slowly opened it and stepped back into the church.

There was a terrible flash of terror. Lee was slumped over, head resting against the next pew. Taylor carefully walked up, about to cry out. In the candlelight Lee looked so deathly pale.

He stood by the general's side, not sure for a moment what to do. "Sir?" he whispered.

There was no response.

Ever so gently he reached out, touching Lee on the shoulder, terrified that when he did so Lee would just simply collapse.

Leaning over, he finally heard a gentle respiration.

Walter stood there for a moment and then began to weep. Taking off his rain-soaked jacket, he balled it up, placing it on the pew by Lee's side. Ever so gently he put his arms around his general and eased him over on his side, the jacket now a pillow. Stepping next to the pew, he lifted the old man's legs and carefully stretched them out.

Lee stirred for a moment. "Roonie," he whispered.

"He'll be all right, sir," Walter whispered back. "Your boy will be all right."

Lee did not stir, lost in exhausted sleep.

Going up to the altar, Walter blew out the two candles. Sitting down in the pew across from his general, Walter Taylor kept vigil throughout the long night.

And thus the Fourth of July, 1863, came to an end.

8:00 AM, July 5, 1863

Littlestown

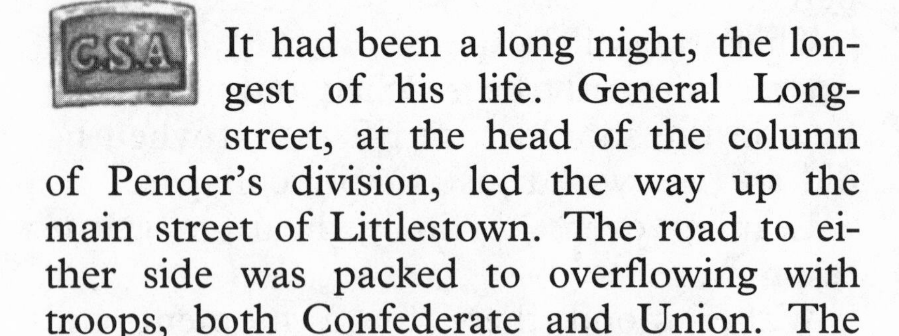

It had been a long night, the longest of his life. General Longstreet, at the head of the column of Pender's division, led the way up the main street of Littlestown. The road to either side was packed to overflowing with troops, both Confederate and Union. The men of Johnson's division cheered his approach, and at that moment, it touched him profoundly.

These were the veterans of Stonewall, and across the last year — since the Army of the Valley had fallen in with the ranks of what would become the Army of Northern Virginia — he had always sensed a certain haughtiness on their part, that they saw their leader, "Old Jack," as the superior of Lee's two lieutenants.

That was gone this morning. Men saluted at his approach, then took off their hats, shouting and waving. Behind him the mud-spattered boys of Pender marched with a jaunty swagger, returning the cheers. A group of Hood's men, drawn up in a small column, each of the men carrying a captured battle flag, fell into the line of march to resounding cheers.

The disarmed Union prisoners, part of a long column of troops now being marched back toward Westminster, had been pushed to the side of the road. They looked up at him, some with open hatred, most with that vague, shocked, distant look of troops who had seen and endured far too much. An officer in their midst stepped forward a pace and saluted.

Pete hesitated, looking down. It was Maj. Gen. Abner Doubleday, left arm in a sling, a comrade from an eternity ago, a fellow graduate of the class of 1842.

"Abner, sorry to see you're hurt," Pete said. "How are you?"

"That was you I faced yesterday at Union Mills, wasn't it, Pete?"

"Yes, Abner."

"A long way from West Point now, aren't we?"

"Yes, Abner."

"And the pledge you made there to our flag."

Pete could not reply.

"Abner, if you need anything, let me know, send for me."

Abner shook his head. "No, Pete, I won't."

"I'm sorry, Abner."

"So am I, Pete. So am I."

Pete drew up, saluted, and rode on.

Hospital flags, hanging sodden and limp in the morning rain, were draped in the doorways of churches and schoolhouses. Every house in town was a hospital as well. Union and Confederate surgeons and orderlies, working side by side, tended to the wounded. Women of the town scurried back and forth, carrying buckets of water, torn-up bedsheets, and blankets.

A grim sight hung in the center of town, a dead Confederate soldier at the end of a rope slung over a tree limb . . . ATTEMPTED ASSAULT OF A WOMAN was written on the sign draped around his broken neck, two provost guards standing beneath the corpse.

The men marching behind Pete fell silent at the sight of him, more than one spitting on the ground at the feet of the dead man as they passed.

Passing through the town, the column worked its way up a low hill, an orderly waiting for them atop the crest, motioning for Pete to follow his lead.

As they crested the ridge, the sight spread out before him was breathtaking.

The fields north of town had become a vast holding area for thousands of prisoners, a long, serpentine column of them now marching along the side of the road in the opposite direction, heading south.

And there was Lee.

Pete spurred his mount, covering the last few yards, grinning in spite of his exhaustion, snapping off a salute as he approached.

Gathered round Lee were Taylor, Hood, and dozens of others. The rain picked up, the sky dark and sullen; but around Lee, at this moment, there almost seemed to be a strange golden light.

"General Longstreet, it does my heart good to see that you are safe," Lee said, riding up the last few feet to him, warmly extending his hand, which Longstreet took.

Pete did not know what to say.

"You were magnificent, General. This victory is to your credit, sir."

"No, sir," and Longstreet started to fumble, embarrassed, "it is yours, sir. Let me congratulate you for this, your greatest victory."

"You were the one who first proposed it."

"It was merely a suggestion, sir. It was your leadership that inspired it."

Lee smiled. "We'll argue about that later."

Longstreet lowered his head, not sure what to say.

"I just received a report from General Pickett," Lee said. "He is stalled just outside of Gettysburg due to the rain, but reports that their Eleventh Corps, and what is left of the Third, have abandoned the town and are moving toward Carlisle."

"They're trying for the river, for Harrisburg most likely," Longstreet replied.

"My thoughts exactly, General. We will pursue them of course. I understand the bridges there are all down, burned by them last week. If this rain continues, Stuart might pin what is left of the Union forces against the Susquehanna and finish that as well."

Pete nodded.

"And Washington?"

"In due course, General. We've cast our net wide," and as he spoke he nodded to the prisoners marching past, "but it is safe to say that maybe thirty thousand of their forces, perhaps more, have broken out. We know their Third Corps, as well as what is left of the Fifth and Eleventh, are back in Gettysburg. I hope we can still pin those. Elements of their cavalry are largely intact, though scattered, and will serve as rallying points for those who are fleeing. That is our first goal, to finish their army.

"Then we need to see to our prisoners,

to move them safely out of the way, and to tend to the wounded of both sides. The losses have been grievous. Our men need rest. We have to push them toward Harrisburg for now, if we can indeed destroy what is left of the Army of the Potomac. Some of the units are so battered, however, that they may need to be reorganized before they can fight again."

"I still wonder about Washington, though, General," Longstreet replied.

Lee fell silent, looking at the column of Union troops passing by along the side of the road, Pender's men moving in the opposite direction. Longstreet pointed to the head of the column. Leading the way were the captured standards of thirty regiments or more. The men carrying them falling out of the line of march, coming up to Lee's side. One of them was Sergeant Hazner, another Sergeant Robinson, who had stopped Lee in front of Taneytown.

For Longstreet the moment was etched like a frozen tableau, the rain-darkened clouds, the mud-splattered, weary prisoners marching past, but in the eyes of more than one a look of steadfastness, that even in defeat there was still pride as they looked at their colors now being presented to Lee.

It seemed that Lee sensed it as well. He stiffened in the saddle, back ramrod straight, and drawing up his right hand, he saluted the captured flags. The Union troops marching past slowed, some stopping, looking on with surprise. A Union colonel, blood-soaked bandage wrapped around his head, came to attention and saluted the colors and Lee as well.

Lee, seeing the gesture, turned and nodded. "Colonel, sir," Lee said, "I shall pray that soon this will all be over and that you and your gallant men swiftly return home to your families."

The colonel bowed slightly. "Thank you, sir, and I shall pray the same for you," he replied, "but, sir, it will not be over until the Union has been saved."

Lee nodded and then looked away.

The colonel fell back into the ranks and disappeared with his men into the rain.

There was a long moment of silence, a soft peal of thunder rumbling in the distance.

"I suppose you heard about General Meade," Lee said, his voice distant.

"Sir?"

"He's dead. They're bringing his body in now."

Longstreet sighed.

"East of here," Lee continued, "about five miles. A regiment of Stuart's cavalry, led by Wade Hampton, came upon him just after dawn. He had a couple of dozen staff and troopers with him. Meade charged. In the melee, Hampton recognized Meade, begged him to surrender, but Meade just tried to cut straight through. He was shot before Hampton could stop him." Lee lowered his head.

"I think I'd of done the same," Pete replied.

" 'My fault, all my fault,' those were the last words Meade said."

"Another old comrade gone," Longstreet whispered.

Lee looked away and said nothing for a moment.

"We press toward Gettysburg today and try to finish what is left of their army, General Longstreet. We must make this victory decisive and so overwhelming that the North will sue for peace. If not, then it will be a march on Washington."

Sunset, July 6, 1863

Marysville, Pennsylvania

US "I think those are our men up there," someone gasped.

Henry, nodding with exhaustion, raised his head. In the gathering twilight, he saw a heavy skirmish line deployed along a low crest, half a dozen guns dug in at the top of the hill.

"Don't move." The voice came out of the shadows from a wooded grove flanking the road.

Henry turned and saw several dozen rifle barrels poised, aiming toward him and his ragged band of men. "Identify yourselves."

"Who the hell are *you?*" one of Henry's men shouted back.

"Damn you, identify yourselves or we'll shoot."

Several of Henry's men started to raise pistols, and he shouted for them to stand and not move. After two days of running, of dodging Confederate cavalry, brushing around the flank of a regiment of Confederate infantry, he was beyond caring. Besides, the fight was out of his men. They had staggered for over forty miles, cutting across fields, hiding in woods to catch a few hours' sleep, abandoning those who could no longer keep up. If this now meant prison, then so be it.

"I'm Henry Hunt, Commander, Artillery Reserve," he paused for a second, his throat feeling thick, eyes filling up, "the Army of the Potomac."

His inquisitor stepped out of the woods, pistol still drawn but now lowered slightly. It was a Union captain.

The man drew closer, looking first at Henry, then at the hundred or so men trailing along with him. The captain sadly shook his head, and then saluted.

"Captain Jamison. I'm on the staff of General Couch, commander of the emergency garrison in Harrisburg."

"Harrisburg?" Henry asked. "We made it?"

"Just beyond that ridge, sir. We finished a pontoon bridge across this afternoon, threw out an advanced guard. I guess you can say I am the advance guard. We've had stragglers, thousands of them, coming in all day, but a lot of Rebs, too, trying to round up men like yourselves. Sorry, sir, but with everyone covered in mud, it's hard to tell who is which at the moment."

Jamison fell in by Henry's side, offering to guide him to the bridge.

"You hear about Sickles and Howard?" Jamison asked.

Henry shook his head. All he knew of the army now was what he had seen with his own eyes these last two days.

"Their corps are over by Carlisle. Been some sharp fighting is the report, but word is they will be here come tomorrow, at least what's left of them, along with what's left of Fifth Corps. Maybe twenty thousand men or so."

"And the rest?"

"You, men like you, sir," Jamison said

quietly, "coming in a couple at a time, part of a brigade from Fifth Corps, a scattering of regiments. A rout, sir. A total rout. The Army of the Potomac has fallen into pieces."

Henry said nothing, too shocked, too weary to speak.

"Seen any of our cavalry?" Jamison asked.

"Not a one," Henry said dejectedly.

"Word is they're reforming over by York. Been some heavy fighting; apparently they blocked Lee from pushing all the way up here. Everyone is so damn fought out and exhausted at this point."

They crested the low rise. Though darkness had settled he could now see the Susquehanna River below, a flickering line of torches and lanterns drawn like a line across the broad river.

"Some general came up yesterday morning with three trainloads of pontoon gear and built that in a little more than a day. They were like ants; never seen anything like it. They're saying, though, it won't hold for long; the river is rising fast."

Henry made his way down the embankment, falling in with hundreds of others shuffling through the mud. In the dim light he could make out, on their caps, the Maltese Cross of the Fifth Corps, the circle of the First, men of the Second and the Twelfth, all moving along silently, the able helping wounded comrades.

As he stepped on the bridge and bid farewell to Jamison, Henry felt as if he were crossing the river out of a dark land of nightmares, the bridge swaying beneath his feet, sentries posted at regular intervals cautioning the men to not march in step, to stay away from the edge, and to keep moving, keep moving.

The lights of the city of Harrisburg shone softly beyond the mists rising up from the cold, churning river; the road along the riverbank was packed with wagons, ambulances, and disorganized troops wandering about. As he reached the end of the bridge, Henry heard sergeants shouting orders, calling off the numbers of corps, then giving directions where to go. Henry was reassured to see a full battalion of guns arrayed along the riverbank, barrels aimed to shell the other side of the river, three-inch rifles, one battery of twenty-pound rifles, the guns obviously straight from the foundry.

Orderlies were waiting, grabbing hold of the injured, taking them to ambulances that lined the street. As each ambulance was loaded up, the driver lashed his mules forward.

No one was giving any orders as to

where the men of the Artillery Reserve should go, and Henry stopped in the middle of the street after stepping off the bridge, looking around, confused, not sure what to do next.

"Hunt?"

He turned and saw by the light of a torch a star on each shoulder of the man calling to him.

The two saluted each other.

"I don't think you know me," the general offered, and then extended his hand, "Hermann Haupt."

"Railroad?"

"Yes, we met just after Second Bull Run."

Henry said nothing. Right now he couldn't remember.

"You were in the thick of it?" Haupt asked.

"Yes, the thick of it," Henry said woodenly. "Union Mills. The charge."

Haupt reached into his breast pocket and pulled out a flask, uncorking it.

"I'd better not," Henry whispered. "If I have a drink now, I think I'll pass out."

"Go ahead, you can pass out on my train."

"Your train?"

"I came up here to build this bridge and get supplies up in case the army got out."

"It didn't."

"I know. But we have twenty thousand men here with Couch."

"Militia?" Henry asked.

"Yes, but it's something. Word is parts of three corps will be in here tomorrow."

Henry was silent.

"So you saw it."

"Yes, I saw it. I was at Westminster as it fell. I saw it all right."

Haupt put his arm around Henry's shoulder.

"General, look at me," Haupt said softly.

Henry raised his gaze and saw the coldness in Haupt's eyes.

"Lee won the battle, but he has yet to win this war. Those are your guns over there," and Haupt pointed to the batteries arrayed along the riverfront. "Some of those tubes were cast less than a week ago. The army will be rebuilt; I promise you that."

"My men, all those men," Hunt whispered.

"I know, God save them, but the Republic will endure. There will be more men and the Republic will go on; that is our strength."

Henry nodded, drawing energy from this man's determination and belief.

"You're coming back with me, Hunt."

Confused, Henry looked at the men

who had followed him out of hell.

"My men."

"They'll be well taken care of. I've put the town under martial law. Every house is open to the troops for billeting. I've got three hundred head of cattle for food and enough rations to stuff every man full.

"But you, sir, I think some people in Washington will want to hear your account, Hunt. So far you are the only general, other than Hancock, who's gotten out from Union Mills."

"How is Hancock?"

"He's in that hotel right over there,"

Haupt said. "Word is he isn't going to live. So you're going back with me."

Henry looked at his men. "In a minute, General."

Henry walked over to the men who had suffered so much with him. They came to attention and saluted. All he could do was nod in reply; words failed him. He took the hands of several, shaking them, and then turned away.

Ten minutes later he was aboard Haupt's train, sprawled out on a straight-back wooden seat, the alcohol unwinding him, and fast asleep.

Chapter Twenty

July 9, 1863

Westminster

"Then it is settled, gentlemen," Lee said, leaning back from the table.

Those around him, Longstreet, Hood, Stuart, the cartographer Hotchkiss, and Walter Taylor, all nodded in agreement.

"I just wish I could have pushed up to that bridge in front of Harrisburg and taken it," Stuart sighed.

"The bridge is gone anyhow," Lee replied, nodding to the captured newspapers, printed in Philadelphia just yesterday, announcing that the bridge had been swept away by the rising flood waters.

Typical of most newspapers, the news was distorted or simply untrue. The lead story declared that the Army of the Potomac was totally destroyed. That was not true. Three corps, the Third, Fifth, and Eleventh, had gotten out with some semblance of command and structure intact. Yes, the victory was complete, but still, their total annihilation, another Cannae or Waterloo, had eluded him. Not to detract from all that had been achieved, and he looked at the count.

Nearly thirty thousand of the Army of the Potomac were now prisoners, half of them wounded. It was reported that at least another seven to eight thousand were dead. Add to that the wounded who had escaped and it was safe to estimate that close to two-thirds of the Army of the Potomac had ceased to exist, but there was still a nucleus, a surviving element on the far side of the Susquehanna, enough to prevent any crossing of that river and a drive eastward toward Philadelphia.

What had been captured was beyond belief. More than two thousand wagons, enough supplies to sustain his army for a month in the field, over two hundred field pieces, though most would have to be shipped back to Richmond for repairs, over a hundred regimental colors.

He scanned the paper again. Draft riots in New York, Philadelphia under martial law, and yet also the proclamation that Vicksburg had fallen, an editor for the paper proclaiming that this Union victory in the West more than offset the losses in what was being called the Gettysburg-Westminster Campaign.

He had hoped that events of the last week would have ended it. It had not, though this campaign was a triumph beyond any ever achieved by Confederate arms. And so still it seemed that it must continue.

It had been costly. Nearly twenty thousand of his own dead, wounded, and captured, though of those captured, nearly all would be back in the ranks within days, taken back when the Union forces abandoned Gettysburg and force marched to Harrisburg.

Harrisburg . . . if only Stuart had been able to seize that bridge, but he knew that dream to be impossible. Stuart had done a masterful job, first demonstrating in front of Gettysburg, holding Meade's attention just long enough to allow the flanking march to continue, pushing the Union cavalry back to the east, and then turning to act as the net to sweep up prisoners. To hope that Stuart's exhausted mounts could be pushed for one final drive was beyond expectations. Exhaustion and the weather had finished the campaign for now. Stuart would maintain a division on the west side of the river to observe Harrisburg, but nothing beyond that could be hoped for now.

He looked at those gathered round him. He had officially reorganized the army this morning. General Longstreet would command the old First Corps, with Pender's and Pettigrew's divisions added to his command. Hood would leave his old division behind with Longstreet and move up to command the reorganized Second Corps. Ewell was gone, returning even now to Richmond, in command of the men from Anderson's division, who were escorting the prisoners on their long march back over the mountains to Greencastle and then Winchester. Hill was gone as well, the strong suggestion that he retire due to health finally accepted.

He looked back at the paper one more time and opened it up. The casualty list for the Philadelphia area filled two full pages, and he shook his head. More than one of his old cadets from the Point, a comrade from Mexico, and others from the days on the frontier were listed there. He closed his eyes for a moment and rubbed them.

"Sir, is there anything else?" Longstreet asked quietly.

Lee shook his head, opened his eyes, and forced a smile. "No, sir. I think it is time we started. Gentlemen, you know the order of march. Let us now see to our duty."

The group stood up, following Lee out

into the street. The scene before them was heart stirring. The battered veterans of McLaws's division lined the street, in marching order, blanket rolls over shoulders, full haversacks and cartridge boxes, all of them with new shoes. As Lee emerged, the cry went down the line, the men snapping to attention, presenting arms, and then spontaneously the cheer erupted . . . "Lee . . . Lee . . . Lee!"

For a moment he was overwhelmed, tears filling his eyes. How they trusted and loved him. He had tried to give them everything, and they had given everything in return. The war was not over as dreamed of, and he sensed that such a dream might very well be impossible in this new age of war, to win it all on just a single battle, though for the moment at least the victory had perhaps tipped the scales back into their favor. What was needed now was yet more audacity and will, and that he knew he had learned again in these last two weeks.

So now they would march on Washington. A forlorn hope perhaps, for the army lacked siege equipment and would go up against an array of fortifications that ringed the entire city. After the casualties of the last fortnight, the need to tend to the wounded of both sides, the escorting of prisoners, he could barely muster forty thousand; but their spirits were high, and with such an army the next step might very well be possible. As he had learned on that night three days before Gettysburg, he knew he had to realize it yet again; that it was his determined will, transfused into the indomitable men before him, that had accomplished so much.

He looked to Longstreet, who nodded, smiled, and then formally saluted while the cheers continued to echo.

Mounting on his beloved Traveler, Robert E. Lee turned south, toward Washington, and a dream of final victory . . . for all things were still possible.

A block away, in the nave of a small Catholic Church, Gen. Lo Armistead at last found who he was looking for. Joshua Lawrence Chamberlain stirred and gave a weak nod of recognition as Armistead knelt by his bedside.

"How are you this morning, Colonel?" Lo asked.

"They say I'll live."

"Yes, I heard. You are a very strong man, Colonel Chamberlain, and so is your brother."

Joshua smiled and laughed softly. It had already become quite a story that everyone was talking about. One of the best surgeons with Pickett's division had worked on Joshua for over an hour, fishing out the bullet embedded in one hip, drawing out splinters of bone from the other hip, which had been pierced by the ball. He'd tried to fashion a small plate from a hammered-out silver coin to close up the hole in Joshua's bladder but then finally stepped back, saying the case was hopeless.

Tom, who had been standing nearby, watching, stepped over to where a Confederate officer lay, waiting his turn for surgery. Tom drew the man's revolver from his holster, cocked it, and pointed it at the surgeon's head, telling him to continue or have his brains blown out. Half a dozen Confederates with weapons drawn on Tom threatened to blow his brains out in turn. The surgeon finally gave a solemn oath to continue, and Tom relented and was dragged away. The surgeon was good to his word and after it was over had Tom released and shared a drink with him.

"My division will be moving out, Colonel," Lo said. "Is there anything I can do for you?"

"My men, you promised about my men. Not being prisoners."

Embarrassed, Lo nodded. "In the confusion afterward, sir, I hope you understand, those not wounded were separated and became mixed in with thousands of others. I personally went before General Lee last night, sir, on your behalf, and he agreed that the promise must be honored. Word is moving along the column, and your men shall be paroled on the spot and escorted back to your lines."

Joshua, eyes bright, nodded, and extended his hand, which Lo took.

"Once you are well enough to travel, Colonel Chamberlain, you and your brother will be paroled through the lines as well. Go home, sir. I understand you are a professor."

"Yes."

"Ah, I envy you, sir. Come autumn you will be back in the classroom teaching again."

Joshua shook his head.

"Don't feel that way, Colonel. You'll recover and your college will be honored to have you back in their ranks."

"No, I'm coming back."

"Back?"

"To the army."

"Why, sir?" Lo asked softly.

"It isn't over."

Armistead sighed and lowered his head.

"I wish to God it was. I thought this would end it forever."

"I wish it was over, too, but not this

way," Chamberlain replied. "You have defeated the Army of the Potomac, but you have not defeated the Republic it defends. There will be a new army, even if I am the only one to join it, but I know there will be tens of thousands more to fill the vacant ranks."

Lo wearily nodded.

"I feared that."

"Thank you for my life," Joshua whispered. "I am sorry that we are enemies. We should not be. I am honored to be able to call you my friend, though I will fight against you yet again."

Lo smiled sadly.

"General Armistead." Joshua sighed, "If there should come a day, a day when it is all different and our roles are reversed, know that you can count on my friendship."

"I hope, sir, that we don't see each other again. I think you know what I mean, until this is over at least. It would be tragic to have to face each other in battle after knowing you like this."

Joshua squeezed Armistead's hand. "God be with you."

"And with you, Colonel."

Joshua, eyes heavy, let go of Armistead's hand. Lo watched him for a moment, worried until he realized that Chamberlain had simply drifted off into a peaceful sleep. Leaving the church, Armistead fell in with the column heading south.

Sunset, July 9, 1863

The White House

"So that is everything you can recall?"

The man standing by the window looked over at Henry with careworn eyes, shoulders hunched, features pale.

"Yes, Mr. President."

"Thank you, sir. Your report has been most thorough."

Henry sensed that the president's remark was a signal that the grueling interview, in which he had spent over two hours recounting every detail of the campaign of the last ten days, was at an end.

Henry stood up, saluted, and then hesitated.

"Is there anything else?" Lincoln asked, and there was a touch of concern, of warmth in his voice, as if anticipating a request for a favor.

"Sir, there is something else."

"And that is?"

"Sir, my men, the men of the Army of the Potomac, in spite of all that happened, they are still the best. There are so many ifs now, but there is one if that should never be raised."

"Ifs?"

"If we had only done this, if only Sedgwick had advanced, or not advanced, if only Meade had listened to Sickles, if only we had moved an hour earlier. That, sir, now, well it is the past."

"Yes, unfortunately, yes."

"Sir, what I am referring to. Never let it be said, 'If only the men had fought better.' My God, Mr. President, I saw them go in, I saw them go in and I saw them die. I saw them die and . . ."

He broke, unashamedly he broke, racked by a shuddering sob, the tears coursing down his face.

Lincoln stepped forward, an arm going around Henry's shoulders. Henry struggled for control but could not stop and for several minutes stood thus, sobbing. At last, embarrassed, he stepped back and looked up. And yet, the look in Lincoln's eyes stilled all embarrassment, all shame, for the president was in tears as well. There was no sound, just a brightness in his red-rimmed eyes and a sudden realization by Henry Hunt that this man had cried countless times in silence, alone, for all that had been done, for all that had been lost.

"Never let it be said, if only we had fought better," Henry whispered. "The failure was in men like me, the ones trusted to command."

"Not you, Hunt."

"Yes, me," and again there was a moment when he had to pause, but then he braced himself, looking straight into the eyes of Lincoln.

"Next time, sir, be merciless when choosing those who command; choose with cold logic and be sure that we know the responsibility given to us, that the lives of our men and the life of our Republic must come before all else. It must come first, or we are not worthy of the trust placed in us."

"I think you did all that you could, Hunt."

"It was not enough."

Lincoln smiled. "I think I can be a better judge of that at this moment, sir."

Henry nodded.

"The men we led, sir, they are the soul of this country; they still are, and always will be. Do not let them die in vain."

Lincoln stood as if struck and then slowly shook his head. "No. And this last battle will not be in vain either, sir."

Henry came to attention and saluted.

Lincoln reached out, extending his hand again, putting it on Henry's shoulder, and slowly walked him to the door.

"May you sleep well tonight, Hunt. Do not blame yourself; the blame is mine now, not yours."

"No, sir, it's not."

Lincoln smiled.

"Don't argue with your president, Hunt. They were my commanders, and in the end their failure was my failure. I'll have orders waiting for you in the morning."

Lincoln looked into his eyes, a look that Henry knew he would carry for the rest of his life. It was a look of a weariness that transcended the mere physical. It reached to the very soul.

"God bless you, sir," Henry said softly, and then he was alone, walking down the stairs and out into the street.

Alone, in his office, President Abraham Lincoln sat down at his desk and looked at the simple five sentence order he had just written out, an order that would go out by telegraph this very evening.

To Gen. U. S. Grant

Sir,

Congratulations on your capture of the Confederate fortress of Vicksburg. It came at a decisive moment. Now we need you here. As of this date, you are hereby appointed to the rank of lieutenant general in command of all armies of the United States. With all possible speed I am ordering you to take whatever steps are necessary to defeat the Army of Northern Virginia and end this war.

A. Lincoln

About the Authors

NEWT GINGRICH, Former Speaker of the U.S. House of Representatives, is the author of five books, including the bestsellers *Contract with America* and *To Renew America*. He is the CEO of the Gingrich Group and an analyst for the Fox News Channel. He holds a Ph.D. in history from Tulane University. Newt serves Secretary Donald Rumsfeld as a Member of the Defense Policy Board, teaches officers from all five services as a Distinguished Visiting Scholar and Professor at the National Defense University, and is the longest-serving teacher of the Joint War Fighting course for Major Generals. In 1999, he was appointed to the U.S. Commission on National Security/21st Century — The Hart/Rudman Commission, which he and President Clinton created to look at national security challenges as far out as 2005.

DR. WILLIAM R. FORSTCHEN is the author of more than thirty works of historical fiction, science fiction, young-adult works, and traditional historical research. He holds a Ph.D. with a specialization in military history from Purdue University and is Associate Professor of history at Montreat College, North Carolina.